West
of the
Midnight Sun

A Novel by John Akers

John Akers

Dedication

This book is dedicated to my grandchildren,
Maggie, James, Zoey, and Deacon.

West
of the
Midnight Sun

Chapter 1

The sun showed it to be a little past high noon on a warm day in early October, with a soft, warm breeze drifting gently out of the east. Two and a half miles to the north, the small band of pronghorn started to stir. They had been bedded down in the thick grass for the past hour, and now a couple of fawns lazily stood and started to move away from the does to feed in the sage. Several more soon stood and joined the fawns feeding slowly toward the west.

Jacob Arrowood pulled his eye away from the spotting scope and looked at his friend Otis Granrud. Otis had given up the watch and was lying with his head on his daypack, hat over his face to block the sun's glare. Only his full red beard was visible beneath the hat, and a low snore was filtering through the lush growth.

"Get up, Otis. Looks like they're movin'," said Jacob as he blinked his eyes to clear the blur caused by squinting through the scope for the last several minutes. "If that big ole buck is close, he will be following for sure, to keep them does in sight."

The rut was in full swing in this eastern part of Wyoming, even though the weather was still warm, often reaching the high seventies during the day. The big buck hadn't been seen at all today, but Jacob still hoped he was close by, lying somewhere in the sparse shade of a cool draw. It was funny how in this barren, undulating land, where you could see for many miles in every direction, these animals could manage to disappear. One minute you could be glassing over several square miles of prairie, seeing nothing but grass and heat waves, and then, as if by magic, thirty antelope would suddenly be running full speed away from you, white rumps flared, vanishing over the horizon.

Jacob and Otis had been hunting together for more than fifteen years on this wide stretch of land. Otis made his living here, running a few cows, and Jacob lived back East. Traveling the fifteen hundred miles every year or so to hunt and visit with Otis and his family was the same as getting a new lease on life for Jacob.

The high-stress job of working within a small office cubicle and dealing daily with a thankless public, combined with playing office politics, was a real mind-killer for someone who craved the quiet solitude of the great outdoors. Some days he was sure he would suffocate if he couldn't escape long enough to draw a fresh breath, and even that was often marred by the caustic smells of the city.

A couple times a year, when Jacob's company would send him to the Denver office for a meeting or training on a new product, he would try to arrange a few off days and make the six-hour drive to the ranch. A day or so working cattle or fixing fence did wonders for working out the kinks associated with cubical life. It never failed to give him a mental boost to help make it through the rest of the year, or until hunting season.

It was a few months back, while repairing a section of

fence torn out by the high spring runoff of the Cheyenne River, that Otis had mentioned seeing the huge antelope buck. Jacob had arrived a few days earlier, after spending a week in meetings at the Denver office. Even though the August sun had baked the prairie to a scorching temperature in the upper nineties, it was still great just to be outside in the fresh air.

"He's the biggest antelope I've ever seen! He'll go at least seventeen inches and with big prongs, but I ain't never been closer than a mile to him. He runs as soon as he sees the truck," wheezed Otis, as he pounded the steel post into the hard, dry ground. "When he comes up to a fence, he don't even slow down, just jumps it like a deer and keeps goin'."

Articles in hunting magazines often tell of how pronghorn have eight power visions and can run all day at fifty miles per hour and will never cross a fence. Most of these so-called experts will have stories of how if an antelope can't crawl under or go around a fence, even to get to water, it will die of thirst rather than try to jump over like a whitetail deer wouldn't even hesitate doing.

"Got the glasses on him a few weeks back. His horns are real heavy and look a little odd, the tips hook to the front," continued Otis as he hefted the heavy post pounder into the back of the old Ford.

"I've seen them jump a fence before but not till after they've tried to find a place to crawl under first." Jacob rubbed a hand along the back of his neck. "When did you last see him?"

"The day before you got here." Otis got into the old ranch truck. "I was goin' to check the float in that big stock tank up in the draw, and when I topped over the bluff, I seen him take off. Six or seven were with him, but they just stood there watchin' him bust and run. Don't know why he's so spooky."

"Must be why he's lived to get so big," said Jacob as he got in the other side of the old truck. "He don't stick around to ask no questions. If something don't look or feel right, he's outta there."

"Let's get back to the house. Work's done for the day, and I could drink a gallon of iced tea if it's sweet enough," said Otis as he turned the key in the old Ford, grinning as it started on the first try and purred like a kitten. Jacob was always amazed at how this old truck never failed to start and run as smooth as it did as bad as it looked. It was seventeen years old and had one hundred seventy-nine thousand miles showing on the dusty odometer, and all of them put on right there at the ranch. It hadn't been on pavement since it left the dealer over in Rapid City.

That was part of what made this lifestyle so special to Jacob. Things never seemed to change, and no one was in a hurry. Even-paced hard work was done every day without complaint, and playtime was thoroughly deserved and enjoyed. Otis was a fine mechanic. All of the ranch equipment ran like a well-oiled watch. Machinery that didn't was just either worn-out completely or beyond repair, for Otis could fix or build just about anything required to operate the ranch smoothly.

"If it's beyond fixin', it's history. Then it's down the road for it," Otis would say. And it would have to be ancient history for an item to be sent down the road because if there was a day of life left in it, it would be running.

The old truck had mismatched fenders and dents in every body panel. The bed sat crooked, and the passenger side window wouldn't roll up. The doors had a habit of jarring open on a rough road, and all the roads were rough. The driver's seat was worn so bad that you actually sat on the floor with only a bunch of folded feed sacks to cushion your butt.

It was difficult for an average-sized man to see clearly over the steering wheel—that is if you could see through the dirty, cracked windshield anyway—but it suited Otis. His frame, measuring at six foot five and three hundred forty pounds, fit fine behind the wheel, and as far as the dirty windshield, he was fond of saying that it got cleaned every time it rained. Otis was the only one who drove the truck, which was a good plan because it was the passenger's job to crawl out to open and close the many ranch gates.

About a mile from the ranch house Otis suddenly slammed on the brakes, and the old truck slid sideways to a halt in a cloud of dust. He then pointed to several white spots a half mile across the prairie. One of the spots was moving away from the others at a fast clip. Jacob grabbed the ten by forty Ziess binoculars from the dash and jumped into the back of the old truck. Steadying himself on the cab top, he picked out the fleeing form in the binoculars.

The buck antelope was only visible for a few seconds, but the picture was forever fixed in Jacob's mind. What a sight! This was by far the biggest buck Jacob had ever seen. Otis was right, as usual; this animal would go at least seventeen inches, maybe closer to eighteen, and the horns looked real heavy with really good prongs. Another thing was apparent even in this brief sighting; the horns did hook to the front.

"What did I tell you!" yelled Otis as he excitedly pounded on the outside of the door with his hand. "Ain't he a beauty? I knew it was him even through this dirty windshield. Let's get to the ranch and find some Windex. I'm gonna' break with tardition and clean this sucker off."

The image of the big antelope was never out of Jacob's mind for very long as he tried to get back in the groove of work once he returned to his nine to five. It was really hard to keep focused on the job, and it seemed the walls of the small cubicle in the office were closing in, with the sole purpose of suffocating him.

There was a stir of rumors in the office about business being bad, and even talks about layoffs. The tech sector of the entire nation was taking a plunge, so why not here too? It was just a matter of time, for you can dodge the bullets only so long before you take a hit. You can only hope the hit, when it comes, won't be fatal.

Jacob had always been a survivor, and he and his family

had been ready to tighten their belts in case the work played out. He would play the cards dealt to him and take things one day at a time. Almost as an answer to his thoughts, the phone rang, and his boss broke the news that there would be a force reduction in about two weeks. Downsizing was the word used so frequently in the workplace, and the word most dreaded.

Jacob and his boss, Mike, had a good working relationship, and Mike had only called to give Jacob a heads-up on the rumors. For now, his job was safe, but he would more than likely be required to take on some additional duties, depending on who lost their jobs. The time on the prairie would be needed now more than ever before. There was no better place to sort out the mind and try to form a plan for the future.

And now, here he was, back on that prairie, trying again for the stalk he had been dreaming about for the past few months. The pace of the grueling nine to five was tucked away in the deep recesses of his mind, and sharp concentration was focused on only one thing: the hunt.

Jacob and Otis had been at it hard for the past four days, and today, although they had seen several bands, there had been no sign of a buck. And no sign at all of the big guy with the forward-hooked horns. It had crossed both their minds that the big buck may have left the country, but neither had spoken that thought aloud. Now they were watching another group. Relying totally on instinct, for they could not be certain the object of their search was with this small band, something just felt right, and Jacob was sure they were on the right track.

Otis normally didn't hunt antelope, too much walking and crawling around in the cacti to suit him. Being out and about the ranch daily to fix a broken fence or tend to the needs of the cows usually kept him only a short distance from the truck. "I ain't about to wear out my boots as long as a truck is runnin'," he would say. But to be with his buddy, he would grudgingly agree to hike along with Jacob at least a few days a year to hunt the way Jacob wanted.

"You ain't huntin' eastern whitetail, Jacob," Otis would say. "We can run you down an antelope with the truck if you want to shoot one. Ain't much meat on 'em anyways."

Jacob would just smile at his friend's comments, not really sure if Otis was serious or not. Even if he was, he had still been wearing out his boots with Jacob for a lot of years.

"You know I don't just want to shoot one, Otis. It's the challenge of the hunt, the allure of the wilderness, the fresh air and the wind in our face," Jacob would tease. "If I just wanted the meat, we'd go into town and get a big steak."

Jacob had hunted most of his adult life. His best hunting buddy was his dad, who, at nearly eighty years old, was as spry as someone half his age. He had been on several western hunts with Jacob and was back home in West Virginia now, preparing for the opening of deer season. It was hard for Jacob to really believe that his dad was no longer a young man. Heck, Jacob was fifty, and after thirty-one years, it seemed his career may well come to an abrupt end. It was hard to believe that too. As much as he wanted to concentrate on the task at hand, his mind was a jumble of thoughts that seemed determined to haunt him.

Jarred back to the present by movement a few hundred yards to the south of the antelope he had been watching, Jacob froze and whispered loudly to Otis, "Don't move, Otis, it's him!"

"What?" questioned Otis sleepily from under his hat.

"It's *him*, Otis. Don't move—just lay still!"

Sure enough, the big buck had been bedded down not far from the does, and as they moved off to feed, he had gotten up to follow. Otis and Jacob had crawled for several hundred yards through a brush-choked gully to get in position behind a large clump of sagebrush to observe this small band of antelope. The big buck hadn't been seen on the ranch for several weeks, and in the past four days of hunting, not a decent buck had been spotted at all. The tactic had been to check every group in case the big buck was lying low somewhere.

Luck was on their side, for normally, if a good buck wasn't spotted within a band from a distance, a stalk was not wasted. Not wanting to take any chances on missing their quarry, though, every band was checked, and there had been several fruitless stalks made the past few days.

The sight of the big buck had instantly caused sweat to bead up on Jacob's forehead and between his shoulder blades. He was much too far away to attempt a shot, so he had to formulate a plan to get closer without spooking the others.

The entire group was standing now and slowly feeding away toward an area of small draws. It might be possible to make a stalk if they didn't drift too far to the west and pick up the hunter's scent. *Keep going in that direction!* Jacob thought as he scooted back to where Otis now crouched. "I'm going to move back down the gully, where it branches off to the north," explained Jacob. "If it don't peter out, I may be able to get a little ahead of them, and if they continue to feed in the direction they're headed, I may get close enough for a shot if he continues to follow."

"We can't move at all till they drop down outta sight," said Otis. "Now that they're standin', we could be busted if they look this way. In a minute or two, when they get into that low gap, you can head out. Maybe by then you will have stopped shakin'."

Not realizing just how excited he was, Jacob noticed he felt the same as when he drew down on his first whitetail buck thirty-five years earlier. Taking a deep breath, he said, while pointing across the prairie, "When I get to that lone juniper, I'll look back toward you. If you see that they've broken and run, wave your hat. I won't be able to see you or them till I get to that tree."

"I'll be more than happy to stay here," said Otis. "That gully is full of them danged cactus. I'll be pulling stickers outta my butt for a month the way it is."

Jacob laughed, but Otis was right. The small cacti were

thick here and always seemed to sneak up on you. The little needles on some of them would go through the sole of a leather boot if you stepped on it just right. But the cacti were a small obstacle to confront when a Boone and Crockett buck like this one was on the line.

Jacob had a long stalk to get to the juniper; about half a mile of gully wound its way up to the tree. In some places the gully was only a foot or so deep, but in others, it was more than six feet. If the antelope broke and ran before he got to the tree, he would be attempting a stalk on animals that weren't even there.

The plan was to make it to the juniper and look back toward Otis to see if he signaled that they had left the country. If Otis didn't signal, that meant the antelope were still feeding in a northerly direction. If Jacob reached the juniper without incident, then he could plan a stalk toward the west, down into the small draws in an attempt to intercept them for a shot.

When there were only about a hundred yards separating Jacob from the juniper, a sweet, sickening scent invaded his nostrils. Creeping another fifty feet revealed the source of this odor. Lying on the southern edge of the gully was a dead cow. Jacob could tell it was a Black Angus, even though it had evidently been dead for several weeks. Otis had mentioned he was missing a cow wearing a yellow ear tag with the number forty-three for several weeks now. Its older calf had been seen and heard bawling for its mother, even though it was old enough to survive fine on grass. The calves were due to be separated from the cows later this month to be sold anyway. Otis figured the missing cow had either been killed by lightning or had breached a fence and wandered onto a neighbor's range.

Holding his breath in an attempt to recover the ear tag, Jacob approached the carcass. If it was visible on top, he'd get it, but if it was buried under the rotting hulk, he'd just tell Otis about it, and they could check for the tag later. He didn't want to waste any time here when the buck of a lifetime could, at this very moment, be heading for the next county. Peering around a clump of sagebrush, toward what used to be the head of the cow, Jacob spied the ear tag—old yellow forty-three. Most of the hide was gone from the head, and the skull grinned hideously at Jacob as he reached for the tag. As he reached out, the brim of his hat caught on the branch of sagebrush and was pulled from his head. In an attempt to catch the hat before it fell into the mass of corruption that was once a cow's gut, Jacob lost his footing, and he fell onto the stinking, slimy carcass along with the hat.

"Crap!" he hissed as he jockeyed for a position to keep his rifle and binoculars out of the mess. "Crap! Crap! Crap!" he grumbled to himself as he picked up the stinking hat, slapping it against the ground to dislodge the clinging maggots, then using the hat to knock the maggots and slime off his pants leg.

Forcing himself to keep from retching, Jacob grabbed the ear tag and stuffed it into his pocket, jammed the hat on his head, and quickly made his way to the Juniper.

Under the low-hung branches of the Juniper, Jacob assessed the situation. Looking back toward Otis through the binoculars, he could see that his friend was looking back at him, but not waving his hat. The antelope were still on course! Quickly trying to plan the route for the final stalk, Jacob scanned the wide shallow draws to the north.

From the Juniper tree, the land slowly sloped downward into the valley and then abruptly rose to a long bluff about two hundred feet high. Along this high bluff was the boundary fence between Otis's ranch and the Robison ranch.

The distance to the fence was almost four miles, with dozens of places to hide a few pronghorn, and from this angle, it was easy to understand how a long-ago war party of a hundred warriors could surprise the Cavalry. From a casual glance, the land looked almost completely flat.

He couldn't see the antelope, but could guess their approximate location, presuming they had continued feeding along at the same pace and observed direction. The wind was still good, coming from the southwest, more a gentle breeze than a wind, just enough to bend the tops of the prairie grass. Even if it changed against him, he still had the added advantage provided by his unexpected dose of dead cow scent. Boy, did he stink; his human odor was surely masked now! Every time he got a whiff of himself his stomach lurched.

He needed to move about six hundred yards to the north to be within range of where he expected the buck to show. Picking out a likely rise in that direction, he started to weave his way through the shallow draws. Popping up often to get his bearings was out of the question. He had learned that lesson quickly on his early hunts. Raising up to keep the antelope in sight while stalking would likely send them streaking off in a cloud of dust, for more often than not, if you see them, they've already seen you. So before he left the Juniper, with the aid of the binoculars, Jacob picked out a particularly crooked fence post in the far-off boundary fence. The fence was high enough on the bluff to be seen from within any of the shallow draws. As long as he kept the crooked post at ten o'clock to his position, he should be able to maintain course to the designated rise, hoping to arrive in time to set up for a shot.

Guessing that the buck, if he showed, would be within three hundred yards of the rise, Jacob felt he would have no problem making a clean kill. The little Ruger .243 had served him well over the years, and he was sure it wouldn't fail him now. If he missed, it would be him, not the gun. Willing himself to remain calm during the stalk of a lifetime, he moved slowly forward.

Constantly aware of the wind, which was still calm and gentle, but most importantly, hadn't changed direction, he eased closer to the little knoll. The only sound was the beating of his heart and the soft crunch of his boots on the dry grass. It took another fifteen minutes to reach the base of the little rise. Jacob stopped to calm his heart and control his breathing.

Inhaling deeply, he knelt to the ground and low-crawled to the top of the knoll. Never rising above the height of the low-growing sagebrush, he removed his daypack and took out the Leica rangefinder, placing the pack down, hoping to use it as a rifle rest. Breaking a few of the small branches off the bottom of a bush to clear the view, he saw nothing on the prairie ahead. Good, he had gotten into position before the band arrived. Now to wait.

Within only a few moments the first of the antelope came into view, still calmly feeding toward the north. They were moving out of a shallow draw into a more open flat area. Perfect, if only the big buck was still with them. The antelope in sight were closely bunched and appeared to be no more than 250 yards to the west. Sighting on the lead doe with the laser rangefinder, Jacob took a reading: 268 yards, well within the range of the little .243. Things were going his way; now if only the buck would show. It would also be better if the antelope were a little more spread out. Bunched as they were, the buck could appear with another antelope between him and Jacob, but there was nothing to do now but wait and hope.

Even though expected, each time another antelope appeared a new jolt of excitement surged through Jacob. Where was the big buck? Did he slip away? Did some small disturbance the others ignored unnerve the buck and cause him to bolt? He was known for being mighty skittish.

Suddenly, seemingly from out of nowhere, there he was, no more than thirty yards beyond the others, at the top of a small rise. He must have been feeding in one of the many shallow draws. Slightly quartering away at about three hundred yards, Jacob was confident he could make the shot but held off for a second or two in hopes the buck would turn full broadside. The wait, though slight, was too long. As the crosshairs were settling just above the shoulder, the buck bolted and started running full out for the bluff and the boundary fence to the north.

Shocked by the sudden turn of events, Jacob lowered the rifle and reached for the binoculars. Sensing a glimpse of movement to his left, Jacob caught sight of a lone coyote skulking through the grass toward him.

That stupid coyote, Jacob fumed, then he realized that maybe the coyote had been drawn to the cow carcass and had followed the scent to him. After all, he had all but bathed in the nauseating smell.

The coyote soon spotted Jacob, then quickly realized his mistake and changed directions just as Jacob sought to pick up the fleeing buck in the binoculars. Although antelope will usually tolerate a lone coyote, they are somewhat wary of a pack, especially if there are young fawns in the band.

The huge buck did not flare his rump as he ran, so the other antelope didn't perceive any danger and continued to feed. The big buck wasn't running full tilt, either, only changing location. Jacob saw that the buck was already halfway to the bluff when he suddenly stopped.

As he focused the binoculars on the buck, his heart leaped with excitement as the buck turned and started running back toward him! Catching a small flash of light on the bluff, Jacob realized the reason for the sudden turn of events; it was the sun reflecting for an instant on the windshield of old Jim Robison's pickup. The rancher was probably on a routine check of his fence, and the spooky buck was startled by the sudden appearance of the vehicle.

Jacob replaced the binoculars with the rifle scope and watched as the buck bounded closer. The only sound was his heart beating against the ground as he lay in wait. The big buck slowed as he approached the other antelope, then came to a full walk but continued past them toward Jacob. *Turn!* Jacob all but prayed, and as if on command, the huge buck turned broadside at less than 200 yards and stopped. Holding his breath and squeezing the trigger, Jacob felt the little .243 bump against his shoulder as the 95-grain Nosler partition was sent on its way. The buck only flinched at the shot, then his legs gave way, and he dropped to the ground as the bullet completed its work.

Time stood still for Jacob as he continued to stare at the fallen buck through his scope, then he gasped a breath as he realized he hadn't taken one since the shot. *It's over,* he thought. It seemed like hours since he left Otis; then again, it seemed like only minutes, but the buck was his to live forever in his memory. Now to claim it.

Slowly standing, he made his way toward the fallen monarch. The buck seemed to grow larger as he approached. He had never even noted the other antelope leaving at the sound of the shot. The prairie was empty except for him and this magnificent animal.

"Thought you were never going to get up and claim that goat," said Otis, startling Jacob. "And man, do you stink!"

"Don't sneak up on a guy like that!" shouted Jacob as he grabbed for his heart. "Are you trying to give me a heart attack?"

"I'm too big to sneak up on anyone," replied Otis. "You're just still up in the clouds, but I can sure see why. That's the biggest antelope I ever seen, and I've seen plenty. Dang, you stink! Did you get that excited?"

"No, I fell in a dead cow to get you this," he said as he handed Otis the ear tag, still not taking his eyes off the splendid buck.

"Old yeller forty-three," exclaimed Otis as he took the tag. "Musta been struck by lightning in that hail storm we had last month. Well, let's take some pictures, and while you do the guttin', I'll go back and see if I can work the truck over this way. Criminy but you stink—you ain't ridin' up front with me."

"Otis, there's two inches of cow manure in the floorboards of that old truck! And I can't hardly smell myself now anyway."

"I happen to like the smell of cow manure, and you *stink*. You're ridin' in the back, but thanks for gettin' me the tag.

Jude will be glad to have it to help keep the book straight. She don't like to write off a missing cow until she's sure it's dead."

Jacob rode back to the ranch house in the back of the old pickup more by choice than because Otis said he'd have to. He wanted to stay close to the big buck as much as possible. Resting the buck's head on his lap, he caressed its neck like he would a loving pet dog, thankful that the good Lord would bless him with such a glorious creature.

Chapter 2

$\mathbf{B}$ack at the ranch, after carefully skinning and butchering the antelope, Jacob rolled the precious cape and placed it in the deep freeze. He would deliver the cape and horns to his taxidermist friend, Jim Farren, when he returned home. Jim was a perfectionist, and Jacob knew the big buck would nearly live again after Jim performed his magic; but for now, after a shower and a change of clothes, Jacob and Otis would head into Oldcastle with the horns for a little dinner and a lot of bragging.

The town of Oldcastle was only thirty miles north, and they knew just where to go for dinner. The Pizza Barn was a gathering place for hunters. It was owned by Tony Iacono, a fellow hunter and friend of Otis and Jacob. Tony had hunted all over North America, and the Pizza Barn was decorated with many beautiful mounts of animals Tony had taken. Hunters would gather there to drool over the trophies and dine on some of the best food in the area. Inch-thick steaks, pasta, and just about any kind of pizza you could think of. Tony was originally from New York, but had relocated and opened the Pizza Barn several years ago. "An Italian can leave the big city, but he can't leave good Italian food," Tony often said.

Tony was seated at the table with Jacob and Otis now, holding the horns in his hands. "You know this buck will score big in the book," he said. "These prongs are close to seven inches."

"I green-scored it before I left at 89 7/8," replied Jacob. "I know it will shrink some before it can be scored officially, but I never even dreamed of making the minimum, let alone the top ten or fifteen in the book."

"I've lived in this area for many years," Tony said, "and I don't think I've ever seen a record book antelope. You must have had one of the top guides to put you on this one." He grinned as he glanced at Otis.

"Yep, he sure did," said Otis seriously. "His guide nearly slept through the whole thing. Woke up at the shot, and it takes a top guide to be able to sleep with his butt full of cactus needles."

They all laughed at Otis's dry humor. Everyone was feeling good, and Jacob was enjoying all the attention the other hunters were showing at the news of the big buck.

Later, after the closed sign had been placed in the window and cleanup was being done in the kitchen, Tony sat with Jacob and Otis and noticed Jacob staring blankly as if deep in thought.

"What's on your mind, Jacob?" Tony asked. "Are you re-living the hunt again?"

"Naw, I was just thinkin' about how, even though this was a great hunt and I've got a trophy of a lifetime, it's not the hunt I've always dreamed of. I mean, I wouldn't trade this day for anything, don't get me wrong, but I still dream of something else. I guess everyone does."

"And just what is your big dream hunt?" asked Tony.

"One of those month-long safaris for Africa's big five?"

"No," replied Jacob. "I've never had a desire to hunt in Africa, but I've always wanted to hunt one of those big Alaska brown bear. I remember looking through dad's *Outdoor Life* magazines as a kid and seeing ads in the back with those great big hides stretched on the side of a building. Sometimes there'd be a story about hunting a big bear that stood over ten feet tall. I can still see the front cover of one of those magazines, where some artist had drawn a big, snarlin' bear jumping out at some poor hapless hunter. I found an old *Outdoor Life* in dad's attic last year from the early sixties, and you could get a fully guided deluxe hunt back then for less than a thousand dollars. Today, that will barely pay for your airline ticket."

"Big game huntin' like that is a rich man's sport," snorted Otis. "If I had the money to spend on a two-week hunt like that, I'd buy me a better truck instead."

"You ever hunted in Alaska before?" inquired Tony. "It's a big land. People think it's overrun with big game, but you could glass for days and not see an animal worth a stalk. Oh, they're there, all right, but with all that territory, a lot of hunters get discouraged real quick."

"I know what you mean." Jacob chuckled. "Several years back I hunted moose there with my father-in-law. On the trip up, I was sure I'd have to hide behind trees to keep from getting run over. The plane landed in Anchorage, and when I saw all those mounted animals in the airport I got really excited. I knew I'd get a huge moose the first day. I guess I was expectin' to see them running in herds like those African plains animals. I didn't see nothin' but birds the first three days. I was sure everything had gone into hibernation the first of September."

All laughed, and then the mood quieted for a few minutes. The silence was broken when Tony spoke. "Otis, you remember my buddy Charlie that stopped by here a few years back, the one that roughnecked down at the Mule Creek oil fields in the early seventies?"

"Yeah," said Otis. "Little guy that left a good job here and headed off to Alaska to work on the pipeline. I always thought he was crazy to walk off a good-payin' job with old Doug's bunch to go traipsing off to Alaska to get his butt froze off."

"That's the one, but he's only little compared to you, ya big ox." Turning to Jacob, Tony continued, "Charlie left here and worked the Alaska pipeline until it was finished, then took a job with one of the contractors on a new oil field project in Texas. He didn't stay there six months before he was back in Alaska. Said the country got in his blood so bad that he had to get back. He's been a professional guide for several years now.

"Next time I talk to him, I'll inquire about his bear hunts. He usually stops by this way every year after season. Seems he's wised up about them Alaska winters and spends the coldest months in South Texas."

"I can't see how I'd ever be able to pay for a brown bear hunt anytime in the near future, Tony. Even if they were going for half-price it would still be too much. A hunt in a good area would be close to ten grand, maybe more."

"Ten grand!" exclaimed Otis. "Do you know how many cows that would buy? I wouldn't pay that much to hunt any animal anywhere in the world!"

"Hunting is big business nowadays," stated Tony. "I attended a fundraising banquet for the Foundation of Wild Sheep last year in Phoenix, where a desert bighorn permit went for over one hundred thousand at auction. One hundred thousand just for a permit to hunt—can you believe that!"

All was silent at the table for a few moments, until Jacob finally said, "Well, I'm just grateful to be able to hunt and fish the amount that I do. It doesn't cost very much, and there is no pressure to fill a tag that you've spent several thousand dollars for. Can you imagine dropping one hundred grand for a tag and getting skunked?"

Everyone laughed at the thought of what a bummer that

would be.

"And look at the bonus you get out here, Jacob," said Otis. "You get to fix fence and work on ranch stuff. You don't get that kinda treatment in West Virginia."

The next several days were spent helping Otis get caught up on the ranch work that took at least two men to do. During the year, Otis would keep a mental note of the chores he could expect Jacob to help him with. The once or twice a year visits were really welcome, for it was a full-time job looking after three hundred head of cattle, mending fences, repairing out buildings, cleaning stock tanks, and keeping all the equipment running. Not to mention being prepared for the sudden emergencies, like a fence washout along the river, or a roof being blown off a shed with wind that could sometimes gust without warning to over fifty miles per hour. A rancher's life was twenty-four seven, and Otis loved every minute of it. He and his wife, Judy, did all the work. for there were no children to help out, or any ranch hands on the payroll. Jacob envied their lifestyle. It was a hard life, but every evening you could sit back after dinner and be proud of the fact that you had done something that mattered, not necessarily to anyone else, but to you. Satisfaction came from seeing the sunset and knowing that when it rose again, anything that was to be accomplished that day would be of your own doing, not having to answer to someone else.

This was the type of life Jacob had always longed for. He and Anna had planned for the day when the girls were grown and out on their own, to have their own little piece of heaven in the mountains, or at least be able to see the snowcapped peaks from the porch of the log home. There was still time for that; he was only fifty years old and in good health. He and Otis could work hard together from sun up to sun down, something a lot of men thirty years their junior couldn't do. Yes, there was still time before he became too old to enjoy the life he dreamed of. The Lord had many blessings to bestow on him yet.

Packed and ready for the long drive back to West Virginia, Jacob said his good-byes to Judy and Otis. As always, Otis followed him out to the truck to shake hands and see him off. They checked the cooler and the condition of the antelope cape packed in newspapers that had been wetted and frozen, and then surrounded by ice-filled Ziploc bags and sawdust, ensuring it would remain frozen for the twenty-two-hour drive. It was always difficult to say goodbye to a good friend, and though they would talk on the phone at least once a month to catch up on the news, Jacob couldn't help but notice the mist in the big man's eyes as Otis grabbed his hand and said, "Be careful on the road, buddy. Call when you get home, and tell Anna we said howdy."

Jacob drove down the dusty road toward the main highway as the sun was just starting to glow on the horizon. For half a day the sun would be shining in his eyes as he made his way east. Taking his time, he usually enjoyed these long drives. If he got sleepy he'd just pull over and take a short nap. He was in no hurry now to get back. He had plenty of time before he had to be at work on Monday. If it wasn't for missing a steady paycheck, he would really think about the early retirement offers being made at the company, although he was really too young to take the small lump sum he'd be entitled to. He would still have to find another job, and there were too many over-fifty guys seeking jobs nowadays.

Even though he was in no hurry to get home, he was really looking forward to showing off the big horns of the trophy antelope to his friends. When he delivered the horns and cape to his taxidermist friend, Jim Farren, the cape would still be frozen. Jacob was looking forward to seeing the buck after Jim worked with it. It would be a proud day when the huge buck was hanging in the family room, and he knew he would never get tired of retelling the story of the hunt to his hunting pals.

****

The winter went by smoothly. Hunting whitetails with his dad, the family get-togethers at Thanksgiving and Christmas. Jacob and Anna's two oldest daughters were living in Florida, but they managed to get home for Christmas. He and Anna loved to take things slowly around the holidays, and having all four of the girls home at the same time was special for the whole family. The two youngest ones were in high school and would be going off to college soon. Kids grow up so fast. He and Anna would be fighting empty-nest syndrome before long. So it was important to stay busy and make every day count, for each one was a gift and should not be wasted.

****

Early in the spring, Otis called and said the calving was finally done for the year. He had been the proud papa of four sets of twins this year and hadn't lost a single calf. The weather had been really mild in the latter part of winter, and the early rains had been heavy. The water table was up, and he should have a bumper crop of hay this year. All good news for Jacob, since he was always really glad when things were going well for Otis. Some years there was no rain, and thus no grass. A big chunk of the money from the sale of the calves was then spent on buying hay to see the breeding stock through the winter. Ranching was a gamble played against Mother Nature, and it was good to hear that Otis had been dealt a good hand this year.

****

One day in late August Jacob and his dad had left early in the morning to scour the hills in search of ginseng and to scratch around under rock overhangs for flint arrowheads. Hunting for ancient artifacts was one of Jacob's passions, and his dad was a digger of 'sang.' The ginseng root sometimes brought four hundred dollars a pound dried and was usually a profitable endeavor. However, Jacob wasn't too fond of the yellow jackets, ticks, and poison ivy that his dad had to wade through, so he spent most of the day under the shade of a rock shelter, sifting through the dirt in hopes of finding an ancient relic. Discovering an arrowhead or knife made of flint in perfect condition was rare but was as addictive as prospecting for gold. The next shovelful could always be the mother lode. The idea of uncovering an artifact maybe eight thousand years old was always exciting. Every time something fashioned by the hand of early man was found, Jacob made sure to pause and reflect on the life of the person who made it. He was reflecting now as he turned the small, delicately formed point over in his hand. Today had been a good dig. He had found two crude corner-notched points, three broken points, along with a handful of flint chips, and this one. Yes, this one was special, about an inch and a half long and made of what looked like gray chalcedony. Apparently archaic, probably of Calf Creek, it was not at all like the local Kanawha flint usually found in this area. What a story this one could tell, if only it could speak. How many hundreds, maybe thousands of years had passed since it was last held in a warm hand? Had its maker been a family man, like himself? Had he traded for the gray stone? Why had a point of this quality been left here, under this rock shelter? It would have been a good place to camp, plenty of room and dry, with the creek running a few hundred feet below. Had it been lost accidentally? Today, it would be like losing a good pocket knife.

Suddenly he was jarred back into the present by a hail from above the rock. "You still down there diggin' in the dirt?" yelled Jacob's dad. "You gotta see the root I just found! Big as a turnip!" Jacob turned to see his dad slide down the hill and come to a stop beside the rock shelter, sweating like he'd run a marathon and covered with brier scratches, some bleeding. A slight swelling was beginning over his right eye.

"What happened to your eye, Dad?" asked Jacob.

"Ah, just a darn yellow jacket. Got me on the neck and back of the arm too," his dad replied, shaking it off like it was nothing. "Look at this baby! Found a four-pronger almost three feet high up in this holler. Three or four more roots like this would almost make a pound."

Holding out the ginseng root to Jacob, he sat down to take a drink of the warm water in the canteen he carried. Jacob took the root to give it a good looking over, and handed his dad the gray point. "Boy, that's a nice one!" exclaimed his dad. "Must be a war arrow. Where did you find it?"

"Right here under this rock, and I ain't seen a yellow jacket all day."

Later that evening, Jacob sat at the kitchen table drinking a cup of coffee as Anna cleaned up from dinner. "I almost forgot to tell you," said Anna. "The caller ID shows a number from Wyoming. Must have come in while I was at the store. I figured it might be Otis checking in. We haven't heard from him in over a month."

Looking at the clock, Jacob said, "It's only six fifteen in Wyoming now. Otis don't usually call until it's ten or eleven here, after he's done for the day. I sure hope nothing's wrong." Getting up and checking the number, Jacob didn't recognize it as belonging to Otis. Fearing bad news, Jacob dialed with a pit of dread gnawing at his stomach.

"Pizza Barn," came a voice at the other end. It was Tony.

"Tony, Jacob here."

"Hello, Jacob. You ready to go on a bear hunt?"

"Bear hunt? Sure, when we going?" joked Jacob. "Is Otis and everything okay? When I saw the Wyoming number on the caller ID I got kinda worried. Didn't recognize the number and thought there may have been an accident or something."

"Naw, everyone and everything here's fine, as far as I know. But I'm really serious about the bear hunt. You still interested?"

Jacob's heart leaped. Now he remembered Tony saying he had a friend in Alaska who was an outfitter. He had almost forgotten the conversation at the Pizza Barn the evening of the big antelope hunt.

"You still there, Jacob?" came Tony's voice through the receiver.

"Yeah, Tony, I'm here. What's the deal? Are you serious?" replied Jacob.

"Serious as Otis sittin' down to dinner," said Tony. "Let me put you on hold till I can walk back to the office. I'll give you the details."

Jacob waited as he imagined Tony walking from behind the counter, around the corner of the dining room, then through the storage room to his cramped little office in the back corner of the restaurant. Almost as if he saw the walk in real time, Jacob heard Tony click back on the phone as he settled into the big worn leather chair that was almost too big for the small space.

"Okay, Jacob, I'm back. Let's see, I wrote all the information down here somewhere. Let me find it."

Jacob heard papers rustling and things being moved around on the big wooden desk as Tony sorted through the permanent pile of clutter. As he was looking, Tony said, "Remember the Alaskan Guide I told you about last fall, my buddy from the early seventies who went to Alaska to work on the pipeline? Well, when he stopped by here on his way to winter in Texas, I told him about the antelope you shot and about your burnin' desire to go on a bear hunt. I also let him know you weren't one of those rich dudes with money to burn but were a real sportsman."

"Yeah, Tony, I remember you talkin' about him. Liked Alaska so much that after the pipeline work played out, he just decided to stay."

"Well, I got some info for you somewhere here. I'll find it in a minute. Somebody has done went and rearranged the stuff on my desk again."

Jacob smiled at the antics of his friend. He remembered Otis once saying that Tony couldn't ever find anything, even if what he was looking for was right in his pocket. "Before you go through a lot of trouble, Tony, I gotta tell you that I couldn't afford a bear hunt even at half-price right now. Christmas will be here before you know it, and I haven't worked much overtime this year. Just meetin' the bills. We aren't starving or anything like that, but I don't have a lot of extra cash laying around. Well, to tell the truth, I could hardly come up with a down payment on a free lunch."

"Just hold on a minute," countered Tony, "you ain't gonna believe the deal we got cooked up for you. Here it is, right where I left it. You ready?"

Jacob listened as Tony explained the situation.

Chapter 3

Tony's friend, Charlie Mason the Alaskan Guide, had called yesterday with a sort of problem. It seemed that Charlie had booked a hunt for a group of four. The four had been in camps together on previous hunts and were very competitive. Two hunters to a guide was the norm in Charlie's camps, but one of the hunters had canceled at the last minute. It seemed he had gotten a much-anticipated promotion with his company and had to start the new job in a new town right away. As he explained to Charlie, he was so excited with the promotion and subsequent raise in salary that he would have no problem forfeiting his deposit on the hunt.

Now Charlie was in a bind. It was too late in the season to spend a lot of extra time trying to find another hunter, as he was already in the bush, setting up camps. If there were only three hunters in the camp with two guides there would be problems, even among friends. One would have a perceived unfair advantage of having a guide to himself. Flipping a coin or drawing straws was out of the question—competitive jerks like this demanded everything be equal. Charlie needed another hunter.

Jacob had been in camps like this before and understood Charlie's dilemma. A bunch of friends would book a hunt together, and most of the time they were well-heeled and could afford to go on any type of hunt they desired. Satisfaction from the experience of the hunt wasn't enough. Oh no, they had to shoot a higher-scoring animal than their buddies. As was often the case, good friendships of many years would be replaced with seething envy. Jacob always thought this type of character was out of line with the hunting spirit. He just loved the adventure of the hunt. The hunt was the prize—taking a quality animal was just a bonus. If what he was hearing from Tony now was correct, then the outfitter was dealing with a small group of childish little rich boys.

Tony continued, "So, Jacob, when Charlie remembered me tellin' him about your burning desire to hunt a brown bear and then his hunter up and canceling, he had me get in touch with you. He's willin' to let you fill in as his fourth hunter for only—are you sittin' down—one grand! Course, that's not countin' your airfare. He figgers the grand will let him break even on the food, guide, and preparing the hide. That is, of course, if you score on a bear. Well, what do ya think? Are ya speechless?"

It took Jacob a moment to believe what he was hearing. "Tony, this ain't no joke Otis put you up to, is it?" he asked warily. "A hunt like that would go over ten thousand dollars."

"No joke. I got Charlie's number here for you to call if you're interested. He will be at this motel in Anchorage tonight, dealin' on what he calls a special hunt. Call him about one a.m. your time."

Jacob took the information and thanked Tony a dozen times for remembering him to his friend. He hung up the phone and sat in silence for a few minutes. He had to think things over and discuss finances with Anna. If he was able to come up with the money, there would be less than a week to make all of the arrangements. He had to be in Anchorage on August the thirtieth, since the hunt started September first, and today was August twenty-third.

"There's nothing to discuss, Jacob," Anna said when he told her. "You have been dreaming about a chance like this all of your adult life. At least as long as I've known you. You were almost an adult when I married you," she added with a smirk.

"How are we going to come up with the extra money?" he asked, letting her remark pass. "It'll take at least two thousand dollars to do this. I'd be worried it'll put us short."

Anna took care of all of the finances. If she said there was no extra money, then there was no extra money. She managed well on her and Jacob's salary. They had everything they really needed, and even a few things they wanted.

Anna was silent for a moment, then she said, "Look, Jacob, this really means a lot to you, and I don't think you should let this opportunity pass. We've got a little cushion put back, and I really do want a bear skin. This could be an early Christmas present for us both—you get the hunt and I get the bear skin."

Jacob knew Anna was serious about wanting the bear. The family room had several animals on the wall from earlier hunts. Elk, moose, deer, and the recent big antelope. Anna didn't hunt but loved the animals. For years they had planned for a log home in the mountains with a great room for all of the trophy mounts. Trophy mounts by Jacob's standards, anyway. Every animal harvested by fair chase was a trophy, no matter what the size.

He walked up to her and took her in his arms, wondering how he ever got so lucky. As he kissed her on the cheek, he whispered, "Thanks, sweetie."

Charlie Mason was sitting on a wooden box containing pots and pans in the large canvas cook tent just erected at the Tippen Creek Camp. This was one of four camps set every season for the fall bear hunts. Charlie had a good area for several types of game. Caribou, moose, bear, and Dall sheep could all be hunted with good success in the Conchuglik Drainage. He liked to manage the bear camps himself, since bear hunting was the main reason behind his decision to remain in Alaska after work on the pipeline played out.

Mason Alaskan Safaris had provided a good living for Charlie over the past twenty-two years. In the early days most of the hunters came for the sheer enjoyment of experiencing the great outdoors. Everyone wanted to visit the last frontier. Game was plentiful too. It was common to see several bears over ten foot during both spring and fall hunts. At least one hunter each season took a bear that would push eleven foot. Now, though, he hadn't even seen a bear over ten feet in this area for years. Moose over sixty-five inches, which used to be common, were scarce now also. A hunter was very fortunate to harvest a moose over sixty inches. Worse, though, was the fact that the yearly profit margin was nowhere near what is used to be. He was getting too old to spend the winters in Alaska anymore, and the expense of living in South Texas while having a business in Alaska was really putting a strain on him financially.

The cost of maintaining the floatplanes alone was nearly a fortune. At least the Champion was paid for. The Beaver was still carrying a note, and with the recent modifications that were necessary for Charlie to continue offering the special hunts, which he started last year, the note was heavy. The extra capacity fuel tanks, along with the performance modifications made to the Pratt & Whitney was money well spent, and if everything worked out as they planned, he would be able to sell the business to Grant in a few years. It would be nice to retire in South Texas. The warm sun was good for his joints.

Grant Gill had worked for Mason Alaskan Safaris for the past eleven years. He was a top guide and Charlie's friend. At thirty-nine years old, he was young enough to take over the business and be successful at it. He had been able to save most of his money, while Charlie had been forced to reinvest his profits into the business. He knew Grant wanted the guide service, for it was in his blood. Charlie really hated to give it up, but he was getting tired. He was sure Grant had the money to make a big down payment, and Charlie would carry the balance for a few years. Heck, it would be like getting a real retirement check.

Early this morning, he had called his friend Tony down in Wyoming. He was sure Tony could find him a hunter to fill the spot here at the Tippen Creek Camp. The four hunters booked were from New York and had hunted with Charlie before. He had never heard so much crying and whining when one shot a bigger moose than the other. Now that one of them had canceled, he knew he'd better fill that spot quickly or he would have a bunch of pouting babies on his hands, and he didn't want to make it rough on the two guides. They had only worked for him a couple of years, and he didn't want them to get mad enough to quit. If business had been better, he never would have booked the four again. Tony had said his friend from West Virginia was a good ole boy and quite a hunter. Charlie hated to put him with one of the New Yorkers, but he was getting a bear hunt for one full week for one heck of a deal. And if he was the type of guy Tony said he was, he'd let the New Yorker tag out first, and then he would have the guide to himself. Good for the guide and good for him.

After he made the call, Charlie met Grant, and they flew the Champion into camp with the last of the supplies. Things looked pretty good. In less than a week, the hunters would begin arriving in Anchorage. He would meet with them for dinner at the hotel, and then he would deliver them to camp the next morning. In the meantime, the two guides could scout the area, and the camp cook and his helper could get enough firewood cut and the latrines set up. Boy, the hunters of today were a spoiled bunch. Most wanted to be waited on hand and foot. A lot of the first-time hunters were shocked to discover they would be living in a tent for ten days. Didn't they ever bother to check into what Alaska hunting was about?

This was probably the biggest reason Charlie wanted out of the business. Dealing with the hunters had become a pain. The cost of hunting had sky-rocketed over the last several years. The guys Charlie liked to hunt with couldn't afford to hunt, and that only left the well-heeled snobs to fill the camps. Well, that wasn't entirely fair—there had been some really decent guys over the past few years. It was just hunters like these New Yorkers who really left a sour taste. He knew all the guys from New York were not like this bunch, either; these four took the cake,

"Want a cup of coffee, Boss?" asked Danny, the camp cook. Charlie jumped, startled out of his thoughts. "Sorry, Boss, didn't know if you were daydreaming or asleep," Danny said, as he handed Charlie a cup.

"Naw, just thinking, Danny. Thanks," said Charlie, taking the cup with a grateful glance.

Just then, Grant entered the tent with a box of supplies. "Danny, how about pourin' me a cup of that mud water too?" he asked as he set down the box. "By the way, Charlie, I forgot to tell you, I picked up the mail this morning, and the insurance on the planes is due by the end of September. They are billing us every three months now."

"Damn!" exclaimed Charlie. "I could buy a new plane every three years for the premium alone. Did you hear anything from the special hunters?"

"That's the good news," continued Grant. "All the checks have cleared. I made the deposit. Mr. Worthington and his son will be here on the thirtieth, early flight. The Germans are to be here the same day, later flight. We can put the four of them up at the hotel and leave out before noon the next morning."

"Good!" exclaimed Charlie. "Especially about the checks clearing. The big beaver is supposed to be checked out and ready on the twenty-ninth. If Tony comes through with his hunter, maybe we can get everything tied together on the evening of the thirtieth. Danny, check things out here, and give Grant a list of anything we forgot. He'll be bringing your New York hunters in on the twenty-eighth. They will want to fish and look around the area for a day or so before their hunt starts. I know you can't wait, so if there is anything you need, Grant can bring it in when he delivers them."

"Yeah, I can't wait, all right; can't wait till they're on a plane back to New York," said Danny. "What about the fourth hunter?"

"If Tony made contact with him and he can make it, I should hear from him tonight. If he's coming, he will be here on the thirtieth. When we leave out with the special hunters on the thirty-first, we'll drop off your hunter here that afternoon."

Jacob paced the floor. He had decided, with a little help from Anna, to call Tony's friend Charlie and accept the offer of the hunt. Airline reservations had been made, but Jacob would be arriving really late, Anchorage time, on the thirtieth. Any delays at all would put him in Anchorage on the morning of the thirty-first. With the time difference, calling Charlie would be well after midnight West Virginia time. Anna was watching the late news when she said, "Will you stop pacing? You're just going to make a simple phone call. The girls are never going to get to sleep if you don't sit down and stop squeaking the floor."

He hadn't noticed, but every time he stepped on a certain spot on the kitchen floor, a board squeaked. "Been aiming to fix that board for years now," he said as he sat down.

"I know," she said. "You just have to remove the ceiling tile downstairs and squirt some wood glue between the boards. You've been saying that for years, all right. But I'm kind of used to it now; lets me know where I am when I walk through the kitchen in the dark."

He smiled as he took her hand. The TV on the kitchen counter was turned down low, but he could see the weatherman pointing to sunny skies over Charleston for tomorrow. In a few minutes, Jay Leno would be giving his monologue. Boy, he missed Johnny Carson.

"I'm going to try Charlie now," he said. "Maybe he's home, and I've gotta get up at six thirty in the morning to take the girls to school."

He took the paper from under the magnet on the refrigerator. He had written down all the information Tony had given him. Charlie kept an apartment in Anchorage during hunting season. Jacob dialed the number and listened as the call rang through.

"Hello?" came a voice at the other end.

"Charlie, Charlie Mason?"

"Yep, this is Charlie Mason. Who's callin'?"

"Jacob Arrowood from West Virginia, friend of Tony's in Wyoming."

"Ah, Jacob, been hoping you'd call."

Jacob thanked Charlie for the offer of the hunt and had a difficult time controlling the excitement in his voice as they confirmed logistics. It was okay with Charlie if Jacob didn't arrive in Anchorage until the morning of the thirty-first, since the flight to Tippen Creek wouldn't be getting away until noon or a little after. The two hunters from Germany would be suffering from jet lag and would want to sleep in for a few extra hours anyway.

After the call, Jacob turned in but couldn't sleep. He was as excited as a kid waiting for Santa on Christmas Eve. His tossing kept Anna awake too, and after a few minutes, she went into the kitchen and made two cups of hot chocolate. Finally, she said, "You should make a list of the things you'll need to take. You know you always forget something."

"You're right," he agreed. "I want to be sure I don't overpack, but I don't want to forget anything important. I can't believe I'm really going, Anna. After all these years, I'm really going."

"I'm glad, and I'm really going too, to bed," she said with

a wink and a smile. "You sit here and make your list. I'll get up in the morning and take the girls to school. Good night, darlin'."

As she got up and left the kitchen, Jacob realized again, for the millionth time, how lucky he was to have her.

Early the next morning Jacob left for the range. He had bought a Ruger Model 77 in .338 magnum caliber several years ago. In the early eighties he used it to take a nice sixty-inch moose in Alaska on his first hunting trip there. That trip had been made with his father-in-law. It was a trip he'd never forget. On several occasions, there had been distant encounters with grizzly bears.

The bears had actually been observed within sight of the tent camp, which was pitched on the sandbar of a small year-round stream. Jacob had gone to the stream one morning with a bucket for water to heat for cleaning the breakfast frying pan. He noticed the huge bear a couple hundred yards across the stream, in the edge of the brush, digging at a stump. At first he was startled, as this was the first live grizzly he'd ever seen without a protective barrier between them. The bear seemed not to notice him, as he was intent on uncovering whatever hidden treasure was lurking around the old stump. The power of the creature was evident, even at such a distance. The muscles rolled under the thick hide as the bear worked at the stump.

Returning to the tent with the water, he had informed the guide of the bear across the stream. The guide, Jerry, remarked that there were plenty of bear in this area, but they were not known to invade an area where human scent was thick in the air.

"Don't come between a bear and his food, or between a sow and her cubs," was Jerry's advice. "Also, don't travel along a noisy stream, where you might walk up on one without being announced. They don't like surprises. Travel along high ground and keep your eyes peeled, and you won't have no trouble."

Jerry the guide was correct, for as soon as the wind changed and the bear scented the camp, he left the area.

Jacob saw bear on two other occasions during that trip, always from a distance. They stirred something in him that would not sleep, for since that time years ago, he had dreamed of returning to hunt the beast.

The faithful old Ruger was still on zero as he cleaned and placed it in the case. He also had to check fire a second gun that had never been used on a hunt. A few years ago, Jacob had won a rifle during a raffle at a big game banquet. It was a stainless Ruger in .338 magnum caliber also. This was the rifle he picked out of the case now; both were going to Alaska with him. He had worked loads for both and wanted to make sure they were zeroed for the same distance. They carried identical scopes and felt the same when shouldered.

A hunter who had been in the same elk camp with Jacob one year had fallen and ruined his gun on the first day of a seven-day hunt. The scope had been busted and the stock cracked badly at the receiver. He had been loaned an old Winchester by one of the guides, but you could tell his hunt was ruined. Being unfamiliar with the loaned firearm was like wearing someone else's boots that didn't fit. On the hunt of a lifetime, Jacob was going to take a backup. He prided himself in having good equipment. The best optics he could afford, well broken-in boots, clothing for any kind of weather, two guns that shot where he aimed, and his small survival kit. He didn't go anywhere without his survival kit. The little zippered case held everything Jacob couldn't survive without. At least that's what he thought. It contained several pencils and a spiral bound notebook, sinus pills, dental floss, aspirin, Alka-Seltzer tablets, two pairs of cheap reading glasses, half a roll of Tums, a hunting magazine, one Leatherman tool, a paperback western novel, roll of mole skin, a small chunk of fire starter, candle, and a couple books of waterproof matches.

For some reason known only to him, Jacob carried this small case with him on every overnight trip. He had for several years, and it had become a habit. It was used to hold airline tickets when flying or road maps when driving. During a layover there was always something to read and reading glasses to read with. After a heavy meal, digging through the bag would produce an Alka-Seltzer or a Tums. There was one time he even credited the little zippered bag of stuff with saving his life.

A few years back, while returning from the DC area, driving through the mountains of eastern West Virginia in early October, a sudden heavy, wet snow had nearly stopped all traffic on the narrow two-lane road. The heavy snow kept falling, and soon the temperature dropped. Pulling off at a wide spot to clean the headlights and remove ice from the wiper had proven to be a bad idea. The little Honda Civic had fast become stuck in the deepening snow. Out of cell phone range and with night settling in, Jacob tried to rock the little car loose, to no avail.

Deciding to flag down the next vehicle didn't work, either. The heavy white snow—over a foot had fallen already—proved to be too much for some of the trees that still carried leaves. Tree tops broke and fell to the highway. Traffic was light on this stretch of highway anyway, as most people drove the interstate. Jacob preferred the scenic route, especially in the fall. But now he was stuck. Resolving to spend the night in the little Honda, Jacob started it up again to warm the car a little.

The snow was already piled up to the bumper, so he knew the exhaust pipe was covered. Crawling into the small backseat of the little hatchback, Jacob folded down the rear seat and found his small metal tool box. Emptying the tool box into the floor, he set the candle from his zippered bag into the bottom of the empty tool box and propped open the lid with a wrench. Taking all of his clean and dirty clothes from the trip to use as blankets, Jacob opened a fresh air vent in the front and settled in until morning. It was cold but not unbearable. The single candle kept the car just warm enough.

A little after daylight the first snowplow drove by, and a highway work crew stopped to check on the little stranded Honda. Jacob informed the foreman that he just loved camping in the snow and drove off with a wave as a few of the crew pushed the little car back onto the roadway.

Jacob never mentioned that little adventure, as Anna hadn't expected him home until the day he arrived anyway. He replaced the burnt down candle with a new one, for he was sure to need the little survival kit again. Yes, this 'survival kit' was a very necessary item.

Back from the range and after a light lunch of Anna's special chicken salad on a bed of fresh lettuce and a dozen saltine crackers, Jacob continued sorting through all the items that might be needed, deciding on what had to go and what could stay. He placed the survival kit in the sure-to-be-needed pile.

His goal was to have only one duffel bag and his rifle case to check on the plane, along with a small carry-on. Looking again over the discard pile, he noticed the plastic gold pan he had bought during the first trip made to Alaska. As he picked it up, he thought back to the day he and Anna's dad had each bought one in the little bait shop just south of Anchorage. They had planned to pan for gold every evening during the moose hunt.

He chuckled to himself as he thought back, remembering how tired they had been in the evening after walking for several miles over the mountains and through the muskeg, the soft, wet, spongy ground that could make a mile seem like a hundred.

Returning to camp after a muscle-killing day brought thoughts of nothing but removing heavy rubber boots and hitting the cot. Maybe, just maybe, a little hot food later, but never was there a thought or mention of wading in a cold stream to pan for gold. The pans were never used.

Jacob held his now and started to put it back in the rejection pile, but he stopped and thought of his father-in-law.

The old guy would never accompany him on another hunt, not after a severe stroke a few years back had left him confined to a wheelchair.

"I'll take this for you, Pop," he said aloud, as he placed the pan in the bottom of the duffel.

Chapter 4

Charlie Mason breathed a sigh of relief. He had just finished a pleasant conversation with the West Virginia hunter and was glad to have spoken with his friend Tony, who had given him the lead on Jacob. Both would benefit from the call, for now there would be four hunters in the camp, and a deserving guy who would otherwise never be able to afford a quality bear hunt would take part in the hunt of his dreams. Charlie truly hoped Jacob would have an experience he would never forget. He seemed like a really nice fellow, the kind of hunter you enjoyed having in camp, genuinely excited at the prospects of hunting, and hopefully harvesting a really nice bear, but more interested in the aspects of the hunt itself than the idea of having to take a ten-foot bear. Most of today's clients seemed intent on a guarantee that they would end up getting a shot at a Boone & Crockett animal, while a real hunter would ask about the area itself. About the piece of paradise that would be their world for the ten days or so afield.

He could tell Jacob was the latter. He wanted to spend every minute experiencing the wilderness and all it had to offer. Charlie thought back on something Jacob had asked: "If I'm lucky and tag out early, will I be able to hang around? I'd be more than willing to help out in camp any way I can." The offer to help had impressed Charlie. He was sure the cook and guides would find Jacob a real pleasure to have around for a couple weeks. In too many recent years, they had been forced to endure clients who would tag out early and then demand to be taken back to Anchorage to the nearest hotel and bar. Some even had the gall to ask for a reduced rate, as they wouldn't have to be catered to for the full days of the hunt. Charlie would most often take them back early to be rid of their whining asses as soon as possible.

Walking into his small kitchen, though, Charlie had to admit to himself that he had met some really great guys over the years. Some even kept in touch with a card at Christmas or a phone call every year or so. He really loved this life and never regretted leaving the oil fields for one minute. It was a hard job at times, but he loved the life and adventure of being an Alaskan Guide.

Taking the old cracked cup from a drainboard beside the sink, Charlie poured it to the brim with strong, hot coffee and eased into the old overstuffed La-Z-Boy that fit him like a glove. He had drunk a strong cup of black coffee every evening before bedtime for as long as he could remember. It never did keep him awake; in fact, after an especially tiring day, he would sometimes doze off before the cup was empty.

Charlie was content with his lifestyle. He had never married, never even had a serious relationship, although there was a very close female friend living near Uvalde, Texas. Hannah Dooley ran the South Texas ranch all alone now that her husband was gone. Six years back, Dean had dropped dead of a heart attack right after breakfast. Hannah and Dean had been Charlie's friends for a long time. Charlie had rented an old bunkhouse on the ranch from them to use as his winter home. After a few years they stopped charging him rent and even helped fix up the old place, turning it into a nice, comfortable little house. It still retained the rustic charm of an eighteenth-century bunkhouse, but with the modern comforts of central HVAC and a custom kitchen and bath.

"You are not a renter any longer, Charlie," Dean had told him that day as he placed Charlie's luggage into the pickup. Charlie's plane had arrived early in San Antonio, but Hannah and Dean were already at the airport to greet him.

"What do you mean 'any longer,' are you kickin' me out? If you are, can I at least stay in the barn tonight? I'm beat," Charlie teased, although he really didn't understand what Dean had implied. He hoped the bunkhouse hadn't burned down.

"I mean, you ain't paying us rent anymore. The bunkhouse has a fresh coat of paint, and me and Hannah want you to have it for as long as you want it. Hell's bells, we ought to be paying you wages for all the work you do around here during the winter."

Charlie's eyes watered up as he thought of how close these dear people were to him. Dean and Hannah were as close as any real family he could remember. It was still difficult to think or talk like Dean was gone. He would always feel his presence somewhere on the ranch.

Charlie had left an orphanage in Iowa on his sixteenth birthday, just walked off and had been on his own ever since. He didn't remember anything about his folks. He didn't even know how he had come to be in the orphanage in the first place, but that was a part of his life he tried never to think about. The way Charlie had it figured, his life started the day he signed up for the pipeline job. He had a way of blocking out uncomfortable memories, but he could never forget the day they lost Dean.

Charlie had been sitting on the bunkhouse porch in the old wooden rocker watching the sun rise, when he saw Dean walk out of the big stone ranch house toward his pickup. Dean threw a friendly wave to Charlie from across the wide field as he climbed into the truck, but he never drove off.

After a while, Charlie began to wonder if Dean had a dead battery or something else causing the truck not to start and began walking across the field to lend a hand.

Hannah came out of the house and walked over to the truck when Charlie was a little more than halfway across the field. His head was down, looking at some fresh deer tracks, when he heard her scream. Heart racing, he ran on to the truck and found Dean slumped against the steering wheel, truck keys still in his hand. He was already gone. Dean's heart had just stopped. They cried together with Dean just sitting there.

Hannah said later that Dean had never complained with chest pains or shortness of breath, and he was not a smoker. When the good Lord calls you home, you stop whatever you are doing, wherever you are, and just go.

Yes, he surely missed Dean. Hannah was a strong woman and did a good job running the ranch, but now she didn't have the zest for it like she did when Dean was alive. The winter before last, she had talked of selling the rest of the cattle, and maybe offering a few whitetail deer hunts. The area produced some really nice deer. The ranch lay between Uvalde and Eagle Pass, and had been in Dean's family for almost one hundred fifty years. Hannah had asked Charlie before about offering a few bow hunts, but it was just in passing. Now he knew she was serious, maybe serious about him too. He could think of a lot worse things to do than settle down with Hannah on a South Texas ranch.

A knock at the door interrupted his daydreaming. "Come on in. Door's not locked!" yelled Charlie without getting up.

The door opened, and Grant walked in carrying a cased rifle. He greeted Charlie and walked over to the stove for half a cup of coffee. Sitting down on the couch, Grant sighed and said, "All the loose ends are tied up now, Boss. If the weather stays good, we ought to have a pretty good season. By the way, I picked up a stack of the new hunting regulations, so the hunters can read up on the game laws. It never fails that someone would want to get by with something, claiming he didn't know the regulations."

"Good thinkin'," said Charlie. "After last season, maybe we ought to start mailin' a copy out to all our hunters and tell them to read and remember all game rules before they even leave home."

The year before, on two different occasions, a couple of Charlie's guides had been offered cash money from hunters to let them take game they did not have tags for. One guy from California had killed a moose, which, after the fact, turned out to be a lot smaller than when the hunter had first seen it. The guide had told the client not to shoot, that there were bigger ones in the area, and it was only the middle of the hunt. Against the guide's advice, the 'seasoned hunter' shot the forty-inch moose, and then realized he should have waited. The guide was offered five hundred dollars cash to cover the dead moose with brush and continue the hunt for a larger trophy. "No one will ever know!" argued the hunter. "Hell, it'll feed the scavengers, and you'll make an extra five hundred dollars."

"No way!" replied the guide. "Your hunt is over! Charlie would have my butt and I'd never guide again in these parts. And besides, it ain't right. You shot this moose, and your tag is filled!"

Another guide in a different camp was offered one thousand dollars from a moose hunter to shoot a really big caribou they had seen. Again, to his credit, and Charlie's insistence on honest help, the guide refused the offer. Any client who showed these characteristics was dropped from the mailing list. Their names were also given to other Alaskan outfitters, as the Alaskan Guide Association, for the most part, looked out for each other's interests. A bad apple could spoil the whole basket, and the 'anti-everything' groups were always looking for more negative press. One of the best game laws, in Charlie's opinion, was one he had helped introduce several years before. It was the No-hunting-same-day-airborne' rule. This regulation really put the skids to a lot of the unethical guide services. A popular method of hunting, for some who just wanted to kill something and cared nothing for the hunt, had been to fly around until a trophy animal was spotted, look for a place to land, then sneak back and shoot the animal. Equivalent to road hunting in the lower forty-eight. This regulation made it illegal to hunt the same day you flew into camp. This gave any game spotted a chance to wander out of the immediate area. It put fairness into fair chase. While the law upset a lot of people, the true hunters were glad, for it enhanced the term 'to hunt.' And with a wilderness the size of Alaska, you could certainly spend a lot of time on the hunt.

Charlie was a real stickler for following the rules, and he expected the same from his staff. Mason Alaskan Safaris had a spotless reputation. They were known for excellent service and controlled an area that produced some really top-notch trophy animals.

Grant Gill was cut from the same type of cloth as Charlie. Charlie recognized that quality the very first time he met the young man. Grant was raised just a little west of Kalispell, Montana. He and his father had come up to one of Charlie's caribou camps about a dozen years ago. Grant had seen a lone, southward-roaming caribou once as a teenager while hunting elk near the west side of Glacier Park along the Canada border. At first, he had taken it as a really weird elk, until a closer look revealed it for what it was. These animals rarely venture south into Montana, but once in a while, some are spotted along the northern edge of Glacier Park.

Grant was impressed by the rack of antlers, but was awed by the pelage of cream and white. What a beautiful animal! A few years later, Grant had managed to talk his dad into a trip to Alaska. Grant had saved his money from working at the local sawmill after school and during the summer, and was able to pay his own way. His father was so proud that he not only decided to go on the hunt, but he also bought Grant a new rifle to take along.

That Winchester model 70 chambered in 300 Winchester magnum was still the only gun Grant would hunt with. It was this trusty Winchester that Grant was carefully cleaning now. Seemed like he cleaned and oiled that gun every other day, whether it had been fired or not. As he pulled an oily patch through the barrel with a string, Grant looked up at Charlie and said, "Charlie, what do you think about raising the price on the special hunts next year? We could easily ask another twenty-five hundred dollars per client. None have even questioned what we charge now. I don't think we would have a problem."

The *special hunts*. Charlie still had trouble coming to terms with these *special hunts*. He remembered back a few months before last season's hunts began, while he was going over the books, filling out the forms for the guide fees and all the other government required paperwork, he noticed again how the profit margin continued the downward trend. It was costing more and more to stay in business, while continuing a first-class operation. Many outfits were cutting their offers to keep the profits in line, but not Charlie. Mason Alaskan Safaris would always be a class act, or there would not be a Mason Alaskan Safaris. That was when Grant brought up the idea of offering the 'special hunt.' At first, Charlie thought the idea was completely crazy and that Grant was just messing with him, but Grant seemed serious. He just hinted at the idea in the beginning, but after a few days, he had a plan that Charlie at least listened to. Charlie thought about it a while and then said, "No way, forget it. I don't want to even think about such a dumb idea."

Grant kept quiet for a couple of weeks as plans were being made for the upcoming hunting season. That is when Charlie got a call from a couple of hunters who had to cancel. By calling early enough, they would get most of their deposit back. This would really hurt the old pocketbook. The government had recently raised the interest rate a little, and people were afraid to spend money on luxury items. The least little thing in the finance world put a fear in people. It did not matter if the rate went up or down; any change in anything outside the norm would cause some people to panic.

"Damn!" Charlie had exclaimed as he slammed down the phone. He had not planned on attending any more trade shows to hawk his business for the year. If he could not secure a couple of hunters to replace the cancellations, he would really be strapped for extra cash during the winter. Every year, he had tried to put a little money into a small fund for retirement, but he couldn't do it like this.

That was when Grant took the opportunity and brought up the 'special hunt' idea again. He noticed Charlie's mood darken as he hung up the phone.

"What's the matter, Boss? Bad news?" asked Grant.

"Couple of hunters canceled," replied Charlie. "The ones we booked at the show in Atlanta last winter."

Charlie and Grant had met in Atlanta that year right after Christmas to attend a big Sporting Goods show. Charlie hated attending these shows. He would see people walk by his booth and pick up a fancy-colored brochure, knowing they wouldn't even look at it.

Most of his business was from repeat customers or their friends. That is why it paid to offer first-class hunts. But sooner or later, the good customers would get older or lose the desire to participate in such a rugged outdoor activity. It was necessary to add new blood to his prospects every year. He did draw the line at attending any more than two shows per year, though, and he was grooming Grant to take over even those.

"Boss, I think we ought to consider them special hunts. I really think we could pull it off," Grant had said.

Sometimes he would address Charlie as boss, and other

times he would use his name. The situation didn't matter. Charlie never knew which one it would be. At first, he got a kick out of trying to guess which would be used. Now he never even paid attention. Grant looked at him now, expecting a comment.

"Get the rest of that apple pie out of the fridge, and I'll pour some coffee. Let's hear this harebrained idea again," said Charlie as he walked into the small kitchen.

Grant sure had a way of selling an idea, and Charlie had been soft for convincing; in fact, he had been desperate for a plan to keep his head above water. After hearing the details, he had agreed, especially since Grant already had a couple hunters eager for the adventure, who were willing to pay.

Looking back now, he was still surprised at how easy it had been to pull it off. Sure, the risk was high, but the money was good, real good.

Chapter 5

After sorting and resorting, Jacob finally had everything packed. He almost had this packing thing down to a science. In the early years, he tended to take too much stuff with him. Items that were sure to be needed while planning a hunt were most often never even unpacked. Usually, you were able to get by comfortably on a lot less than originally thought.

As he was zipping his one carry-on closed, the phone rang. A few minutes later, Anna came in and said, "That was your mom. She wants the girls and us to come up for supper this evening. She's made a bowl of potato salad and a big thing of banana pudding. I have to call her right back and let her know if you would rather have fried chicken or chicken and dumplings."

"Oh boy!" exclaimed Jacob, his stomach already rumbling at the thought. "Tell her to fry the chicken and not let Dad into the banana pudding till we get there."

Anna was glad she would not have to cook this evening.

The cooking wasn't so bad, but she sure hated to clean up the kitchen, and Jacob's mom was a great cook. The girls loved to tease around with their grandpa. He and Jacob sometimes acted like a couple of kids themselves. It would be a great evening and a good send-off for Jacob.

The supper was great, as usual, and after his second helping of banana pudding, Jacob carried his bowl to the kitchen sink. Anna and the girls were helping Mawmaw with the dishes. The girls had always called their grandparents Mawmaw and Pawpaw, the same as Jacob had called his. One day, he hoped he and Anna would have some little ones calling them Mawmaw and Pawpaw. It seemed like only yesterday his girls were running around the house in their little footy pajamas, wanting a story read. Every time Jacob was getting ready to go away, even for only a few days, he would get a melancholy feeling.

"Come on, Jacob; let's get out of the kitchen and go upstairs. I've got something for you," Jacob heard his dad say as he started up the stairs.

Following his dad up to the little den that, many years before, had been Jacob's bedroom, he noticed how spry his dad really was. In twenty years, would he be able to run up the stairs as his dad had just done? He sure hoped so. Entering the room, Jacob sat in the corner recliner as his dad settled into his own easy chair. Reaching over to the lamp table, he retrieved an object and tossed it to Jacob, saying, "I want you to take this with you. You gave it to me for Christmas over twenty years ago. Never used it. I want you to skin that big bear out with it."

Jacob looked at the stainless steel Kershaw skinning knife. Turning it over, he noticed 'JGMT 81' written on the back of the leather sheath. Jacob's dad always wrote or scratched somewhere on every gift. The letters stood for 'Jacob Got Me This,' and 81 was the year 1981.

He smiled and said, "Dad, if someone gave you a solid gold watch, you'd get a nail and scratch 'so-and-so got me this' and the date on it, wouldn't you?"

"Why not, it'd be mine, wouldn't it?" answered his dad.

"Yeah, I guess it would. I'll carry this with me and skin out the biggest bear in the woods. I won't even wipe the blood off. I'll give it back to you dirty," said Jacob as he tested the sharpness of the six-inch blade against the hair on his arm. After shaving off a small patch, he returned the knife to the sheath. A Kershaw knife came from the factory razor-sharp. "Thanks, buddy. I'll take care of it. Wish you were going with me," he added.

"Couldn't go now anyway," his dad answered. "It's the middle of sang season, and I plan on diggin' a couple pounds this year. Besides," he added as he grinned, "there's a bunch a yellow jackets I ain't met yet."

Saying their goodbyes, Jacob, Anna, and the girls left for home with the last of the potato salad and a little banana pudding. Jacob would see to it that the pudding would be gone before bedtime.

About eleven o'clock that night, Anna found Jacob sitting on the front porch in the dark in an old rocking chair. "It's late," she said, "don't you think you'd better get some sleep? Your flight leaves at six a.m." She sat down in a chair beside him, and he reached over and took her hand.

"I'll sleep on the plane," he said. "I've got a box of Dramamine in my carry-on."

"Only one box?" she teased. Jacob feared motion sickness the way some people feared germs. She was sure the Dramamine would knock him out until the plane landed.

"Come on, sweetie; let's sit in the swing for a while."

He said, moving to the end of the porch, still holding her hand. They sat quietly for a few moments, swinging slowly to the music of the crickets and creaking of the swing chains.

Jacob placed an arm around Anna, pulling her close. She knew he was starting to feel a little sad. He always slipped into this mood before a trip, even if he was only going to be away for a couple of days. She was a little sad too; it always seemed so empty around the house when he was away. Work and the girls always kept her busy, but when the sun set she wanted her family together. Although this trip was a dream come true for Jacob and she was extremely happy for him, the next three weeks would drag by for her. Jacob interrupted her thoughts. "Anna, see that big ole moon shining? While I'm away, come out and look at it every night, and when I look up and see it, I'll know you're looking at it too. Even though we'll be thousands of miles apart, we can be close with our hearts through that big ole moon."

What he said touched her deeply, and while some might think it a lame attempt at being romantic, she knew he loved her and had spoken through his soul. She truly loved this man, and for a second, a spark of fear moved through her body. She quickly dismissed it as only dread of him leaving for a short time. Anything could happen, even on a short trip to the grocery store. She didn't dwell on those things, only trusted that God would bring him home safely.

"I love you," he said as he held her tight and kissed her in the warm glow of that big old moon.

****

Early the next morning, before sunrise, Jacob boarded the plane, and before it reached cruising altitude the Dramamine started kicking in. A little after noon he was staggering through the Seattle airport toward the departure gate for his connection into Anchorage. He had changed planes in Pittsburgh but hardly remembered the take off and had slept until the stewardess reminded him to stow the seat tray in preparation for landing in Seattle.

Fully recovered and alert, he glanced at a monitor that reminded him of his two-hour layover. His watch showed quarter till one and was still set to Eastern Time. It was still early morning in Seattle. Approaching his gate, he decided to sit a few sections away, where it was less crowded. The next departure from this gate was a direct flight to Dallas, scheduled to leave in fifty minutes. Taking a seat near the window, he noticed the dreary, overcast sky. *Typical Seattle weather,* he thought. *How do people live here? It's so depressing, the majority of the population must be on Prozac.*

Someone had left a morning paper in a seat nearby, and as he scanned the headlines, he noticed a man take the seat across from him. The weary traveler looked like a salesman, dressed in a wrinkled business suit, but Jacob noticed first the snakeskin cowboy boots he wore. As the man sat, he splashed coffee from a cup he was carrying all over those 'pretty' boots. "Damn!" the man exclaimed as he grabbed a napkin and wiped at the coffee. Looking at Jacob, he grinned and said, "These are the best genuine imitation snakeskin boots money can buy. Bought 'em just for this trip to Dallas. Want to look like I fit in down there among all them cowboys."

Jacob wasn't sure if the man was serious or kidding, but before he could comment, the man stuck out his hand and continued, "Name's Randy Hawkins. I'm a sales agent for Pacific Distribution. I supply products to the oil industry. Goin' to Dallas for a trade show and sales meeting. How about you?"

Jacob shook the guy's hand, but before he could reply, Randy's cell phone rang, and he became instantly engrossed in a conversation that seemed to upset him. Jacob could hear him ranting something about someone named 'Harry' and 'He can't do that' as he walked toward the window. Jacob took the opportunity then to leave and make his way to his own departure gate, grateful that his time of business meetings and office politics were behind him for a while, at least for three weeks.

****

As Jacob approached the gate check-in, Grant Gill was delivering the three New York hunters to the Tippen Creek

Camp. Danny, the cook, was standing at the crude dock on the small lake as the plane floated near enough for Grant to toss a rope. Grant stepped onto the dock to give Danny a hand at securing the plane, and then proceeded to open the rear door for the hunters to deplane. As they gathered their luggage, Grant introduced the clients to Danny, who shook hands all around. Tossing a brand-new and fully stuffed duffel to the dock, Grant rose and said, "Danny, I brought you a few customers for that fancy new restaurant you just opened here on this pretty picturesque lake." Turning to the hunters, he continued, "Fellows, I guarantee this to be the fanciest place within one hundred miles."

Everyone chuckled except Danny. One of the hunters by the name of Tom reached down to pet Danny's miniature dachshund, Emily. Danny's little dog never barked; she was always ready to roll over and have her belly rubbed. Tom and Emily became fast friends as he knelt to feed her a piece of his beef jerky.

The other two hunters, Carl and Homer, walked over to the edge of the mirror-smooth lake and discussed tossing a few flies before lunch. Most likely, there would be fresh trout for dinner.

"Your fourth hunter will be dropped off tomorrow afternoon, Danny," said Grant. "Have the guides done any good with tying up a few critters for the guys?"

"Shrop spotted a couple of big boars yesterday about three miles up the valley," replied Danny, "and I saw a bull well over sixty across the lake about an hour before you dropped in. He'd be a nice one, if anyone's got a moose tag."

The rest of the gear was hauled up to the tents, and Danny's last-minute supplies were stored away. Grant discovered the lunch to be mighty fine, but would never let on to Danny. As he got up to leave, he threw two quarters on the table. Grinning at the New Yorkers, he said, "I always leave a tip—helps the cook pay for his correspondence course in Advanced Culinary Arts."

Giving Emily a pat on the head, he walked out of the cook tent, stretched, and said to Danny, "Got to get back to Anchorage before dark and get the Beaver loaded. We'll stop by here sometime tomorrow afternoon with your other guy."

Giving Danny a parting pat on the shoulder, Grant was soon banking slowly to the south. As the last of the water dripped from the pontoons, he glanced down in time to see a big bull moose step out of the willows.

****

The sky was sunny and bright as Jacob's flight touched the tarmac of the Anchorage Airport. As he made his way toward baggage pickup, he paused often to admire the mounted animal displays. He took the time to read the brass plaques on each, giving the hunter's name, when and where taken, along with the name of the taxidermist who had done the work. Moose, caribou, Dall sheep, mountain goat, muskox, wolf, wolverine, black bear, and even walrus, were all displayed in their wild glory. Beautiful works of art, all proclaiming the last frontier.

Even here, there was no slowing the push of humanity. Crowds moving in every direction, always in a hurry; rush-rush-rush. Most people never even took the time to notice the animal displays. Standing near a huge walrus mount, Jacob could catch the sounds of voices parading by. Japanese, Chinese, German, Australian, French, and Arabic, mixed with English, all wanting to get someplace else. The Anchorage airport was truly a stepping stone where west meets east.

Approaching the carousel, Jacob noticed his duffel bag had already arrived. As he off-loaded it, his gun case appeared. So far, so good. No lost baggage. Hoisting the duffel to his shoulder, with the carry-on secure under his arm, Jacob picked up the gun case and stumbled toward the doors to catch the airport shuttle. Reservations had been made for him at the Golden Lion Best Western in Anchorage. A short ride later, he was standing in the lobby, starting to feel a touch of jet lag. He wasn't even sure of the correct local time, only that he was tired and hungry.

He needed a quick shower and a bite to eat. First, he needed to dump the luggage and phone Anna of his safe arrival. As he picked up his key and turned to leave, the desk clerk handed him an envelope with his name on it. In the room, Jacob opened the envelope to find a note from Charlie Mason, inviting him to meet in the hotel dining room for breakfast the next morning at seven a.m.

Jacob phoned Anna and then showered; he was asleep before his head hit the pillow.

****

Waking with a start of near panic, Jacob knew he had overslept. Glancing at his watch, he saw that it read nearly ten a.m. Almost sure the plane with the other hunters was already far away from the city, he jumped from the bed in a cold sweat. Almost as suddenly, he realized with a rush of relief that his body was still operating on Eastern Time; in fact, he hadn't even reset his watch. Local time was closer to five a.m., so he was actually up early.

Turning on the TV as he dressed and hearing the weatherman predict a warm, clear day, Jacob was suddenly overcome with excitement. The hunt of a lifetime was really about to begin. He was determined to savor every minute. Walking into the lobby, he picked up a copy of the local paper and a cup of coffee. He still had close to ninety minutes before breakfast, and his stomach reminded him that he hadn't taken the time to get a bite the night before. He had been more tired than he had realized. But now he was fresh and excited. There was no one else in the lobby as he sat to read the morning news. Glancing into an alcove to his left, Jacob noticed the namesake of the motel. A huge stuffed African lion was leaping out toward the main lobby from a bed of silk grass.

The taxidermist was a true artist, for the effect was realistic. A plaque above the entrance gave the information on the hunter and when the animal was taken, along with a plug for the taxidermist. The former owner of the motel had made the encounter with the lion in 1978. While the animal was magnificent, Jacob still had no desire to hunt or travel in Africa. He was drawn to the cool, crisp mountains.

The restaurant opened at six a.m., and he was the first customer. The waitress brought a steaming cup of coffee, and Jacob informed her of the need to wait until seven to order, as he was meeting others for breakfast.

"Are you one of the Charlie Mason hunters?" she asked as she set the coffeepot on the table.

"I sure am." He grinned. "I've been waiting on this hunt all my life."

"Charlie is a good man, and he runs a first-class outfit. You should have an experience you'll never forget. Keep the pot here, and I'll take your order when the others arrive — and welcome to Alaska."

Jacob was nursing his second cup of coffee when he heard a hearty laugh, followed by something indistinguishable said in a thick German accent. Looking up, he saw four men enter the dining room and take seats at a huge, round table across the room. Two of the men looked to be father and son, and were wearing identical large white Stetson cowboy hats and belts with big silver buckles. The other two were a contrast of differences. The one speaking was a tall, painfully thin man wearing a heavy yellow wool sweater that looked to be several sizes too large, although the sleeves looked too short. The other fellow was very short and heavyset. He wore a fancy hunting jacket with leather patches on the elbows and a little string tie around his thick neck.

The ever-efficient waitress was at the table immediately with fresh coffee. Filling their cups and setting the pot within reach, she turned to leave and almost ran into two other men, who were coming in behind her. She spoke to them for a moment and pointed to Jacob. Both men nodded and approached Jacob's table. The older man smiled and stuck out his hand and said, "I just bet you're Jacob Arrowood. If you are, I'm Charlie Mason, and if you ain't, well, hell, I'm still Charlie Mason."

Jacob took an instant liking to the man's friendly nature and wit. He returned the handshake, saying, "Yes, sir, I'm Jacob, and it's a pleasure to meet you, Mr. Mason."

"Charlie will do. *Mr.* Mason was my father. And this ugly young feller with the growling belly is my partner, Grant Gill."

"Pleased to make your acquaintance, Jacob. I am starvin'. I say we go meet the other fellows and get something to eat. I haven't had a bite since lunch yesterday at Danny's camp." Winking at Jacob, Grant continued, "I'd swear Charlie could live a week on one bologna sandwich."

Ignoring Grant, Charlie said, "Danny is the cook and camp boss at Tippen Creek, Jacob. That's where we'll drop you off this afternoon. It's a good area, and we take some nice bears outta there."

Before Jacob could reply, they approached the round table, and the four men stood up while introductions were made. Charlie had met the four earlier, but Grant, and of course Jacob, had not.

"If I get your names wrong, I apologize," said Charlie, speaking to the four. "These two fellows here are Grant Gill, my partner, and Jacob Arrowood, a hunter friend of mine who will be riding with us as far as the Tippen Creek camp."

Jacob noticed how Charlie had introduced him as a friend. Charlie would be an easy guy to like, and he did stumble with the "cowboys' " names. The tall, thin fellow was Alex Huber, and the short, stocky man was Lukas Bauer, both from Germany, but he introduced the others as Jack Washington and his son, Chaz.

The son quickly corrected, "My name is Chad, Mr. Mason, and our last name is Worthington."

"Sorry about that, Chad, and here I thought I'd mess up on these other two fellows' names," Charlie said as he took a seat.

Everyone chuckled at Charlie's little blunder. Everyone, that is, except Chad, and Jacob wondered if the young man really wanted to be here. He looked to be about twenty-five or so, and Jacob noticed a gold-and-silver Rolex on his wrist. The kid would probably never have to worry about money, but he just didn't look happy.

The conversations over breakfast began with a few questions concerning the hunt, the expected weather and the like, but soon turned to business. Jack Worthington owned several luxury automobile dealerships in the Houston area and was planning to open another in Lubbock, Texas. Chad had recently married, and the couple was moving to Lubbock, so Darla, the wife and recent law school grad, could take a position with her father's law firm. Jack wanted to open the new dealership so Chad would have something to do. Alex and Lukas were with Mercedes-Benz and spent a lot of time doing business in America.

Jacob and Grant were completely excluded from the exchange, while Charlie occasionally grunted. Grant downed the last of his coffee, stood, and said, "Sorry, fellows, but I've got to run. I need to make a few stops before we head out." Looking at Charlie, he continued, "Boss, I'll take the pickup and finish loading the plane, and you can tie up any loose ends here. The van's in the parking lot, all gassed up. Anything else you need me to do before I leave?"

Charlie scratched his head and answered, "I think we're good here. We'll stop at the sporting goods before we leave town, in case these gents need any last-minute items."

"In that case, I'll see you folks at the plane," Grant said. Looking at Jacob, he asked, "Jacob, do you mind going with me? I might could use a hand."

Jacob almost knocked the chair over as he stood. He knew he didn't fit in with this bunch and thought Grant felt the same way. Charlie threw a wave as they left, but the other four only resumed discussion on the business deals. As Jacob left the room, he heard Charlie grunt.

****

While Jacob checked out of the hotel, Grant took his duffel to the truck and had pulled to the front door as Jacob walked out into the cool Alaska air. Climbing into the passenger side, he said, "I sure want to thank you for rescuing me in there. I don't seem to mix well with the 'high-rollers.' I was startin' to feel as outta place as a porcupine in a balloon factory."

"1 know exactly how you feel. That's why I'm so glad Charlie takes care of that part of the business. We get all kinds up here, and Charlie has a way of letting the bullshit go in one ear and out the other. It would be awful easy for me to offend some clients 'cause I sometimes speak before I think. The boss has been tryin' real hard to teach me how to keep my mouth shut, 'cause we depend a lot on repeat business."

"Have any of those guys hunted with you before?" asked Jacob, as they pulled into the parking lot of a small sporting goods store.

"The Germans were here a few years ago and took a couple of nice sheep. They were in another camp, and I didn't get to meet them, but Charlie says they're real serious about their hunting and don't mind spending big bucks on a trophy hunt. The Worthingtons I know nothing about. I understand Jack has hunted all over the world, but mostly in Africa. According to Charlie, he's a big supporter of one of those fancy international hunting clubs—you know, a club for well-heeled hunters where the members get together to smoke cigars, drink, and brag. Jack Worthington is supposed to have a huge trophy room at his home in Texas full of 'Gold Medal' animals. I guess that's some kind of award recognition his club gives out. I don't think he hunts North American game, or any that would require an effort. Too much of a challenge, I guess.

"I never could see going to Africa and ridin' in a Land Rover up to a big herd of animals and blastin' away. Be kinda like shootin' buffalo in the Old West, I guess. But do you know why Daddy Worthington wants a big bear?" Before Jacob could answer, Grant continued, "Charlie says he's going to have a full-body mount of it fighting a big long-horn bull. Wants to put 'em in the lobby of his wife's office building."

"I know he's in the car business, but do you know what his wife does?' asked Jacob.

"Charlie said something about her investing other people's money in the stock market. I never did trust the stock market myself. I guess she's some kind of independent broker or something. Only stock market I'm familiar with is the kind we used to sell our cows at down in Montana."

Jacob laughed and said, "I don't trust the stock market, either. I lost all of my retirement money there, but I think she might be trying to represent the Bulls and Bears of Wall Street."

"Lost all of your retirement money—damn that's tough!" declared Grant as he got out of the truck. "I don't have any retirement money saved up yet. I've been puttin' any extra cash into this business of Charlie's. I hope to buy him out in a year or so. I have to pick up a few things in here, Jacob. Do you need anything before we head out to the plane?"

"I really need to get a pair of ankle-fit hip waders. My old ones have done dry-rotted. In fact, I bought them up here several years ago while on a moose hunt with my father-in-law. Seems like only yesterday, though," Jacob reminisced.

They entered the small well-stocked sporting goods store, and the owner, an old crusty-looking fellow by the name of James Harper, recognized Grant and almost ran across the floor to greet him. "Grant, my boy, are you getting ready to head out?"

"Yeah, Jimmy, going out to load the last of the stuff now. Needed to pick up a couple boxes of ammo first, and this fellow needs a pair of ankle-fits. Don't hold him up either, you old bandit, or we'll start shopping over at the Walmart."

"I should charge him double just 'cause he's with you!" countered the old man as his eyes sparkled at the chance of a fight. "Soon as Charlie shows up I'm gonna suggest again that he fire your ass."

"Charlie will be stopping by in a little while with our latest group, and they've got money to spend. You just might make enough to take tomorrow off." Grant placed two boxes of Winchester .338 cartridges on the counter.

"I was gonna take tomorrow off anyways. They're havin' a big sale at Walmart, and I don't want to miss it," Jimmy said as he rang up the sale, then, turning to Jacob, he added, "Them ankle-fits on the shelf by the window are your best bet, young fella. You can wear 'em all day—most comfortable brand I've ever carried. Made in Canada, not China. Wouldn't give a damn nickel for them boots made in China."

On their way to the plane, Grant gave Jacob the story on Jimmy. When Charlie first came to Alaska, he was given the job on the pipeline as a welder's helper. Old Jimmy Harper was the welder. Born in Alaska, the old guy had been to the lower forty-eight only once and said he didn't like it because it was too hot. He was one of Charlie's first camp cooks, but as he got older, he decided to open up the sporting goods store. Said the bigger stores carried mostly junk, and he wanted to give his customers the best-quality merchandise available. Grant and Charlie always brought their hunters to Jimmy.

Chapter 6

Mason Alaskan Safaris kept their planes at a small private airstrip about an hour and a half north and west of Anchorage. Located on a small lake, the strip could accommodate several floatplanes. Charlie wintered the planes here and rented his own hangar. The owner was a good friend and lived on-site.

Grant pulled the pickup down to the edge of the dock, and Jacob got his first look at the plane. He could see the look of pride on Grant's face and the way he grinned as Jacob admired the aircraft. Jacob didn't know much about airplanes, but he did appreciate the beauty of a really cool machine, whether it be an automobile, tractor, or, in this case, a floatplane. This was bigger than the other small single-engine airplanes he had seen flying around, and the paint job was beautiful. Starting at the propeller to a quarter way back, it was a brilliant white fading to a beautiful ice blue, and that faded into a deep gray for the last third, including the tail section. The painter was truly an artist, for the fading effect made the color change almost without notice. The airplane almost seemed to be in a perpetual shadow.

"Charlie insisted on a novel color scheme, but I was more interested in performance," stated Grant. "The power is almost double what she started out with, and there are extra fuel cells to give her tremendous range. You sure don't want to run dry in some of these mountains, but the biggest expense was the upgrade in the electronics."

Grant continued to praise the plane and her abilities as he and Jacob loaded the supplies. After everything was aboard, Jacob climbed inside for the first time. Right away, he had a question. "Uh, Grant, I see two pilot seats and four passenger seats."

"Yep, she'll carry pilot, copilot, four passengers, and a truckload of cargo," answered Grant.

"You, Charlie, the two Germans, and the two cowboys. Where am I going to ride?"

Grant laughed as he clapped Jacob on the back. "Why, Jacob, old buddy, we don't follow all the FAA rules up here. You get to be part of the cargo."

"The cargo!" exclaimed Jacob. "You don't happen to know a fellow in Wyoming by the name of Otis Granrud, by any chance?"

"Who?"

"Never mind"

Within the hour Charlie arrived with the other hunters. While they stowed their gear, Jacob went into the little office to visit the bathroom, take a Dramamine, and give Anna a call. He informed her that the big adventure was about to get underway. Told her to hug the girls tight and that he loved them all.

He got back to the dock just as the other hunters were boarding. Charlie and Grant took him aside and explained that he was to make himself comfortable in the tail section of the plane, where all the gear was stowed. The soft stuff was put in last, so he could make himself a warm, cozy nest.

He would be let off for his hunt at the Tippen Creek Camp as the first stop. The other four hunters had paid big bucks to hunt a special trophy area.

The flight to Tippen Creek would only take a few hours or so, and he would be the only one who could stretch out and take a nap. Grant handed him a set of headphones and explained where they plugged in. Music would be piped in to the passengers, but Jacob would also be on a channel that would allow him to speak with the pilot or copilot if necessary. This was a feature that allowed Charlie and Grant to keep in touch over the noise of the engine, if one had to be in the back of the plane while the other was flying.

Jacob wanted to be settled in before the plane took off. He wasn't sure if the Dramamine had time to kick in, so he hurriedly arranged the sleeping bag rolls and tent bags into something that rivaled a first-class seat on a 747.

He had just snuggled in when Charlie cranked up the engine and started to taxi across the water. A moment later the plane was airborne. By the time cruising altitude was reached the Dramamine kicked in. It and the drone of the engine, along with the sound of Patsy Cline's "Crazy" had Jacob asleep and dreaming of huge bear tracks in the wet sand within minutes.

****

Danny stepped out of the cook tent into the cool, clean, rain-washed air. The smell of the forest mixed with a hint of fresh-brewed coffee filled his nostrils with every breath. It had rained steady all night. The drops hitting the tent had made for a relaxing sleep. And now the strong, hot coffee was putting the spring back in his step. He was so glad that he had given up cigarettes last year. He was now able to smell and taste everything, even his own cooking.

He could see that Carl and Homer were already at the

edge of the lake casting flies. They would appreciate the little pot of coffee he was taking them.

Emily was following a few paces behind as he approached the two fishermen, when Homer suddenly let out a whoop as a small trout hit his fly.

He was in the process of lifting his line out of the water near the shore when the little trout stuck. His surprise and momentum carried the six-inch fish out of the water and right into Emily's waiting mouth. She never missed a beat as she spun around with the fish and headed back to the cook tent.

Danny was just as surprised as anyone but kept his cool and said, without cracking a smile, "Taught her that trick when she was just a pup. Usually don't let her keep the small ones, though. Want some coffee?"

Carl and Homer looked at Danny and then at each other, not sure whether to believe him or not. Danny sat on a big, smooth rock and poured the coffee and asked if Tom had decided to sleep in. Today would be a good day to catch a few extra winks, for tomorrow would be the start of the season's hunt and everyone would be out early.

"Tom's been chompin' at the bit ever since you mentioned that big moose you saw," declared Carl. "He's walking around the edge of the lake, lookin' for fresh sign. He's sort of a camera buff and is hoping to get some good pictures."

"In fact, there he is now," said Homer, pointing up the lake.

Tom joined them a few minutes later, and said that he had indeed seen fresh moose tracks across the lake, but no moose.

"Just where did you see those tracks?" asked Danny, looking across the lake.

"Right over there." Tom pointed to where a big bull moose was now standing in the shallows across the lake.

"Yep, I bet those tracks were purty fresh," said Danny with a grin that showed his missing front tooth. "Breakfast in twenty minutes, fellows," he added as he headed back toward the cook tent.

The two guides, Shrop and Buck, helped Danny clean up after breakfast. The three hunters returned to their tent, bellies full of Danny's special sourdough pancakes, as the misty rain started to fall again. Danny was starting to worry, and the guides tuned in to his mood right away. They both knew what was on his mind.

"Fog's holdin' in real tight," declared Buck as he set down a bucket of clean water. "Weather report said it was supposed to clear up this mornin'."

"I know, and that's what's got me worried," said Danny.

"Charlie and Grant are both top bush pilots, but neither one can land on a lake they can't see. Hell's bells! The lake is barely big enough to land on in clear weather. I shut my eyes and pucker up every time I land here with 'em," said Shrop, as he dipped a soapy plate in the rinse water.

"It's still a couple hours before they're due to get here, but it don't look good for us gettin' our fourth hunter today. Grant was supposed to bring me some more salt and a box of bar soap too." Danny paused, then continued, "I can finish up in here, fellows. Go ahead and take advantage of your lazy day. One way or another, we start bear hunting tomorrow, but keep your ears peeled for the sound of that plane."

****

The strong purr of the engine was a sweet sound to Grant's ears. He grinned and turned his head to Charlie but noticed the boss's attention was directed toward the northwest. Looking in that direction, Grant also saw the dark clouds in the distance. Just then Charlie turned, and Grant noticed the concern in the older man's eyes.

The flight had started in warm weather with calm winds and clear skies, but after crossing the first small mountain range, the sky became a little overcast. Morning fog was common this close to the coast; however, by noon most had dissipated in the warming sun. Alaska weather could change in a minute. A warm, clear morning could lead to snow by evening, especially this time of year. And the weather forecast had called for warm, dry days and cool, dry nights.

Suddenly they were flying into a steady rain, not a storm, but a light, steady rain, the type of rain farmers loved but bush pilots hated. No lightning, no wind to push it out of the area. This type of weather formation could find a valley and settle in for days, until the heavy clouds were empty.

Grant's disposition quickly changed to despair. He knew they would not be flying out of this very soon, and there was no way he could land on the little lake at Tippen Creek.

He thought then of the little lake. On the maps it had no name, just one of a thousand small lakes in Alaska fed by snowmelt that really had no significance, except to the fish living there and the bush pilot who needed a place to land. On occasion, when the lake filled to overflowing, the runoff would flow down the valley for a mile or so and dump into Tippen Creek.

The camp was given its name for this creek, which was a prime salmon run. The perfect place for a bear camp. Charlie had been very fortunate to have secured this particular hunting area.

"Looks bad, Grant," came Charlie's voice over the headset, jarring him back to the present. "Looks like we're screwed for landing in this crap. Unless we fly out of it in the next twenty minutes, we'll need to make other plans."

****

Danny heard Emily give a short little yip. He was not as surprised at what she might be barking at as he was that she barked at all. The little dog never made a sound, but something now had her attention. Then he heard it too. Hurrying out of the cook tent, he nearly ran into Buck and Shrop.

"We were just coming to fetch you, Danny," said Buck.

"Only Charlie's plane sounds like that."

The powerful sound of the floatplane's engine filled the air, and they knew it was circling the area. Maintaining a safe altitude, they also knew she could never land in this soup. The drizzling rain continued to fall, and the fog was getting thicker. The dock was even hidden from view, and it was less than a hundred feet from the front of the cook tent.

The three hunters joined the group, and they all stared up through the drizzle as the sound of the plane faded away. Danny was the first to speak. "Well, I can't understand why they didn't land. Grant knows full well I needed that salt."

"You mean they really would try and land in this stuff?" asked one of the hunters in disbelief. "I can hardly see the lake when I'm standing on the dock."

"Well, hell yes they'd land in this little drizzle," teased Shrop, catching on to what Danny was doing. "This crap ain't nothing. I was with Charlie one time when he landed in a full-blown blizzard!"

"Come on, fellers, it's lunch time, and I got a big pot of beef stew simmerin' and a pan of my famous cornbread." Danny headed back into the cook tent.

****

Charlie felt someone tap him on the shoulder and looked around to see Chad scream something about flying in circles. Charlie pointed to his headset and reached to the console and flipped a switch, cutting off Chad's music and opening a talk path between them. "What you say?" asked Charlie.

"I asked WHY we are flying around in circles. I paid a lot of money for this so-called special hunt of yours. *Why* are we not getting on to it?"

"Sorry, Chad, but we were just signaling one of our other camps," Charlie said, barely able to hold his temper. Turning around and reaching again for the switch, he added, "By the way, Chaz, my boy, your daddy paid for these hunts." He then flipped the switch, sending Johnny Cash's "Ring of Fire" into Chad's already burning ears.

Charlie hadn't liked the boy's attitude from the very beginning, spoiled little bastard, and now wasn't the time to take his crap. He had to figure something out fast because he had a lot to lose. Damn these special hunts anyway. He'd had a feeling something was going to foul up the works.

Grant interrupted his thoughts. "Hey, Boss, no problem. Let's just take Jacob with us."

"What? Are you crazy? We can't get him involved in this."

"Calm down, Charlie. Just think for a minute. We've got a lot riding on this hunt. We stand to clear, in only a few days, more money than a really good normal season brings in. You know you need the money, right?"

"Sure, we need the money!" answered Charlie, a little irritated. "We still can't drag Jacob into this. He didn't agree to take the risk like these other guys."

"Let's talk to Jacob, then, and let him decide. Hell, Charlie, we can't just quit and go home. You know as well as I do that this is make it or break it for Mason Alaskan Safaris. Three days, four at the most, and we'll be covered for the year and be able to start next season in the black."

Grant had a way of selling his point, and Charlie knew what he was saying was the truth. The survival of the business depended on a few years of these damn special hunts. For some reason, he had a nagging uneasy feeling, though. They had planned well and even made a couple trips to the hunt area without any hunters. Both times, they had been sure to take extra jerry cans of fuel, just in case. These were stashed away now at the campsite, along with a few other items from last year's hunt. A few tarps, ropes, charcoal briquettes, even a Dutch oven was left in a covered fifty-five-gallon drum.

The two hunters Grant lined up last year had both taken record-class bears, both scoring the first day. In and out in less than seventy-two hours, and there was no reason this year should be any different. Still, the fact that he didn't have a legal right to hunt this area bothered him. It wasn't like hunting in a National Park, though. Maybe he wasn't even breaking any state game laws, and it was for the survival of the business.

The clients were fully aware of the risks, and though they were able to afford to hunt anywhere in the world, he was giving them an adventure. Yes, an adventure involving the thrill of getting by with something most considered illegal and potentially deadly, unless everything went without a hitch. Precisely why he was reluctant to involve Jacob. If Jacob had reservations, Charlie would dump the deal. He wanted complete buy-in from anyone concerned.

"Well, Boss, are we going to ask Jacob or what?"

Jacob was in a deep sleep, warm and cozy in his nest among the baggage, when he heard a tinny voice call his name. "Jacob . . . Jacob, are you awake? It's me, Grant—wake up."

"Yeah, Grant, I'm awake now. Are we there yet?" answered Jacob groggily as he sat up a little straighter. He could see Grant looking in his direction through the big rearview mirror in the cockpit.

"Jacob, we have a slight change in plans and need to get your okay before going on. Your headset is on the same channel as mine and Charlie's. The other guys are still hearing music. We can't land at Tippen Creek. The whole valley is fogged in. These other guys have paid big bucks for this special hunt, and we need to take you with us. How would you like to have an almost guaranteed shot at a world-class bear?"

Jacob couldn't believe what he thought Grant was saying. "I'm not quite sure I follow you, Grant."

"What we're saying is this: if you agree to go along and kinda work as a camp cook or packer for a day or so, then after these guys tag out, you and I will go out and find you a monster. I can almost guarantee you an eleven-footer or better."

"Are you kidding? Why would I not agree to something like that? What's the catch?"

"Well, the catch is that we have to fly quite a ways, and we really don't have rights to hunt this area. It's kind of like our secret, private hunting reserve."

"You ain't going to sneak into Denali or someplace like that, are you? I don't want to get arrested."

"No national parks or protected areas. We'll be hunting wild, free-ranging bears but not in our normal hunting areas. No game wardens to worry about. It's just a little more risky than the other camps. We have to land on a glacier."

"On a glacier? That's ice. How are you going to do that with a floatplane?" asked Jacob, a little more confused.

"This glacier is huge, and a few miles up from where it meets the ocean, it smooths out enough to hold a few melted pools that we can land on."

Jacob thought about this for a few moments. He wasn't really concerned about landing on a glacier. If Grant felt he could land safely that was good enough for him. The location might be some other outfitter's hunt area, which didn't bother him either. The game didn't belong to any individual or group; the game belonged to everyone, and he had a legal bear tag, good for one bear, and as long as it wasn't chained up or in a cage it was fair game. Before coming on this trip he had no idea where they were going to let him hunt. Charlie needed an extra hunter, and through good friends and good fortune, that hunter was him. Now he was being offered a chance to hunt where the well-heeled hunted. He'd be crazy to turn down this offer. He was sure the Worthingtons and the two Germans had paid far more than a thousand dollars for their hunt. Heck, this was great. What a deal, and all because of a little rain and fog. He'd never look at an overcast sky the same way again.

Trying to keep the excitement out of his voice, he said into the headset microphone, "I'll be head cook and bottle washer, packer and skinner, no problem. I'll have a fire goin' and coffee ready before the Germans get the kinks out. Thanks for the opportunity, fellows."

"Fair enough," answered Grant. "Go on back to sleep; we'll wake you all just before we land."

Grant was satisfied, and Charlie felt somewhat better too, although he felt Grant hadn't been completely honest by not revealing all the details to Jacob. However, in a few days, they could drop Jacob off at Tippen Creek, and he could fish or help out the guides, if he wished, for the duration of his hunt. Either way, he was sure to see that Jacob enjoyed this experience. Tony had pegged him correctly, and Charlie had liked him from the beginning, might even invite him on a South Texas whitetail hunt sometime.

Jacob curled in among the sleeping bags and covered himself with an old wool blanket. The sound of an old Jim Reeves song coming through the headset echoed in his ears. He couldn't believe this. Was it really happening? He was sure to have stories to tell for a long time. The hunt he'd only been able to dream about. He knew he'd never be able to go back to sleep. He was too excited. A few minutes later, though, he was dreaming again of huge tracks in wet sand.

Charlie dozed a little as Grant kept the plane on course. The throaty sound of the recently modified engine had lulled him to sleep. The airplane was performing better than expected, and the top cruising speed had increased dramatically. The enhancements had been money well spent, and he was sure to miss this plane if Grant did indeed buy the business. For a while he found himself dreaming of Hannah and the little bunkhouse in Texas. Maybe he would cut out a little early this year and leave Grant to fend for himself during the last hunt of the season. It would give the young man a chance to experience the reality of being in charge without having the boss to rely on to make the decisions. He was sure Grant would step up to the plate. The business would be in good hands.

"There she is, Boss," he heard Grant say through the headset. "Looks just like she did last year."

Charlie sat up straighter to see the huge glacier appearing in the distance. The sky here was clear and sunny, the glacier shining like a wide silk ribbon placed delicately from sea to mountain. He marveled at the wild beauty of nature seemingly unchanged since time's beginning. Dark boulder-strewn slopes dotted with spruce crowned the head of this raging river of ice frozen in time.

Flipping the switch, Charlie informed the passengers they would soon be landing. Chad's headset was in his lap, his head lolled back, asleep, and the elder Worthington elbowed him awake.

All were soon looking out the windows save Jacob, who was still confined among the baggage. Peering through the cargo net strapped to each side of the plane, he could sometimes catch a glimpse out a window, but the effort left him nauseated. Fearing he would make himself sick, he curled back into his nest, breathing deep and even with eyes shut.

The airplane circled once above the fjord to allow the group a view of the tremendous calving cliffs giving birth to icebergs the size of skyscrapers, with only their top floors visible above the rolling ocean.

Heading inland, the glacier was a maze of deep crevasses mingled with jagged points of ice. Here and there, rivulets of water ran through a jumble of dirty white and blue mixed with dark gray and black shadows seeking a way to the sea.

A mile or so farther along, the glacier smoothed, and its surface took on the appearance of a great blue-and-white desert, complete with gentle dunes, over which lay clear melted pools, some as big as small lakes. One of these lakes was where Grant now pointed the plane. The pool had formed at the left bank of the glacier, against a towering wall of melting ice.

The wash from the prop slightly disturbed the pool's surface as Grant flew low, making the climbing turn lining up for the landing. Pulling gently back while cutting power to the engine, the plane's left float skimmed the pool's surface a few seconds before the right. A moment after the right float touched the water, the left float made contact with a thick ridge of ice lying just below the surface, resulting in a crashing jolt as the float was ripped from the plane. Realizing too late the clear pool was shallower than it first appeared, Grant tried to compensate by increasing power, causing the damaged craft to career out of control. Spinning wildly, the plane lurched across the shallow pool, sliding up on the ice and crashing prop-first into the towering wall of white.

Surprisingly, no one yelled out during the crash-landing, but now that they were still, the plane was filled with groans and curses. "Is anyone hurt? Is everyone okay!" shouted Charlie through the chaos.

"I feel like my damn neck is broken!" cried Chad as he threw his headset to the floor.

"I'm all right," said the elder Worthington, "but Lukas is bleeding!"

"It looks worse than it is," said Alex, as he examined the cut on his friend's forehead.

Jacob was struggling to climb from beneath a stack of tents and duffels when, from outside the plane, they heard a loud, grinding groan. "Oh, GOD NO!" screamed Grant as the sound of a tremendous crash filled the plane.

Then silence.

Chapter 7

Jacob awakened to the sound of dripping water hitting the plane's surface close to his head. He was very cold and felt as though he was smothering. His head hurt and his legs felt cramped. He tried to move his right foot, but it was stuck. The baggage was mashed tight around him, and it was pitch-dark. Fighting waves of panic, he relaxed and drew in a deep breath. Freeing his arms, he removed the blanket and sleeping bag covering his face. Touching his forehead, he found a painful lump the size of a hen's egg. Able to breathe more freely now, he tried to sit up, but hit his sore head against the smooth metal roof of the plane. Seeing stars, he fell back. Something was dreadfully wrong. He remembered the roof being a few feet above his head, then he recalled the loud crash following Grant's scream. Whatever had happened had led to the knot on his head and the roof closing in on him.

"Grant!" he yelled. "CHARLIE!" he screamed at the top of his lungs.

No answer. Struggling to free himself, his breath coming in ragged gasps, panic and pain gripping him again, he suddenly stopped, forced himself to lie back, and tried to regain control. Calming a little, he assessed his own body for damage. Finding pain from only the blow to the head and being cramped in an awkward position, he decided he wasn't hurt, thank God. His next problem was how to free himself. Touching the airplane's roof, he followed it forward with his hand until it almost touched the floor a few inches from his right foot. His foot was squeezed between the roof and the floor. A little tug and it was free. The baggage pressed in all around him. Turning on his back and pushing with his feet, he managed to mash some of the luggage farther back into the tail section. This done, he was able to clear a space to the closest side wall of the plane. He had to be able to see, so rolling over again, he felt around for the nearest duffel. Finding the zipper, he searched blindly through the underwear, socks, and shirts — no flashlight!

The next one produced a small penlight from someone's shaving kit. The little beam of light gave him comfort as he continued his search. A short time later, he had found a larger light and a small camp axe.

The little axe just might do the trick; it shouldn't take much effort to chop through the plane's thin aluminum skin. Not having much room to swing the axe, Jacob struck a short, hard blow and was surprised to feel the metal give a little. Two more such chops and there was enough of a slit to peer through.

He could barely make out the ground. He was either in deep shadow or it was dark. A few more minutes of chopping and he could make out the tree line. It was dark. He had been out longer than he first thought. The cool air entering the small hole gave him a little more comfort. He could breathe freely now and didn't feel so claustrophobic. Catching a few more deep breaths, he decided it would be best to get comfortable and wait until morning to enlarge the hole. He feared the worst for his friends, but tried not to think about it. He could hear nothing at all from the front section of the plane. He called out again several more times, to no avail. He forced himself to remain calm. He couldn't smell any smoke and couldn't really detect the strong smell of fuel. He listened intently for any groans or sounds of movement but heard neither. There was nothing to do now but try to keep warm and wait for daylight. He looked at his watch to find the crystal had broken. He lay back, staring into the darkness, and sometime later, fell into a fitful sleep.

Jacob dreamed of sniffing and scratching sounds all around him. Opening his eyes to light streaming in through the narrow gash he had chopped, he still heard sniffing and scratching. Something moved past the opening. Leaning closer for a look, he beheld a pair of yellow feral eyes staring back.

Grabbing the axe, he slammed it into the side of the plane, making a loud crashing sound that sent the wolf fleeing, as he had hoped. Yelling and beating the metal wall let them know this strange beast was still alive.

Chopping a horseshoe-shaped gash roughly two foot square within the confined space took the better part of an hour. Wiping the sweat off his forehead with the blanket, being careful of the knot, which was much smaller but still very sore and tender, Jacob turned and pushed at the flap of aluminum with his feet. Feeling as if he had just opened a tin can from the inside, he managed to squeeze through the jagged hole onto the ground.

Standing and stretching, he was totally unprepared for what he now saw. Taking a few steps backward, he stared at the tremendous mass of blue-white ice resting on what was left of the plane. A chunk fully forty feet high and half as wide had sheared off the massive cliff, completely crushing the airplane's fuselage. Only the tips of the wings and the small tail section had been spared. What could be recognized of the rest was less than a foot thick. He looked in horror at the water dripping from the cliff as it splashed in a shallow pool of pink water surrounding the crushed metal.

Knowing now what had drawn the wolves, Jacob reeled in shock and sat back hard on the ice. Quickly regaining his feet, he moved around the plane, checking to see if, by some miracle, someone else had maybe been thrown free. Six people's lives snuffed out in an instant! Such a horrible thing to happen. What could he do? How could he just go off and leave them there? Feeling completely helpless, he moved several yards off to sit slowly down beside a small boulder. He had to think, had to plan, had to keep calm. There was nothing he could do for the others, that was obvious.

He was sure Search and Rescue would be looking for the plane once it was apparent they were overdue. How long had they planned to be gone? Grant had said three or four days. No one would be looking for them for at least five days. He would have to make the best of this terrible situation. There was enough food and water for a few weeks at least. He would gather all the flashlights in case of a flyover at night, a much better idea than trying to build a signal fire.

His breath was coming in gasps. He knew he was in shock. "I must stay calm," he said aloud. "Just relax. I'm the one who survived — it's okay, just relax."

Jacob sat by the small boulder for the better part of an hour. A million things seemed to course through his mind. Every few moments he would look at the wreckage, then gaze off toward the mountains.

The glacier wound its way up through the valley until it curved around a high, smooth hill and was then lost from sight on its journey toward the majestic peaks beyond. Jacob studied the smooth hill and decided to go there in hopes of better understanding exactly where on the Alaska coast he was. There may be a hunting camp, or even a small town nearby. Better to make a hike now than to remain here for a week and find out later he could have walked out in a few hours.

He could hear Otis now: "You mean you camped out on

an iceberg for seven days when you could have walked down to a 7-11 and made a phone call!"

Trying to be as respectfully silent as possible at the wreck-turned-tomb, Jacob retrieved his rifle and daypack and began the long hike to the hilltop, leaving the glacier far below. The old game trail he followed was very steep in places and required many rest breaks. He was resting now, after crossing a particularly tricky talus slope. The loose rock fragments had caused him to lose his footing several times.

Catching his breath, he gazed into the valley beyond the frozen river. The verdant forest seemed to go on forever. A few open parks of lush grasses dotted the far hillside, while the stark gray cliffs above hid patches of snow.

Several areas were showing the bright hues of autumn caused by cold, frosty nights. It was only the first of September, and he could tell that recent snows had already dusted the high peaks. The new snows were a brighter white than that leftover from last year. But this far north, a blizzard could blow in July. This land was magnificent and the vistas breathtaking, but he would hate to think of having to face one of the brutal winters here.

Placing his water bottle back inside the pack, he was soon on his way, and after a while, reached the top of the hill. A cold wind blew across the summit but soon died away as Jacob sat on a sun-warmed rock. Taking his binoculars, he looked back the way he had come. Far below, the glacier crept toward the ocean. He had a hard time locating the downed aircraft but soon spied the tail section peeking from under the huge mound of ice. The color of the plane caused it to blend perfectly with the ice and shadows. It would be virtually impossible to spot it from the air.

A few miles beyond the wreck he could make out the ocean, mile upon mile of coastline in both directions, but no sign of habitation. Only vast forests as far as the eye could see. The foothills at his level gave way to the mountains beyond. Scanning the sea revealed no vessel of any kind. The only things floating were several icebergs of varying sizes.

The cold breeze was beginning to blow again, so Jacob moved off the warm rock to lean back against it. Facing the ocean, he began trying to determine which direction the search party would come from. He had no idea how long they had flown. He had slept most of the way and could only guess which direction led to the Tippen Creek Camp. He guessed it really didn't matter. Grant was sure to have filed some sort of flight plan with someone. He would hope the bush pilots were required to do that.

He could tell by the way his shadow was slowly creeping toward the ocean that it was getting to be past noon, and he had a long walk back. As bad as he hated to, he knew he would have to spend the night in the plane. Tomorrow he would find a comfortable campsite close by.

As he was getting to his feet, a cold realization hit him. His breath choked in his throat. His heart stopped in his chest and then started beating faster. It was as if the elevator door opened and he started to step in, only to see no elevator, just a deep, dark shaft. Hyperventilating, he sat down hard and stared toward the ocean. "No way — it *can't* be!" he said aloud.

Chapter 8

Jacob sat in disbelief for several long minutes. Realizing his situation could be much worse than he had first imagined, he continued to watch his shadow growing longer, stretching slowly toward the ocean. Something was wrong, really wrong, for the sun was behind him! Sitting on the Alaska coast facing the ocean, the sun would be in his face, even this time of year.

He must be on an island or severe curve in the coast, but he had seen the map of Alaska often enough to know there was no island this large off the coast. If he was near Norton Sound, surely he would see evidence of habitation, boats or something. Even Kodiak and the Alaska Peninsula were said to be almost crowded by Alaskan standards.

Grant had said they would be flying northwest and would drop him off at the Tippen Creek Camp, which was on the way. Being stuck in the back of the plane, he hadn't been able to see any landmarks or anything, but it had saved his life — or condemned him to a slow death at the mercy of the elements.

No! He would not think such things. His first instinct was to survive and return home. The accident had only happened yesterday. He would force himself to stay calm and formulate a sensible plan.

The late evening shadows were claiming the wreck when he returned. Evidence was clear that the wolves had been scratching around again. They were wasting their time, of course, as getting at the bodies would be impossible.

Jacob climbed in through the opening he had made and bent down the flap of metal behind him. Knowing six people were lying dead a few feet away didn't bother him any more than being in a mausoleum. There was nothing he could do. He did hope that each one had been prepared to leave this life. Eternity was a long time, and everyone had to choose between Heaven and Hell. This he believed with all his heart. Silently, he prayed for each of them and their families. He prayed for his own safety and for Anna and the girls. He was really tired, but troubled sleep came slowly.

Jacob slept without moving and awakened to the soft patter of rain against the metal tail section. It reminded him of the way the rain sounded on the tin roof of the deer hunting camp he and his dad had shared for many years. It had been his job to get up and get the old coal-burning stove going. As the chill left the cabin, his dad would be up asking for coffee, for he would always be the first one out to start the day's hunt. Very seldom would they have breakfast, but they managed to climb out of the tree stands and be back to camp for lunch. Oftentimes, after his dad had hit the woods, Jacob would sit back and listen to the quiet and the soft crackle of the coal in the stove. He loved those times, especially after a stressful week at the office.

The rain now was steady but seemed to be tapering off. The past two days had been like a bad dream, but the shock of the situation was beginning to wear off. Now came the time to think and plan carefully. A little thing like getting wet and chilled could cause him to take sick. Slipping and falling could break a leg. These things could prove fatal in this situation, so he had to really think of his own safety. His survival depended on not taking unnecessary risks.

He needed to first take inventory of the items at his disposal. He hoped someone had brought along a GPS. He knew there was one in the cockpit because he remembered Grant commenting on how he didn't know how they had ever been able to fly without one. In the cramped space, he began a search of the first duffel.

As he searched through the baggage, Jacob considered himself extremely fortunate that all of the gear survived the crash. Most every item stashed in the tail section could still be used, for nearly everything was geared toward wilderness living. The wealthy clients owned only the very best, and most of the clothing could be worn. There was even a pair of new boots in his size. Who in the world would bring a pair of new boots on a trip like this? Even with old, comfortable, worn-in boots you could get blisters.

He did not want to speculate, though, on an extended stay, for hope of a speedy rescue claimed first priority in his thoughts. At the moment, he wanted to get a better idea of exactly where he was stranded. A map had been located in the side pocket of Charlie's briefcase. And looking through the last duffel produced a new GPS still in the original box, surprisingly, in Chad Worthington's belongings. Upon opening it, a small card fell out, revealing it to have been a Christmas gift from his father.

The rain had stopped, but Jacob was too preoccupied to have noticed. The air was only light jacket cool as he exited the wreck. Powering on the GPS indicated low battery, but the unit locked on to the fixed satellites long enough to give a brief reading before dying. The coordinates confirmed his fear, that he was west of the Alaska mainland. He hurriedly wrote the readings in the margin of his notebook. According to the brief reading and Charlie's map, he was somewhere on the Russian coast.

Stunned again at the heavy reality of his predicament, Jacob considered his options. For some reason, he remained surprisingly calm. Some deep determination dominated his thinking.

How in the world had Charlie and Grant pulled this off? This was Russia, for heaven's sake. Maybe with the breakup of the Soviet Union, the mutual fear level had dropped, but they had still been sneaking into a foreign country. People just didn't do that.

Grant had mentioned the fact that fishermen from both countries shared fishing waters and sometimes traded. One of Grant's friends supposedly supplemented his catch by trading blue jeans and cigarettes for fish. But surely the Russian military monitored all flights with sophisticated radar. Maybe it was possible to evade them, but not the sharp eyes and ears of the American bases. What if a small aircraft wasn't considered a threat? Maybe the locals just got along better than Washington and Moscow.

Whatever the speculation, his plight was confirmed. Jacob was stuck on foreign soil. If a search party covered every square mile of Alaska, they would still be searching in the wrong location.

Even with this knowledge and the fact his situation appeared hopeless, Jacob remained calm. From where this inner strength came he wasn't sure, but the fact remained, he intended to somehow survive.

Jacob took his knife and carved into the soft metal of the exposed tail section at eye level. When finished, he stood back and read:

This wreck contains the crushed bodies of:
Charlie Mason, Grant Gill, Jack Worthington, Chad Worthington,
Alex Huber, Lukas Bauer
The Mason Alaskan Safari flight crashed on Sept. 1, 2002
I, Jacob Arrowood, am the sole survivor

Satisfied at this spur-of-the-moment deed, he gathered his rifle and daypack, setting off to locate a suitable campsite. Before he had gone far, he decided it may be proper to go back to take a few photos of the wreck, just to have a record of the terrible event, even though chances were slim that anyone would ever see them.

Reaching the small rise above the wreck, his eyes were drawn to a boulder field located on a level bluff above a broad valley about a quarter mile away. Setting off in that direction soon brought him to an old game trail leading south, but not too far away from his intended objective. It would be much easier to follow the trail, as the undergrowth had become denser and the way steeper.

Taking the trail proved to be the correct option. Within thirty minutes, Jacob was indeed standing in the middle of a group of boulders, some the size of a small house. The level bench lay at the foot of a narrow talus-filled chute leading higher into the treeless mountains. It made no geologic sense to him why these huge boulders came to rest here. There were no others to be seen anywhere around, and he had a commanding view of the valley below.

The boulder field covered roughly two acres, and the initial investigation disclosed a small, fast-running stream emerging from under a jumble of rocks at the foot of the narrow slope. The cold, clear water wound through the edge of the boulder field before spilling downward, losing itself quickly in a thick stand of willows. Following the run with his eyes, Jacob could see the stream dumping into a small river deep within the valley. The river, at this point, tumbled in cascades, surging its way hurriedly toward the ocean some three or four miles distant.

He decided the area to be a suitable spot for his initial camp. Protected from the worst of the wind, having a ready source of water, and being close enough to the crash site to see or hear any attempt at rescue made it perfect. He noted also an ample supply of firewood in the blowdowns along the trail.

Locating two of the giant stones nearly touching at an angle, forming a large V, Jacob was shocked to see a couple fifty-five-gallon metal drums partially covered by an old green canvas tarp. Further inspection revealed several full military-type fuel cans and a couple empty plastic bottles of fuel stabilizer. Inside the drum, along with ropes and tarps, he was even more surprised to find a Dutch oven, complete with charcoal.

He decided that this unexpected blessing had to be a stash left by Charlie and Grant, and this was later confirmed when Jacob noticed the letters 'MAS' stenciled on the fuel cans. The same as on a fuel can he had seen in the back of Grant's pickup.

Two trips and several hours later, a very tired Jacob Arrowood sat near the dying embers of a small campfire within the protection of the two boulders. Most of the time had been spent gathering two large stacks of firewood. One he placed here for warmth and comfort, and the other on the far side of the boulder field for cooking fires. He wanted to make sure nothing snarling came looking for food near the tent in the middle of the night. All food items had been placed in a waterproof bag and hoisted high in a dead spruce tree near the cooking fire pit.

Three four-man tents had been in the plane. One was now his home for the time being and was set at the apex of the two giant rocks. The tents were of high quality, complete with full rainfly and made of tough waterproof material. Two had been a forest green color and one a bright blaze orange. A four-man tent slept only two comfortably, a fact Jacob found now pertained to the expensive ones, as well as the cheap ones he was used to. He had enough room for his sleeping bag and personal items. Most everything not immediately needed was left stored in the plane. His little zippered bag, rifle, and daypack were kept close at hand. Soap, towels, boots, and an extra jacket also found a place.

He had selected a green tent for fear of being seen by the wrong people. He wanted to be certain that when he was rescued, it was by Americans. It was too early in the game for him to consider himself desperate enough to risk being captured by the Russians. He smiled at that. "Captured by the Russians," he said out loud. Maybe he had watched too many spy shows on television. He really wasn't sure what would happen if someone other than his own people found him. The language barrier was sure to be a problem. Would they consider him a threat, maybe just shoot him?

"I can hang out here for a while," he said aloud. "I'm not dumb enough to go looking for trouble."

The sound of his own voice disturbed him. It was the sound of someone who was very worried. Worried that he may never be found. After all, who knew he was here? Did anyone know this was their destination? Anyone other than those poor fellows mashed flat over there in that wreck?

Almost on cue, the mournful howl of the wolves reached him, drawn again to the smell of blood around the plane. He could see them in his mind, sniffing and pawing, trying to get at the source of what had drawn them. The metal flap he had made was bent down, and he had stuffed a sleeping bag tight into the space where the roof met the floor. How long the ice would keep the odor contained he didn't know. He had hoped to use the plane as storage for the extra rifles and other gear he might eventually need. He didn't intend on staying here long at first, but now he didn't know. He didn't know.

It was full dark now, and he looked up at the sky as a dazzling display of the northern lights flashed across the heavens. No man-made fireworks display could ever compete with nature's own. "Lord, my fate is in Your hands. I'm trusting You completely to see me through this trial." Jacob poured water on the dying embers and crawled into the tent.

Chapter 9

Shrop tossed the dregs of his coffee on the ground and looked over at Buck. Both had been sitting in front of the cook tent for the better part of an hour, watching Danny pace between the tent and the dock, Emily keeping in step closely behind. "Danny, you're makin' a ditch in the ground. If you don't sit down purty soon, lake water's gonna be flowin' back here to the cook tent," said Shrop as he stood to put his cup in the pan of now-cold soapy water.

"Yeah," added Buck. "You gotta figger thays a good reason they ain't showed up yet. They'll be here in the mornin'. The guys have to be at the taxidermist tomorrow afternoon."

It had been nine days since Danny heard the sound of the floatplane over the fogged-in lake. Two days after that, the sky cleared and had been clear ever since. He certainly expected them back before now. Grant had said they would be back in four days, five at the very latest. He sure hoped Buck was right. Charlie did make it a point to have a plane in camp by the morning of the last day of the hunt to give the successful hunters extra time to make taxidermy decisions or meat shipping arrangements. Someone would always fail to include time for these things in their travel plans. In the past, at least one hunter a year would say he was really rushed to catch a return flight, and could you guys have my meat cut and shipped for me, or would you take this to a good taxidermist and have such and such done? Charlie or Grant would be happy to take the client, but made sure the hunter himself negotiated with the butcher or taxidermist and was given the time to do so.

Danny knew he was a worrier. With one more ten-day hunt scheduled after this one, he sure hoped it went smoother. However, all three hunters on this trip had managed to take a bear. No huge trophies, but at least no one would go home empty-handed.

When the fourth hunter had been unable to land, Danny about had a fit. He and the guides were stuck being forced to pacify the three who had paid for a one per two hunt. Shrop came up with a plan at the last minute that seemed to work out just fine. In fact, it was really a better deal for the hunters. After talking it over with Danny and Buck, Danny dropped the idea on the hunters, and they loved it.

Rather than two hunters per guide, each would have his own. Danny had guided for years and had only agreed to be the camp cook a few years earlier. He loved cooking and planned to buy a restaurant later, but if guiding for a few days brought harmony to the camp, he was all for it. Everyone agreed to help out at mealtime and did so. The so-called New York hunters, soon referred to as *the guys*, turned out to be some likable fellows after all. A might standoffish at first, they soon pitched in and attempted to carry their own weight. Homer even offered to cook an entire supper himself one evening. It was a tasty meal, although a little on the spicy side. Things hadn't been so bad after all. He was probably worrying about nothing.

When Danny stopped, Emily stopped. "Maybe you guys are right, but I just got a real uneasy feelin'. I just ain't felt good about somethin' since I heard the sound of that plane flyin' off."

"Listen, Danny," interrupted Buck, "we done got the hides fleshed and ready, and next week's wood is cut and stacked. This hunt turned out just fine. Charlie and Grant know what they're doin', so just stop worryin'."

"Well said, Shrop. If they don't show up by this time tomorrow, we can all start worryin'." Looking toward the lake, he added, "Here come the guys now, and they got fish for supper."

****

About this same time, Jacob was preparing to fry some fish of his own. Two days before, he had made a trip back to the wreck to retrieve some fishing line. He had found a spool loaded with a thousand feet of hundred-pound test braided fishing line while going through all the stuff in the plane. He remembered Grant saying that Charlie loved to fish for halibut whenever he could get away, but he only found line, no rods or reels.

The small, cold stream at the edge of the boulder field spilled into several small pools on its journey to the river, and each of these pools contained a healthy population of trout. Trying to catch these with the braided line was similar to fishing with a rope; however, he managed to land enough for supper. It was here he spied the first bear sign. A deep print of a huge front paw was embedded in the soft mud at the edge of the farthest pool. He had almost forgotten his reason for being here in the first place, until he saw the bear track.

Lightly breading the gutted trout in corn meal and placing them in the pan of hot oil, he couldn't get the sight of the track out of his mind. He had been so immersed preparing his camp and dealing with the terror of the crash and loss of lives that he hadn't given a thought to hunting. He actually hadn't seen much game at all. A few sheep far off on the high ridges and a young bull moose feeding in the shallows of one of the trout pools was all he had spotted. Of course, he had been anything but quiet, not being in hunting mode. He sure didn't want to sneak up and surprise some big critter while out gathering firewood.

After seeing the track earlier this evening, his mind was a little more alert. As the smell of the frying trout reached his nostrils, he wondered if any other nostrils had been reached. He was glad the cooking fire was well away from his sleeping tent. Maybe he would leave his light jacket here too. It was covered with smoke from the fire. Yes, good idea, this would be his chef's coat. He would pull it up high off the ground, along with the cooking gear.

Eating the trout right from the frying pan, he paused with a forkful halfway to his mouth, sensing movement. It turned out to be only a small fox lurking amongst the rocks, hoping for a leftover tidbit. Almost a week he had been here, and suddenly, he was jumping at shadows. The bear hunt of a lifetime had brought him here to begin with, and now he was being unnerved by the sight of one track.

Glancing over to his sleeping area brought a feeling of comfort and safety. He had placed the tent in the V of the two boulders. At the apex, the boulders almost touched, and he could barely squeeze through. He had put the drum, now containing some of the things he might find handy, here. This made it much easier than making trips back and forth to the plane. He only went to the plane now when it was truly necessary, for the feeling of death seemed to overpower the place. The half-mile distance was almost too close.

He had worked almost a full day dragging long poles fashioned from saplings with the limbs removed. These he placed atop the boulders from one to the other and covered this framework with a couple of the old olive drab tarps. This kept the tent and a fair area in front of it dry in almost all but the wind-blown rain. There was ample room on both sides of the tent to stack firewood and still allow room to walk.

The past several mornings Jacob had awakened to the soft cadence of rain marching across the old tarps, and still, the immediate campsite had stayed dry. The vast valley now lay covered in a thick mist, and although the sky revealed a billion stars, the scent of rain was heavy in the air. The days seemed to be growing shorter and the nights noticeably cooler, but maybe that was just his imagination. He really didn't have any knowledge of the weather patterns here. The same might be said for July at this latitude.

Suddenly, an overwhelming sadness engulfed his spirit. This should have been the day that he called Anna for the first time since heading into bear camp. He was scheduled to fly home in the morning. She would be frantic with worry by tomorrow. A few days from now, all who knew and cared for him would be sick with anxiety, and there was nothing he could do. He could imagine his family clinging together, crying and praying, and it broke his heart. He could only imagine the grief they would be feeling, not knowing if he was alive or dead. There could never be closure unless his fate was known, and Anna would hold fast to any glimmer of hope.

Stowing the cooking utensils, Jacob set aside a can of glowing embers before extinguishing the cooking fire. These he carried to the fire pit in front of the tent and kindled his small evening fire. Retrieving a pen and the spiral bound notebook from the small zippered case, Jacob began writing by firelight. He penned the first of his many letters to Anna, beginning with an account of all that had happened since he had last spoken with her. He mentioned the plane crashing and him being the only survivor, but for some reason, he didn't write anything about his whereabouts, except to tell her the accident had occurred during an attempt to land on a glacier. He felt it best not to speculate on that until he knew for sure.

It seemed a month had passed already without hearing her voice. Jacob wrote long into the evening, writing things he should have said more often but didn't. Finally giving in to sleepiness, he crawled into the sleeping bag, dreaming of family and friends he may likely never see again.

The sadness carried over into morning. Rekindling the fire eased his mood a little, but he could still feel himself sliding into a deep depression. He could see it had rained a little again in the night, but he hadn't heard it. Now the clouds were giving way to a glorious sunrise. This truly lifted his spirits a little more, for this place was without a doubt the land of his dreams. If the situation were different, he would be giddy with excitement.

Drinking the last of yesterday's warmed-over coffee, he remembered something in the wreck he wanted to retrieve. Banking the coals under a few scoops of dirt, he started toward the glacier, but rather than take the normal route, he decided to climb a ways up the hill behind camp, which would give a better view of the vast valley, while bringing him down on the wreck rather than the usual climb up to it.

Jacob stopped a few hundred yards above camp and observed the breathtaking view. All of God's handiwork lay before him, from the newly dusted snowcapped ridges, to the vast ocean in the distance. Nestled in between, forests and fields were crowned in all their autumn splendor, while the fast-flowing river matched the azure sky above. Anna would love this place, and his dad would literally go wild. Jacob could only imagine a little cabin perched on the bench where he now stood. Why did things have to be so difficult? Seeing this very spot in his dreams for years, only to be here now with the weight of the world on his shoulders.

Continuing around the side of the hill soon allowed Jacob a view of 'Dead Beaver Glacier.' While writing to Anna, he had started assigning names to the various features he encountered. His camp was now Rock Camp, and the little stream behind it he called Little Rock Creek, which eventually flowed into the Blue River. Grant had said something about the plane being a Beaver, thus Dead Beaver Glacier.

Here, he observed the wreck, a little below and to his left, at a completely different angle. He could plainly see the gouge made in the bottom of the shallow pool, where the plane had made its fatal slide. Something undetected until now caught his eye. At the edge of the shallow pool, about two hundred yards away from the wreck, lay the float, which had broken away on contact with the ice. Also the sheer size of the glacier was apparent, for it was actually much wider than suspected, at least half a mile at this point. The smooth section suddenly gave way to jagged upheavals mixed with deep crevasses a mile or so down the ice-choked valley.

Jacob marveled at the raw, harsh side of nature displayed in this river of ice, wondering how deep the ice must be, for its surface lay far above the neighboring valley.

Instead of venturing on to the wreck, Jacob descended the hill and followed a ridge toward the broken float. At the foot of the hill ran a previously undiscovered small stream. Feeling a desire to quench his thirst before going on, Jacob removed his daypack to retrieve his filter flask.

The filter flask had probably saved him from many bouts of stomach distress. The plastic quart container had lids at both ends. By removing the red twist-off lid and filling one half with water from any source, you could then let the water gravity feed through the micro filter in the middle and be assured of clean, cyst-free water at the other end.

Stooping to fill the flask, Jacob noticed the water to be a little warmer than the frigid ice water at Little Rock Creek. Sitting back to wait for the water to filter through, he thought about how he came to buy the filter flask in the first place.

Several years ago, he and Otis had been scouting the national forest area north of the ranch for elk sign. The morning started out on the cool side, but the temperature had soon climbed into the mid-seventies. Coming upon a small stream, Otis knelt and slurped a big mouthful of the cool water. Turning to Jacob with water dripping from his bushy red beard, he smiled and said, "I just love the taste of this clean mountain water. It sure tastes sweeter than the water back at the house."

Continuing on upstream for another minute, Otis suddenly stopped, turned pale as a ghost, and started to gag. Jacob let out a side-splitting laugh, pointed, and said through the tears, "That's why the water tastes so sweet, Otis!" There, lying in the stream, was a half-rotted mule deer carcass with the water flowing gently through the rib cage. Otis didn't become physically ill over the incident, but it inspired Jacob to buy the filter flask at the first opportunity.

Warm Creek, as Jacob now referred to the little stream, flowed to the sea through an almost hidden ravine with a tree-lined ridge on the right and the rocky slope on the left that led over into Dead Beaver Glacier.

Movement from above caught his eye as he ascended the rocky slope. Suddenly three caribou bounded over the edge, almost on top of him. As surprised as he, the three made a mad dash for the tree-lined ridge across the creek. Recovering from the near head-on collision and seeing the last of the three disappear into the willows, Jacob topped the slope just in time to intercept a half dozen more of the animals heading in his direction. Having time to react, he decided now would be a good time to supplement his dwindling food supply, so he elected to shoot the smallest caribou. It fell dead at the shot, scattering the rest.

As the sound echoed across the glacier, Jacob approached the animal to begin the arduous task of butchering the meat. Now only a few hundred yards below the wreck, Jacob noticed the damaged float lying a short distance away.

Skinning the animal and putting the hide hair side down, Jacob placed all the usable cuts of meat on it, and then he had an idea. Taking a closer look at the float, he saw it was almost torn in half from striking the ice ridge. And the struts fastening it to the plane's fuselage had ripped the top section almost completely off, leaving a section roughly shaped like the front half of a canoe.

Just maybe, with a little work, he could fashion a crude sled. The light aluminum would pull easily across the ice and might also be of use in the snows that were surely soon to fall.

In less than an hour Jacob arrived at the wreck towing his sled full of meat. As always, approaching the wreck gave him a solemn feeling. He had begun to think of it as a memorial to the poor fellows trapped within.

Quietly, he retrieved the item he needed, which was an old army surplus ammo can. The can now held a few boxes of Winchester .338 ammo, which he could use, but he mainly needed it for its waterproof design. It would now be used to protect things that needed to be kept dry at all costs.

Chapter 10

It took the better part of the day to get the meat hauled back to camp and put away. Jacob had constructed a cold storage locker into the bank near where Little Rock Creek emerged from under the boulders. Lining a hole dug into the bank with flat rocks and using a larger flat rock for a lid, he achieved a refrigerator that would impress Fred Flintstone. Meat placed in a waterproof bag and stored inside should keep for days.

Although he hated liver and heart, it was on the menu for tonight. He had always been told it was good for him, and he felt that keeping healthy should be top on his list of things to do. "By Golly, if I'm going to freeze to death, at least I'm gonna be healthy when I do it," he muttered out loud. "And I'm gonna take me a vitamin too."

Rummaging around in the tent produced a large bottle of multi-vitamins. He had found a bottle in each of the Germans' kits and had carried one back to camp. He knew he had already lost weight, but he also knew it was weight he needed to lose anyway. He really felt better physically than he had in years; it was only the mental games he found extremely difficult to deal with. As long as he kept busy doing some sort of physical activity he could cope with the situation, but he sure dreaded the quiet evenings, when his mind would wander.

The writings to Anna helped. When he wrote, he felt as if he were actually speaking with her. He anticipated her answers and it soothed him. He would talk about the girls tonight and how much he loved each of them, remembering things they did when they were little. Knowing the weather would soon be unbearable — in fact, a blizzard might blow up any day now, for the nights were getting considerably colder — he began to think maybe spending the winter in a Russian jail wouldn't be so bad given the alternative. While cleaning the supper skillet, he had an idea. He decided to make a hike down to the beach to see if maybe the area had been visited by any local fishermen. For all he knew, there may be a village or town along the coast somewhere relatively close. He remembered looking far in both directions the day after the crash with ten power binoculars and seeing no sign, but still, there may be habitation over the horizon.

Before turning in, Jacob gathered together items he thought he would need for tomorrow's hike and stuffed the daypack. Starting to build up the fire to have light to write by, it hit him how tired he really as. Hauling the caribou meat and dragging the improvised sled had taken its toll, or maybe the wonderful meal of heart and liver had made him sleepy. Whatever the reason, he decided to forgo the writing tonight and get a good night's sleep. Banking the fire, he crawled once again into the sleeping bag and soon dreamt again of the big track in the sand.

The rising sun found Jacob standing on a high bank above Warm Creek, deciding on which of two game trails he should take into the valley. The shortest of the trails led close to a swampy-looking area that was sure to be nothing but muskeg, fit only for moose and not for a man in his fifties carrying a rifle and heavy pack. The other led along higher ground but crossed a long, steep slope of loose shale. Choosing the latter, he continued toward the coast now a little more than a mile away.

From the high vantage point above camp, Jacob had determined approximately where Warm Creek met the coast. This was his destination, and then he planned to walk the beach in the direction of where the Blue River emptied into the ocean.

Stopping to catch his breath after crossing the slippery slope, Jacob scanned the sea for any type of craft, only to catch glimpse of a lone fluke disappearing beneath the gentle swells. The sea looked to be very calm this morning, and he had all but forgotten the possibility of seeing a whale. Grabbing for his binoculars, he focused on the spot in time to see the steamy spray as the great mammal exhaled. Diving once more, it was gone, and although Jacob watched the area for several minutes, nothing else appeared. A few birds fed on and near the beach, the larger ones more than likely gulls and the smaller ones probably puffins floating nearer the shore, their colorful beaks bobbing for small fish just beneath the surface.

For a moment he marveled again at this wild and wonderful place. He found himself thinking of how he could happily spend the rest of his life in this majestic piece of paradise, and an instant later being overcome with sadness that he just might indeed. The sharp cry of a fish eagle broke his melancholy, and he pushed onward.

In little more than an hour Jacob stood catching his breath and gazing along the beach close up for the first time. He noted that it was made up of pea-sized gravel in a rainbow of colors, more so than common beach sand. Here and there a large boulder lay half buried. A myriad of shore birds chased the gentle surf, hoping to find a tasty morsel being uncovered, while others dived among the many small icebergs calved from the nearby cliffs of Dead Beaver Glacier, which lay at the head of a long, narrow fjord.

The beach ran from the ocean inland perhaps eighty yards before stopping at a sandy bank about head high, topped with a thick growth of willows.

Jacob picked a sun-warmed waist-high boulder for the place to take breakfast. He hadn't bothered to fix even a cup of his precious coffee before starting out this morning, and now his growling stomach said it was time to stop. Digging into the daypack produced two cans of potted meat, a tin of sardines packed in olive oil, and a Ziploc bag half full of broken crackers.

He elected to dine on the sardines, and as he opened the small, flat can, he thought of old Johnnie Morgan. It's funny how sometimes a sight or smell can trigger a long-forgotten memory. He hadn't thought of old Johnnie in many years. In fact, he was sure the old guy had died several years ago now.

Johnnie Morgan was a man of small physical stature, not much over five feet tall, with thick white hair cut to about a half inch all over his head. He wore thick horn-rimmed glasses and he loved guns. Not much of a hunter but one heck of gunsmith. After retiring he had taken gunsmithing up full time and turned a small backyard one-car garage into a gun shop. Jacob had bought his first hunting rifle from Johnnie. The old guy was unique; for one reason, he was the only Johnnie Jacob knew who spelled his name with an *i-e* instead of a *y*.

Johnnie's shop looked to be a disorganized mess, when, in fact, everything was in reach. He had little shelves at the back of his workbench that held at least a hundred sardine tins. He always said they were easier to find stuff in rather than digging around in deeper cans or boxes. The tins held an endless supply of tiny nuts and bolts, sears, clips, pins, shims, or anything else a competent gunsmith would need.

Johnnie also loved the outdoors and solitude. He had a rustic hunting camp in the mountains that he used often to just get away. It was near the area where he grew up, and although he had given up hunting years before, he was always there during deer season, simply because he enjoyed the visits from old friends who were sure to drop by.

Once, about twenty-five years ago, he had invited Jacob and his dad to the camp for the first week of hunting season. Jacob had never killed a deer, so he could hardly wait to get to the mountains. There was no electric in the camp and only a coal-burning stove for heat and a few gas lights. Water came from a spring in the side of a hill, and the only bathroom was a small, crooked shed with a crescent moon carved in the door. But Johnnie did have a propane stove, and he loved to cook.

Jacob and his dad arrived about an hour before sundown and were greeted by a smiling Johnnie standing on an unstable-looking porch. He proudly showed them into the little two-room cabin containing a main room and a small bedroom with one small bed. Two old worn-out couches and a ragged easy chair draped with an equally ragged quilt surrounded an old rusty coal-burning stove. The floor around the stove crunched with ashes, and a wooden box against the wall held lumps of coal. It was the prefect deer hunting camp.

The weather had turned cold, and as the sun set, a light snow began to fall when Johnnie pointed to a neighbor's camp far across the hollow, where a soft yellow light spilled from the windows. "My neighbor done went and got electric run up to his camp. Next thing you know somebody will be wantn' to build a shoppin' center around here somewhere. Hope I never live to see it." Turning to Jacob's dad, he continued, "You fellers can bed down right here on the couches. I'll get up in the mornin' and fix you a hearty breakfast, and since I won't be doin' any huntin', I won't wake you till it's ready."

It had just gotten full dark when Johnnie announced he was going to turn in. "Up here, I sleep with the sun," he said. "Make yourselves at home. You won't wake me once I hit the cot. Oh, yeah, how do you like yer eggs?"

Jacob finished the sardines and crackers, then stowed the can in the Ziploc bag, placing both in his daypack. Taking a drink from his canteen, he smiled as he replaced the lid, recalling the breakfast old Johnnie had made.

Jacob and his dad had sat relishing the warmth from the old coal stove, planning the next day's hunt for a few hours after Johnnie had gone to bed, but the soft popping of the burning coal soon lulled them to sleep too.

"Get up, fellows! The lights are already on across the holler. Them fellers will be out ahead of ya if ya don't shake a leg!" Old Johnnie yelled, while flipping eggs in the hot skillet. "Hot coffee's in the pot, and there's sausage and hash browns on the table. Biscuits be ready time ya get dressed."

Jacob and his dad groggily dressed and sat down to the hearty breakfast. Johnnie kept spooning food onto their plates and pouring coffee in their cups. As Johnnie started to fill the cups for the fourth time, Jacob said, "Not another drop for me, Johnnie. I'm about to bust already."

"Mighty fine meal, Johnnie, but I'm full too," said Jacob's dad as he pushed his empty plate away.

"Be gettin' daylight soon," said Johnnie, and again, he pointed across the hollow as he added, "Them boys over there must be headin' for the woods, cause the lights just went out. Better git a move on."

"What time is it, anyway?" asked Jacob to no one in particular.

"Don't know," answered Johnnie. "I don't keep no clock up here. Like I said before, when I'm here, I keep time with the sun."

Jacob's dad walked over to check his wrist watch he had placed on a little table with his truck keys. He looked at the watch, hit it against his palm, and checked the time again before shouting, "It's only three minutes past midnight!"

"No way!" exclaimed Jacob as he grabbed for his own watch. "Mine has five minutes past!" Looking at his dad, they both then turned and looked at Johnnie.

"The hell you say! In that case, I'm going back to bed," said old Johnnie, and without another word, he went back to bed.

Jacob and his dad looked at each other for a moment, then both gave a little I-don't-believe-it laugh. Here they both stood, fully dressed, stuffed to the gills, with six hours to go before daybreak. Old Johnnie had gone to bed so early that when he awoke, he assumed he had slept all night. When the lights went out across the hollow, the guys there were just going to bed, while Johnnie thought they were leaving to hunt. Filled with too much caffeine to allow them to sleep, the two hunters sat until daybreak, often looking at each other with a shake of the head, the only sound being the soft pop of the fire and old Johnnie's snores echoing through the cabin.

Jacob's mind returned to the present day on the beach as the sound of angry seagulls stirred him from his reminiscence. Curious about the commotion, he donned the pack and eased around the boulders to a bend in the shore. In the near distance lay what looked to be a dead sea otter or small seal, and perched on the carcass was a large bald eagle.

Completely ignoring the gulls, the eagle's attention was directed to the edge of the willows, where movement soon revealed a wolverine intent on securing an easy meal. Teeth bared in a threatening grin, the wolverine danced side to side with an occasional growl and mock charge as he slowly approached, confident his brutish behavior would intimidate the eagle into surrendering his claim.

For a moment the eagle sat motionless, but as the wolverine closed in, the eagle suddenly leaped high into the air on powerful wings, leaving the gulls focused on how to steal from the new owner.

Jacob's gaze followed the eagle as it rose and was surprised to witness its sudden graceful turn into a rigid diving attack toward the unsuspecting intruder. Before the wolverine could react, dagger-sharp talons stabbed into its meaty neck, while a sharp, curved beak pierced its left eye. The eagle held on like a cowboy riding a bronco while the terrified wolverine tried to dislodge its tormentor.

Realizing quickly this meal would cost more than he could pay, the defeated bully broke free and scrambled for the safety of the willows, resulting in the winner screeching a final insult while performing a victory lap before settling once again on his prize.

Raucous laughter from the gulls faded into the distance as Jacob made his way farther along the beach. One thing he noticed was the lack of anything man-made littering the shore. No plastic of any kind, no bottles, cans, fishing line, nothing! It was as if no human had ever set foot here. This was pure nature in pristine wholeness.

After another mile the beach widened to more than a hundred yards and now consisted more of common beach sand and less boulders. A small freshwater stream spilled out of the thickening forest and down the bank in a little churning waterfall. A small pool gathered near a very large tangle of driftwood before continuing on to meet with the ocean.

Jacob puzzled as to why the huge mass of driftwood had come to rest at this location. Some of the pieces were almost two feet in diameter and smooth, as if they had been finely sanded. Deciding this was a good spot to refill his canteen, he removed the pack and took out the water filter. Leaning the rifle against one of the drifted logs, he filled the container and set it aside to filter.

Placing the binoculars against his eyes, he scanned the ocean once again for any sign of a vessel. Moving his head slowly from left to right along the horizon showed only the same empty waters, and just as his vision reached the shore, something caught his eye that caused a sharp intake of breath.

Far up the beach, three bears emerged from the willows. Moving around the tangle for a better view, Jacob saw the bears to be a large sow followed by a small cub. The third bear appeared to be almost as large as the sow, possibly a previous year's cub that had been allowed to stay in the family group. Cubs would normally stay with their mother until a new cub was born, forcing her to give the older ones the boot to fend for themselves.

Jacob smiled as he watched the small bear splash in the surf as mother dug around in the sand. The scene played out before him like an episode on the Discovery Channel, the cubs chasing the surf, only to have the surf chase them back. The young, larger bear had unusually light-colored ears, almost white compared to the dark chocolate color of the rest of him. He instantly assumed they were big brother and little sister out with mother bear for breakfast. No way of knowing for sure, but this scenario seemed to work.

Carefully moving forward to one of the few boulders for a better look, Jacob knelt behind it to rest his elbows to better steady the ten power binoculars, only to find another player had entered the scene. From the willows emerged a huge boar grizzly, bounding swiftly toward the unsuspecting group. A warning roar from the mother caused both cub and 'White Ears' to look up. The small cub looked toward her, and the other toward the advancing boar. White Ears, seeing the boar charging toward him, panicked and turned to run, only to receive a glancing blow from a huge swiping paw. He tumbled, regained his footing, then managed to escape into the underbrush. The other was not as fortunate, for before it could decide what to do, huge jaws had clamped about its neck.

Giving one pitiful scream, the cub went limp, causing the enraged mother to attack. Although the giant boar appeared nearly twice her size, the mother was on him in a second. Dropping the cub, the boar turned to face his attacker in a meeting of teeth and claws.

Jacob watched in stunned silence as the hair and blood flew, most coming from the sow, for within a few moments, she lay still. The huge boar stood over her, mouth agape and panting for a full minute, before picking up the dead cub, only to move a few hundred feet farther up the beach before stopping again. He placed an enormous front paw on the cub and proceeded to tear away large chunks of flesh, gulping it down fur and all.

Jacob paled as the grisly blood-covered beast gazed in his direction, seeming to make eye contact. A shiver went through him as he lowered the binoculars. Even though he knew large males often preyed on cubs, the reality of witnessing it unnerved him.

Reaching the mouth of the Blue River now seemed less important, maybe even a bad idea. Surely the stream contained many spawning salmon, which would make it a magnet for more of the bears. No, he decided to head back to camp. It had turned colder during the last hour, and the graying clouds moving in from the sea spoke of rain. He could take his time and make it back before dark; he sure had plenty to write about this evening.

Turning to go, he suddenly froze, fear washing down his body as if ice water filled his spine. In his excitement over watching the bears, he had inadvertently moved about thirty yards away from the tangle of driftwood, committing the terrible mistake of leaving his rifle and pack.

Now his pack lay in shreds, small pieces blowing over the sand, while between him and his rifle stood a tremendous bear even larger than the boar that now fed on the cub.

Chapter 11

Hannah Dooley stood back with her arms folded over her chest, smiling at the sight before her. Her plan had come together even better than she had first hoped. Dean's old friend, John McCoy, in San Antonio, had been a big help in doing most of the leg work, but it had been her idea and she was very pleased.

Two years before Dean's untimely death, he and Charlie had found an old 1951 Ford pickup truck on a nearby ranch in an old shed. They had been helping their neighbor, Andy Arthur, install a new stock tank when the three stopped for a rest break in the shade of the dilapidated old building.

Noticing a dust-covered vehicle inside through a wide crack, Charlie had just had to investigate. "Dean! You gotta see this!" Charlie had yelled with excitement. "A genuine '51 Ford pickup. Shoot, I was born in '51!"

The old truck had seen better days, and the 1963 license plate attested to the fact that she had been sitting for a while.

Four dry-rotted tires, a missing headlight, and several generations of mice nests under the hood pretty much guaranteed they couldn't drive her home.

Charlie just had to have that truck and asked the neighbor if he would consider selling it. Winking at Dean while Charlie wasn't looking, Andy said in a serious voice, "Don't believe I could ever part with the old girl, Charlie. She's been in the family for quite a few years. Besides that, this one is a very rare model—weren't too many made with only one headlight."

Actually, the rancher hated the old piece of junk. Andy's dad had traded for it many years earlier in hopes of using it on the ranch, but it was always breaking down, leaving the driver walking most of the time.

"Well, if you ever decide to sell it, you let me know. I'd sure like to try and fix her up," said Charlie as he ran his hand over the dusty old fender, distracted enough to not even catch the joke about the one headlight.

Later in the evening the stock tank had been placed and leveled, and while Dean completed the water connection, Charlie wandered over to the old shed again. Andy chuckled to himself as Charlie bent down to inspect under the old truck.

"Turn on the water, Andy, and let me check for leaks. I'll adjust the float, then Charlie can back-fill the ditch."

Andy turned the water valve, then walked over to the old shed, where all he saw of Charlie was his legs sticking out from under the old truck. "Charlie, you better keep your eyes and ears open for rattlers if you're going to crawl around in the dirt. I killed a big one last week right where you're layin' when I came down here to check on where to put the tank."

Charlie eased out from under the truck with eyes as big as saucers, and when he stood up, he said, "Man! I never even give snakes a thought; when you said that, I could just see 'em crawlin' all over me! How big was the one you killed?"

"Ain't seen a snake around here in years," Andy said with a grin. "I just wanted to see how fast you'd move."

"Hey, Charlie!" yelled Dean. "Bring the tractor on over, and let's get this ditch filled in, but watch out for rattlers when you climb in the cab. Andy seen a big one sleepin' on the seat last week."

Charlie rolled his eyes and took the good-natured ribbing. It was just his turn, probably next time he and Dean would pick on Andy.

Andy's wife, Helen, was a great cook, so she didn't have to try too hard to get Dean and Charlie to stay for supper. After they ate, the three men retired to the front porch in time to see the sun disappear below the low hills to the west. Andy lit up his old brier pipe and took a few puffs to get the right glow in the bowl, and then he asked, "Charlie, do you have two dollars in your pocket?"

Charlie looked a little surprised at the question, but replied, "No, Andy, I really don't. I didn't even bring my wallet with me. I've got about a dollar's worth of change in my pocket, though. Why?"

"Well, I been thinkin', and I've decided that old truck is only worth about two dollars, and that's what I'll take for it."

Before Charlie could react, Dean said, "Hey, I've got a dollar. Me and Charlie could maybe pool our money and buy it." Looking over at Charlie, he then added, "Charlie, I'll sell my half interest in the truck to you for five dollars."

Charlie didn't say a thing. He only looked at his two friends, figuring they were up to something again, but then Andy said, "Seriously, Charlie, you are more than welcome to that old heap if you really want it. I've been planning on tearing down that old shed anyway. Only reason I haven't is because I didn't want the hassle of cleaning the junk out of it. You haul off that old truck, and after the next rain, I'll just burn her down and cover up the ashes. You'd really be doing me a favor if you took it."

The saying 'one man's trash is another man's treasure' proved correct, for Charlie was like a kid with a new toy. The next day they hauled the old Ford to the ranch and made room for her in an equipment shed that was only a short walk from Charlie's bunkhouse. Every spare moment Charlie got for the next two weeks was spent going over the old hulk, removing this and sanding that. With Dean's help, they secured four old patched inner tubes to temporarily inflate the old dry-rotted tires enough to roll the pickup outside. Charlie liked working in the sun, and if it looked like rain he could push the old girl back inside.

One evening, during supper, Charlie produced a color photo from an auto parts store calendar showing a bright red 1951 Ford pickup. "This is how old Sally is going to look after her makeover. But I've decided her motor is too tired to fix, so I think I'm going to find a late-model three ninety and an automatic for her."

Dean had made the suggestion of replacing the engine after he and Charlie found the old one locked tight and full of rust. A hole in the block from a thrown piston had allowed water inside.

Work on the old truck took second to the daily chores around the ranch, and soon Sally was just another old piece of neglected junk taking up space. Hannah had seen Charlie on several occasions during the last few years remove the old tarp he used to cover the truck and stare in thought, only to replace the tarp and leave the shed. He sometimes spoke of finishing the project because it was something he and Dean had begun together but couldn't seem to get into it. He just missed his buddy.

Now Hannah smiled in anticipation of the look on Charlie's face when he saw what she had done. Her plan had started to come together even before Charlie left for Alaska early this spring.

During a Christmas shopping trip to San Antonio last year, she had run into John in a mall parking lot. She heard the throaty rumble and looked around to see a beautifully restored 1970 Chevrolet Chevelle pull into the space beside her. The grin on John's face was infectious as he recognized her. Greeting her with a warm embrace, the bear of a man spoke kindly of Dean and, with a tear in his eye, changed the subject to the old Chevelle.

The two friends were having lunch when Hannah brought up the story of the old truck at the ranch and how Charlie and Dean acted like two schoolboys with their first automobile when they first got it. She was in the process of pouring dressing on her salad when the idea struck her. She decided she would have the work done herself and excitedly told John of her inspiration.

And so, with the help of good old John McCoy, she was now staring with complete satisfaction at the end result, a beautiful, bright red, fully restored 1951 Ford pickup.

John had managed to locate the engine and transmission needed right after Christmas, and after pulling a few strings, had both rebuilt before Charlie left the following spring. Then the rush began. The day after Charlie's departure, Andy Arthur helped her load Sally on a goose-neck trailer, and she hauled the ugly old truck to San Antonio. John took over from there, having all the work done to represent the photo on the calendar.

She couldn't help but laugh, for she thought that even with a makeover, Sally was still an ugly girl. Just a shiny ugly truck, but Charlie would think her a beauty. His birthday was October fifth. He was due back on the second, and she would have to keep him away from the shed for a few days. Satisfied with money well spent, she was sure this birthday surprise would be one he would never forget.

Chapter 12

Jacob realized immediately his serious mistake, very probably a deadly mistake. He had carelessly walked away from his rifle. He could see the dead branch pointing toward the sky on the driftwood log where he had leaned it, but that was on the far side of the driftwood pile.

The terrible brute was sniffing at the remains of the pack, which now lay strewn between him and his only means of defense. Something dropped from the mouth of the bear, and Jacob noticed the crumpled remainder of the sardine tin. The beast had not yet seen him, although it was less than forty yards away, pawing and ripping through the pack's contents.

Moving his eyes to the left, Jacob noticed the near side of the driftwood tangle at maybe twenty yards. He was nearly standing in the surf, so there was no place to hide. Trying to swim away wasn't an option, either, for he was a terrible swimmer, and in this frigid water the bear would be on him before he could get waist deep. His only hope was that the bear would turn and walk down the beach away from him.

Glancing beyond the bear, Jacob relived his nightmare as he saw the great tracks in the sand led toward him. The creature had emerged from the willows less than a hundred yards down the strand. Had the bear picked up his scent? Was he being stalked?

The cold breeze blowing in his face did nothing to stop the sweat pouring down his body. Eyes glued to the hulking mass of muscle, Jacob was reminded of the bear they called Bart he had seen on television. This animal was as massive and likely had never seen a human, unless maybe Charlie or Grant or one of their special hunters last year.

The beast moved a few feet toward Jacob, swaying its huge head with each step, causing a new drenching of cold sweat, when suddenly it stopped. Seeming to sense something amiss, it slowly raised its massive head and locked a pair of black, beady eyes on a pair of terrified brown ones.

Neither beast nor man moved. Jacob recalled the first line of defense when confronted by a bear: drop in a fetal position and play dead. A split second later, he sprang for the pile of driftwood!

He'd managed three full strides before the bear reacted. With less than half the distance to cover and the element of surprise, he figured he may have a chance if he could locate a hole to dive into. The only one was a narrow opening under a large, knotty log wedged at an angle, nearer to the bank than he would have liked.

With a quick glance at the charging bear, he dove for the opening, scraping his back in the process and banging his knee. Digging and throwing sand like a badger, Jacob clawed his way under the pile of logs, breathing as if running a marathon. Feeling giddy with the prospect of making good his escape, he was entirely unsuspecting when he felt the vise-like jaws clamp down powerfully on his right foot!

He hadn't heard a sound from the bear until he felt himself being forcefully dragged backward, then the rumbling growl became the most horrible sound he had ever experienced. Stiff with fright, he never moved, and his heart surely stopped when the excruciating grip released, only for him to be violently turned over on his back. Instinctively moving both arms to cover his belly, a huge front paw roughly knocked his left arm aside, only to pin his bicep firmly to the ground. He was sure the crushing weight would break his arm as he raised his left hand enough to grab a handful of long, thick hair, the meaty muscles beneath as hard as iron.

Terrified beyond belief, his mouth yawned wide in a silent scream as his right hand suddenly brushed the handle of the knife his dad had given him. Without a thought, he withdrew the knife, fully knowing it would be of no use against the monster endeavoring to kill him. The ugly beast's eyes bored into his, while its wet nostrils expanded with a rush of air and mist as it exhaled in anger. Then, as if on cue, the big, ugly mouth opened, and he breathed in the fetid breath. He felt a huge drop of hot saliva fall on his cheek as he glared at the huge yellow fangs. Raising its head with a victorious roar, the bear then closed its mouth and looked Jacob straight in the eyes.

The wet nostrils inhaled and then exhaled forcefully as the jaws opened once again, this time for the kill. As the open maw descended, Jacob again reacted clearly on instinct as he thrust the fist holding the knife up past his wrist, into the huge gaping mouth. With the butt of the handle fully pressed against the tongue and the point of the six-inch blade against the roof of the bear's mouth, the powerful jaws acted on reflex and clamped shut, forcing two inches of the blade out the top of the bear's snout.

With a bellow of rage and pain, the beast jerked its head, trying to dislodge the offending object, spraying Jacob's sweating face with blood and saliva. Frantically pawing at its jaw and rubbing its face in the sand, the bear fought at the knife, slinging bloody slime, finally managing to break the blade with a snap, while Jacob lay frozen with fear. Somehow his brain registered the snap of the blade over the bear's agonizing roar, and he quickly concentrated on disappearing, farther this time, into the tangle of driftwood.

Moving with breakneck speed through openings a rabbit would find difficult, Jacob clambered and burrowed, kicked and plowed his way to the back of the pile, soon reaching the sandy bank.

Covered with sand and sweating profusely, Jacob pulled his knees to his chest, shut his eyes, and tried to calm himself. Shaking uncontrollably and nearly hyperventilating, he peered through the thickness of his confined space to catch a glimpse of the retreating bear far down the beach, still worrying at his snout.

As his breathing slowed nearer to normal, he spoke aloud a prayer of thanks for his survival and felt the pain of his injuries for the first time. He throbbed and ached from head to foot, especially foot, but his first concern was to retrieve his rifle. Less than twenty feet away, he could make out part of the stock still leaning where he had left it.

Freeing himself from the tangled sanctuary proved to be much more difficult than entering. He found himself trapped at every turn but managed to struggle out after wondering how in the world he had managed to work himself into the middle of this mess in the first place. He decided that with the right incentive a man could do most anything.

After hobbling to retrieve the rifle, he removed his boot and sock to happily find no broken skin, only ugly, purple bruises where the teeth had clamped down. The ankle felt sprained and was starting to swell, so he replaced the boot and laced it tightly. His left knee was also bruised and stiff, and he had suffered a nasty scrape on his back. A new knot had formed on his forehead in exactly the same spot as the one from the plane crash.

Hardly an hour had passed since he had witnessed the mother bear and cub being killed farther up the beach. His deadly ordeal had lasted only a few minutes but seemed like hours. The image of those gaping jaws would be permanently burned into his mind for the rest of his life.

The sky had become overcast, and a light, cold rain started to fall. This was all he needed right now. "Bear hunting my ass!" he said with disgust. "I could be home right now, watching television."

Glancing down, he saw the handle of the knife that had saved his life sticking out of the sand. Retrieving it, he found it still had two inches of blade left. He wondered if he would ever get a chance to explain to his dad how he had managed to break the knife. If he made it back to camp, he would write to Anna of today's adventure, so there would at least be some hope of someone knowing what he had been through, if the letters were ever found.

During the next hour the temperature had dropped another ten degrees, and Jacob was really getting cold. The remains of his pack had been blown into the ocean by the stiffening breeze, which had gusted at times before the drizzle set in.

He had found nothing to use to start a fire; all of his supplies were gone. As a last resort, he would try to kindle something with a cartridge from the rifle. Breaking a bullet open would produce enough powder to ignite some dry tinder with only a minor spark. However, keeping enough dry firewood gathered would be a problem with his bum legs. He even thought of trying to set the tangle of driftwood ablaze, but the soaking rain made that a problem. He was really tired and just wanted to sleep, but the threat of hypothermia scared him, and he knew he had to do something soon.

Glancing up the beach, he saw the carcass of the mother bear, and, without much thought to anything else, he started toward her. Wincing with every step, he hobbled nearer. The old sow lay on her side with her back toward the sea, appearing to be asleep if not for the unnatural angle of her head, obviously the result of a broken neck, and the blood showing on the sand. The sow had fought bravely for her young but had been dispatched quickly with a powerful blow to the neck, the boar's main quarry being the cub.

With his core temperature dropping, he knelt at the belly of the bear and began to skin the animal with the stub of knife. Cutting around the tops of the legs and splitting the belly skin, he worked with shivering hands to loosen the still-warm hide.

The soft rain had turned to sleet as he struggled and finally managed to roll the carcass over to free the other side, dropping the knife several times before the task was completed. The incoming tide had reached the feet of the dead bear before Jacob had freed the raw skin, dragging it now to the slightly undercut bank.

With barely enough room under the bank to shelter him from the icy rain, and only then if the wind continued blowing out to sea, Jacob wrapped himself in the fresh skin, the heavy hide pressed tightly against him. Praying the wind didn't reverse course, he found himself thanking God over and over for his survival thus far. The shivers soon subsided, and his calming body now allowed the pain of his injuries to throb with each beat of his heart. The steady rhythm soon settled him into a fitful sleep.

Chapter 13

In his dream, Jacob and Anna were asleep back to back under the heavy quilt. Sleeping in a cold room with heavy covers reached back to his childhood in a hollow of the Appalachian Mountains. In the Cabin Creek coal fields, he and his little brother slept this way, drawing from each other's warmth. Jacob's mother would turn off the open gas heaters at night, and the brothers would crawl into the big bed under mounds of quilts. It was common on cold winter mornings to find the drafty single-pane windows covered with ice on the inside.

Anna gently nudged him. *Let me sleep a few more minutes,* he thought. She nudged him again, more forceful this time. He must have slept through the alarm.

He felt a small rush of cold air and realized his head was under the cover, the reason for not hearing it. He hated that clock. The irritating electronic buzz always started his day off on a sour note. More than once he had threatened to trash it and get one of the old wind-ups with the bell alarms. One like the kind that had lulled him to sleep as a child with its soft *tick-tock, tick-tock*.

He yearned for the good old days, but Anna liked the big bright red numbers. She could wake up in the middle of the night, look across the room, and easily see what time it was. She nudged him again. *Okay, okay, I'm awake.*

Jacob's eyes snapped open, the dream fading as the musky smell of the raw hide assailed his nostrils. Something was touching him, something alive.

His heart clenched at the sudden thought of the big, furry beast with the knife blade sticking out of its snout. It had come back to eat him!

He had slept with the rifle at his side and was gripping it now, but wrapped in the hide, he would never be able to free himself quickly enough to wield it. The awareness of all the injuries returned, his breathing labored now with pain as well as fear.

One chance . . . He screamed with all the strength he could muster and fought to free himself, hoping the noise and surprise would startle the creature long enough to mount a defense.

The tactic worked, for as he threw aside the bristly blanket, the creature beat a hasty retreat, kicking up sand as it tore across the beach, running nearly a hundred yards before it stopped to look back with a puzzled expression.

Jacob's battered body ached in a dozen places with every thump of his racing heart, his throat, already raw with thirst, now burning as a result of the scream that still echoed in his ears. Relief surged through him as he realized the creature of his nightmares turned out to be the bear with the white ears. Even so, other bears may be nearby, so he cowered in the sheltered bank and listened for other sounds above the crash of the surf; there would be no more sleep tonight.

Later, when the rain had stopped and his ragged breath showed a mist in the cold, damp air, he painfully crawled out of the stiffening hide, looking and listening carefully, though the only sounds were the gently crashing surf accompanied by cries of the gulls quibbling over breakfast. Several bald eagles defended the carcass of the mother bear from each other and the other scavengers demanding their share.

Jacob was so thirsty. 'Water, water everywhere and not a drop to drink.' Long ago, he remembered reading that somewhere. "My water bottle!" he said aloud. He remembered setting it by the pile of driftwood to filter. Maybe it was still there.

Standing made him light-headed, and for a minute he felt he would throw up, but the feeling soon passed. The driftwood pile lay only a couple hundred yards down the beach, but in his condition would feel like miles. The cold air made him want to cover himself with the old hide, but the added weight would only make the walk more painful. He decided to hurry as much as possible. If the fresh water was still there, the cold trek would be worth it. One thing was for sure, the rifle would go if he had to drag it.

Halfway to the pile the squawking of seagulls drew his attention toward the sea. A few hundred feet off shore, several dark fins could be seen breaking the surface. At first Jacob thought of huge sharks, but then, upon closer examination, he identified the fins as belonging to a small pod of killer whales feeding.

Stopping to catch his breath, he looked through the binoculars and saw that several sea lions were trying in vain to escape the huge jaws of a carefully orchestrated attack. A shiver went through him as he watched a normal design of nature being played out before him. Everything here was food for something else, and only by the grace of God and a Kershaw knife had he been spared being the main course at yesterday afternoon's banquet. The memory would haunt his dreams for years to come, if he was lucky. Right now, his main goal was to somehow survive the next few days.

Skirting the edge of the driftwood tangle, Jacob spied his water bottle exactly as he had left it. The cold, clear water had formed a thin film of ice, which brought instant relief to his raw, parched throat. Never had a pint of water tasted so good. Things taken for granted, in the right circumstances, became more precious than jewels. Here he stood in one of the most beautiful places on Earth, a land of his dreams, and yet the very basic necessities of life mattered most.

The cold water chilled his insides and made him more aware of the cold air. He needed to find a way to stay warm, for even the slightest breeze could cause real problems, and more rain would be fatal now, in his weakened condition.

He refilled the water bottle, and as he turned to set it aside, a glint in the sand caught his eye. Inside a nearly worn away paw print lay the top of an aluminum can, which, on further examination, turned out to be an intact can of Vienna wieners. Manna from Heaven! Just maybe some of the heavier items from his pack could have escaped being victims of wind, surf, and claw.

Half an hour's search turned up a treasure trove of items: a military issue spoon and fork set still snapped together, and the real prize, a magnesium fire starter keychain with a broken plastic compass and two keys. The fire starter had been carried in his pack for several years, and it had never been used. He had no idea what the two brass keys were for; more than likely there were a couple of padlocks somewhere back home in his little workshop in need of keys. No doubt he had wondered where these were every time he ran across an old padlock lying in a box of junk.

Turning the little magnesium block over in his hands and running a finger down the flint striker insert, he took inventory of what he had: a little food, water, a way to make fire, a rifle, and up the beach, a soon-to-be-stinking bear hide. He looked up and said aloud, "Thank you, Lord."

Deciding to set up a temporary shelter within the driftwood tangle, to be nearer his water and firewood source, stirred him into action. Within an hour a niche had been dug into the sandy bank beneath the tangle, and a small fortress built around it. Nestled in a small depression in the sand, a small fire flickered, bringing much-needed warmth.

It had been easy to get the fire going. Shaving off small pieces of the magnesium block with the broken knife and then sparking into the shavings had ignited what dry wood he could find into the life-giving little blaze. Most of the driftwood in the pile was so water-soaked it would never burn, but he was fortunate to find several pieces dry enough, along with the encouragement of some dry grass, to get the fire going. He thought of how the simple things in life were often the most important. His meager possessions were, at this moment, more valuable than a stack of gold.

Building the fire up a little to keep it going, Jacob decided he was warm enough to hobble up the beach to retrieve the heavy old hide. Even with the fire going, it would be much more comfortable to sleep on it than the cold ground.

The air felt a lot colder after Jacob left the warmth of the fire, and he hurried as best he could toward the spot under the sandy bank where he had spent the previous night huddled in the raw hide. The bear skin looked like something he would normally avoid getting near, let alone use as a blanket, but desperate times called for desperate measures. Dragging out the skin, he tried to shake off some of the sand, but the heavy weight of it only aggravated his sore muscles, so he settled for draping it around his shoulders. He noticed that a part of the hide felt warmer than the rest but attributed the sensation to the sun shining on a part of it during the day. Halfway back to his new shelter, though, he noted that the sun was completely hidden behind an overcast sky.

The hide was a welcome addition to his new shelter, and by placing the skin side down while arranging a part of it up against some driftwood, he soon had almost all of the wind blocked. The cold, gentle breeze blowing in from the sea barely fanned the fire, and the bank would protect him from most rain if it started again.

After a day or so spent here, he felt sure he could get back to his main camp. He would eat a few of the little wieners tonight and the others tomorrow morning, hoping a warm night's rest would put his swollen foot on the mend.

The fire had produced a hot bed of coals, and its warmth soon made him drowsy. Five minutes after adding more wood he was dead asleep.

He had failed to notice the small pair of eyes staring at him from beyond the driftwood pile.

Chapter 14

Danny sat behind Charlie's desk with a million things going through his head. Charlie's answering machine was completely full, and the phone continued to ring. He knew it was someone else seeking information about the missing plane and the fate of the hunters and crew or a volunteer of assistance. He had no information and was just as concerned as everyone else; he just didn't know what to tell someone if he didn't know anything himself.

The last call had been from Jesco Isenberg, the pilot who had been the rescuer of Danny and his people from the Tippen Creek Camp. Jesco had flown over the camp while returning with a group of his own hunters and noticed the frantic waving on the shore below. Upon landing, to the relief of the haggard group, he soon made arrangements to return and ferry everyone out.

Danny's camp had remained in good spirits during their extra six days in the bush. Although everyone had concern over the plight of the missing party, the hunters deemed the circumstances a grand adventure. Danny, on the other hand, suffered with his worry on maximum overload, for he knew the true gravity of the situation. And now the weight of it began to take its toll.

Looking over the list of names and phone numbers scratched on the legal pad, he knew it was time for him to start returning the calls. The list contained the first dozen callback numbers taken from Charlie's answering machine. Shrop was manning the other phone at Charlie's little kitchen table. He was so glad that Bill Shropshire had stuck with him. More than a crusty old guide, Shrop could be counted on for about any task. Danny was grateful for the help, so he unplugged the phone at the desk and stuck it into the connection to the fax line. He had to get back with these people, even if he couldn't offer them much information at all.

Charlie should at least have told him where the special hunt area was. You never fly off into the wilderness without someone knowing your destination. Usually the many Alaskan pilots kept within their own hunt area, flying from camp to camp and back to their home base. If ever there was a reason to deviate, they would file a normal flight plan with someone, but neither Charlie nor Grant had left any information. He and Shrop had combed through every drawer and file but found no information regarding where they could have been heading. The map on the wall only indicated the location of the known camps. They could have flown off in any direction after the flyover at Tippen Creek.

Danny sat back in the old worn leather chair, shut his eyes, and gave a deep sigh. He couldn't even give the searchers a hint of where to begin to look. Hell, he was only the camp cook, why should he assume so much responsibility? Because it had always been so. People had always deferred to him, due to his serious nature and dedication to friends and employers. That may be why most all of his employers had become his friends.

He stretched out his arms in an attempt at relaxing the taut muscles in his upper back and let them slowly drop toward the floor. Almost at once he felt a warm lick on his hand and looked down to see Emily staring up at him with her big, sad eyes. Smiling, he gave her a loving scratch behind the ears, and she returned to the old rug in the corner as he sat up to the desk.

Scanning the list again, dreading the first call, for he had no real information to share with anyone, he noticed the name and number for an Anna Arrowood. The name Arrowood didn't register with him as being the name of any of the special hunters. Then, as suddenly, he remembered the fellow who was to be his fourth hunter in camp, the guy who landed his dream hunt for a pittance, unable to land due to the fogged-in lake. Less than two weeks ago, and now it seemed like months. This poor lady must be beside herself with worry. He would call her first.

Anna answered the phone on the first ring, even before the caller ID had displayed the number. "Hello?" Her voice broke as she spoke.

"Mrs. Arrowood? This is Danny Parker, calling for Mason's Alaskan Safaris—"

"Oh! Mr. Parker, please tell me Jacob is safe. What happened—?"

"I know you're worried sick, Mrs. Arrowood," Danny gently interrupted, "and I don't exactly have any bad news for you, but please let me explain what little I do know."

Anna listened carefully, hanging on to every word for a thin thread of hope. This past week had been the longest and most difficult in her life. Trying so hard to keep an upbeat and positive front for the girls, she barely kept the torment and worry tearing at her heart from the inside hidden. Every night, what little sleep came was the result of the sheer exhaustion of crying when alone. Her own prayers, along with those of her church family, kept her from losing her sanity completely.

The girls weren't children anymore, and they had her inner strength. She could tell how distraught they were by their forced bravado. "Dad's all right. He just can't get to a phone. The dumb plane probably won't start and he's trying to fix it for them. You know if something's broken, Dad will figure out a way to get it patched up."

They fed from each other's courage, and Anna could feel that the hugs were tighter and lasted a little longer than usual, and everyone's eyes seemed to be a little redder. She was so proud of the children, beautiful young women now. She and Jacob had done well. "We make pretty babies," she often told him. People had always commented about the pretty Arrowood girls.

Danny Parker finished by saying it wasn't unusual for a bush pilot to be a few days overdue for any number of reasons. Anything from bad weather to a mechanical problem could cause a delay, and the good news was that no one had reported finding any wreckage. He promised to call her again when he heard anything at all.

She thanked him and hung up feeling only slightly better. The girls had been hovering around her, so she repeated everything Mr. Parker had said. Afterward, they held hands and prayed for the safe return of Jacob and the others. The girls volunteered to call family and friends with the latest news and left her alone with her thoughts.

The sun had long set, and the day had been warmer than usual for this time of year. It was full dark when she decided to go sit in the swing on the front porch for a little while. Telling no one in particular to call for her when they had Otis on the phone, for she needed to speak with him herself. Poor Otis had called every day seeking information about Jacob. She knew the big man was greatly concerned for his friend.

With her little dog curled up in her lap, Anna gently put the swing Jacob had built for her into motion. The warm breeze felt comforting on her skin as she closed her eyes. Thoughts of their years together came pouring into her mind with a flood of emotion. Fresh tears ran down her cheeks as she opened her eyes, to see the big full moon hanging above the trees on the hill.

Chapter 15

A small pocket of moisture warmed and then quickly heated into steam. The building pressure resulting in a miniature explosion, causing a loud pop in the damp firewood. The sudden noise startled Jacob from a sound sleep. He felt completely warm and comfortable for the first time in many days, free from most of the aches and pains that had recently plagued him.

He had been dreaming when the popping of the fire awakened him. Dreaming of mowing the grass at home of all things. Anna had just brought him a cold glass of her sweet iced tea, and he had cut the throttle down low on the old mower and was reaching for the glass when the mower backfired, as it sometimes did at idle. The sound of the fire pop corresponded with the backfire of the old mower. Funny how things like that happened. That glass of iced tea sure would have tasted good. Anna always made his tea really sweet with pure sugar, none of the artificial stuff. She would sweeten it before adding the ice, when the tea was still hot. This way the sugar would melt completely. He hated to have undissolved sugar floating around in his iced tea.

Reaching to place another piece of wood on the fire, he thought he saw movement beyond the edge of the firelight but quickly discounted it as only dancing shadows cast by the fire through the driftwood tangle. He would have to work on not seeing ghosts and monsters at every turn, for every thought of the bear encounter caused a cold sweat to form on his back. Pushing that memory aside because, for now, he was warm and safe, he retreated back into the protection of his cozy nest.

As he lay there pondering all that had transpired this last couple of weeks and just before sleep claimed him again, his mind filled with yearning for his family, his Anna. With heavy eyes glancing toward the heavens, there, framed by the driftwood, shone the big old moon. Something in the way the face seemed to smile at him gave him comfort, for this was his link to Anna. He loved her so. Would he ever see her again?

Early morning arrived with a rush of cold wind, stirring the ashes of the now-dead campfire into a sleet of black snow. The little dark blizzard coated Jacob's face as he emerged from beneath the smelly old hide. The greeting set his mood for the day. The land had lost its beauty, and hunger clenched his belly in a painful grip. It would be so easy to cave in to the situation and call it quits, for all common sense branded his plight as hopeless.

Staring toward the cold, foamy surf, his mind formed a vision of little girls laughing and playing in the emerald water. The sun shone brightly, and the sand felt warm on his feet. Warm breezes caressed his body as Anna's hand found his. The huge beach umbrella provided a comforting shade from which to watch their children scamper about the wet sand as the gentle waves washed up the beach.

Something tugged at his heart as the vision quickly faded, to be replaced by sense of dread. The overwhelming desire to remain within the tangle nearly consumed him, but somewhere deep within the recesses of his psyche, he once again heard the faint sound of children laughing. With the laughter came a firm determination, so he crawled out into the open, dragging the old hide along. Gathering up his few possessions and taking a thin, sturdy piece of driftwood to use as a walking stick, he set off.

Mid-morning found Jacob only two miles farther along the beach. The dreary, overcast day, accompanied by the nagging hunger pangs and throbbing in his foot made him so frustrated he could hardly stand it. He refused to stop, for his goal was to reach the permanent camp before nightfall. Stubbornness kept him moving. Good fortune would be to find a little food along the way; bad fortune would be to become food along the way.

Try as he might, the lingering images of the great bear wouldn't leave his mind, receding into the background only to leap forward at the slightest sound or sudden movement, causing a racing of the heart and rapid breathing. This fear soon won out over frustration and stubbornness. A healthy dose of fear could keep you alive.

The cold wind continued with no reprieve, causing his eyes to water and blurring his vision. Seeking a moment's refuge behind a head-high boulder, Jacob scanned the distant foothills for the protruding bench that held his camp. Upon locating it, he noticed far in the distance where the huge glacier emptied into the sea. Although the river of ice itself couldn't be seen, the slope leading up to it seemed to overwhelm the little bench of his camp.

Carefully studying the land from this perspective, he decided the quickest direction to his goal would be to cut cross-country. The land was a little higher here, so the cross-country route shouldn't be very marshy, and the trees would protect him from this aggravating wind.

Shifting the heavy wet hide, which had become a burden as well as a blessing, he picked his planned route into the mountains. The smelly old skin had surely saved his life and was now blocking the cutting cold of the wind, for which he was grateful, but he really missed his warm Gortex parka. With every moment and every step forward, he gained more respect for the tough old mountain men. That hardy breed had to be part animal in the way they coped with the elements.

A well-worn trail led through the willows, and a thorough search of the area revealed only moose and small animal tracks. Just maybe the rich salmon streams behind would keep the big bears occupied until the time for hibernation. Muttering a short prayer for safety, Jacob turned from the beach and entered the stand of willows.

The trail reminded him more of a narrow tunnel, and with every cautious step, he felt as if his breath was leaving his body. Near panic seized his chest, and several times he started to turn back to the beach, but then the narrow trace gave way to more open land as the elevation increased. The path led up a small hill, and at the top, the trail forked.

Jacob stopped to catch his breath and looked back the way he had come. He felt a little ashamed at having been so fearful while walking through the willows, for from this angle they looked peaceful, gently swaying in the breeze, but he didn't think there was anything that could make him go back through them again. He had been legitimately scared, and he still couldn't shake that feeling.

Breathing a little easier at not feeling so hemmed in, he studied his options. The path to the left led down to skirt the edge of the willows for a short way before turning back to the right into a long, narrow valley. The direction was correct but had the promise of being somewhat marshy. It could lead into some of the muskeg flats that were to be avoided at all costs.

Being cold was bad enough, but being wet and cold could be a killer. He'd stick to the high ground. The trail to the right was not as direct and looked quite rough, but was clearly the only sensible choice.

The first hundred yards or so was rocky and steeper than

expected but eventually leveled onto a wide, grassy knoll surrounded on three sides by a thick spruce forest. The open side was the way he'd entered, and he turned around to check his back trail once again. This uneasy feeling of being followed was really grating on his nerves.

Something shining ahead caught his eye, and upon closer examination, a small clear teardrop-shaped lake could be seen through the trees. At the far end of the lake, a narrow stream trickled out of the rocks through a small stand of dead timber. The old evergreen trees must have once stood on dry ground, but as the little lake grew in size the water soon caused their demise. Stark and bone gray against the dense green, they were drowned and dead.

Protected somewhat now from the steady breeze and with the exertion of the steep climb, Jacob felt warm and tired. The grassy knoll with the lake view would be the perfect place for a snug little cabin. He and Anna had often dreamed of a place like this in the mountains of Wyoming or Montana.

Choosing a spot at the edge of the lake to rest for a spell, he became aware again of the hunger that gnawed at his belly. The audible growl it made caused him to jerk his head toward the tree line. The subtle sound startled him and he had to smile. Jumping at hearing his own stomach growl was slightly funny, even now.

Yes, he thought, Anna would love it here. He could envision the little cabin with the wraparound covered porch, rocking chairs on all sides. Mostly, though, she would love the water and how it reflected the blue of the sky and merged with the evergreens in a painting only nature could create.

Gazing over the lake, he noticed for the first time the small strip of ice lining the water's edge, only an inch or so out onto the calm surface, but a prelude to colder times ahead. "How many days longer can I really expect to survive here?" he asked himself aloud. His very next thought was a sudden urge to get back to his journal. There were so many things left to be said; to Anna, to the girls, his parents and close friends. He prayed that coherent words would continue to come to him in the next however many days he had left.

As he turned to leave the water's edge, he stopped to survey the mountain beyond the trees at the far end of the lake. In the distance he could make out the bench, where he hoped his camp remained intact. From this angle the campsite looked to be no more than a bump on a slope that led to the higher mountains, the peaks of which were already white with a new coating of snow. The crash site lay in the glacier valley over the high ridge to the right.

Deciding to skirt the lake to the east through a small stand of spruce, he then would slowly pick his way up the steep slope. Eyeing the general direction of the feeder stream, he wondered if this water came from a branch of the one by his camp that he called Rock Creek. He knew it flowed in a series of small cascades into the valley but could easily split on the rush to the sea.

This small lake had no outlet that was apparent but probably seeped into the ground and helped to feed the marshy muskeg flats in the valley to the west. With a parting glance, he pulled up short at movement near the dead trees across the lake. An eagle was landing on a broken branch at the top of the tallest dead spruce, folding its wings as it stared intently at the lake. Probably looking for lunch, Jacob thought, just as the huge bird leaped from his perch and silently glided out over the water. With hardly a wingbeat, it descended toward Jacob, and with barely a ripple on the surface, snatched up a large trout.

Amazed at the sight, Jacob stood still and marveled at the raptor as it fought for altitude. Seemingly hovering as the great wings fought the air for purchase, the hunter with its prey slowly defeated the pull of gravity and gained height above the lake. As if in slow motion, it rose with sound determination to a flight path that would be directly over Jacob's head. As the big bird approached, struggling to maintain a hold on its prize, for a reason he never knew, Jacob instinctively threw the walking stick into the air, spinning it akin to a baton tossed by a drum major.

The effect was instant, for the eagle reacted in such a way as to drop the trout almost at Jacob's feet. With an angry cry, it banked over the lake and was soon cursing in an avian voice over the distant valley.

Jacob fell on the flipping fish as the stick splashed into the edge of the lake. Elated at his good fortune, he whooped with excitement as he claimed his prize, stomach growling in concert with laughter.

Flame-seared trout had never tasted so good; in fact, he couldn't remember any meal being more satisfying. Sated, he relaxed near the dying coals of the small cook fire. With a good hike still ahead and with a healthy burp, he covered the coals with dirt and, with newfound strength, stood to resume his trek.

Movement at the edge of the trees drew his attention. The familiar feel of ice water filling his spine froze him in place as the bear stepped out of the forest.

Chapter 16

Otis stared in dismay as Bertha's life blood poured onto the dry Wyoming prairie. A thickening pool formed around his worn boots even as he pondered the grave situation. Big Bertha, as she was affectionately known, was the old Ferguson tractor with a big powerful Perkins Diesel engine that had served the ranch faithfully for several years. She had now become only a heap of scrap in the middle of the hayfield.

More than three-quarters of the huge field lay spotted with the big twelve-hundred-pound round bales; six hundred and four to be exact, for he was making the final count for the day when the old tractor threw the rod through her belly.

The morning had started off on a sour note, with the threat of rain in the forecast for tonight. At any other time rain would be welcomed, often prayed for, but not now. Not when he needed the hay to be dry for baling. Baled wet, it would mold and could make the cattle sick or worse, and last night, he had dreamed of his buddy Jacob. He hardly ever dreamed, but in last night's event, he and Jacob had climbed an old dead cottonwood to poke into a honey bee's hive. They had noticed honey running out of a knothole several feet above their head and were bound and determined to harvest a pound or two.

He didn't even like honey, and when the bees attacked, he lost his grip and fell. On his way to the ground he awoke. He couldn't get back to sleep for thinking of his buddy. They had had no word out of Alaska, and although the authorities continued to give Anna hope, he was expecting the worst.

Days of air search by nearly a hundred planes had found nothing, nothing at all. The bush pilots were a tight brotherhood and would not give up when one of their own was down, but so far, nothing.

Otis felt especially sad for Anna and the girls; he'd talked with them nearly every day and knew he and Jude would soon have to make a trip back East. They needed him and he needed them. Anna was a strong woman and would never give up hope. Maybe he could draw from her strength.

A subtle stirring behind him caused Otis to turn away from Bertha's demise. Old Bob and Jennifer sauntered around a hay bale; Old Bob dropped the halter rope as Jennifer began to sample the fresh-rolled hay.

"Knew she was gonna play out before ye finished the day," croaked Old Bob matter-of-factly. "Heard that knock in her belly clear down in the river bottom."

Otis stared at the little old man with the tobacco-stained beard and the fuzzy white hair peeking from beneath the brim of a ragged old Stetson. The hat could have been old when Jesse James was a young man. Old Bob's faded and patched bib overalls were wet but not dripping.

"Yep, was just finishing up my laundry when I heard her quit. Surprised she lasted this long with all that racket she was makin'. Ya know ya still got hay to bale. Guess you'll have to pile it in a big stack. I'll help ya tomorrow, if ya want me to. Don't worry, it ain't gonna rain. I'd help ya today, but I got a lot of stick to place. Spotted me a big new dog town over next to the Robison place."

Otis had to grin at the little old man in spite of his new load of problems brought on by the death of Bertha. Old Bob hardly ever spoke much, but when he did, he said everything on his mind at once. You couldn't get a word in until he was through.

He was correct in the fact that without a tractor large enough to operate the round baler, the remaining hay would have to be stacked, or maybe put up in small square bales. It would be a lot of work with the small tractor, but Otis felt amused at the seriousness in which the old guy stuck to what he considered to be his sole present purpose in life.

"Got me a load of the best sticks I had in a while," he said as he nodded toward Jennifer.

Otis followed the nod and noticed the little donkey staring directly at him, almost seeming to smile as she chewed on a mouthful of the fresh baled hay. On her back, balanced perfectly and bound to a homemade pack frame, was a large bundle of dry sticks and limbs gathered from along the river. Otis knew at once why they had been gathered, for the results could be witnessed in remote prairie dog towns throughout the area.

Old Bob felt he was on a mission, a mission of one, and, of course, Jennifer. He would spend days gathering just the right sticks, haul them out to the dog towns, and carefully place them in the burrow openings. When his task was complete the dog town would resemble a small forest of dead sticks.

To his way of thinking, the sticks would provide handy perches for hawks and eagles while on the hunt. A main source of prey for the big birds happened to be the little rodents. The feathered hunters would perch on the sticks and wait in ambush for an unsuspecting dog to venture out.

A common dog town would be located on the treeless prairie, where the slightest shadow or hint of danger would be loudly reported by the town's many lookouts. When a soaring threat was spotted, the whistle of alarm was given, and all would quickly scurry to safety.

In his own way, Old Bob felt he was evening the odds a little because, for some reason, he just hated prairie dogs. Otis hated the little rodents too, but not to the extent of Old Bob. Most people thought the little animal to be cute and harmless, maybe because they were called prairie dogs instead of the more appropriate prairie rats, but whatever they were called, they were a real source of irritation for the rancher, who often spent a considerable amount of time and money to eradicate the dog from their range.

Cattle would sometimes step in an old burrow entrance and break a leg, especially if the hole happened to be covered in snow. The little pests also ate the grass, including the roots. The cows would eat the grass down short, but it would grow back, but the dog towns were soon void of all plants except the nasty little cactus. And then there were the rattlesnakes and fleas. Walking through a dog town could oftentimes leave a fellow covered with fleas, and the rattlesnakes also fed on the dogs and would get comfortable in the cool burrows.

Old Bob didn't feel a sense of duty to the ranchers; the weird little fellow simply hated prairie dogs, and since the ranchers benefited from his overeager desire to eradicate the pests, he was left to his eccentric ways.

Otis studied the small-framed man and felt a little privileged to again be having an actual conversation with Old Bob. Most of the local ranchers had only seen Bob at a distance, for as soon as he caught sight of someone, he changed directions. Otis was the only person who didn't send him hightailing it the other way.

A few latecomers to the area actually thought the stories about the little recluse had been made up because they had never seen him. Those who had seen him knew nothing about his past or where he came from. In that respect, Otis was included; even though he had known Old Bob most of his life, he knew nothing of the old man's past.

Yes, Otis felt privileged to call the little man his friend, and he also knew the little guy sometimes sought him out for conversation as he had now, even if he never stuck around long. Only one other time could Otis remember Old Bob having tolerated a stranger, and maybe even then it was because Otis himself was there.

Several years ago Otis and his buddy Jacob had been pursuing a particular mule deer buck with an above-average set of non-typical antlers. Opportunities for as good a buck, or in one case, a better buck, had been available, but Jacob's stubborn streak left him only interested in this one, maybe due to its unique set of non-typical antlers.

The buck appeared to be aware of the game, for after several busted stalks, it soon became evident dark would catch them before they could make it back to the old truck, if they could find it at all. They had misplaced the truck on more than one occasion over the years, for the undulating prairie could be as deceptive as the middle of the ocean at times, and much worse after dark. And after dark, especially on a moonless night, the cactus monsters came out to attack. The nasty little devils were bad enough in full daylight, but they couldn't be avoided in the dark.

This time Otis had been caught up in the moment and had really lost all sense of direction. The day had been overcast, and he knew if Jacob found out he was a little turned around he'd never hear the end of it. Just as he was about to admit the fact, he noticed the derelict old windmill against the darkening sky. Old Bob's place lay just over the rise, and he owned an old pickup that had looked worn-out even back when Otis was a kid.

Otis knew the old truck ran because Old Bob once said he had rigged up a few twelve-volt lights inside his shack to read by when he couldn't sleep. Otis had given him an old hundred-foot extension cord to connect to the truck battery, which powered the lights. Old Bob would run the engine every week or so to keep the battery charged, though he never drove it. He much preferred the company of Jennifer, and once said she could gas up on grass, which was much cheaper than gasoline. Otis was sure Old Bob would loan the truck, especially if Otis promised to haul a few things back out for him.Within a few minutes the two were descending the gentle slope to where Bob called home. A ramshackle collection dominated by the two rough-hewn log structures still looked the same as when Otis first saw them many years ago. The low, flat sod roofs were still covered with a dense growth of the hateful little cactus. Otis's father had explained how the cactus formed a dense root system on the sod roof that not only served to hold the roof together but soaked up any water from a rare rain, as well as working to keep the inside cooler in summer.

Otis rarely visited this part of the ranch, but the story of how the two old buildings came to be flooded his memory when he noticed the small, flat boulder where he had sat when his father told him the story. The boulder seemed much larger back then, as he and his dad shared a moment gazing over the valley. Otis could almost smell the pipe tobacco as his dad took a deep draw and used the old brier pipe to point toward the buildings.

The old homesteads were exactly alike; both measured about ten by twenty feet and were separated on the short ends by a space of about eight feet. The story was that in the mid 1800s, a couple had homesteaded two sections of land. The young man and woman were not married, so each was able to file a claim on their own section of land. The line that separated the sections ran between the two buildings. Being a shrewd couple, they each improved upon their separate homesteads and took care to make sure all legal papers were in order before they married and connected the dwellings, with a sod roof forming a sort of breezeway between.

Much of the exterior today remained in the original condition; the appearance sat unchanged after more than a century of drying summers and freezing winters. Old Bob had carefully removed the sod and cacti in sections before replacing several rotting boards. Then he managed to replace the prickly roof so that it looked untouched. Inside, he removed a foot of the dirt floor, giving much-needed head room, before overlaying it all with flat inch-thick stone cleaved from an outcropping where the rock had naturally eroded into large, flat slabs.

An impressive patio of sorts made from the same material spread out from the front of the first building. Here is where Otis and Jacob encountered the old hermit as he placed a few pieces of dried wood on a small smokeless fire.

"Heard you two stompin' around out there for the past hour. You dun skeered off every critter within a square mile," Old Bob croaked without turning around. "Ain't got no rabbit left, but thay's plenty of coffee."

This had been the only time Otis could ever remember the old man welcoming a stranger. He recalled the day he first laid eyes on Old Bob. He had turned eight years old that spring and was pulling handfuls of new green grass to feed to a little calf with a bum leg. The little bull calf's mother had stepped on its right front leg soon after he had been born. The little fellow was trying to stand up for the first time when the accident happened. His inability to keep up with his mother and her unwillingness to stay with him, meant that he was soon abandoned. Otis's father discovered the little guy limping alone as a pack of coyotes closed in. Rescued in the nick of time, he was brought home.

"This here calf is for you to take care of, Otis," his dad had said. "You do a good job and you can have half the money when we sell him. Start yourself a savings account."

Otis didn't understand much about what a savings account meant, but he did know about money, and half-a-cow money would make him rich! For a couple weeks he had been feeding the calf four times a day with a big baby bottle. To supplement the milk diet, he had started to pull handfuls of fresh, green grass, but Limpy, as Otis had started calling him, would have nothing to do with it. He'd sniff at the offering but wouldn't take a bite.

Otis nearly wet his pants when he heard the strange voice behind him say in a scratchy tone, "That thar calf's too little to be eatin' grass, Son, but give him another month and he'll find it fer hisself. Is your pa around?"

Otis turned to see a wiry little man carrying a bent-up gasoline can. The man didn't look to be much taller than Otis, who had always been big for his age, and he had a kind face with several days' growth of salt-and-pepper beard. Curly hair of the same color poked out from under a sweat-stained Stetson hat.

Sensing the little man meant him no harm, Otis pointed to where his father's feet stuck out from under the side of an old pickup. Nodding slightly, the stranger crossed the yard and was soon in conversation with Otis's father.

The memory of that first meeting was still fresh in Otis's mind as he recalled how ancient the little man looked all those years back. He couldn't have been that old, for he didn't look that much older now. Maybe some folks are just born to look old all the time.

Otis had felt something of a connection that day as he watched the little man carry on an animated exchange with his father. Seems his car had run out of gas a few miles back down the county road. The little man was still talking, while Otis's father filled the can with gasoline and offered a ride back to his car. The pickup needed a test drive anyway, to see if the irritating rattle that had aggravated him for weeks had finally been found and fixed.

Otis looked expectantly at his father as the two men got into the pickup; his father caught the look in his son's eyes and jerked a thumb toward the pickup bed. Sporting a grin from ear to ear, Otis bounded in with a practiced leap as the truck started to pull away.

A few miles down the dusty road, in the edge of the sagebrush, sat an old blue Studebaker covered in dents and dust. The windshield contained spiderweb cracks, and the ugly front bumper dangled on one side, held up by wraps of rusty baling wire. While pouring in the gasoline, the little man looked Otis in the eye and simply said, "I hate this car."

With a thanks and a wave, the little man soon disappeared in a cloud of dust, the old car dragging a tailpipe, creating a small spark each time the metal struck a rock. Otis figured that would be the last time he'd ever see the little man, but a few days later, an old Dodge pickup pulled into the ranch yard.

"Where's yer pa, Son?" Old Bob asked by way of a greeting as he hopped spryly out of the dusty old truck.

Otis pointed toward the workshop at the side of the barn as his father walked out, wiping his hands on an old rag. Old Bob reached his hand into his overall pocket and withdrew a wrinkled dollar bill and reached it forward as he said, "Come to pay ye fer the gas."

"No need for that," replied the other man. "A neighbor should help a neighbor."

"I ain't no neighbor, and I always pay my debts," he said, shaking the dollar. "Please take yer money."

Otis's father took the dollar with a concealed smile, for he had instantly liked the little fellow. Debt paid, Bob seemed satisfied, and then he asked, "Do you know of a place where a fellow might camp for a few days near some water? I kinda like this country and might have a hankerin' to maybe stick around these parts for a week or ten days."

Otis's father hesitated for a moment, then said, "This ranch runs for little more than two miles along the river south from here. River water is fine for washing but not much for drinking. A clean spring seeps outta the bank about halfway down on the east side. Site of an old Indian camp back in the trees. I keep that little area fenced off from the cows, but they're all up in the north pasture this time of year anyhow. You're welcome to camp there for a spell. Everything beyond my last cross fence is BLM land."

"Thank ye kindly," replied Bob. "I'll keep my campsite clean." And with a tip of his hat and a wink to Otis, he climbed into the old pickup and left without another word.

Otis encountered Old Bob about a month later and about every month or so since. The old guy never left.

"What're studyin' about, Otis? Ya ain't heard a word I been sayin'. Ya act like yer mind's a million miles away. Something's bothering ya more than just this busted-up old tractor."

The concern in the old man's tone touched Otis as he snapped out of his reverie. "Sorry, Bob. Guess I was wandering off in my head for a minute. Just got a lot on my plate these days. Thanks for your offer to help, but I'll get the rest of it with the small baler, and if you're sure of your weather report, I'll be okay."

"If I know anything for sure, it's my weather perdictin. Ain't no rain in the forecast. And just remember, if somethin's botherin' ya and they ain't nothing ya can do to fix it, then yer wastin yer time if ya worry about it. Come on, Jennifer, we got work to do too." The little donkey grabbed a parting mouthful as Bob took up the halter rope.

"Take care, Bob," Otis said as the pair departed. Taking one more look at Bertha, he started toward the pickup and kicked at an anthill in frustration. *No more work today,* he thought. *At least not until I call Anna.*

Chapter 17

Jacob froze at the sight of his worst fear manifested before him. A huge mass of flesh covered with chocolate brown hair and slavering jaws full of razor-sharp teeth. Four-inch claws ready to rip him to shreds.

Vibrating like a tuning fork, knees weakened to the point of collapse but unable to move, he stared at the beast. On the verge of losing bladder control, breath racking his chest with gasps, he tried to raise the rifle, but the butt stock seemed to be stuck to the ground. All he was able to do was grip the barrel with a sweaty hand. The other held the walking stick, and the old hide lay on the ground behind him. He was acutely aware of all his worldly possessions for some reason, which made no sense. Willing himself not to move, he only stared at the bear.

The bear seemed not to notice him. It only sniffed the air as it turned its head side to side. Maybe it was trying to locate the source of the cooked trout. The smell had to have permeated everything around, including him. He remembered sitting and inhaling the wonderful smell as the trout cooked.

Dumb! he thought now.

Regaining some of his composure, he continued to stare as the bear appeared to change before his eyes. No longer was it a snarling beast ready to devour him, but a smaller bear. Still close to four hundred pounds, it was not the thousand-pound monster that filled his mind and hid behind every bush. This creature appeared to be unsure of itself, almost to the point of being afraid. It kept looking left and then right, as a person checking the traffic before crossing the street would.

That's when Jacob noticed the bear's ears, almost an ivory white! A cord of recognition was struck. It was the bear from the beach! He wondered briefly what he was doing there. Still, it was a bear, and he wanted no part of bears, any bear. Mustering newfound courage, in his deepest voice, he shouted, "GET!"

The effect was immediate, for the big cub jerked, turned, and scurried quickly for the timber. Jacob followed it with his eyes as it vanished down the back trail. Breathing a sigh of relief and feeling his heart regain normal rhythm, he stood for a moment longer before hoisting the hide and resuming his trek into the mountains.

The last hundred yards proved the most difficult; an ever-steepening talus slope giving way to large, loose boulders ended at a sheer rock face too high to climb. This area, from below, had looked to be only a few feet high, but facing it up close, it was every bit of ten feet.

Out of breath, Jacob rested as evening shadows grew ever longer. The days seemed noticeably shorter, and he reasoned sooner than later the sun would fail to even rise above the horizon. Despair joined weariness and threatened to consume him. He thought, *What's the use?* But every time discouragement settled over him, firm determination chased it away. The survival instinct manifested itself as a powerful drug. He had to keep going. In reality, only several days had passed since the crash, and here he was having thoughts of giving up! Then he remembered the journal. He had so much left to write; his heart was full of things unsaid. He had to put these last thoughts into words for Anna and the girls. Surely it would be found someday and sent to his family.

Leaning against the cliff to draw the last bit of heat from the sun-soaked rock, he looked left, then right. Neither way promised the easier solution, for the stone face turned out of sight in both directions. The camp had to lie just above this last obstacle. Figuring one direction to be as good as the next, he turned to the right, and in only a few yards a crack was revealed. With little effort he was able to climb high enough to toss his belongings up over the lip. In another moment he was staring into the middle of his old campsite. He'd had no idea he was this close!

The camp appeared the same as when he'd left, save for a tent peg loosened by the wind. Suddenly overcome with exhaustion, he didn't even stand, but crawled the few feet into the tent. Feeling under the mound of sleeping bags, he found the journal. Falling back into the mound with it across his chest, he fell into a deep sleep.

The night passed quickly without movement or a dream. Lying on the lumpy mound in the same position proved enough to thoroughly render all of his joints stiff, and he awoke rested but sore over his whole body. Groaning, he shook out the stiffness and arose to build a morning fire.

The stockpile of firewood needed replenishing. This chore would be addressed first, for the weather felt like a change was about. Dark clouds filled the valley, moving in from the ocean, and the air held an odd stillness.

Two armloads of firewood later, the loose end of the tent flapped severely as the wind marched through the camp in howling gusts. A fine mist of cold rain accompanied the wind. After a few minutes the wind calmed a little, but the rain picked up in intensity. A few minutes later, big drops pounded the ground and seemed to turn to ice as soon as they hit. Jacob rushed to beat in the loosened peg and secure the tent. The heavy canvas tarp stretched on the boulders over the tent strained at its tethers. Fearing it would be blown away, Jacob started adding more lashing, but before the task was barely underway, the wind eased and the rain turned to snow.

Under the ever-darkening sky, the snow fell in big flakes. The heavy clouds rolled over the peaks, pushing the morning light toward the horizon. With the days already shortening noticeably, Jacob feared this current prelude to winter would soon be the rule and not the exception.

Hurriedly gathering his belongings from yesterday and dragging them under the shelter, he also saw fit to go back and get the old hide. This he dragged to the back of the shelter and spread it hair side up behind the stack of firewood. Maybe one day soon he would scrape the hide and try to preserve it — after all, it had saved his life.

The snow fell steadily for most of the day, a light, fluffy powder two feet deep by early evening. Between efforts at scraping snow from the sagging tarp, Jacob sat in front of his tent and wrote in the journal. The warm fire provided comfort, but the writing brought on a deep sorrowful feeling. As much as he missed his family, he was more concerned about the anguish they must feel because he was unaccounted for. He knew everyone was worried sick, and there wasn't a thing he could do about it. At most, he could put his thoughts into words in hopes they could be read by his family one day, to help bring closure.

The smoke from the fire melted the snow on the edge of the tarp above enough to allow a row of icicles to form. He could see the flickering reflection of the flames sparkle like the lights on the family Christmas tree. Sadness clutched his heart in a tighter grip as he thought of Christmas mornings when the girls were small. The season would soon be upon them again, and he wondered how they would fare without Dad. He wondered how he would fare without them, or if he would still be among the living in a month or so. Would the snow melt and allow a few more mild days, or would this cold weather only get worse and stay until spring?

There were so many unknowns. A few more mild days might permit the gathering of a large stash of firewood; maybe allow a little time for hunting. A moose or another caribou would help to fill the larder, but it would only prolong the inevitable. And then how much firewood could he gather? How much would it take to keep him warm for six months of brutal cold? He could see no way for him to survive the winter in a tent. He needed a miracle to see him through, and while he truly believed in miracles, he didn't believe God granted them indiscriminately. Maybe it was in God's plan for his life to end here. Whatever the outcome, God was in control. Anna always said that.

The real battle to come would be the one in his mind. Already, he felt rational thinking losing ground to blind despair. The small glimmer of hope he had grew dimmer with each minute. He would drown quickly if he allowed negative thoughts to possess him. So he started to sing out loud.

"My home's in Montana, I wear a bandanna, my spurs are of silver, and my pony is gray!" He sang out loud as he made himself a good dinner from the stash of food Charlie had packed in the barrels. Dessert was a can of cling peaches in heavy syrup.

His spirits lifted a little, and being warm and dry, a down parka and thick wool pants surrounding a full belly soon resulted in heavy eyes. Humming the Montana song quietly, he noticed the icicles had grown to over a foot, reflecting the firelight beautifully. With a smile, he stowed the coveted journal and crawled into a thick sleeping bag. Sleep brought an end to the day and a night of dreaming of little girls around a sparkling Christmas tree.

Two feral eyes gazed past the dying fire into the darkening shadows beyond. Once again, the familiar scent found its way to his nostrils. The smell of what he needed was mixed with the unusual odors that didn't frighten him as much as before. Instinct told him what he needed was near. His mind was unable to comprehend the changes that had left him shaking for the past several days. Before, when things caused the shaking, he was able to find comfort near the familiar scent, and he wanted that comfort now.

The shaking grew stronger as he waded through the soft powder. He had waited through the night and for all of today, staring at the strange objects. Nearing the unknown caused the shaking to increase, but comfort was very near. His need for it overcame his fear. Slowly, on silent feet, he crept forward, and although the odd smell grew stronger, he found what he needed. Circling once, he curled up on the old hide. The shaking eased immediately, and soon he too was asleep.

Chapter 18

Otis hated flying more than anything else he could think of at the moment. He remembered why as soon as he got on the plane in Rapid City. The seats were meant for normal-sized people. His knees were rubbed raw, and he had a terrible queasy feeling in his stomach, but this was one flight he had to make. He'd insisted on accompanying Anna to Alaska. She wouldn't sit still, waiting on news concerning Jacob. Determined to go, she had scraped the money together for the trip, and Otis was to meet her in Seattle. He couldn't blame her, either. He was just as anxious for news.

The plane had touched down exactly one minute before he would have had to use the barf bag. Three minutes earlier he had discreetly located it in the seat pocket. The screech of tires on the tarmac was as welcome a sound as 'supper's on' after a long day's work, but he doubted he could ever eat again. He stumbled through the airport like a lost kid, until a kind old man showed him the flight schedules on the television monitors and pointed him in the right direction.

Anna met him with a hug at their departure gate. The trip had been arranged to allow them the same flight to Anchorage. He noticed how sad and drawn she looked, but she still managed to smile. He loved her friendly smile, and the hug had a comforting need to it. She held on to him a little longer, and when she finally pulled away, he noticed the tears in her eyes.

"Oh, Otis, what am I going to do?" she asked in a quivering voice.

His words were choked too as he said, "It'll be okay, Annie."

An awkward silence followed them to a row of seats near a window. Dropping carry-on bags to the floor, the friends prepared for a two-hour wait. Small talk dominated the conversation, or what there was of it, for both avoided talking about the reason for being there. Any news of Jacob's situation had been quickly shared. And the news was that there was no news at all.

Otis had tried to convince Anna that making a trip to Alaska would accomplish nothing, but she could not be persuaded otherwise. She felt she had to be where Jacob had last been. Maybe drawing something from his lingering spirit, the essence of his excitement must have permeated everything. That little boy excitement of his was what filled her mind now as she looked out the window at the dreary sky. Could any answers be found, or was Otis right? Maybe when they arrived, some new information could be had.

"Annie, I'm gonna take a walk. Don't go nowhere," said Otis as he lifted his bulk from the uncomfortable seat.

Anna smiled at him as he stood; he always acted like he was trying to protect her. She knew it was a tough thing for him to do, this flying. She knew how he hated it, but she also knew he would do anything for her. Otis was a true friend. "Don't forget the gate number," she called after him. "You get to fly again in about two hours."

"I can hardly wait," he mumbled as he strolled off.

Anna tried to occupy herself with a copy of a Seattle newspaper, but her mind couldn't concentrate on any of the articles. As soon as she started to read something, a noise startled her or someone would move nearby, and she would look up. A busy airport provided a thousand distractions, and this one was sure to hold the record for the loudest public address system. Over and over it seemed, the same announcement was being made for a Mr. Sautemoto to report to gate D-41.

Several minutes later Otis appeared carrying two boxes of buttered popcorn. "Here. I brought you something to eat," he said as he handed her one and sat beside her, causing the seat to groan as it took his weight. "My favorite vegetable is popcorn."

She smiled as she took the popcorn. Otis had a way of talking that always managed to somehow lift her spirits. She'd never thought of it until now, but wondered if corn was a vegetable. As she pondered this, she heard someone say, "Excuse me" and looked up to see a lady pulling a rather awkward rolling piece of luggage that wasn't quite rolling. One of the wheels looked bent and wasn't cooperating with the others, causing the piece to weave from one side to the other as the rather slight woman tried to control it. She managed to steer it past Otis and Anna to a seat nearly across from them.

Anna smiled as she caught the woman's eyes and was startled, as she seemed to recognize her. She felt as if she knew this woman, felt connected in some way. She couldn't help but stare for a moment, but quickly looked away, trying not to appear rude.

"Looks like you got a bum wheel on your cart," Otis said as he got up from his seat. "You mind if I take a look at it?"

He'd already started to turn the luggage over before the lady could reply. "The caster seems to be bent. One of them baggage handlers must have dropped it or something," he said as he grabbed the wheel with a meaty hand and bent it straight. "There, rolls good as new now."

The woman thanked him profusely for his open kindness, which caused Otis's cheeks to redden. Before he could respond, the overly loud announcement came again for Mr. Sautemoto to report to gate D-41; his party was waiting.

The flight to Anchorage was uneventful, and Otis hardly spoke a word. As the plane rolled to the gate, Anna thought she would have to pry Otis's hands from the armrests. The color of his face had mostly returned to normal by the time they got to baggage claim.

An hour and a half later, both travel weary, they were checking into the Roaring Lion Hotel. Otis made sure that Anna was settled into her room, and he reminded her that he was just across the hall if she needed anything. He treated her like she was a little sister, although she was at least five years his senior. As he was leaving, he stopped, and Anna could tell he was about to say something.

"Wonder why they named this place the Roaring Lion? You know they ain't never been any lions up here in Alaska. It's almost too cold for people."

She smiled at his attempt at levity. Otis always tried to cheer her up and make her laugh. He could act so serious and found humor in nearly everything, but she knew he was speaking from the heart when he said, "Annie, I promise I'll do everything in my power to help you find Jacob. He's my buddy, and I love him too. Anyway, you get some rest, and in the morning I'll find out where we need to go. Make sure you keep your door locked, and remember I'll be right across the hall."

She nodded and thanked him again for making the trip with her. She noticed before he quickly turned away that the big man's eyes were misty and his lip was quivering. Wondering what information, if any, she would find out tomorrow, her heart ached as she sat on the side of the bed.

****

Danny Parker hung up the phone and stared out the window. It had been several weeks since Charlie's plane went missing. Many hours of many days had been spent searching in ever-widening circles, and still, nothing had been found. It was as if the plane had simply disappeared. All of the normal flight paths between Charlie's known camps had been searched from every direction, and still nothing. Now, within the last ten minutes, he'd received two calls from people seeking answers he didn't have. The Alaskan authorities had maintained contact with families of Charlie's hunters, and Danny had been grateful for that. The Worthingtons' attorneys had initially called every day. One young lawyer seemed to be upset mostly because no bodies had been recovered. Actually blaming Danny for the situation, he complained, "Do you have any idea how difficult it's going to be to file life insurance claims if you can't provide proof of death?" he whined. Rather than tell the attorney where to stick his insurance claim, he simply hung up the phone. Checking the caller ID, he refused to answer any more calls from that area code.

These last two calls were different. These were from people who had traveled to Alaska seeking a little hope, and his heart went out to them. He told them to come by anytime but didn't know what he could say to ease their pain. He felt he owed them all the time and consideration he could give. He too suffered, because Charlie had been a close friend for years, and although the chance was extremely slim at finding any survivors, the fact that no wreckage had been found meant they couldn't rule out the chance all were alive somewhere awaiting rescue.

Anna and Otis arrived at the Alaskan Safari office to find Danny Parker involved in a conversation with a woman. The woman was facing away from them as they entered, but upon hearing the door open, she turned. Both she and Anna startled at the recognition; it was the lady from the airport with the bent luggage wheel. Otis didn't notice as he busied himself closing the door. When he turned, he immediately smiled and asked, "How's your wheel holdin' up, ma'am?"

Introductions were made, and Anna soon realized why she had felt a connection with this woman. Hannah Dooley had traveled to Alaska also seeking hope. The women seemed to bond instantly through common grief, and were soon trying to console each other.

Danny took an instant liking to Otis. The two men discussed in depth the rescue efforts and the feeling of helplessness Danny felt. On nearly every other occasion when a bush plane had gone down, some evidence had been found within a reasonable amount of time. At least the information with which Danny was familiar. Even the Alaskan Safari planes maintained an above-average safety record but still had two planes go down within the last five years. No deaths had resulted, only minor injuries, but this was different. Charlie's plane had simply disappeared. The lakes and ponds had been checked. From the air, these bodies of water would reveal a sunken plane. Those in the area were clear enough and shallow enough not to conceal a plane the size of the Beaver.

"I don't know what to say or do, Otis. The search will continue for a while, but soon the weather will be too bad. I just don't know . . ."

Otis could tell this man was suffering; he too had a good friend missing. Words weren't necessary, for a feeling of despair permeated the room.

Chapter 19

His feet felt as if they were frozen. Jacob opened his eyes to a bitter cold morning, much colder than any of the others. Dawn cast a dim light into the shelter, allowing him to easily find the Coleman lantern, although he nearly broke the ash sock before getting it lit. More for the heat than the light, Jacob was grateful as he warmed his hands. Building a fire was the first order of business, without a doubt.

His firewood stack had frozen together, while the still air seemed to grow colder. A dark, clear sky showed no clouds. No wind blew, and the normal sounds of morning were silent. Long minutes later, flames licking the wood, Jacob shivered before his fire. The little blaze grew in slow motion, as if it too hated the cold.

Jacob would never know about the visitor who shared his shelter for most of the night. The big cub, surrendering to instinct, had roused as the night grew colder. Leaving as the heavy snow continued to fall, he simply walked away into the darkness. The comforting scent of his mother faded as a stronger urge overtook him, the need that allowed his species to endure for eons. It was nearing time for the deep sleep of hibernation. The snow fell long enough to cover his tracks as he followed through on nature's plan for him to survive the winter, leaving behind another who had no idea how he could survive the same.

Alternating his back and front to the fire, Jacob finally stopped shivering. But an even deeper cold formed inside of him. This could not go on much longer, and he knew it would get colder and darker before too many more weeks passed. Should he just surrender to the inevitable? Crawl in his sleeping bag and freeze to death? The huge stock of firewood he had managed to gather would only last so long. This discussion with himself occupied most of his waking hours, but he somehow forced it into the back of his mind, despite the fact that, with the sudden cold front, he knew time was short.

After a meager breakfast, Jacob had decided he would stay here at the camp for two more days, just to see what the crazy weather would do. Back in West Virginia, a cold snap like this would be a prelude to the onslaught of winter, only to give way to several days of unseasonably warm temperatures, not unlike a second Indian summer. He could only hope, for he knew nothing of the weather patterns this far north . . . and west. He knew nothing of this place.

If he deemed the winter had set in for the season, he would make the trek back to the plane, secure the journal after writing his decision, and wait inside. Just wait. At least within the plane, the scavengers couldn't get to him and scatter his bones. This way, if the plane was ever found, at least his family would have closure. Boy, he hated the thought of going back to the wreck. It was only a cold tomb for the others, and now it would be his. He knew the feel of death was there, and he only hoped the cold would cover the smell.

His fate decided, he threw another log on the fire and,

with a macabre sense of humor, recalled that he had read that a body felt warm and comfortable just before freezing, a much better fate than being eaten by a bear.

The young bear had never been this far into the mountains, having spent all his life feeding and living along the coast in the willow flats. He had followed his mother into the foothills on occasion to munch on the tender spring grasses, and along the feeder streams in search of the fat protein-rich salmon. They had spent his few winters in dens closer to the coast, but this high, rocky terrain was a foreign land; rich for exploring, and while searching for a place to winter, he meandered to and fro. Soon his wandering led him to the wrecked plane. Sniffing and pawing revealed strange new scents, along with some that were now familiar. The investigation soon complete, he turned, following the rocky trail paralleling the glacier. This soon forked toward Warm Creek and on down into the valley. He hesitated for a moment, turning to look back the way he had come. Torn between conflicting urges, he chose the strongest and ambled toward the valley below.

On the afternoon of the second day of the cold spell, Jacob noticed a sudden change in the weather. For nearly forty-eight hours the wind had been completely still, and now a faint warm breeze blew in from the south. So warm that the icicles were soon dripping in a symphony of splashes.

The warming trend continued throughout the night, and by mid-morning the following day, Jacob noticed on the small thermometer hanging outside his tent a reading of forty-three degrees. Warm enough for a bath. Soon a large pan of water steamed over the coals.

Amazed at how a warm bath and clean clothes can lift one's spirit, Jacob actually hummed a little tune while cooking the evening meal. Again, things had changed suddenly, all dependent on the weather. Warm weather was the key to survival, but how long could it last? Was nature teasing him?

As soon as the thought entered his mind, he knew the

answer. No, of course nature wasn't teasing him. This was just a case of being in the wrong place at the wrong time, just plain bad luck. Abruptly, he questioned this thought too. Another mental tug-of-war started forming. He would endure these arguments with himself often, sometimes several times a day. He was constantly reminded of what Anna would say and what he really believed too. 'God is in control.' But was saying God was in control just a way to accept that whatever happened was okay? What choice did he have? What was God's role in this? Maybe God's plan was for him to freeze to death here, or to be eaten by a bear, or . . . maybe freezing to death and then being eaten by a bear.

Okay, a revision of plans. First thing tomorrow, he would hike to the wreck site and secure the journal. He remembered seeing a high-quality aluminum gun case in the plane. The precious document would be secure inside until found, or at least for several years, depending on how fast the glacier moved. The wrecked plane sat on its very edge. The ice river could even melt quite a bit and still leave the plane on the rocky side slope.

Maybe he should leave it somewhere else? No. Shaking his head to clear his thoughts, he knelt down and prayed out loud: "Lord, I don't know what tomorrow may bring. I don't know how long You will allow me to live in this land. I don't know anything, except You alone are in control. I only ask that someday you will allow Anna and the girls to know what happened to me. Please keep them safe, and let them know that I love them. And, Lord, when the time comes, I would ask that You not let me suffer too much. Your will be done, in Jesus' name . . . Amen."

With a renewed sense of purpose, Jacob spent the rest of the day working the old bear hide. He was surprised at how well it had held up given the rough treatment it had endured. He hadn't treated it with much care, but was well aware he was alive because of this old hide. By nightfall Jacob had the hide scraped and ready for tanning. Very little of the hair had been lost in the scraping process, and it was cold enough under the shelter for the hide to keep for a while. He would need some animal brains to finish the tanning process.

Tomorrow, he would go hunting. Fresh meat would provide a welcome change in diet, as well as provide the natural tanning material. Now he wished he had paid more attention to what his old buddy Dave Lyons had told him about the brain tanning process. Here again, a situation or abstract thought brought to mind a vision of the past. Was it just the loneliness that rekindled these thoughts? He hadn't thought of Dave in years, and now the long-past conversations seemed as recent as yesterday. Dave had always considered himself somewhat of a modern-day mountain man. He belonged to a group of black powder enthusiasts, who made their own flintlock rifles and such. These guys gathered at annual rendezvous to act like a bunch of early nineteenth-century trappers. He remembered Dave telling him once about a recent rendezvous he had attended, where he'd acquired some authentic brain-tanned deer hide to make a period set of buckskins. He described the fringed jacket and pants he planned to make as lovingly as a new bride describing her wedding dress.

He really took his hobby seriously, and Jacob admired his skill and knowledge of the early trappers. Dave stressed the rules of rendezvous, where all items had to be authentic; from shelters and cooking utensils to clothing and weapons. The general public was invited to attend these outings, enjoying the shooting and tomahawk competitions, observing craft-making and such, but they couldn't venture into the actual camp. The camp proper was reserved only for the real buck skinners, where every item was required to be period only. Jacob had listened to Dave explain how the members weren't allowed to wear sneakers or any modern shoes. No radios, modern matches, bottles, or cans of food were allowed. Everything, he stressed, had to be authentic reproductions or originals.

Jacob remembered listening intently to Dave's sincere explanation of the rules and regulations required for being a proud member of the Black Powder Society, and when Dave had stopped to take a breath, Jacob had asked him with a twinkle in his eye, "Dave, you mean to tell me that not a one of you fellows wear your Fruit of the Looms under your buckskins?"

The look on Dave's face was priceless. He stammered and stuttered for an answer, and Jacob had just laughed. Then they both laughed. Dave had a great sense of humor. He could be a hundred percent serious one minute and then full goose silly the next. And, he could laugh at himself. Dave was a good guy.

Reminiscences like this had helped to keep Jacob sane. As long as he could conjure up good memories he would be okay. They helped to keep the dread at bay. Making the most of each minute and living day to day was the immediate key to survival for the time being.

By early morning the next day Jacob stared down onto the remnants of Charlie's plane. The weather held, with the gentle warming breeze still wafting in from the south. He was glad his approach was also from the south, so, with the wind to his back, he drew toward the aluminum tomb. The sensation he felt was hard to grasp; for under this mass of ice and twisted metal lay the remains of the last people he had seen. Maybe the last humans he would ever see. Forcing the thought from his mind, lest he fall back into despair, he hurriedly recovered the aluminum gun case. The fine rifle it contained was carefully laid aside and replaced with the precious journal. Taking one last look at the spiral bound notebook that contained the expressions of his heart, he thought of things left unsaid that could fill volumes. Words he would never be able to say to his future grandchildren, advice he'd not be able to give to future sons-in-law.

"Quit thinking like that!" he admonished himself out loud, the sound of his own voice nearly startling him. Exiting the plane, he carefully bent the metal flap to cover the opening.

Recovering his rifle and shouldering his pack, the old thrill of the hunt soon began to surge, lifting his spirit. And with a spring in his step that hadn't been there since before the fateful crash, he walked away from the wreck.

Later that same evening Jacob paused from rubbing a paste of moose brain into the hide of the old mother bear to check on his meal of the young moose's backstrap as it sizzled over the fire. He had not walked a hundred yards from the wreck before spotting the young moose lying below the edge of the ridge beside a muddy area of snowmelt. The secluded bench below the ridge held a depression that contained an often used mineral lick, for a well-used trail led from it into one of the many valleys below.

He had never before ventured into this area because the terrain had always looked too steep. Wanting to keep the warm breeze to his face, he walked to the edge for a better look. Surprised to see the easy trail, he then noticed the bedded moose. The animal never flinched at the shot, and the fresh meat helped to restock his dwindling supplies. He still had several cans of fruits and vegetables, but all meat was gone. He knew this, but until his recent redirection, he hadn't cared. Now, determined to make the best of every day, a good meal became important again. His mouth watered at the sounds of hot drippings sizzling in the coals.

Chapter 20

Many, many miles away to the southeast, another sizzling was taking place. This sizzling was anger uncommon to the normally mild demeanor of one Otis Granrud. All day he had worked alone, gathering and separating the calves from the cows. The calves had done well this summer, fattening nicely on the abundant grass, the first good grass in four years. Each should carry at least seventy-five pounds more than the average of the past several years.

This fact should have had Otis in high spirits, but he was in a low emotional state. He had even refused help in separating the stock. Normally, gathering the animals would be the work of two or more, but Otis hadn't wanted any company. After returning from Alaska he had just wanted to be alone. Judy had seen him brooding and knew the way he felt. She had politely refused help when a few neighbors had called and offered.

Tomorrow morning the truck would arrive to load up the

calves for transport to the big feedlot in Iowa. A small operation like Otis's had exactly one hundred calves to load, but when he made his final counts there were only ninety-eight. Two of the fat calves had squeezed through a space between the head gate and a post. He'd been meaning to straighten the post since before the Alaska trip, when he had bumped it with the tractor, and now his procrastination had allowed two calves to escape. He may not have noticed until morning, but he'd checked everything before supper, and a calf was trying to squeeze through.

Now, after counting twice and coming up with the same number, he knew for sure that two were missing. Usually they would hang close, bawling and trying to find their mama, but these two were nowhere to be found. The cows were being held in a pasture close by, and the constant noise of bawling caused by the separations seemed to be driving him crazy. Any other year the commotion wouldn't be noticed, and everything would settle down anyway once the calves were gone; but this year, the noise sounded louder and really grated on his nerves.

Crossing the lot to the old faithful pickup, he noticed the driver's side front tire was really low. Giving it a swift kick that stunned his leg, he cussed under his breath and headed for the shed for an old tire pump. He'd also known the tire had a slow leak and had planned on fixing it too, but lately, his world had come unglued.

Tossing the pump into the pickup bed among the tangle of barbed wire, broken posts, and other fencing tools, he gave the freshly pumped tire a gentle kick. Satisfied with the solid thump, he cranked over the engine and headed over to the pasture containing the cows.

Sure enough, one of the escaped calves was found bawling as he walked around the outside of the wire-fenced pasture. The spunky calf would be nearly impossible to catch alone if he decided to run. His best chance at a successful capture was to keep the calf moving to the right along the fence. Herding him into a corner formed at a cross fence, Otis managed to get a rope around the calf's neck. Tying the other end to the pickup's rear bumper, he managed to gently lead the stray animal back to the holding pen. This recapture took little time, so he decided to temporarily wire up the breach with a few twists of old barbed wire.

One down and one to go, with little over an hour of daylight left and the other escapee nowhere to be seen. A black calf should be easy to spot against the short, yellow grass of the prairie. And the only direction not blocked by fences was to the west, where the flat land rose to a high bluff. This high piece of ground was where Otis headed, but he had to drive north to access the old ranch road to the top. Driving cross-country would only serve to drive more cactus needles into the already worn tires of the truck. This time of the year, the ground-hugging cactus needles were dry and harder than any other time. Always sharp but mostly flexible while growing, in the fall it seemed they dried to be hard, sharp, and hateful. Otis's dad had always said these high prairie cactus needles were like a deer's antlers, soft during the growing season but hard in the fall.

Topping the rise with the sun still a hand's width above the horizon, Otis eased the old ranch truck along the edge of the bluff. Movement in the valley below caused him to pull up short. The spectacle unfolding before his eyes caused a grin to replace the scowl buried in the red beard.

A large calf stood at the edge of a small prairie dog town, something else Otis had meant to deal with before it grew into a city. But this dog town had sprouted a small patch of sticks, and in the middle of the sticks, with a bundle on her back, stood Jennifer, staring toward the calf. Easing between them, ever closer to the calf, moved Old Bob on cat feet.

Otis couldn't hear from this distance, of course, but he knew Old Bob was talking softly and cooing to the calf. A moment later he slipped a length of rawhide around the calf's neck and led him over to one of the sturdier sticks jammed into the ground. He tied off the loose end and sauntered over to Jennifer. With a look and wave in the direction of the truck, he led Jennifer away into the valley.

Shaking his head, Otis could think of no one else who could have walked right up to that ornery calf; the animal had stood still as if in a trance. Old Bob would be sure to ask for his length of rawhide the next time they met, so Otis tied another rope to the calf and left the rawhide connected to the post. He knew Old Bob would be back to this dog town soon.

Before full dark the last fugitive was back in the pen, and Otis had just sat down to supper when the phone rang. He continued to pick at his food, while Judy conversed with the caller in hushed tones. Occasionally, she looked up at him, and he knew they were sometimes speaking of him. In a few moments, Judy handed him the phone. It was Anna.

"Hello, Annie," he said as cheerfully as he could. "You bout to get settled back in from your trip?"

"Yes," she replied, the sad tone still strong in her voice as she continued. "You know, Otis, you were right about making that trip. We didn't learn anything at all, but I'm still glad we made it. I felt a connection to Jacob there, and that might be all I ever have to hold on to."

He felt more than heard the quiver in her voice, but she continued, "The lady we met, Hannah Dooley, we promised to keep in touch. That fellow who owned the outfit, Charlie Mason, he was her dear friend."

Otis knew this, but he let her keep on. He knew she was trying to tell him that they must accept the fact that the chance of finding Jacob alive was very slim. He knew it too but wanted her to come to grips with it on her own.

"Otis, I now know how those wives and mothers with husbands and sons missing in action during the wars must feel. Closure is a big part of healing, and we must prepare ourselves."

She was trying to comfort him! Jacob was a dear friend, but he was Anna's husband and the father of their children.

"Otis, the facts don't look good, but we must continue on. Jacob would have wanted us to. Part of me will always expect him to come walking through the door at any time, but I'm just going to pray for God to give us comfort. I'm not saying I've given up but just that we must go on. Do you hear me?"

Hardly able to get the words out, he agreed with her. She then told him of speaking with Mrs. Dooley every few days. It was good they had connected; the women would be able to comfort each other.

They talked for a few more minutes, and when he hung up the phone, he knew they had to accept things at face value and focus on tomorrow. It still wouldn't be easy, but he felt better knowing that Anna was a strong woman. Things would eventually be all right for him too. But he made up his mind right then that he would never participate in another antelope hunt.

Chapter 21

The weather held fair and unseasonably mild for the next four days. On the afternoon of the fourth day, the warm breezes stopped suddenly. For over an hour, a complete stillness shrouded Jacob's world. He noticed the change immediately. The last of the moose meat being smoked over the fire hung in long strips. He had constructed the smoking rack a little to the side of the fire to allow the gentle breeze to blow smoke over the meat. Now the smoke rose straight up from the fire, missing the meat altogether.

It had taken most of a day and a half to recover all the meat from the moose, and then, in the evening and throughout the night, he had kept the smoky fire going to cure some of the meat. He had napped occasionally, between bouts of feeding the fire. He had never cured meat before, other than to make deer jerky in the oven at home, and he really only wanted to dry this enough to keep for a while. The task was now complete with these several remaining pieces. The better cuts of the backstrap should keep for a while stashed in his Fred Flintstone refrigerator.

As he gathered them up, the least little noise sounded unusually loud. A stick snapping in the fire popped with a strange clarity; the thud of his boot on the hard ground carried a weird echo. The odd silence enhanced every resonance. For the first time, the placid gurgling of the small stream beyond the camp could be heard distinctly. As quick as the eerie quietness arrived it was gone, replaced now by the breezes again. But this time they came from the north; still gentle but much cooler.

Jacob sensed another cold spell on the way, making him even more thankful for the moose meat and the time to care for it. He had placed the cured meat in one of the fifty-five-gallon drums, which he'd dragged under the protection of the shelter. Now he hurried to gather as much firewood as he had room for under the shelter also. Not wanting to be caught by sudden extreme weather without the necessities, he made a trip to the stream to fill his water containers, checking the rope tie-downs around the encampment.

Satisfied everything appeared to be in order, he kindled a small fire in the pit in front of the tent and settled in for the evening. Not yet sleepy and not having cleaned his rifle in a while, he dug through one of the duffels for a cleaning kit. Finding the compact kit, he rolled the duffel back, only to uncover the broken-bladed Kershaw knife. Turning it over in his hand brought back memories he'd hoped to forget. In fact, he had tried so hard to forget, it suddenly occurred to him that as recently as the few days before, when he shot the moose, he had let his guard down.

Yes, he had made several trips back for the moose meat and not once checked to see if something else had claimed the kill before approaching. He'd been lucky, for each time, he'd blindly walked over the ridge to the moose without checking first to make sure the way was safe. The thoughts of what could have been the outcome of his lackadaisical attitude brought beads of sweat to his brow.

Finding a string, he hung the knife at eye level next to the exit of the tent, to make sure it was seen every time he went out. The broken blade reflected the flames of the campfire as he cleaned the rifle, remembering in vivid detail how the blade came to be broken.

The cold, gentle breeze matured into a full wind by the time Jacob put away the cleaning kit. His shelter tarp flapped loudly as it strained its tethers. Easing out of the tent, he again checked the restraints outside the boulder enclosure, retying a knot here, adding another rope there, until he felt reasonably sure the cover would withstand anything but a full gale. The tarp was heavy and of the best quality. Charlie hadn't skimped on his supplies.

Back under the shelter, he checked his provisions and rolled a few of the bigger rocks he could handle to fill in cracks between the boulders. He'd placed the old bear hide hair side down over a couch-sized boulder near the fire. He figured that any drifting smoke may help in the tanning process. There was not enough wind here to blow it away, not that it really mattered anyway; he'd only worked on it to wile away the hours and keep his mind occupied. "Always do something!" he had said out loud many times. "Keep from going crazy, even if you have to start talking to rocks." The thought of this brought a chuckle. "If you start talking to rocks, it'll mean for sure you've gone crazy."

At night he had started to force himself to recall memories from the past, picking one and then trying to recall as much detail of it as possible. After crawling into his sleeping bag, the routine was to have his talk with the Lord over the day's happenings and asking protection and comfort for Anna and the girls, his family and friends, and anyone else he could think of. Then he would recall some tidbit from the past, a hunt, a birthday, an arrowhead dig with his dad, building forts as a kid with his brother, Gary; anything to keep from thinking of the dire situation surrounding him.

This concept proved to work effectively, for his mental attitude had improved considerably over the past several days. Maybe it was only the change in the weather, but he hoped not, for if that was the case, things were to change again soon if this cold wind was any indication.

The hot rocks were ready, and Jacob placed them one at a time into the small barrel that had been used to store Charlie's supply of flour and sugar. The container of fire-heated rocks continued to radiate heat throughout most of the night; a metal lid on the barrel provided a warm seat inside the tent. Another small barrel upended over the coals of his carefully banked campfire ensured an easy start in the morning. This nightly ritual complete, he settled in for another night. The cold wind had stopped blowing by the time the tent flap was zipped down.

Lying in the dark, he concluded he would have to locate another more permanent campsite if he wanted to have even a remote chance of making it until spring. He may have already waited too long, but up until a few days ago, he had given this concept up completely. Now, though, he knew it was something he had to attempt. The idea of living day to day might keep most of the dread away, but realistically, he knew a better plan was necessary, and he didn't have much time. The weather proved to be unpredictable; bitter cold changing seemingly overnight to spring-like warmth. This he knew would end all too soon, for the temperature would surely fall to well below zero. He'd watched too many programs on the Discovery Channel to think otherwise.

While Jacob sought sleep, the snow fell, small, placid flakes at first, quickly growing into leaf-like clumps. Silently, they floated down as Jacob searched through the volumes of memories for something to occupy his mind as he sought rest. In that somnolent state before deep sleep, he thought of a hunting trip with his dad many years ago.

In the low gap near Jim Town that mild November day, he had stumbled upon the remnants of an old root cellar.

Further investigation disclosed scattered cut stones of an old homestead. Resting for a moment on one of the moss-covered stones, he thought of the family who once lived here, eking out a life deep in the forest of still-rural West Virginia. Life must have really been tough back then for those hardy folks.

He remembered kicking around in the leaves, uncovering his first antique bottle, a beautiful root beer-colored *Pratt's Distemper and Pink Eye Cure.* Something so fragile, manufactured to be thrown away after use, somehow fascinated him by surviving intact so long. The crude old bottle had a story to tell and started a new hobby that would last for years. He could see every distinct, colorful example on the backlit shelves occupying the end wall of his little office back home. Even now, whenever afield, he kept his eyes peeled for old bottles, although he was very doubtful he'd find any here.

Wondering what Anna and the girls would do with his prized collection, he thought of the young bottle-digging friend he'd met a few years ago. Jason Arnold, a young man fifteen years his junior, was a bottle-digging rascal. He lived in a small town in southeastern Ohio, spending every spare moment poring over old fire maps of small towns in and around the area.

A fire map, most notably a Sanborn Map, consisted of town plots from the mid to late eighteen hundreds. Every building in a defined town was plotted on the map, including the outhouse or privy locations. Every privy location was akin to an 'X' on a treasure map. Gaining owner permission to probe for these privies proved quite easy once you explained to the landowner what you had in mind.

Probing consisted of using a thin, solid metal rod to probe into the ground, hoping to locate the stone lining of an old privy. Once a site had been located and the perimeter determined, the probe was carefully inserted into the center area. Any glass encountered would be felt in the metal rod.

In the time before modern garbage collecting, glass and

pottery rubbish was typically disposed of by tossing it into the hole of the outhouse, while combustible refuse would be burned. When the privy pit became nearly full, a new pit would be dug nearby, and the first removed soil would be used to fill in the old pit. Oftentimes these abandoned pits would line the back part of a lot. Over many years one house may have ten or more pits.

A hundred fifty-year-old privy consisted only of fine, rich soil, and maybe some very valuable antique bottles.

Early one spring day a few years earlier, Jason had gained permission to probe an area above a small town along the Ohio River, not far from his home. When he had approached the old fellow working on a lawn mower, he really didn't know how to ask about looking for old privies in his backyard. The old gentleman seemed friendly enough once he guessed Jason wasn't trying to sell him something. As they exchanged pleasantries, Jason commented on the old John Deere lawnmower with the faded paint and how they seemed to last forever. The old man said he had bought it brand-new in 1962 and had replaced the tires five times, and his eyes took on a quizzical look as he noted the strange-looking T-handled rod held in Jason's hand.

Jason readily explained the probe's intended use and quickly gained access to the man's backyard. The old fellow explained how he had planted a garden there for several years, and it was still too early in the season for tilling and planting.

"I always plant by the almanac," said the old man. "Still, you might get a late frost that'll kill everything. If you dig up any rocks, toss 'em off to the side with the others, so I won't run over them with my tiller."

Jason thanked the old man, and as he walked through the dead brown remnants of the previous year's garden, he noticed how the bench ran for several hundred yards below sheer sandstone cliffs and just above the little town. It was easy to conclude where the old dwellings had stood in relation to the newer houses following the banks of the river, for a small number of the structures were holdovers from the eighteen hundreds. The old two-story buildings faced the river road, while the back of the top floors opened onto wide covered porches with direct access to the bench. The wide bench served as a backyard for small gardens and the outhouses.

Jason probed around the edge of the overgrown garden that afternoon and was excited to find a row of promising spots along the back edge, near the sandstone cliffs. He noticed how some spots coincided with the icons on the Sanborn maps. His unusual activity sparked the interest of a few of the neighbors, and before long he had acquired permission to check out the bench behind more houses. Promises to refill and reseed any ground disturbed, along with his affable manner, earned Jason enough promising land to feed his hobby for a year or more.

One of the hot rocks shifted in the metal barrel and bumped the side loud enough to startle Jacob fully awake. Closing his eyes again, he recalled how excited Jason sounded when he called to tell him about the good fortune in acquiring such a promising place to dig. The two arranged to meet the following Saturday, and at 8:30 that morning they were standing in a hole almost three foot deep. Several broken pieces of good bottles were lying on the ground. The shards indicated the bottles would be from the late eighteen hundreds.

Drifting deeper into sleep, Jacob continued to dig. The memories became dreams, and the sensations became real as his mind recalled in detail the looks and feel of being above the little town on the Ohio River. A few hundred feet farther along the bench, among several other boulders, stood a large, cube-shaped rock covered on the top with moss. Taking a break from digging at about noon, the two ate from their bagged lunches and decided to explore among the boulders for possible old dumpsites.

Rounding the large rock, Jacob noticed the carved characters. Someone long ago had carved D.M.B. and a date of 10-5-1854 in the sandstone. What made the characters unusual was that they were upside down. Why would anyone take the time to carve their initials and date upside down?

The carvings were facing the cliffs, which began about fifty yards farther up the gentle slope. Glancing in that direction, Jacob soon had the answer. High at the top of the cliff, an open space revealed dimensions the size of the rock chunk Jacob stood beside; approximately nine feet high by fourteen feet wide by eleven feet deep. This massive block had cleaved from the cliff and rolled to where it stood today, sometime after 1854.

This area, tangled with sleeping vines and small trees, was situated beyond the normal property lines and, from the looks of the littered ground, had been the local dump for many years. Jason had busied himself by scratching around in a natural cavity under the big stone, a den dug by some animal, probably.

"Hey! Look at this!" he exclaimed as he withdrew an almost-complete cobalt blue squat soda. The bottom edge revealed a triangle-shaped hole, and the bottle was half-full of compacted dirt.

"A Pomroy soda! I've never seen one this color, and it's busted," he continued with excited disappointment.

"It's hard to tell what's under here," said Jacob as he took the old piece of glass, holding it up to the sky to reveal its true color. "We should investigate this further. This may well be the jackpot we've been looking for!"

Within a couple of hours a hole big enough to accommodate two people and one entrenching tool had been excavated under the boulder. Two complete squat sodas in shades of aqua and the top of an olive green Drakes Bitters had been uncovered, along with several pieces of rusty unidentifiable junk and a few slickers—the bottle diggers' term for nondescript common bottles with no embossing.

Holding the Drakes Bitters shard, Jason mused, "If this Drakes was complete, it'd be worth about fifteen hundred dollars."

"Just wipe the tears outta your eyes and keep digging," Jacob answered, receiving the shard from Jason.

The color was perfect. Green of any shade was a top color for a Drakes Bitters. The embossing ST DRAKE'S 1860 and PLANTATION was visible on the three-stepped roof of the cabin-shaped bottle, but that was all. More parts of the bottle may be found, but all would be only worthless pieces of green glass. A treasure may yet be found here, but not today, for the evening had fallen, and the modern-day prospectors had no light. Plans were made to return the next Saturday.

Rain was in the forecast the following Saturday as Jacob made the hour-long trip from home. As he crossed the Ohio River his cell phone rang. It was Jason, with the news that he had been called out to work. Jacob decided to dig alone, since he was only a couple miles from the site by then. If he had known earlier he would have stayed at home, spending the day in his recliner watching the History Channel.

With a thermos of hot black coffee and a couple of doughnuts in a baggie stuffed into his daypack, Jacob trudged up the steep bank to the big rock. The sides of the entrance hole under the boulder were piled high with excavated dirt and uncovered junk.

The whole area had undoubtedly once been used as a community dump. Digging under the boulder proved quite a bit easier than digging through the tangle of vines and roots around it. Trash and junk of more modern times could be found all over, but the huge boulder had protected the really old stuff underneath. Deep moss covered most of the boulder, and even a few small, stunted trees grew out of the accumulated soil on top, their gnarled roots stretching down the sides in a quest for water.

Always on the lookout for snakes, Jacob shoved his backpack into the hole before he entered. More prepared this time, he removed a small lantern from his pack equipped with a new six-volt battery. He also took out an eighteen inch square piece of foam salvaged from an old sleeping bag pad to act as a seat.

There was barely enough room to sit at the bottom of the excavation without your head touching the bottom of the rock. A little housekeeping was in order, so the first few minutes were spent scraping the loose dirt from the boulder bottom. "At least now it won't be falling down my neck," Jacob soliloquized as he arranged his digging tools within reach.

A small trowel, a stiff brush, and the indispensable entrenching tool made up his arsenal. He spent a few more minutes cutting out a small ledge near the exit and placed a flat stone the size of a dinner plate there. On this he would place any good bottles he found, to keep them safe. The year before, Jason had found a near perfect Red Spring Saratoga, only to break it by dislodging a small stone that proceeded to fall gently on his prize find. The gentle tap by the stone caused a crack to form completely around the base. Making a choking sound with visible panic, he had quickly picked up the bottle, watching in horror as the whole bottom fell away. Unable to stomach the event, he just decided to pack up and go home; he was so sick he didn't dig again for a month.

Jacob was filling the bucket for the seventh time when the rain started. Scooting over to the entrance, he tossed out the dirt and thought of how convenient it was to be able to dig with a roof over your head, for open-air privy digging could be mighty uncomfortable in the rain.

On his next probe with the trowel, he heard the gentle 'tink' of metal striking glass. Carefully, he removed over a hundred years of accumulated dirt to uncover the side of a straw-colored bottle. Large embossed letters could be seen. "Hot dog!" he exclaimed. "Please don't let it be broken."

A few minutes later, Jacob sat holding a beautiful Hartley's Peruvian Bark Bitters. Even with it half full of dirt, he could see it didn't have a chip or crack. Carefully setting it on the makeshift shelf, out of harm's way, he leaned back and admired the specimen. "Just wait till Jason sees this," he said out loud.

Deciding to capture the moment, he rummaged through the pack for his camera. Arranging the bottle on the stone shelf for a good angle, he snapped a few pictures. Noting what a good job he had done constructing the shelf—for the bottle just fit, with about a half inch between the top of the bottle and the bottom of the rock—he snapped a couple more.

Turning back with newfound enthusiasm, he noted the trash layer extended for only about twenty inches, then gave way to hard-packed sandy soil. Scooting over to where he had uncovered his treasure, he used the stiff brush to sweep the entire side of the hole free of loose dirt, tossing it out of the hole. The effect was to reveal several more pieces of glass, mostly colored.

His heart raced in excitement as he carefully broke down more of the wall; the rain coming down harder as he dumped another bucketful. A trickle of water flowed into the entrance and formed a small puddle, which slowly sank into the ground. Several more minutes of furious digging uncovered two White Sulphur Springs / Greenbrier VA mineral water bottles. One had a bad lip chip, but the other looked near perfect. He knew these bottles dated to pre-1863, for later bottles had been embossed W.Va. after West Virginia became a state from part of Virginia.

Suddenly, a loud *POP* of breaking glass interrupted his reverie. Thinking for a moment his buddy Jason's work had been called off due to the rain and he had arrived and was playing tricks, Jacob turned to the entrance. Panic seized him and caused his body to freeze when he realized that was not at all the case. His prized Hartley's Bitters lay in pieces, but what caused the breakage stopped his heart; the huge boulder was sinking before his eyes! Already, his escape had been compromised. How could he have been so stupid as to undermine the big rock? This, along with the rain, had softened the soil enough for the several-ton stone to sink into the hole, the hole he had dug!

Scrambling back, he began frantically digging an escape route out the other side, but the more dirt he moved, the quicker the rock sank! Not fully grasping his fate, the rock soon pressed his back until breathing became nearly impossible, and he was being crushed to death!

Chapter 22

Jacob fought panic and struggled for air, the weight of the boulder pressing against him, forcing him facedown into the sleeping bag. He was cold, he was sweating, he was awake, but the weight kept pressing, making it more and more difficult to breathe. It had only been a terrible dream, so why was he still pressed under the rock, fighting for breath?

As his mind slowly cleared and his right eye focused, he could see the bottom edge of the flour barrel—the flour barrel? A hand lay next to it, his hand. He wasn't being crushed under a boulder along the Ohio River. He forced it to touch the barrel. It was cold. The hand was the only part of him that could move. His left arm lay under his chest, and he slowly worked the sleep needles out until he forced it up by his head and out of the sleeping bag.

Now fully alert, he realized the foundation of the nightmare and how it had paced in conjunction with reality. The heavy, wet snow must have buckled the canvas shelter, also ensuring the collapse of the tent, which he could see was draped over the barrel. Pulling both arms back, he tried to push himself upright, but it was no use, like trying to do a push-up with a sumo wrestler on your back. Rolling a little side to side served to open a little space around him, but he was soon drenched with sweat, which would be fatal if he couldn't extract himself soon and get a fire built.

It had to be near dawn, for even being trapped under everything, there was still enough light filtering in to distinguish items around him. Raising his chin off the ground and pulling his elbows under his chest allowed him to take a deep breath, and arching his back, he managed to create a little more space. The snow was wet enough to pack, and after a few more minutes he was able to get his knees beneath him.

After what seemed like hours Jacob stood outside surveying the damage. A fire was blazing, the smoke trailing straight up in the still air. At least two feet of wet snow covered everything, but it was already starting to melt. With unpredictable weather again playing tricks and the temperature well above freezing, which could last for days or minutes, Jacob had serious decisions to make. He could salvage part of the big tarp, which had ripped down the center, dumping the load of snow on the tent, but staying here for more than a few days was out of the question.

The rest of the day was spent gathering only some necessary items and sorting through the rest. Another temporary camp was set, and a healthy fire set to blazing a little larger than needed, but the big flames yielded extra comfort somehow.

He decided he would concentrate on finding a suitable shelter tomorrow, hopefully a large animal den with no occupants. He needed to train himself to think like the primitive people who lived here twenty thousand years ago. It had come to this: A twenty-first century man facing the same challenges as his prehistoric ancestors. The few modern items at his disposal hardly made him an equal to those of old to whom this was a part of daily life. At least he didn't have to worry about saber-toothed tigers chasing him. As soon as this thought entered his mind, and for the first time since realizing he was somewhere in Siberia, he thought of Siberian tigers. His knowledge of tigers was limited to only the pictures he'd seen and the old gasoline and cereal commercials. Tony and his friends could live a thousand miles away, or this could be their main area of habitation. He didn't need to worry about tigers and bears fighting over who would invite him to dinner first.

By early evening the supplies were sorted into three stacks. A small one that he would need immediately, and another that could wait and be transported to the new shelter if and when he found one. The third contained items that, until recently, he had felt he couldn't do without but now seemed to be almost unimportant. When it came down to a life-or-death situation, only a few things were really necessary, and there was always the cache at the plane.

With the rifle close at hand, Jacob sat staring into the fire, wondering again what the dawn would bring; wondering if his family was safe and warm, and if they had given up hope of ever seeing him again. His closing prayer was for the wreck to be found some day and his journal to somehow make its way to Anna.

****

The white-eared bear sniffed all around the opening between the rocks, staring into the void with hesitation. Turning away, he stopped, turned back, and sniffed some more, then ventured closer. Satisfied the information revealed no apparent threat, he risked a few cautious steps inside, stopping to let his eyes adjust, then continued. Initially, the upward path narrowed to a tight squeeze that subsequently opened wider and turned downward, deeper into the mountain. A short distance farther, the way leveled, then stopped at a small dome-topped room littered deep with the debris of countless years' occupation by numerous tenants. Sticks, twigs, dry leaves, and evergreen boughs, even small bones and feathers, covered the floor to a depth of several feet in places.

A long crack in the floor, wide enough to wedge a huge paw, snaked its way along one side of the den. Through this had fallen much of the nesting material used over the years, requiring each new occupant to add to the mix, but the bear was satisfied with what he found, and with a few turns and scrapes, he settled in for a long sleep.

****

The next morning the coals were still glowing as Jacob added wood to the fire. A few minutes later the pan of snow had melted and the water was steaming. Taking advantage of the milder weather, he decided to bathe as best he could while waiting for the coffee, and before the hour had passed he was ready to leave. He had carefully packed a small backpack with only essential items for a few days. When a suitable winter camp had been found, he intended to return here and to the wreck to take stock of everything that could be transported for use through the winter.

Leaving his favorite Ruger rifle, he picked up an older Model 70 Winchester with open sights chambered in .338 Winchester Magnum. The old gun had been well cared for, and he paused to wonder which of the fellows resting inside the plane may have owned it. Was he indeed the lucky survivor?

A few yards away from the camp, he stopped. "Which way?" he asked aloud, as if expecting someone to answer. Turning completely around, he studied the far vistas. The way he traveled from the beach experience was out of the question. That way offered only marshy ground and close-growing willows. Nothing in the way of a shelter could be found in that direction, and the path up over the pass toward the wreck revealed only the glacier and strong winds. That left only two options. One route led down into the valley between the mountains, with the glacier filling the high valley on the other side toward the north. This course would provide the most undemanding hike, although a survey through the binoculars revealed little in the way of shelter-providing rocky crags or caves.

That only left the path into the smoky valley beyond the mineral lick where the moose had been killed. He remembered seeing several game trails converging in the area of the lick; one had to lead to a promising area for shelter. Added luck would be to find a place that offered an ambush site near one of the trails to the lick.

As he passed, Jacob stared at the remains of the moose. The bones were scattered, as the scavengers had grubbed for the remaining morsels. Dried mud held the littered tracks of the visitors; however, no evidence of a bear could be seen, so the giants of his nightmares must have taken to the dens for a long sleep.

The game trail chosen looked the most promising, as it seemed to lead into rough, craggy country. He followed a narrow path along a steep cliff. The high, smooth walls rose almost a hundred feet on his right, and the bank to his left dropped steeply into the foggy canyon. There was little change in elevation as the trail led gently up and down for the next half mile or so.

After a while Jacob stopped to take a short break on a large boulder resting on a wide area of the trail, almost completely blocking it. Only a very narrow trail skirted around on the canyon side. The boulder was half buried in the ground, but it was easily determined to have fallen sometime in the distant past from a spot in the cliff. A shallow cavity twenty feet up on the face matched the boulder, and Jacob pondered why the huge stone had suddenly let go and fallen. There appeared to be no other cracks radiating out from the opening. The bottom of the shelf looked to be level from his view from below, but failed to offer anything but a respite from bad weather. The overhanging top would provide protection from steady rain or snow, unless the wind came from up the canyon. No way could this provide a winter shelter. Deciding to continue on, he had to use both hands to help climb down the off-side of the boulder he had merely walked onto from the up trail side.

He continued to scan every break in the rocks for something promising, but after another hour the path turned down toward the damp lower ground. With a feeling of frustration, Jacob decided to search in another direction. From a nearby high point, he could observe the trail just followed and access his options.

The bench of his old camp lay far to his left, out of sight beyond the turn of the peak whose melting snow fed Little Rock Creek. Just to the right of this and a little past stretched the mountain range holding the distant river of ice he had started calling Dead Beaver Glacier. The narrow foggy canyon he had just traveled opened below and behind him, into the dense willow flats filled with the swampy ground, and eventually, this led to the coastal bay.

Suddenly he felt the despair of loneliness settling in again. This land held such beauty, with unspoiled vistas as far as the eye could see; a land he had always dreamed of exploring and enjoying with fresh air, clear-running streams, and abundant game. How ironic it all seemed now, and then he felt the small stings against his face. The cool, gentle breeze that had been at his back only a moment before unexpectedly now came from the front, colder, and with the first hints of sleet. He knew he couldn't afford to be caught out in cold, wet weather and fought down a sudden surge of panic. "Play it smart and stay alive," he said aloud, as he gathered his belongings.

Before the backpack was settled on his shoulders, Jacob had decided that his best option was to make for the cavity above the boulder back a ways up the trail. This late in the season, the days were short enough, and as it was, the day was more than half over anyway. The trail wasn't steep, and if the weather didn't turn really bad, he could afford to spend the rest of the day and a night on the shelf. He remembered a shallow draw choked with dry brush not far below the boulder, where he might be able gather enough dry wood for a small fire.

Before getting halfway to his destination, the cold, misty rain turned to fine ice granules, making the trail very slick. By the time the boulder was in sight, the ground was covered with an inch of the stuff, under which lay a covering of smooth ice where the rain had frozen. Jason carried a small bundle of dead branches and hoped he could find something else to burn, or it would be a really uncomfortable night.

Stopping at the base of the boulder, he surveyed the shelf above with a little more scrutiny. It vaguely reminded him of a miniature Mesa Verde, and it looked dry. Also from his vantage point below, there appeared to be evidence of some sort of abandoned animal den, which would provide additional fire-making material.

Unable to climb the slick boulder with his arms full and the rifle slung over his shoulder, Jacob chose the narrow trail around. It happened in an instant. On the third step, the ground gave way and he was falling. Dropping the bundle in an attempt to regain footing and grab onto the boulder, the rifle slipped off his shoulder, along with a backpack strap, which bound his arm.

Falling a short distance before hitting the slope belly down, he slid feetfirst, quickly gaining speed. Glancing up as he hit the water, he glimpsed the sliding rifle an instant before it struck him in the middle of the forehead.

Jacob was unsure how long he had been out. His head throbbed, and his torso was freezing, but he had a strange sensation in his legs. They felt as if they were slowly moving, with almost a floating sensation and were oddly warm, at least compared to the rest of his body. At first he had the terrible fear that he may have broken his back and his legs were paralyzed. His arms failed to move at first, but he soon realized the backpack straps had slid down around them, slightly cutting off circulation and causing them to feel asleep. Something was pressing into the top of his head, and as he raised it off the ground, his rifle slid butt first under his chin, stopping at his chest.

Struggling a little to free himself of the backpack, he gingerly felt his forehead and winced as he touched the goose egg between his eyes. The exact same spot that he had already injured twice before! The skin wasn't broken, but it felt stretched tight enough to burst. Slowly, he turned his body over to determine the cause of the strange feeling in his legs. As he turned, he heard and felt the water splash and saw that he had slid into a shallow, slow-moving stream, but unlike the other streams, this one wasn't flowing with ice water but was almost warm. His upper body was covered with a half inch of frozen sleet, and this warmer water may have been all that kept his core temperature high enough to prevent him from freezing to death, or at least developing hypothermia.

It took a few moments to stand, and the cold air immediately attacked his wet clothing, stealing the warmness from his legs and bringing a cold chill up his back, causing his head to throb. Dizziness made him stumble as he looked around for the bundle of sticks. He desperately needed a fire, but only a few of the sticks could be found at the edge of the stream. The others had no doubt floated away.

Looking up the bank from where he had fallen, it was obvious there would be no way to climb the hundred feet or so back up to the boulder; it was now covered in ice and much too steep. He had been lucky to have slid down the slope, for if he had taken a tumble, he would surely have been hurt much worse, maybe even killed. Nothing appeared to be broken, and he wasn't bleeding. His vision wasn't blurred, so he doubted he had suffered a concussion. If he could get warm, he could survive the knot on his head.

A glance downstream revealed more of the same steep, slippery walls and no sign of likely shelter or firewood-providing trees. With a sudden feeling of panic, he willed himself to remain calm, even as the cold penetrated deeper into his legs. Turning about, he gathered his belongings and stumbled upstream, where the little canyon narrowed even farther as it veered off to the right, away from the trail.

Around the bend, the small creek tumbled over and around rocks and small boulders, and travel became more difficult. The canyon also split here, with the stream flowing from the right fork. The dry fork provided the easiest travel and led to a jumble of huge boulders that promised shelter, but as Jacob started in that direction, he noticed the top of a large, dead tree trunk showing above a rock jutting out from the side of the canyon a few hundred feet farther up the right fork. He was shivering violently as he made for the tree, hoping to find a source of dry wood. He knew he wouldn't last much longer without a fire. Already, the numbness could be felt in his legs, and stinging needles pierced his feet.

The top of the old dead black spruce had broken off about ten feet up, and the shiny gray of the trunk left standing had caught Jacob's attention. The broken top had fallen across the narrow canyon and lodged in a way that the dead limbs were left intact. Although a couple inches of frozen sleet covered the top, the lower-hanging branches were dry. As Jacob approached, he startled a small squirrel-like animal that chirped excitedly as it ran across the treetop and disappeared into a hole in the dead tree trunk.

Immediately, Jacob started breaking small limbs and, with a shaking hand, reached into a cavity at the bottom of the old tree trunk to gather dry handfuls of decayed wood from the inside. He carried a half-full book of old military surplus waterproof matches in his shirt pocket, and the magnesium fire starter was in his backpack. If the matches were still good, using them would be quicker. He dropped the first match, and the second one sputtered and went out, but his numb fingers managed to keep hold of the next, and within a few minutes, the lifesaving flames crackled the dry wood into a small fire.

The warmth only managed to bring a little feeling into his numb hands, while the shivering in his body continued. He would need a bigger fire to dry out his wet clothes. He had started considering setting the tree trunk on fire, when he noticed the sizzling sound coming from the fire and noticed the snow falling heavier and the wind picking up. Standing to break off more limbs, he first climbed around the dead trunk to gather some of the large slabs of damp bark, to bank his fire from the wind. That's when he noticed it! There was a small, dark opening behind a boulder in the side of the mountain. The little creek was flowing out of a four-foot-high cavern entrance. Slipping back down the bank to his already snow-covered pack, he retrieved a small flashlight. Returning to the opening, he cautiously crouched to peer inside. The small beam exposed smooth cavern walls that widened to about eight feet, and, initially, there was not enough head room inside to stand up. The small stream flowed along the right side, allowing enough room to stoop and walk beside it. In the beam of his light, he could see that about ten yards farther in, the ceiling sloped upward enough to allow him to stand, and a few more yards farther than that, he would barely be able to reach the top with his hand. Beyond that, he could see the tunnel made a turn that was past the help of his light.

Jacob was so excited he nearly forgot the cold. Ducking his head, he entered slowly, not forgetting for a second he could be crawling into a bear's den. Cautiously moving beside the stream until he was able to stand up, his eyes slowly adjusted to the darkness. With the help of the flashlight, he could make out that the cavern continued for several more yards before making a turn to the left. Shivering again, partially from being thrilled at this discovery, but mostly from the wet clothing that was beginning to freeze, he turned to retrieve his pack and rifle, admonishing himself again for walking away from the firearm.

Outside again, the glare off the snow nearly blinded him and the air felt even colder. Squinting, he noticed the heavy falling snow had already put out the fire, so gathering an armful of the dead branches along with his other belongings, he chided himself again on how stupid he had been for entering the cave without his rifle. He'd been lucky again, but promised himself not to do anything else without thinking of the potential danger.

At a place about forty feet inside, the floor widened, so he dumped the branches there and hurried back for more, along with a handful of the dry tinder from inside the tree trunk. A few minutes later he had a warm fire again, and as soon as the smaller branches caught, he returned for more. After a few trips he'd gathered a sufficient amount of firewood to allow a sizable blaze. His wet clothing soon started to steam as the life-giving warmth slowed his shivering. The fire soon heated the smooth wall of the cavern enough to reflect heat, allowing Jacob to become a little drowsy, but first he wanted to look into the cavern beyond the bend. Turning the corner, he discovered the cavern narrowed to about three feet, with no room to walk past the stream. Leaning around in the weak beam of the flashlight, he saw the passageway turned sharply and the narrowness continued.

Returning to the fire, he added a few more branches and lay with his head on the pack and his back to the fire, his mind dwelling on how close he had actually come to dying. If he hadn't stumbled upon the cave, the chances of surviving the night would have been very slim. The big knot on his forehead throbbed with every beat of his heart, but if he hadn't taken the fall, he'd be miserable trying to camp on the narrow ledge above the boulder, worrying about tomorrow.

"Thank you, Lord, for providing this cave and this fire," Jacob said aloud as he closed his eyes.

Outside, the snow continued to fall, but inside, Jacob slept in the warm comfort of his new discovery.

Chapter 23

Jacob awakened to the little stream's soft gurgling and the continued warmth provided by heat radiating from the walls of the cavern. He had slept soundly for about an hour, and for the first time in many days, it had been a restful sleep. A threshold had been crossed, for he had found shelter, even if it consisted of only a narrow six-foot-wide stretch of hard ground beside a stream at the present. He still had many things to gather before the onset of winter. He understood well the dangers ahead, but also knew the necessity of focusing on one hurdle at a time.

The fire had mostly died down to glowing coals, so he added the last of his branches to build it up. These had been a little damp when gathered, and the fire smoked somewhat as they caught. Jacob noticed immediately that as the little column of smoke rose, it also drifted into the cavern instead of toward the entrance. He watched as the smoke slowly made its way deeper into the mountain, and realized for the first time that the cavern didn't carry the normal musty, damp smells usually associated with being underground.

Excited and wanting to explore further, he realized more important matters needed to be addressed first, so he stood to gather more wood and prepare for the night in his new and much-appreciated shelter. It was then he felt the slightest movement of air drifting from the entrance, which told him that there had to be another opening somewhere to pull the air through, another plus for his new home.

It was completely dark by the time Jacob had gathered enough fuel to keep the fire going through the long night. He had managed to break all the smaller branches and gather a pile of dry chunks of decaying wood from inside the dead tree. He also pried slabs of the loose bark free, although these proved to be really damp, but would dry sufficiently if placed near the fire. The snow had stopped falling, and the air was cold and still as he carried in the last load. With a full canteen and enough food for another day, he would be comfortable until tomorrow, when he'd start the arduous task of moving his supplies and gathering necessities for the long winter ahead.

The fire cast ghostly shadows on the cavern walls, and Jacob couldn't help but wonder what he would find farther into the cave. It may stop shortly after the turn, but there had to be a crack somewhere to allow the air to move. The small flashlight he carried already showed the signs of weakening batteries, but he had several more, as well as a few lanterns, in his supplies. He decided that further exploration would have to wait, for he could hardly afford to step in a hole and break a leg, or even worse, fall over another cliff in the dark. From here on out he would think before making any move that may result in danger, and would pay closer attention to avoid doing something stupid. Not knowing if some animal had already claimed the cavern, he thought it prudent to build two small fires, one between him and the outside entrance, and another farther inside, nearer where the tunnel made the turn.

He would remain between them, with the rifle always within reach.

The next morning Jacob found a game trail out of the narrow canyon that met with the trail he had taken a few days earlier. His head still hurt whenever he touched it and was too tender to for his heavy cap, so he opted to wear an old wool stocking cap he always carried in his pack. The old camp on the bench was less than three miles away and mostly uphill, so he would be hauling supplies down a snow-covered trail. He formulated a plan as he walked, and it involved returning to the wrecked plane.

****

Three days later, a very tired Jacob sat staring at what looked almost like a mountain of supplies. He was proud of his accomplishment, for the idea of using the pontoon torn from the plane as a sled had proved to be sound. Chopping the top until it resembled a cross between a canoe and a kayak took some work with a camp axe, but the beat-up aluminum device held a good load and pulled fairly easily down the trail. Going back up the trail empty took a little longer, and both ways would have been impossible without the snow, which, in hindsight, was a blessing.

The weather had remained cold, but there had been no wind and no more snow. The sky remained a dull gray, and he hadn't seen a hint of the sun for two days. When it had peeked over the horizon, the shadows remained long. He'd never given much thought to how far north one had to be to experience the six months of darkness, but he could tell for sure the days were getting shorter. When the sun came up it was farther to the south and made a long arc before setting again.

There was something else he had failed to do, though. He had not kept track of time, hadn't even thought of it till now. He had no idea exactly how many days it had been since the accident. How long had he been stranded here? On one hand, it seemed like only yesterday, and on the other, it seemed like months. He had lost all track of time, but he had started making a mark on the cavern wall for every day he spent there. He'd chuckled as he made the mark this morning, thinking of the cartoons he had seen of unfortunate prisoners marking their days.

He remembered the movie where the fellow had been stranded on an island and talked with a soccer ball. He feared madness almost as much as he feared the bear, so he decided to read aloud to himself every evening. He'd found an Alaska travel guide with some of the gear but was thrilled to have found his Bible in the duffle he'd left on the plane. Anna made sure he took it with him on every trip. Most times, he never removed it from his suitcase, but still drew great comfort from knowing it was there.

Every item he'd packed for the trip was with him now, as well as most of the other stuff from the plane. This was the last trip for anything that might prove useful he'd brought, for he never wanted to visit the wreck again. He'd left his journal, but he'd cleaned out the rest. As he held the Bible now, he vowed to start at Genesis and read some every evening.

He thought again of the fellows still in the plane and wondered if any of them had given their life to Christ. He hoped they all had and glanced up in the direction of the wreck. As the crow flies, it lay only about a mile or so away, and from the edge of the glacier, you could see down and over into the general area of the cavern. With all the twists and turns, it was hard to pinpoint exactly.

As he started to unpack the last load, some movement above the trail caught his eye. Several of the big snow sheep he'd only seen from a great distance were crossing the ridge above him. These sheep resembled the bighorn sheep he'd seen in Montana and in the Black Hills, but these had even larger horns; on the big rams, the horns made a curl and a half. He'd never seen them this close, and hidden as he was within the entrance to the cavern, he knew they couldn't see him. His next plan had been to hunt, and now the game was coming to him. He glanced down at the Bible in his hand and couldn't help but feel the blessing.

Easing inside, he grabbed his Ruger 7mm mag and chambered a round. The sheep were still much too far away for a shot, but their general direction of travel might bring them close enough. "Lord, I know You have given these to me, and I thank You," he whispered.

Jacob crouched behind the rock at the mouth of the cave for over an hour before being presented with a shot. Earlier, the sheep had disappeared from sight for quite some time, and he feared he'd lost them, when suddenly, they stepped out less than two hundred yards away, almost at eye level. Jacob aimed for the big ewe in the lead and centered the crosshairs behind her shoulder as she stopped. Sighted in at three inches high at a hundred yards, he could almost see the hair it would hit as he squeezed the trigger. The round was still climbing as it hit the sheep in the spine, and she fell where she stood. With their leader down, the rest were confused and, not used to the sound of gunfire, didn't spook. Jacob chambered another round and sighted on the large ram bringing up the rear as he stepped forward. At the shot, the ram bolted, as did the others, but within fifty yards the big ram collapsed. The remaining sheep ran straight up and over a place where Jacob knew he would have a difficult time climbing.

Jacob managed to field dress both animals before full dark and had them moved closer to the cavern. He packed chunks of snow around them and covered both with the turned over makeshift sled. The next couple days would be spent curing the meat.

By noon the next day a sizable drying rack had been constructed and a sled full of fuel gathered. Now the thick smoke rose through the meat as Jacob cooked a stew of sheep meat and freeze-dried vegetables. He had been surprised at the amount of staples that had been stashed in the barrels at the camp on the bench—flour, sugar, coffee, salt, pepper, and several packages of freeze-dried vegetables. If he rationed well and continued to have successful hunts, he shouldn't starve for a while. He'd found a well-stocked first-aid kit, along with a bottle of aspirin, a big bottle of multi-vitamins, and even a bottle of Vick's Nyquil.

While gathering firewood for the curing fire, he'd come upon a small pond nestled in a little valley that he was sure was full of trout. He would catch as many as possible until it froze over. Already, ice rimmed the edges, except where a stream entered on one side and flowed out the other.

Packed away somewhere was a backpacker fishing kit, complete with an assortment of hooks and lures. It was a kit of very high quality, belonging to one of the ill-fated hunters who had no doubt hoped to spend a quiet afternoon fishing. Jacob decided he'd put it to good use; instead of fishing for fun, he'd be fishing as if his life depended on it, because it did.

The smell of the cooking stew made his mouth water. It was bubbling at a high rate now and the juices thickening. Giving it a good stir, he set it aside to cool a little, while he added more damp wood to the meat-curing fire. After a good meal, he'd planned to dig out a flashlight with a good strong beam and, along with one of the gas lanterns, explore the cavern a little further. He'd hoped to find a little wider spot to make his permanent camp, since the current location was becoming quite crowded with all the provisions he'd hauled from the wreck. And he would like a separate place for his food stores.

With a belly full of savory stew, Jacob burped as he rummaged through the stores for a pair of ankle-fit hip waders he'd packed away. Surely the further exploration would require frequent forays into the stream flowing through the cavern. He'd be wise to dress for the occasion, and this time he had opted to carry someone's .44 magnum revolver instead of a rifle. The handgun would be much easier to wield within the confined spaces he knew he'd encounter, and heaven forbid he run into anything with sharp teeth and claws. Shuddering at the thought, he checked his light pack and headed out.

The path along the stream diminished as the cavern narrowed, and soon it was necessary to walk in the water. The depth ranged from ankle-deep to almost reaching the knees, and on two occasions, he passed cold water flowing into the stream from small fissures in the cavern sides. The left side of the passage soon bulged out to further narrow the course, and in one spot, the depth reached a little above his knees, and he had to brace himself against the sides to keep his footing on the round rocks of the stream bottom.

At one point, water splashed over the top of the wader on his right leg, and it didn't feel as frigid as the ice-cold rivulets flowing in from the sides. The main flow evidently came from far underground, having regulated its temperature to cave levels. He remembered his dad, who had worked in the coal mines in West Virginia, telling him how the underground maintained about the same temperatures year round.

Shining the light ahead, he was unable to see very far, as the cavern continued to follow a curving course, and it was also evident the ceiling was curving downward. He could now reach up and touch the smooth surface of the ceiling, the height had diminished so much. Another twenty yards and his cap touched the top in places, and either his eyes were adjusting, or there was a hint of light up ahead. He decided it may be the flashlight beam reflecting off the surface of the water.

The passage narrowed down even more as he rounded another slight bend, and his light revealed numerous smooth protrusions in the sides and top. Reaching a point where the cavern roof dipped sharply down to only about three feet above the water, he bent down to look, only to have one of the smooth rocky protrusions announce its presence by slamming into his already sore forehead. The bill of his cap had blocked the small outcropping from his line of sight. The shock and pain in his head and neck caused him to see stars. Blacking out for a second, he sat down hard with a splash in the stream, dropping the flashlight, which floated away behind him, still burning brightly. Instantly, his waders filled with water as it surged around his waist. His moans of pain echoed off the cavern walls as he sat there with his eyes tightly shut, willing the pain to subside.

As the bass drum playing inside his head began to subside, he opened his eyes to see the beam from his flashlight dancing around on the cavern walls and ceiling. The light was bobbing in the water a few feet behind him, caught in a gentle eddy between two rocks. Glancing ahead farther into the cavern, he was surprised he could see without the aid of the flashlight. Blinking to clear the cobwebs, and to make sure the blow to his head wasn't causing him to imagine things, he slowly turned and recovered the flashlight, which he turned off. Still, there was enough ambient light to dimly make out his surroundings. Turning around again and leaning down closer to the water, he looked ahead into the cavern, only to have his breath catch in his throat.

Chapter 24

Otis felt really tired and worn-out. Leaving well before daylight this morning, he had been on a mission, and as he pulled the old livestock trailer down the dusty road toward the ranch, the sun painted the evening sky in vivid shades of orange and pink. In addition to all his other ranch chores, for the last few days, he had taken time to fence off a special section of pasture that butted up against a south-facing bluff bordered by a narrow draw, which contained a watering tank. A quarter mile yet from the turn-off road, he could see that the draw was already in shadow. Some of the light snow from three days ago still remained in those shadows, although the temperature had reached into the low sixties that day.

The weather had held pretty well for the last week, allowing for easy maintenance on the five other tanks serving the ranch's stock watering needs. A severe cold snap with temperatures in the single digits had surprised them two weeks ago, causing the tanks to ice up. During a long cold spell, every morning required breaking the ice to allow the stock to drink.

The tank in the shaded draw, like all the others, had once served as a tire on a giant piece of earth-moving equipment. Ranchers had discovered that these huge tires made excellent water tanks once a sidewall was removed and the rim hole near the ground had been filled with bentonite, fine white clay mined locally. Wyoming bentonite was a much sought-after product used in the drilling industry, and a few inches of it packed into the hole for the rim made for a watertight seal.

The big tire lying on its side filled with water made for a much better tank than the galvanized metal ones sold at the big feed stores, for these rubber tanks proved to be virtually bulletproof, a requirement in an area where irresponsible hunters sometimes used the tanks for target practice. A bullet hole in a metal tank wasted precious water, while the big rubber tire would seal itself off. He remembered several years past, when he and Jacob had wrestled this particular tank in place. Someday he'd find some use for the old bullet-riddled galvanized tanks he'd stacked over near the shop.

Jude had thought him crazy for thinking up this latest plan, but once his mind was made up, she knew she was wasting her time trying to change it. He'd had a good reason to leave before daylight this morning hauling the stock trailer down to Arapahoe, Nebraska. He had to be in Arapahoe to pick up his passenger, who had arrived in style, riding up from Woodward, Oklahoma, in a shiny new livestock trailer pulled by a big Ford Powerstroke with a custom paint job.

Otis had decided on a whim to do this, mostly as a way to cope with, as well as a way to honor, the memory of his buddy Jacob. Early the week before, while checking the float in a tank, he'd decided on the plan after awakening earlier than usual that morning with thoughts of Jacob weighing on his mind again. The idea had hit him suddenly as he sat on the side of the tank, staring across the tall grass to where a small knoll rose slightly above the otherwise flat pasture. This knoll was where Jacob had crawled to when making his stalk on the record book antelope.

That day had played out over and over in Otis's mind a million times. He could almost remember every word of their conversations that day. He remembered vividly the comment Jacob had made while glassing out the rolled-down window of the pickup. He'd said without taking the binoculars from his eyes, "Otis, you know, what this ranch needs is a Watusi cow."

"A what?" Otis grunted.

"You know, one of those cows you see on the National Geographic Channel with the really big horns. The skinny ones the natives over in Africa herd around. Yep, one of those would be really cool. I've never seen one up close; you could be the first rancher in this part of Wyoming to have one."

He knew Jacob was just funnin', but he would mention it again every now and then. Otis never carried the thought any further, mainly because the Black Angus cattle he did raise required enough work without adding in some fancy newfangled cow he knew nothing about. However, the more he considered it, the more curious he became. "Nah," he said aloud with finality. "The last thing I need around here is something else to feed and take care of."

Making sure the float worked freely, he'd hurried back to the ranch and typed the words 'watusi cattle' in the search bar of Jude's computer. Within an hour he'd gleaned enough information about the Ankole-Watusi cattle to consider pursuing his crazy idea further. From what he gathered, it wouldn't take much extra work to actually have a token Watusi here on the ranch. They were said to be of a gentle nature, and they could sustain on poor forage and limited water, but most of all, he was fascinated with the photos showing the bovine's unusually large horns. These huge horns grew to be six feet in length and were honeycombed with blood vessels to thermo regulate body temperatures. Blood moving through the horns is cooled by moving air, not unlike the radiator on his old truck.

As he read on, he discovered the breed had been brought to the United States in the early sixties, and there was even an organized group, the World Watusi Association. A few phone calls later and he had firmed up a deal to buy a pig-in-a-poke, or better, a big old bull in an open-top cattle trailer.

His passenger's official name was Wentzel's Champion, as written on the bill of sale and the Ankole-Watusi International Registry form he carried. The huge, young, sixteen-hundred-pound bull with the thick seventy-inch horns had been raised to be a champion breeder, but genetic testing revealed an undesirable trait, resulting in the great bull's promising career being terminated before it started.

Jay Barnette, the wealthy owner of a ranch specializing in champion Ankole-Watusi, had no use for an animal that couldn't increase his bottom line or add to his huge collection of trophies and blue ribbons, so it was 'down the road' for Wentzel's Champion.

Otis's friend Tony had provided the tip leading to the purchase. During casual conversation with a visiting diner at the Pizza Barn, Tony learned the gentleman's son worked for the Barnette Ranch. The fellow was heading back home to Montana after a visit and remembered the amazing pizza he'd enjoyed a few years earlier and decided to stop again on his way through Oldcastle. One thing had led to another, and within a few days of the tip, Otis was making plans for the quick trip to Nebraska.

Turning in a large sweep, Otis stopped when the rear of the trailer came even with the pasture gate. "Well, Wetzel, we're home," he said aloud as he turned off the pickup's engine. "Wetzel?" he repeated. Where had he heard that name before? "Wetzel," he said again as he remembered. Several years ago, Jacob had brought his dad out with him. The old fellow had carried a Thompson Center black powder rifle that must have been six feet long, and he could hit a prairie dog at a hundred yards off hand with that muzzle-loader. He kept saying that was how Wetzel would do it. Otis finally found out he was referring to Lewis Wetzel, an Indian fighter and early frontiersman of the 1700s. Jacob's dad admired this character immensely and read all he could find on his exploits.

Reaching for the Ankole-Watusi International Registry form lying on the seat, he exited the truck. Squinting at the document in the waning light, he read the name aloud with feigned magnitude, "Wentzel's Champion."

Crumpling the form in his hands, he tossed it in with the other miscellaneous junk in the back of the old pickup and said to the bull, as he walked back along the trailer, "As long as you're on this ranch, your name is gonna be Wetzel."

With the pasture gate open, Otis let the ramp to the trailer down and looked inside. The brown-red bull with the scattering of white spots looked back at him with bright black eyes, the muscles of his neck and shoulders brawny from carrying the weight of the massive horns. "Come on, Wetzel, let's have a look at your new digs before it gets too dark."

The big animal hesitated only a second at the command, then ambled slowly toward the exit, stopping within inches of the man, turning its head until the wet nose moved against the bib of Otis's overalls, the coarse hair between the heavy horns touching a woolly beard nearly the same color.

Otis reached a callused hand up to stroke the huge animal's jaw. Two bigger-than-average creatures instantly understanding each other, a bond was formed between the new friends, and when Otis finally turned, the big bull followed him through the gate.

Early the next morning, Otis decided to check on Wetzel before starting on the long list of chores he needed to complete in order to prepare the ranch for winter. Exiting the grove of cottonwoods, he was surprised to see two other figures at the fence, one of which carried a load of sticks on her back. Old Bob and Jennifer seemed to be having an in-depth discussion with Wetzel.

Pulling the pickup to a stop near the gate, Otis got out, left the door open, and approached the group. "Well, whatta ya think?" he asked.

Old Bob replied while keeping his eyes fixed on the big bull. "Does this big, ugly critter have a name yet? I'm sure Jennifer would like to know."

"I call him Wetzel," answered Otis.

"Ahh, Le Vent de la Mort," whispered Old Bob thoughtfully.

"Leave him where?" asked Otis, puzzled.

"Not leave. 'Le Vent,' as in, Le Vent de la Mort, or 'Death Wind,' the name the Indians gave Wetzel." Old Bob snorted. "Don't you know nothin' 'bout important American history?"

"I don't have a clue what you're jabbern' about. What does American history have to do with a Watusi Bull?"

"You just said this critter's name was Wetzel, didn't ya?" asked Old Bob, taking a wheezing breath and gesturing with his arms in disgust. "Well, the Indians back East in the olden days was scared to death of Wetzel — that's Lewis Wetzel, the greatest Indian fighter ever did live. They called him 'Le Vent de la Mort,' which was some Frenchy name for 'Death Wind.' He was known to sneak up on a passel of Indians without makin' a sound, scalp a bunch ov'em and run so fast the rest couldn't ketch him. Ya see, he was really mad at them cause a bunch of 'em masakreed his family. Fella name of Zane Gray wrote a few books about him one time. You really oughtta read somethun once in a while. How did you wind up with this miserable-lookin' varmint anyhow, and what in tarnation caused his horns to grow like that?"

Otis couldn't help but get tickled at the little old man's ability to jump from one subject to another without taking a breath. The entire time Bob was talking he had never taken his eyes off the bull and had yet to turn to face Otis, but he continued his tirade.

"We was headin' for that new dog town over by the Seabolt spread early this mornin', when all the sudden, ole Jennifer here threw up her head and made a dash over this way. Didn't know what got into her. She never moves that fast—was droppin' sticks and everything. I takes off after her, pickin' up the sticks as I went, and when I topped over that rise yonder, I seen her down here nose to nose with this ugly brute. What are ya gonna do with him, anyway? I ain't never in all my born days seen anything like this. Where'd ya get him, or better yet *why* did ya get him?"

When Bob slowed down long enough to take another breath, Otis explained how Wetzel came to be here. As he did so, his voice cracked a little at the mention of Jacob.

"No word on your friend, huh?" Bob asked with concern, his manner changing sincerely in an effort to comfort. "You know somethin', Otis?" This time the little man turned to look Otis in the eye. "I had me a strange dream a little while ago. Ya remember couple weeks back durin' that cold spell? I woke up in the middle of the night freezin' to death. Durn stove went out, and I could hear my teeth chattern', and they was a layin' clear over on the table, where I leave 'em. Well, I gets up and stoke up the fire, and when I quit shiverin', I went back to bed and went right back asleep. That's when I had this here dream. In it, me and Jennifer was a walkin' across the prairie through about a foot and a half of snow, just ploddin' along, ya know. Well, we come up over this little knoll, and down on the other side, when everything leveled out, I saw this here little lake, kinda like a big pond. It should have been frozen over as cold as it was, but it wuzzent. And in this pond set a nekked feller. I just guess he was nekked, 'cause all I could see out of the water was from his belly up." Old Bob stopped talking for a moment and rubbed his scraggly chin thoughtfully. "Now that I think about it, he may have been standin' and not settin'. Anyways, as I got closer, I could see that this fellow was that friend of yours. Never did say nothin', but he sure didn't look cold, either. Then I woke up and didn't dream no more. See ya, Otis. Take care yourself. Let's go, Jennifer."

Without a look back or uttering another word, Old Bob

led Jennifer back the way they'd come. Otis leaned back against the gate watching the pair amble away, pondering the meaning of Bob's dream, if there was even a meaning to think about. He heard Wetzel move closer and felt his wet nose touch against the back of his neck. With a shiver, he turned to scratch his big new buddy under the jaw.

Chapter 25

The panorama held him mesmerized. He could neither move nor breathe at the sight before him. The size of the place made him feel small after the cramped confines of the narrow cavern. After a few moments of gaping, the pain in his head forgotten, he took a tentative step forward. Through the filtered light, he beheld the smooth ceiling curving at least thirty feet above him. He couldn't take it all in at once, but at first blush, the place reminded him of the cliff dwelling at Mesa Verde that he and Anna had visited that summer, except this place held no man-made dwellings.

In the shadows to his left and ahead, he could see additional openings of different sizes, but he couldn't tell if they were other cavern entrances or just cavities in the rock. The floor, though, mainly of smooth stone, rose and fell in several places, and he could make out several pools of water seemingly connected by a common stream, and he could hear the sound of falling water like a small waterfall somewhere. There were also several huge, smooth, flat boulders scattered around. But the focal point of it all lay to his right, at the source of the light. An immense wall of ice in translucent shades of blue curved away, giving the impression of being inside a gigantic opaque, wavy sphere. The aura of it all had his breath coming in gasps; he had to almost force himself to breathe. Stumbling onto this place had been totally unexpected.

He naturally gravitated toward the ice wall and noticed the air immediately became much colder, reestablishing the knowledge that his waders were half full of water. He sloshed his way to the edge of a small rock face with the ice wall still some fifty feet away, although it curved back at the top, meeting with the stone wall above. In this spot, he again felt as if he were standing at the entrance to Mesa Verde, looking out over the valley below, but in this case, the valley view was blocked by way of a massive wall of ice.

Vivid shades of blue dominated the sight before him; a colossal undulating wall curved from high above and met the ground twenty feet below; the black, sandy earth below was cut by a gentle stream flowing along and cutting under the ice. To his right, the stream flowed between the ice and the rock wall for another fifty yards, until the ice again met the wall, and at that point, the stream completely disappeared under it.

Stepping back, Jacob knew he could spend days exploring the vast network of rooms, niches, and crannies, but he also knew he must empty his boots and dry his legs, for he was starting to chill. Part of the shaking could be attributed to excitement, but he was really getting cold, despite the fact that the temperature was above freezing.

Finding a suitable rock, he sat and removed both waders, wishing he had the means to build a fire here, rather than having to wade back to his camp; even though firewood lay less than two hundred yards away, it would be a cold walk. Deciding to leave the backpack, for it would be something less he would be moving to this new location, he removed the extra batteries for the flashlight and took out the old ones. The dunking the light had taken resulted in very little water entering, but the beam had noticeably dimmed just the same.

Fresh batteries resulted in the desired effect, and when he shined the bright beam toward another room farther back in the cavern, something caught his eye. A few dried sticks littered the floor; at least, they looked like dried sticks from where he sat. Further investigation revealed they were not only a few dried sticks but an incredible amount of dried sticks, twigs, small bones, and leaf litter. A huge pile of the stuff nearly filled the room and rose nearly to the height of his head.

Walking around the heap, he saw the oblong room contained a jagged vaulted ceiling with several long, deep cracks and fractures. It seemed the litter had fallen into the cavern from above through one of the breaks. On the other side of the pile, the room narrowed into another opening. It was difficult to envision the immensity of this labyrinth — one cavity led to another. Although this one held no pools or streams that could be seen, he had no idea what lay farther into this part of the mountain. Further exploration would have to wait, though, for the shivering had intensified, and a warm fire would need to come first.

The armload of litter burned hot and smokeless. He'd built the fire alongside one of the clear pools, where he could see the wall of ice, and while his wet pants steamed over the fire, releasing their moisture, he contemplated the makeup of this strange and beautiful cavern. Only a short while ago, his prospect of living beyond a few days seemed slim indeed, and he knew it was not simply dumb luck that had brought him to where he was now. He had been grateful to have been led to the little ledge beside the stream, but now, being blessed with this cathedral, which came with a supply of firewood and fresh water, seemed too much to comprehend.

Upon closer examination, it was revealed that the several pools were not supplied from the same source. This one near the fire contained clear, cold water fed by a small flow from a crack in the cavern wall, and tasted as cold and sweet as any natural stream. However, the three other pools in the main room were connected by a common flow that had cut a deep groove in the floor, indicating it had been flowing for quite some time. In some places the stream flowed in the bottom of a channel about four feet deep, and in other locations the evidence exposed dry trenches connecting equally dry basins, indicating the watercourse had changed over the years. The temperature, while cold, was not uncomfortable, and humidity, even with all the ice and water, seemed low. The slow movement of air currents within the cave system must have prevented the musty dampness usually associated with wet caverns. Also, there was very little dust; his hand had come away clean when he drew it across the floor.

Reaching to check and finding his pants required more drying time, Jacob added more of the cave litter to the fire. As the flames caught, he looked again toward the ice wall blocking the front of the cavern, noticing the dim light diminishing even further, signifying the short day drawing to a close. It appeared obvious the ice wall had to be part of the glacier. He could only imagine the view across the wide valley before the ice filled it; most likely a clear mountain river running cold on its way toward the ocean. He remembered the climb to the high ridge, where he first observed from a distance the clear pool on the ice where the plane had met with disaster. He recalled seeing the tail section protruding from under the monstrous chunk of ice, the final resting place of the entire group but him. He'd never felt more alone at that moment than any other time in his life.

The sun had reflected that day off the pool, masking the deadly up thrusts of smooth ice that had spelled disaster for the plane. He followed the path of the glacier on toward its meeting with the ocean and noticed how quickly the appearance changed. High up the valley at the pool level the ice looked flat and smooth, but about a mile farther down, the course dropped steeply, resulting in a vicious change to dark, brooding crags and crevasses.

Adding a few more sticks to the fire now, he wondered at exactly what point under the ice this present location was; if he were to guess, he would say it would be at the lower end of the smooth, level section just above the descent. Deciding to evaluate the area a little closer on the next trip outside, he retrieved the now-dry britches and headed back to his camp along the stream. A hot bowl of stew would really hit the spot, and he needed a good rest before moving all the stores to his new home.

It took most all the next day to move the supplies, and a trip outside disclosed a clear, cold day. The distant sun felt good on his face as he gathered together the cured meat. He had a good supply, and it would last for quite a while if he rationed it smartly. Hunting would be required again before long, but for now, he was anxious to survey the cavern and secure the ideal spot to set up his permanent camp.

The quarter-mile tunnel to the outside would require a little improvement; he had come to that conclusion the fourth trip made hauling supplies through the water. Investigations confirmed that the warm stream could be diverted with a little work, encouraging it to flow over the lip of the cavern and under the ice. The small stream forked, and a part of the flow poured over the cave lip anyway, so damming the tributary flowing through the tunnel would make travel much easier. All of the water flowing couldn't be eliminated, though, because many rivulets emptied from cracks in the wall. The first part entering from the main cavern caused the most travel problems, for that was where the tunnel was at its narrowest.

Jacob felt reminiscent of a person moving into a new house, deciding on which room to paint, carpet colors, furniture, etc. For the first time since the crash he had hope, and hope was as important as food and water; the prospect of actually surviving the harsh winter now seemed to be a good possibility, if he could keep from falling off a cliff or into a hidden crevasse that is. Or catching pneumonia, or getting eaten by a bear; come to think of it, his throat had been feeling a little scratchy since taking that dip in the stream.

He'd been using a small LED headlamp to free up his hands during the move, so when he lit a lantern, he wasn't expecting the difference it made. The cavern's rock walls nearly sparkled with color, and what he thought to be a layer of ice across the way was revealed to be a vein of quartz-like mineral running along the far wall at ground level, curving upward to disappear into the gloom.

A nearby room with a naturally angular opening caught his eye, and he moved closer to investigate. Standing in the wide entrance, he discovered a small room with a mostly level floor, the walls containing several naturally formed niches or recesses, one of which brought a smile to his lips. It was as if the little room had been made to his specifications, especially the small alcove. Walking over, he placed the lantern inside and stepped back. The opening measured about ten feet wide by not quite five feet high, cutting back into the wall at least another six feet. The nearly perfectly level floor started about two feet off the ground, and when he turned around, it sat as if settling down on a very hard sofa.

An hour later, with a small fire built at the entrance to his new bedroom, Jacob ate a small meal. With his back to the room, he noticed that what little smoke rose from the fire drifted into the main cavern. Dipping a handful of small sticks into a nearby pool, he returned and placed them on the fire. The wet sticks caught, and as the steam and smoke drifted away, Jacob followed the path it took with the beam of his flashlight. The trail rose slowly toward the arched ceiling, but within a few feet of it, some drifted into the room containing the pile of sticks and disappeared through the cracks in the top, but most traveled horizontally and disappeared into a tall, narrow opening in a far wall. Out of that opening also flowed the main course of the stream filling the warm pools. Tomorrow, he would explore this passageway. Maybe another exit to the cave complex could be found in that direction; he wanted to get started mapping out the maze of warrens converging in the main cavern.

The small alcove where Jacob had chosen to place his numerous sleeping bags, ground pads, and clothing made for a warm and cozy place to sleep. Three loaded rifles leaned against the walls of his 'bedroom' in various places, and the .44 mag revolver stayed near the rolled bag he used for a pillow. He also carried it in a holster whenever he moved around inside. Although he felt rather safe, he felt more comfortable with this protection, given the possibility of stumbling onto something big and scary. He'd bet every grown man, if he was being honest, would admit to having some little boy fears of the dark. With several flashlights and loaded guns at hand, he felt more capable of defeating any of the monsters lurking in these dark caverns.

Before turning in for the night, Jacob remembered something else he'd brought from the wreck. Rummaging around in his provisions, he found it; although when he had been gathering the supplies from the plane, he had picked it up a few times only to end up tossing it aside, in the end, he'd put it in his duffle. Now he was glad he had, as he held up the little crank lantern. Winding the crank for a couple minutes charged up the internal battery, giving power to the row of LEDs that provided a bright white light. A switch allowed three, six, or all twelve of the tiny LEDs to burn; twelve allowed enough light for reading, and three furnished a comforting glow, providing for a good night light.

Warm in his sleeping bag with the small lantern against the wall behind him, Jacob lay on his back, noticing the tiny sparkles in the ceiling. The minerals in the sleeping alcove reflected the soft light's radiance, giving the impression of sleeping under the stars. As his lids grew heavy, he repeated to himself over and over again the child's nighttime prayer his mother taught him long ago. The same prayer he had taught his girls: "Now I lay me down to sleep; I pray the Lord my soul to keep . . . "

Early the next morning Jacob started damming the stream leading into the exit tunnel, and before long, most of the flow had been diverted over the lip of the cavern. The chore had proved easy, considering all the smooth, flat stones found littering parts of the floor. The filtered light coming through the ice also allowed enough illumination for the task to be completed without the need for a lantern. Being able to distinguish day from night would keep his system in some semblance of normalcy, providing he was located far enough south not to have to face the six months of full darkness associated with far northern regions. But then again, this region could receive a thick covering of snow that would further diminish the transmission of light through the ice. Thoughts such as this crossed his mind often, and he was getting more adept at dismissing them, finding it better just to take one day at a time and deal with situations only when they arose. "That doesn't mean going about unprepared," he said aloud, startled at the sound of his voice echoing throughout the chamber.

A permanent fire pit was constructed, and a couple of flat seats built with the flat stones, along with a larger flat rock laid across the far side of the pit to serve as a warming stone. Jacob stood back to survey his work and laughed out loud when he noticed he had built two seats. "As if I'm expecting a guest," he said.

While sorting and storing things, he unrolled the old bear hide at the base of his sleeping nook. It served as a rug beside the bed, something to keep his feet off the cold floor. Rummaging a little more, he found his small digital camera in one of the kits, and when he turned it on the low battery display was not lit yet, indicating a good charge. He immediately took a couple photos, one of himself, using the self-timer. He vowed to provide a visual record as long as the battery held a charge.

By early afternoon Jacob was feeling poorly. He had come

down with the head cold he was hoping to avoid. The stuffy nose and headache made him want to do nothing but lie down, so after heating up a hot cup of watered-down stew, he retired to his 'bedroom.' He'd suffered through hundreds of these aggravating colds, some of which really brought him to his knees, but every time, he had been able to endure at home with a mother or wife to help him through if his misery became too severe. Once, when he was very young, he'd had pneumonia. At least, that's what his mother had told him; he didn't remember the episode, and he was never too keen on going to see a doctor.

Gathering his meager pharmaceuticals together, he withdrew to the warmth of his sleeping bag, hoping his system was strong enough to withstand the bug and see that it did not develop into pneumonia. So many things could get him here, from falling from a cliff, to being eaten by a bear, or dying from a sickness. However, all things considered, he was probably safer in the cave than walking the streets of a city.

It was the third day before Jacob felt well enough to move around much. The previous days had been spent with bouts of fitful sleep, followed by restlessness, along with a fever. Later the past evening, the sweating had started. He didn't think the miserable night would ever end, but now remembrances of it seemed only a blur, and his fever seemed to have broken. Still feeling weak, but without a headache, most of the cold symptoms seemed to have disappeared for now, with none of the feared 'rattling' in the chest. With clear lungs and only slightly stuffy sinuses, he felt more secure, in that he would avoid pneumonia and could now work toward developing a routine of some sort. Staying busy would be the key to staying sane.

The breakfast he'd prepared tasted unusually satisfying this morning, another sign he was on the mend. As he ate, his eyes wandered to the narrow opening in the far wall of the main room, into which most of the smoke drifted. He'd been so busy earlier, except for the past few days he spent 'under the weather,' he had postponed the exploration plans. Maybe he'd check the passage out today.

"Yep, that's what I'll do," he said. He had started speaking out loud often, finding the sound of his own voice a comfort.

Chapter 26

An hour later Jacob stood at the entrance to the narrow passage, a light backpack outfitted with the necessary items for a day or so traipsing in the unknown. Upon closer examination, it could be determined that the narrowness of the opening was caused by a large piece of stone that had broken from the solid wall, partially blocking the route. Once past, he found the rest to be wide, smooth, and on a slight upward incline, with the walls slanting toward one another until they met ten to fourteen feet above the floor; a narrow trench varying from one to two feet wide and about four feet deep ran parallel to the path. Water could be heard gurgling in the trench.

In several places, the beam of the flashlight revealed indications that the passage had been widened on purpose; however, Jacob dismissed the crude marks as natural striations and not rudimentary scores made by man-made tools. The path and trench wound through the passage for another two hundred feet or so, until they diverged. The trench disappeared into a tall, vertical crack running from floor to ceiling, while the path veered to the left, climbing a little steeper, and a dim light could be seen another hundred feet up, where the path took a slight turn to the right.

Reaching the top, where the path leveled, Jacob was again met with an unexpected sight that left him speechless. He found himself looking down into another great room, this one with a clear steaming pool of water the size of a large backyard above ground swimming pool, but what amazed him the most was that he could see the sky. A full sixty feet above the pool and another forty feet above his location on the path was a slender opening above another smooth wall of ice.

The huge room below disclosed a shape not unlike a half-domed symphony hall; the open side was blocked by another smooth wall of ice, but in this case, the rising heat had melted an opening at the top, allowing the steam to escape. The top of the ice wall, eroded smooth by the warm steam, angled away at the top, allowing a narrow view of the sky, at the moment displaying a beautiful cloudless blue. Where the steam met the stone ceiling at the opening, it condensed enough to cause a steady patter of droplets falling in a shimmering veil. The top extended beyond the base, allowing the water to fall away without splashing onto the floor of the cavern. The lip of this cavern matched that of the one where he had made his camp, lending to the conclusion the two caverns once shared the same view of the great valley.

The path he was on continued farther around the rim of the amphitheater, curving gently downward to meet with the floor. Reaching that level, he stopped, amazed at the scene before him. Steaming water bubbled up from a spring where the wall met the floor, reminding Jacob of a smaller version of the Dragon's Mouth hot spring he had witnessed when the family had taken a vacation to Yellowstone Park. The hot water flowed from here into the large clear pool, giving the impression of being no more than four feet deep at its deepest.

The bottom looked to be covered mostly with dark, coarse sand.

A colder small rivulet trickled into the pool from under a huge, smooth boulder. This had to be the source of the foggy valley he had detected from his first observation from the ridge above the wreck. The fog had been thicker on cold, frosty mornings, but he had given no thought to it being caused by a hot spring—a hot spring sharing space with a glacier!Engrossed with the hot spring, pool, and wall of ice, Jacob had failed to immediately notice a sight that now made his breath catch in his throat: Evidence that someone *had* been here before him! He had started to sit on an indentation in the large boulder, when he noticed it was not a natural occurring notch, but something that had been cut there by design; a step leading to another and another that led onto the flat top of the boulder. These were the same cut marks he had seen at the beginning of the passage, the ones he had attributed to natural striations. There could be no mistake, and taking a few steps back, he could see an alcove in the wall above the boulder. All this was hidden from his view while walking the narrow path above the pool.

The natural light filtering through the opening above the ice allowed him to ascend without the aid of a flashlight. Carefully, he made his way to the top of the stone, where another flat rock served as a short, narrow bridge into the recess. When his eyes adjusted to the gloom, he stood paralyzed for a moment at what he saw.

Two long, curving beams, forming an arch over ten feet high, stood at the smooth back wall. The thick beams attested to great age, being yellow-brown, scarred, and cracked, but they were still standing strong. A big flat-topped stone nearly as large as a small car rested between the arching beams, and on this, there appeared to be a pile of rubble. Walking slowly closer, the glow of his light fell upon the wall, and the illumination divulged numerous petroglyphs carved into the smooth stone. Pictograms from an earlier age, possibly several thousand years old, stood out as if carved yesterday. Goose bumps covered his body as he took in the images: representations of animals with huge racks of antlers, others of fish showing mouths full of jagged teeth; the likeness of a great bear surrounded by stick figures of men with spears. Even many centuries ago, the monster haunted the lives of men. Then he saw the rendering of a beast with great curving tusks; now the beams forming the arch beside him took on new meaning as he reached out to caress the ancient warm ivory.

Removing his backpack, he placed it on the flat stone to remove the camera; as he did so, he disturbed the pile of rubble, some of it crumbling, revealing the items within. Jacob paused at the gentle sound like pieces of glass hitting the stone behind the backpack. Investigating the sound, he noticed several white objects had slid down the pile onto the stone.

Retrieving one of them, he stared in wonder at the beautifully knapped stone blade! Never had he beheld one of such striking perfection, not even in the artifact magazines he and his dad had drooled over. The large fluted specimen looked to be one of the rare Clovis points he'd only seen in photos; but he'd also read that no stone tools resembling the Clovis type had ever been found anywhere in Siberia, or anywhere on the Asian continent, for that matter. Clovis, Dalton, or Folsom were the only fluted point types he could recall, or maybe this was something completely unknown. He'd never actually seen one, let alone held one in his hands!

Carefully, he replaced the point where he found it and took several pictures of the items in situ. He was living in the moment, forgetting, for the time being, the state of affairs his life was in. If only his dad could be in on this discovery. After the photos, he cautiously sifted through the pile.

Hidden within potato chip-sized dark brown flakes of what may have been leather pouches at one time, he found fourteen more of the fluted points. All were made of the stunning, almost translucent white stone; some of them had fine veins of yellow running throughout. Also mixed within the pile were a hundred or more beads of the same material; probably at one time strung together with a long since deteriorated cord.

But the object he now saw made the others pale in comparison, and his hands shook as he reached for it. Carefully, almost reverently, he picked up the carving of a shark or whale, actually a killer whale in an arching dive as if breaching the surface; it was made of the same quartz-like stone but with much more of the yellow gold striations. Why would these items have been left here? Who had left them, and how long ago? Were they maybe some type of offering? Did these ancient people think the gurgling hot spring to be some sort of god, or something sent by a god? Was this considered a holy place?

Placing the object with the others back on the stone, a thousand thoughts running through his mind, he stepped back and took a few more photos with the little digital camera, after which he noticed the battery indicator showing less than half charge. He felt a little dizzy, maybe because he had been hyperventilating for the past several minutes. He looked again at the array before him, no doubt a major archaeological discovery, but who would ever know?

Turning, he walked slowly across the short bridge and down the stone steps. He felt tired, almost exhausted. With the excitement of this new discovery and the weakness from the recent illness, he wanted to rest, rest and think. He stared into the hot pool of steaming water and, without a moment's hesitation, he removed his clothing and eased into the water. It was hot! It reminded him of the pool at Chico Hot Springs in Montana, one of the only two hot springs he had ever been in, the other being in Thermopolis, Wyoming.

Hunting trips with his dad and a family vacation had been the reasons for those visits. He remembered clearly the evening sitting in the steaming spring in Montana, with snow falling in huge flakes.

The heat permeated his body to the core, and as he slowly became accustomed to the warmth, it seeped into his limbs, all but melting his bones. The soft, coarse sand molded to his bottom, and he lay his head back and shut his eyes, fully enjoying the relaxing sensation. He opened his eyes after a few moments, to see the sliver of sky high above and smiled as he saw through the escaping steam that it was full of huge, soft flakes of snow.

Jacob soaked and even dozed off for a few minutes. He hadn't been completely warm throughout since the crash. A big fire warmed only the side facing the fire, but this was all-encompassing. How quickly his circumstances had changed; only a few days ago he had feared freezing to death, and now he had his own spa and was in possession of what might be a priceless discovery. But who would ever know but him? None of these things could buy him a plane ticket home, or even a three-minute phone call to let his family know he was safe. Everything in life was relevant only to the state of affairs at the time.

Sweat was running down his forehead and onto his unshaven face; he dunked his head and licked at the water on his lips. It didn't have the mineral taste or smell; this pool contained clear, sweet water, only it was hot. Digging his feet into the sand, he also noticed there was no silt disturbed.

Now was a good time for a bath, so, without any soap available, he scooped handfuls of the sand and proceeded to scrub his body. Feeling something in his right palm other than sand, he glanced down to find a smooth yellow nugget, instantly bringing to mind a resemblance to a Raisinet, the chocolate-covered raisin candy he loved.

Realizing with shock that he actually held a piece of gold, without another thought, he did what he'd seen done in TV Westerns: he bit into it and left a tooth mark in the soft metal and then laughed out loud. He was as unprepared for this find as with the artifacts, and it caused another stunned surge to flow through his body. Looking toward the altar stone, he realized that those yellow veins in the artifacts were also gold!

Looking up toward the heavens, he screamed, "Is this some kind of joke!" He threw the nugget across the pool, his elation instantly turning to frustration.

He'd worked really hard the past few weeks at curbing his emotions and keeping them under control when he felt anxiety creeping up on him. Maintaining a clear mind while under stress required constant practice, he knew this, so he sat back and forced himself to relax. So what if within the last twenty minutes he'd made a major archaeological discovery and now might quite possibly, literally be sitting on a fortune in gold? "Yeah, so what?" he voiced his thoughts.

Working his hand down through the sand almost a foot before touching a smooth stone bottom, he brought a handful up again and gently shook off most of it under the surface, revealing another small piece of the yellow metal. "At least I won't be bored this winter," he announced.

Jacob crawled into his sleeping nook early that evening; the soak in the hot spring, while relaxing, had acted to drain his strength and now, with all the pent-up tension gone, he just wanted to sleep. The ambient light in the cavern had darkened considerably, most likely the result of the heavy snow falling. It would likely cover the somewhat translucent ice and reduce the filtered brightness even more. Giving the crank lantern enough turns to provide an hour or so of the comforting glow, he settled back to review the happenings of the day, which would be a great deal to process.

He picked up the little camera, which was of no use now, given that he had no way to charge it, and removed the small memory card and laid it on his Bible while he arranged the sleeping bags to a more comfortable position. Satisfied that his bed was now more comfortable, he reached for the Bible and heard the soft clink of the memory card hitting stone. Knowing he would surely lose it, he stuffed it between the spine and leather cover of his Bible. It was a snug fit, but at least the photos would be safe as long as he had the Bible. Opening the book to First Corinthians chapter two, he started to read in the dim light, but found he just couldn't concentrate; he couldn't stop thinking about the ones who must have been here before him.

In his mind's eye, he saw rough hands carving the petroglyphs into the wall; the natural light from the unblocked cavern opening illuminating the curved wall, while the gurgling sound of the hot spring echoed nearby. Thousands of years before the first stone was placed for the Great Pyramids, these carvings were already ancient. What kind of life did this early artist lead? What great beasts he must have seen in a land that, for the most part, had remained unchanged. How different was he from that man? Other than the fact the artist had his family close by. Thoughts darted through his mind rapidly, until all became cloudy and, once again, he succumbed to sleep.

Chapter 27

White Ears was restless. He had come out of his deep torpor to sounds and smells familiar and comforting. For the past three years of his life, he'd shared the time with his mother, and then last year, they were joined by his sibling; however, his world had recently changed, challenging him to fend for himself. Natural instincts had guided his path, but he was still confusingly linked to these strange smells and sounds.

Intuition ingrained into his kind since time's beginning had led him to seek out this place during the days of bitter cold, but now, even though the snow fell in huge flakes, the air was much warmer, and he was hungry. He had managed to pack on a thick layer of fat due to the abundance of fish in the area and their willingness to be easily caught. He was already much larger than the average cub his age, mainly because he sated himself at every opportunity.

The big pads on his paws found purchase on the rocky, snow-covered trail that evening, and when it forked, he hesitated at which direction to take. Relying on sound and smell rather than sight, he heard the squawking of the jays and ravens before the scent reached his flaring nostrils.

Lumbering in the direction of the fracas, he soon caught scent of a bouquet that made the drool drip from his muzzle. Several ravens had converged on a pile of sheep entrails that had previously been in possession of the jays, resulting in a shrieking protest at losing their prize. Without pause he moved in and claimed the meal for his own, managing to knock one of the ravens to the ground as it wavered over another morsel, its life ending under a huge paw. The unlucky bird soon joined the gut pile as the main course for his evening meal; the jays voiced their approval at the justice.

Charged with a full belly, his aimless wandering soon brought him to the drying racks near the cavern opening, where the latent smells of burnt wood and dried meat caught his attention. Pawing and digging through the snow brought the crude racks down, and he soon grew tired of this and moved to the breach in the rock. A plethora of scents caught his attention here, some strange and new, others old and familiar, but none threatening; so after only a moment of uncertainty, he entered and sniffed around at the recent campsite.

In a spot near the wall, one odor stood out among the others, causing him to draw up short. He tasted and smelled the air, then followed his nose farther into the mountain until he located what he sought. Here, he quietly circled once and lay down.

Jacob's sleep proved to be deep and restful; the long soak in the hot spring had done more than unwind his keyed-up body but had also managed to relieve some of the stress on his mind. His dream was filled with visions of a wide, verdant valley dotted with great beasts, and he observed this marvel from the cavern mouth, no wall of ice blocking his view. He'd spent the morning working the white stone, knapping the last of a group of ceremonial points the shaman had asked him to make.

Shaking the small stone flakes from his finely made leather apron, he stood and walked closer to the lip of the cave, to give closer scrutiny to the actions of a small herd of shaggy animals browsing in the thick brush along the river. Noticing their strange behavior brought concern that they may have already detected the small assembly of hunters creeping toward them through the tall grass. The group had left the cave only a short while ago; they surely could not have gotten close enough to spook the small herd so soon. The gentle, warm breeze was blowing toward the hunters from the direction of the river, so the animals could not have winded them, and their eyesight was too poor to have detected the slight movement of the grass as the hunters advanced.

The old shaman, Na-too, had requested the ceremonial points to be made of the white stone, and Ja-kab had been chosen to craft them, even though he was not the principal stone worker for the loosely gathered clan. Most all of the hunters in the group knapped their own points, but Ja-Kab was known for his finely detailed work, which was much sought after. His small family was well dressed and well fed, the result of trades he'd made.

The old shaman, Na-too, was guardian of the sacred grotto, where the Great Earth Mother sent forth the bubbling water heated without fire.

Na-too watched over the grotto, as had his father and his grandfather before him. That special gift had been given to their ancestor many lifetimes ago, when the injured hunter had crawled into the cave after being severely wounded by the great cat. He had stumbled upon the cat with the long, curved teeth just after it had made a kill of the very animal he himself had been stalking. Rounding a curve on a narrow, ice-covered trail, the young hunter had hoped to have the deer cornered with no place to escape, but the cat had been waiting above, unseen, and made the kill first.

His surprise at seeing the cat so close and with no place to run led him to make an attempt to leap off the smooth rock face into the thick branches of a tree, just as the beast sprang to sink the long, sabered fangs deep into his thigh. The fall to the ledge below severely sprained the ankle on the already-injured leg. Looking up to see the big cat with his own blood dripping from one of the great teeth, he knew it would find an easier way down to complete the grisly task. As the beast turned away, he knew his time was short, but unknown to him, the cat had only looked down from above, then returned to his meal.

The young hunter despaired at his plight and, unable to return to his small group camped far down and on the other side of the great valley, decided his only choice was to drag himself into the cave he now lay before and protect himself as best he could. He would either bleed to death, freeze to death, or be eaten by the cat. With only his spear to protect himself, he examined the wound to find a deep hole in the flesh, with shiny white bone showing at the bottom, but not as much blood as he had first thought; the real pain came from the rapidly swelling ankle.

Dragging himself backward deeper into the cavern, he almost fell into the hot pool of water; he'd been so intent on looking out for the cat that he hadn't even noticed the pool behind him, or the warmth of the place. He took dried herbs from the leather bag around his waist and soaked them into the hot water and applied the poultice to the wound. The cat never showed itself, so after a little while, he crawled back to the opening and gathered ice to pack around the swollen ankle.

For two full days he lay there, quenching his thirst with melting ice and periodically soaking the ankle in the hot water. On the morning of the third day, he heard a shout from below and was ecstatic to see that a member of his hunting party had ventured so far up the valley in search of him. The injured young man mustered all the strength he had left to respond, but the effort caused him to black out. The searching hunter thought a dead man had called out to him from this strange place, and then the dead man moved, another sign that this sacred place contained great power! Na-too was told the story of how his ancestor had survived the fangs of death, only to be healed by the sacred waters.

Ja-kab knew the advancing hunters couldn't see their intended quarry. They had planned the stalk with the hope that the small herd would be grazing in the same area for some time. The youngest of the seven young men had noticed the shaggy beasts descending into the valley before the sun had risen enough to burn the fog away.

Mammoth were a rare sight. None had been seen in the valley since before the season of snow, and that time had now passed, for the new grass had greened and stood taller than a man's head. Without doubt, something else had aroused their suspicion, for the three old females of the herd had gathered the others behind them. Possibly the scent of a pack of wolves had startled the group, except for the old bull, who seemed oblivious and continued eating, stripping the branches from a small willow.

As Ja-kab stared at the old bull, movement in front of the females caught his eye as a huge cave bear stood up on its hind legs; the brute easily stood eleven feet tall, able to look a fully grown mammoth level in the eye. Unimpressed, the old females moved in unison toward the bear, causing it to give ground. Not used to being challenged, the creature tried to exert dominance by letting loose a deep, guttural growl, a move that had no effect on the determination of the old cows. The lead cow hit the bear just as he dropped to all fours, bowling it over in the grass, out of Ja-kab's sight. The old cow continued through the grass as the bear sought to escape, running across the valley, directly toward the cave where Ja-kab stood.

A little over halfway to the cavern, the bear stopped, stood up again, and looked back toward the mammoths, who trumpeted in unison as a warning. The bear seemed to have gotten the message, for it dropped down and continued on a path toward the cave. Ja-kab watched as the beast came closer, until it passed beneath the lip where he was standing. Not daring to move for fear of drawing attention, he stood stock-still.

The bear stopped for a moment not ten feet below the rim, huffing belligerently. Ja-kab had never been this close to a bear of this size, only having seen their kind from a distance before now. The coarse hair of the monster moved in conjunction with the ripple of powerful muscles, and the rank odor of the beast floated up to envelop him.

Jacob opened his eyes, the strange dream still fresh in his mind as he turned to lay on his back. There wasn't enough light as yet to see his surroundings, but glancing to his left, he could make out the faint glow near the top of the ice wall that indicated the short day was soon to begin. A soft sound had awakened him, a gentle *huff* if he recalled correctly. The dream he was having had appeared so vivid, the sleep so deep, he was only now returning to the present. His mind's eye could still see every hair on the big bear's back, even the grass seeds and plant burrs caught in that hair, and the raw, wild smell emanating from the beast still lingered.

In fact, as he inhaled, he could still detect that odor. How was that possible, though? It was only a dream. Then he again heard the soft rush of air that had awakened him. His body stiffened. Was he still dreaming, or was there something near? Ever so slowly, he turned his head in the darkness. A weak glow came from behind the thinner ice, not an adequate amount of light to see anything, but still evident. Suddenly, even that was blocked by a darker shadow! Paralyzed with fear, he only stared, as a dim outline materialized as the dark shadow moved closer. A huff sounded again, followed by wet sniffing noises, then two small lighter-colored areas could be perceived moving with the shadow.

Fully awake now, he realized this was certainly no dream, but a nightmare! His arms were inside the sleeping bag, and the handgun lay only inches behind his head, but he dared not move. The sniffing was growing closer and louder, the fetid hot breath bringing back memories of the bear attack. And it was about to happen again! There would be no escape this time; he was trapped! Just as suddenly, the shadow backed away, allowing for a clearer shape to form in the growing light.

The recognition was immediate; the surviving bear with the white ears! He was much bigger than remembered, but it had never been this close before, either. How did it get here? How did it find him?

Still, Jacob was afraid to move. He only stared at the beast, and the beast stared back! Able to distinguish better in the increasing light, he could make out that the bear was sitting on its haunches, looking into the sleeping recess. Could it sense the fear that gripped Jacob, preventing him from moving, even if he wanted to? Two sets of eyes locked together, each set trying to perceive the intent of the other; the bear suddenly looked away, stood up on all fours, and quietly disappeared into the darkness.

Jacob lay there for what seemed like several minutes, although only a few seconds had passed before he could breathe again. He couldn't understand how the bear happened to be here. How did it find him, and why? Now that he had time to reflect, it did seem that it had almost been stalking him ever since the time on the beach several weeks ago. Had it really been several weeks? It sometimes felt as if he had been stranded for months. What reason could this bear have to follow him?

Slowly, he extracted himself from the sleeping bag and sat on the edge of the little alcove. The dim glow through the ice provided enough brightness for him to see the immediate surroundings, and there was no sign of the bear. Had it gone out through the narrow tunnel to the outside, or was there another entrance known only to the bear? Was it lurking somewhere in the shadows?

As soon as Jacob's feet touched the old bear hide, he seized on a possible answer. Maybe the bear was following the old hide, something that linked him to his mother. After all, he had imprinted on her smell all of his life, and even though other scents had recently mixed with what he knew, enough of what he identified with her was also there. In that case, he might return, so, to develop the theory farther, Jacob dragged the hide across the cavern floor, to the far side against the wall. This placed the water channel between Jacob's bedroom and the old skin, but would still allow him to see it from a distance of about sixty feet.

For the rest of the day Jacob talked out loud and sang a number of old songs, anything to make his presence known. He sorted through a bunch of his stuff and relocated the gold pan from the bottom of a duffle bag. He studied the dry streambeds within the cavern and chose the first location that indicated where there had been a small waterfall at one time. The break in the ditch fell for only several inches, but here Jacob dug through the coarse, dark sand until he reached the solid bedrock, another eighteen inches down.

The sand near the bottom was of a slightly finer consistency, and he took a pan of this to the nearby stream. He squatted and dipped the edge of the pan under the surface, going through the motions of gold panning as he'd seen done on television.

Almost right away, he saw a few flakes of bright glitter, only to watch them spill over the lip of the pan and be lost in the stream. Several more times this happened, until only a little of the sand remained, along with four small, heavier nuggets the size of white rice. Jacob removed the little pieces of gold, and as he held them in his palm, he thought again of the wealth this place must hold; and all for naught. Then again, maybe this gold had value to him after all. He couldn't use it to buy a mansion, but maybe it could buy his sanity, give him a reason to get up in the morning! That was it; he would work his claim as a job, eight to five every day, as long as he was able.

Chapter 28

Jacob continued to toil in the sand pit below the dry falls, while being ever vigilant for the return of his uninvited guest. Too soon it seemed, the light dimmed as the day again moved into evening. He had been so engrossed with his task that he hadn't even stopped for a midday meal. The gold found thus far almost covered his palm, but since he'd never undertaken a task like this before, he really wasn't sure of his accomplishment. Would this be considered a rich strike? Was this real gold? He believed it was. In the movies and stories he'd read about, only a few gold prospectors ever found the 'mother lode.' Mostly, they just wandered the desert, leading a sorry-looking burro with a bunch of clanging supplies strapped to its back.

He smiled as a vision of Old Bob and Jennifer was brought to mind; Old Bob fit the description perfectly. He could picture Jennifer with a load of picks and pans instead of a load of sticks. He paused in his work a moment as he savored a memory. He and Otis had been unable to locate the old gentleman during his last visit to the ranch. They had even taken a ride out to the old shack Bob called home, but there was no sign of him or the little donkey. Otis had left a small box containing salt, sugar, and coffee in an old wooden crate on the rickety porch, covering it with a flat piece of rusty tin. He hoped the old codger was doing well and wondered if he ever had done any prospecting. How would he react to this cavern under the ice?

Somewhere in the blackness a rock fell, and Jacob jumped. Every sound startled him; perhaps the bear had moved on, but still, if the big cub had found another way inside, then that way would allow other things to enter too. What if there were several entrances into the cave system? The possibilities of what may take him by surprise caused his stomach to knot. Maybe it would be better if the bear did return; at least he could keep an eye on it, maybe even use him for a watch dog.

Too keyed up to sleep, Jacob cautiously made his way to the hot spring, shining the flashlight into every shadow along the path. He spent the next couple hours soaking, letting the steaming water ease tense muscles, alternately wondering how much gold lay buried in the sand around him and how many pairs of eyes were watching.

Several handfuls of sand revealed nothing, although he was sitting in a different spot than where he found the nuggets, and his continuous looking around also revealed nothing. If he wasn't eaten alive, he would eventually get around to panning everywhere possible, really work the prospecting as a way to keep his mind focused and his muscles toned.

His greatest fear remained going mad, and he was determined to avoid this at all cost; he also had to be wary of other things invading the cave system. So far, he had seen no other sign of habitation by any animals. The only indication of anything or anyone being here before him was the artifacts and the petroglyphs, and that was before the openings had frozen over. But the bear had found a way inside; hopefully, it had followed the scent and followed his trail through the tunnel.

Soon the hot water relaxed his tense body as much as he felt was necessary to allow sleep, so with ever wary steps, he returned to the main chamber. He built up a small fire to heat some stew, glancing every few moments at the old hide across the way.

The last of the natural light now departed, and Jacob sat before the small fire holding a bowl of hot stew, a tin of coffee cooling by his side. At every small noise, either real or perceived, he pointed the beam of a flashlight across the way to illuminate the old bear hide. Each time, the light revealed only the old hide, nothing on it or near it. Looking to the sleeping nook, he knew if he ever hoped to sleep again, he would need an alarm system.

The opening to his sleeping room was too wide to construct any sort of door or barrier, but he could manage to arrange a few poles with hanging empty cans or something; anything to make a noise if disturbed. He was a light sleeper, so it wouldn't take much. Best to stay armed, just in case.

Cleaning up from supper, he decided to take the next day off from his new job and go hunting. He still had a good supply of dried meat, but he knew he should add to his larder whenever possible, and he also needed to cut the few saplings to construct the warning device.

After a mostly sleepless night, Jacob greeted the dawn at the mouth of the cavern. The air was cold and completely still. A dark gray sky draped the land like a shroud, and the crunch of his boots through crusty snow seemed magnified ten times. The sudden shriek of a hawk startled him; the sound seemed to come from only a few feet above his head, forcing him to fall to his knees for fear of being attacked. Recovering, he looked up to see the offender circling two hundred feet above.

The strange auditory remained, even when he reached the top of the high ridge. The sky appeared close enough to touch, and far into the distance he could see the ocean, the huge icebergs distinct; their blue and white hues in perfect focus. The normally hazy view at this extreme today appeared clear. Even at over two miles, he could even hear sounds of the sea and the calls of the gulls, which appeared as slow-moving white dots.

Breathing in the cold, crisp air, he sat and scanned the long, narrow fjord through binoculars, noting the newly formed sea ice rimming the beach. In a month or so, most all of the huge bergs would be trapped until late spring, unless the current allowed escape sooner. He wondered how much winter snow the area accumulated, and how far the mercury would drop before the spring thaw. Most importantly, when would that occur? The harsh winter could last six to eight months. Could he really make it that long?

He turned slowly, scanning for a place close by to harvest some strong, thin saplings, and was relieved to see a small basin containing a copse of willows. The thicket grew in a ravine protected from the wind near the cavern entrance. He'd not noticed this ravine before, as it was one of several that converged with the warm stream and that he would have completely missed if he had not been at this altitude.

The whole of the immediate area lay like a wrinkled blanket and would be difficult to navigate without often climbing to a high vantage point such as this. Following a game trail worn to the dirt through the snow soon led into the grove that, in actuality, encompassed a much larger area than it initially appeared.

A short while later, as he was gathering the willow saplings, several sets of animal tracks were discovered coming and going from yet another trail leading into the thicket; although he saw no animals, this appeared to be a very good place to hunt. If his approach had been a little stealthier, maybe he would have caught one of the animals leaving the grove, for some of the small cloven tracks were fresh, indicating small sheep or deer.

It was a godsend to locate such a place only a short distance from the cave mouth. He studied the approaches and was careful to pile the willow tops in a location to provide an opportunistic browser a reason to stop within an easy rifle shot from the ridgetop nearest the cave entrance.

It had been a full week since the visit to the little glen of willows. He'd spent two days constructing a formidable fence with swinging gate just in front of his sleeping nook; at intervals along the fence, he suspended empty cans containing several small pebbles to rattle around if disturbed. An enraged grizzly would make short work of destroying the results of many hours' labor, but he still felt confident he would be able to rest better at night. His uninvited guest had yet to return, though. The next several days were spent working the gold claim, and the evenings involved soaking away the muscle stiffness in the hot springs. Panning gold required many hours of stooping, squatting, and bending, but the hours passed by quickly and the little pile of gold grew.

Subsequent visits to the outside revealed the curious weather pattern had held; no wind, rain, or snow, only a steel-gray sky that held low over the land, resulting in the strange acoustics. A pebble falling from a cliff a hundred feet away resonated with the sound of a glass marble being dropped on a hard tile floor.

Early one evening Jacob climbed the short distance to the ridge overlooking the little glen. As he eased himself over the crest, movement below immediately drew his attention to the narrow trail leading up from below. A dozen or more dark shapes weaved through the shadows, and contented sounds of grunts and snorts carried up through the still air.

Entering the grove, the passel of hogs spread out through the willows. A dark row of coarse hair standing stiff down their backs defined the large adult males. The smaller females, some accompanied by even smaller piglets, stopped occasionally to root around in the damp leaf litter covered in patches of frozen snow.

Thoughts of sizzling bacon and fried pork chops entered his mind as he leveled the rifle. Four quick, carefully placed shots still echoed as three of the larger pigs lay motionless on the ground, a lucky fourth one escaping with the others as the last shot kicked up the snow as they disappeared from sight.

With the echo of the gunfire fading away, Jacob stood to make his way into the grove. He approached the largest hog first, and as he made an initial cut to field dress the animal, warm escaping air from the cavity frosted in the cold air, rising straight up until caught by a sudden light breeze.

The unexpected waft quickly advanced up the ridge, followed by a constant gentle cold wind blowing from the northeast. By the time he'd moved to the second hog, tiny sporadic flakes of ice crystals could be felt on his face. Being familiar with the unpredictable nature of the weather patterns and how quickly things could change forced Jacob to pick up the pace with the task at hand.

By field dressing the animals, the carcasses would be allowed to cool, then they would be cut into manageable portions for the chore of transporting the meat over the ridge to the drying and smoking racks. He was thinking of the firewood needed to process his bounty and was intently focused on making careful cuts when it happened. From behind, he was caught off balance and pushed facedown into the fresh gut pile, a weight between his shoulder blades keeping him there. He felt the warm puff of air on the back of his head an instant before something wet and rough snaked across the back of his neck.

Chapter 29

Otis's troubled mind was far away as he drove the old pickup across the auto gate toward the east pasture. He had gambled and lost; now the ranch was in trouble. He approached Wetzel's paddock and noticed his big friend was already hurrying on the way to the gate to greet him.

Stopping the truck a few yards from the enclosure gate, he shut off the engine and just sat there, trying to gather his thoughts. Wetzel was puzzled at this. Otis would normally spring from the truck with an enthusiastic greeting for his big friend. Wetzel would wait for Otis to pull open the gate, reach up and grab the bull's loose cheeks, and give his great head an affectionate shake and rub.

The great beast sensed a change and bumped the heavy gate with his head; it slowly squeaked open on rusty hinges, for it was never locked. There was no need, since Wetzel would never wander off. He preferred the comfort of his compound, where all his needs were met and the daily visits from Otis provided all the companionship he required. Occasional visits from Old Bob and Jennifer were a bonus, but today, he detected something amiss as he slowly approached the rolled-down window of the old pickup.

Otis looked up at the approach and spoke for the first time, "Hello, old buddy. I guess I'm just outta sorts today, sorry."

Otis exited the truck and shrugged into his heavy canvas coat; his breath frosted in the cold morning air as he draped his arm over the great neck. He and Wetzel turned to re-enter the enclosure, as most of their visits took place just inside the entrance, and that's where Wetzel led him. If Otis needed to talk, he would listen at their usual spot.

Wetzel instinctively sensed the despair in Otis; the animal had no idea what or why, of course, but the change compared to his usual jovial greeting was apparent, even to the mind of the big bull. Otis started talking as if Wetzel understood every word and would somehow offer advice, same as always, but, this time, the despondency was evident.

He had a meeting scheduled the next day with the new president of the small bank in town. Cattle prices had been low last year, but they were even lower this year. The calves sold the day before had barely covered the cost to raise them. If he failed to secure the loan to carry them through the winter, he'd have to sell most all of the breeding stock.

Money had been tight for the last couple of years, and even with limited funds and near drought conditions, Otis had muddled through. Jude had been able to sell honey from the bees she kept, more than Otis would have guessed when she came up with the 'bee idea' seven years ago. Otis had found the first hive in an old cottonwood tree that had been split by high winds; the split section had fallen across a five-wire fence, and he had been nearly eaten alive by the wild bees when he started to remove the offending trunk. To hear him tell the story, he was ambushed by millions of angry bees as soon as he touched the chain saw to the wood. In reality, he had suffered less than a dozen stings and had left a running saw on the ground and his pickup nearby as he fled to the house seeking Jude's help, knowing the bees were after him.

Otis had always hated anything with a stinger, and Jude had to be the one to retrieve the chain saw and pickup. She had also managed to locate the queen after the insects had calmed a little, moving her to an old abandoned hive box that had been back behind an old shed. By the next day most all of the colony had followed her to their new home. A big chunk of the damaged comb and honey was placed in the box in hopes the hive would survive. Not only did they survive, but they thrived, and by the next spring Jude had added several more colonies to her apiculture hobby. Otis never ventured near the colonies, insisting the bees could smell his fear and would attack him en masse if he got too close.

The millions of wildflowers growing on the ranch made for a very light-colored, sweet honey, and soon friends, neighbors, and even strangers were stopping by for a jar. After a couple years, Jude's hobby had become another small source of income, but it all came to a halt with the drought. Fewer flowers meant less honey, and soon the hives started to die off. Maybe some of the bees just packed up and left, but the honey business nearly ended.

The entire problem had been carefully explained in detail to Wetzel, and it almost seemed as if the big animal listened with the sympathy of a loyal friend who would soon offer words of encouragement. Otis was anxious regarding tomorrow's bank appointment.

His family had been doing business with the small hometown bank since before Otis was born. The previous bank president, Mr. Ryan Dhooge, had met Otis when he had visited the bank for the first time as a small child. The banker had lifted Otis off the floor and sat him on the edge of his desk, while his father completed the paperwork on the ranch's first new tractor.

Years later he had financed Otis's first vehicle, a sweet

little 1956 Chevy pickup with a fresh rebuilt motor. Mr. Dhooge had agreed to the seven-hundred-dollar loan even though the truck was over ten years old. He felt confident the sixteen-year-old Otis would never miss a payment, and refused to let Otis's father co-sign either. He said the young man would feel more responsible if he shouldered the burden alone.

Otis had managed to pay the loan off not only on his own, but a few months early. He had worked evenings and weekends at the big feedlot east of town to make the money. There was no pay for the work done at the home ranch; that toil was considered chores and had to be done before the paying work started.

Now, after many years, some fat and some lean, Otis maintained his business relationship with the small hometown bank. At least that was how it had been up until a few months ago. That was when the depository had been acquired by a large out-of-state financial institution, and Mr. Dhooge had retired rather than conform to the procedures that had dramatically changed with the acquisition.

He'd heard that the small hometown feel had been quickly replaced with terse new regulations, which rendered old, faithful customers to being considered only a number. The new bank president was a short, unpleasant-looking man in his late fifties, who wore a perpetual frown, as if he was being punished for taking the job. Otis dreaded the meeting. He could envision the reaction by the little pompous squirt at being approached by a man twice his size, asking for a financial favor.

Otis had only seen him through the floor-to-ceiling glass wall of his office on the two occasions he'd been in the bank since the changeover, and both times, he'd had a phone to his ear and seemed to be ranting and gesticulating, red-faced, over something. While none of the conversation could be heard from across the room, when their eyes met for only an instant, the little president had immediately turned his back.

****

Otis arrived in town the next morning an hour before the bank opened. He sat in his old truck, feeling the swarm of butterflies doing aerobatics in his stomach. He intensely hated being in this position. He had always been independent, relying on his own hard work, and now he was being reduced to groveling. His future and the future of the ranch depended on the outcome of what would no doubt be a short meeting.

Glancing down at the Seiko Titanium watch Jacob had sent him for Christmas several years earlier, he saw it was time. He hardly ever wore the watch, partly because it fit tight, even though the band was adjusted out as far as it would go, but mainly because he was afraid he may accidentally scratch or damage Jacob's gift.

The truck door squeaked angrily when he opened it, and he didn't even notice that it failed to shut completely as he closed it. Beads of cold sweat beaded up under his cap, and the butterflies increased their aerial tricks as he crossed the street and entered the bank.

Almost two hours to the minute later, Otis walked trance-like out onto the sidewalk. Without stopping to look for traffic, he crossed the sleepy street toward the truck. Luckily, no vehicles had been approaching from either direction, and halfway across, he noticed the door hadn't shut all the way and made a dreamlike note to oil the hinges, which would be for the first time.

Approaching the pickup from the rear, he stood and rested his beefy forearms on the badly bent tailgate and gazed intently at the loose mix of fence repair tools and debris in the bed. Picking up a short piece of rusty barbed wire, he turned it absentmindedly in his hands, feeling the tips of the sharp barbs. A dog barked in the distance.

The meeting with the new bank president hadn't gone the way he'd been prepared for. The man had walked out from behind the big desk and met Otis halfway across the room with a genuine smile and a firm handshake. Otis was ushered over to a comfortable leather chair, and the bank president asked him how he liked his coffee.

"Black will be fine, sir," Otis murmured as he sat, taken aback by the man's genial manner.

"Call me Pip, and I won't have to call you Mr. Granrud," came the reply as the president went to a small alcove and returned with two cups of steaming black coffee. "Now, what can I do for you on this fine morning?"

Purvis Irving Pinehurst wasn't anything like Otis had expected him to be. His preconceived notion had been totally wrong. The conversation had started with small talk that quickly put Otis at ease; not the type you usually get from a used car salesman, but a sincere desire to get to know someone. In the first hour, the exchange revolved around hunting, fishing, old trucks, horses, and cowboys.

Pip, as he preferred to be called, as opposed to Purvis or Irving, had several framed black-and-white photographs of Hollywood Western cowboys on the walls of his office. Randolph Scott, Gary Cooper, John Wayne, Andy Devine, Eddy Waller, Gabby Hays, and Audie Murphy to name a few, and Otis knew them all.

Born and raised in Zanesville, Ohio, young Purvis had always wanted to be a cowboy, and after several years as a banker in Columbus, he'd jumped at the chance to move West after the acquisition. As he explained to Otis, the biggest challenge he'd faced since the move was convincing the home office to allow the bank to retain the hometown feel. He'd argued that keeping the current customer base was paramount, since most of them had known no other financial institution, Otis being a fine example. He had prevailed in the end and assured Otis the bank he had always depended on wouldn't change.

Maybe that explained why the banker was ranting, red-faced, on the phone the first time he'd seen him. He felt like he'd known the little banker for years after only a two-hour meeting. He had even invited him out to the ranch for a little bird hunting after Pip had revealed his passion for the sport, along with the fact that he'd managed to acquire a nice collection of Model 21 Winchester side by sides over the years.

It was the last hour of the meeting that Otis found difficult to believe, even though he had ask Purvis twice if he'd understood the banker correctly. Otis had explained very carefully his current financial situation, but in a nutshell, the unforeseen equipment breakdowns, feed costs above norm due to a multi-state drought, and the low price of beef had all combined to put a strain on cash flow.

A few years ago he had gambled on the market and used anything of value for collateral, along with nearly all his savings, to purchase a section of land that bordered his ranch. This acquisition had nearly doubled his holdings, greatly improving his water rights. In hindsight, the decision may have put everything he had in jeopardy.

Purvis had listened intently, while occasionally looking down and shuffling through a small stack of papers on his desk; then, when Otis finished speaking, the moment of silence in the room seemed thick enough to cut with a knife. Finally looking up at Otis, the banker smiled and said, "Otis, even though all this data is in the computer, I pulled your file yesterday evening in preparation for this little meeting. You've been a customer of this bank since you were sixteen years of age. It looks as if everything you've ever bought on credit has been financed through us, and you've never been in default and never missed a payment. This says a lot for your responsibility and your character, and I consider it my responsibility to help you any way I can."

The banker went on to explain a new government loan guarantee established for ranchers meeting certain qualifications and other financial avenues they could pursue. The final results still had Otis's head spinning, thus the need for Purvis to explain twice. In a few days, Otis would return to sign papers consolidating all outstanding loans under one at a fixed rate almost three points lower than current, and it would be ninety days before the first payment came due, meaning no payments at all through the winter.

"I'll never get used to calling him Pip, though. Couldn't even call a dog that," he said aloud as he made the turn east over the auto gate toward the ranch. "Can't wait to tell Jude the news."

****

Early the next morning Otis was back at the paddock, and Wetzel immediately sensed the change in demeanor, even before the still-squeaking truck door had been shut. They met at the gate, where the big bull lowered his head down for a scratch between the bosses of the huge horns. Great puffs of frosted breath escaped the flared nostrils as Otis greeted him.

"Well, big fellow, I took your advice and got everything straightened out at the bank. Worked out better than I expected even. Now I gotta concentrate on gettin' those fence posts put in the ground 'fore the snow starts flyin'. Supposed to be a real nasty one blowin' in from Montana in a day or so."

With a spring in his step not seen in a while, Otis approached the pile of posts stacked outside the enclosure. He grinned at the memory of how the bundle had first come to be on the ranch.

A few years earlier, Jacob and his father had arrived, ready for the fall hunt and pulling behind their pickup the sixteen-foot utility trailer with the normal load of camping gear and an ATV, but also with a strapped bundle of one hundred genuine West Virginia locust fence posts. Jacob had boasted about how he would guarantee these locust posts to last forever in the dry Wyoming soil, as they lasted nearly forever in the wetter ground in the East.

Otis had really appreciated the unexpected gift; however, the following year, he'd told Jacob in partial banter that those danged old locust posts were so hard that the fence wire had to be welded on, and that the longer they dried the harder they got. Without missing a step, Jacob had replied that he'd only guaranteed that they'd last forever, either sticking in the ground or lying on it, and never said anything about putting fence wire on them.

Otis's mood darkened a little while loading the fourteen posts he needed today as he thought of his buddy. He would give Anna a call for the latest update later that night. He knew she still held out for hope, and he even tried to encourage her as much as possible, but he'd about reached the conclusion that he would never see Jacob again and was doing his best to try to come to terms with that.

Chapter 30

The pressure on his back eased a little, but Jacob remained still as he felt the rough, wet object slide across his neck again. With both eyes squeezed shut and breathing as calmly as he could through the one nostril not plugged with hog guts, he realized he had been licked and prepared himself for the crushing bite. Afraid to move and not knowing what else to do, he braced himself for the worst, until the weight lifted completely, and few seconds later a loud *WOOF* sounded a few feet to his right.

His face already turned in that direction, he dared open his eyes to slits, catching sight of the huge, hairy creature moving slowly away toward one of the other hogs. Careful to remain as still as possible, he watched as the animal sniffed around the gutted hog and casually licked at the warm entrails. He recognized the beast as a bear and relaxed only a little as it turned enough for one of its white ears to be seen.

The cub seemed bigger being only a few feet away and

with the daylight, and Jacob remained still, not knowing how the animal would react around a fresh kill. The bear sniffed a few more times and then moved on to the other hog; this one he pawed at as he sniffed and easily turned the hundred-pound animal over and sniffed some more. Apparently satisfied, he lay down behind it and rested a huge paw across the still-warm body and looked at Jacob as if to say, "This one is mine."

Still apprehensive, Jacob slowly moved to rise up, but remained careful not to take his eyes off the bear, which only opened its big jaws to yawn, revealing a mouthful of sharp teeth. There appeared to be no immediate sign of danger, so he proceeded to remove the two hams from the hog he had been working on and tie them together with a short length of small rope. With guarded movements, he gathered his few belongings and slowly made for the top of the rise, looking back often to check on the bear.

At the top, he paused once again before starting down the other side. Back down below, the bear was tearing at the hog's carcass, seeming oblivious to Jacob ever being there. Jacob made the decision then to alleviate himself of a potentially deadly situation.

Moving out of sight below the ridge, he dropped the hindquarters and his pack, checked the rifle, and eased back up to the ridgetop. The bear was still facing him, with his chin resting across the hog's body, appearing to be resting.

Jacob took a steady rest across a small boulder and settled the crosshairs on a spot just above the bear's snout. Shooting down at this angle, the bullet would enter the brain and continue on into the spine. He didn't want to take a chance on only wounding the animal. He really didn't want to kill it, but he also knew he would have enough problems surviving the winter without facing the unpredictable notions of a brute that could slay him at any moment.

He took a breath and was holding it, slowly applying pressure to the trigger, when he noticed the bear's eyes through the scope. He knew a bear's vision was fairly poor and it couldn't possibly see him at this distance, but at that moment, the dark eyes seemed to bore into his soul. He even noticed the white hair on the ears moving with the breeze.

Releasing the trigger pressure, he continued to stare for a moment, realizing he was probably making a big mistake, but he just couldn't kill this bear. Maybe it would eat him sometime over the next few weeks or months, if he even made it that long, but whatever the case, he'd made up his mind for the moment.

The trek down the slope proved for unsteady footing with the swinging of the heavy hams, and there was still a lot of meat left to carry back to the cavern. He'd been contemplating whether or not to build up more drying racks outside or attempt to construct a way to smoke the meat inside. The natural draft of the cave system would carry out the smoke, if he was be able to devise something, although, at the moment, he was having trouble concentrating on anything but the bear. Would he still be in the little basin when he returned? He may have to shoot him yet if he was still there and acted the least bit aggressive.

On the next trip, Jacob decided to leave behind the rifle and carry only the .44 magnum handgun and a pack frame. He could strap a more balanced load on the frame, and maybe save a trip or two by carrying more at one time. His aging legs were growing weary with each step up the steep ascent. He hoped he'd made the right decision about leaving the rifle behind, but at the last minute, he decided to at least carry it to the foot of the steep slope. He'd leave it there and trust his luck to the handgun; the bear might have eaten his fill and left already.

At the top of the ridge, he saw that he was wrong. The bear was still there, and the snow around the hog it had claimed was stained pink with blood and gore. Looking back down the slope, Jacob could barely see his rifle far below, leaning against the small spruce, where he'd left it near the mouth of the cavern. When he turned again, the bear seem oblivious to his presence, but he probably hadn't noticed him yet.

Jacob stood there for another few moments, and then decided to make some noise as he descended, making sure the bear was aware of his return. Singing "From the Halls of Montezuma" loudly, he was halfway into the basin before the bear looked up; from its red-smeared muzzle hung a long pull of entrails. The animal stared for a moment, then resumed its feast, unmindful at the intrusion.

Cautiously, Jacob approached the hog he'd been dressing and continued his work, careful not to turn his back toward the bear. He was close enough to hear the crunching of bones and gristle as the bear ate his fill.

Returning for the fourth, and hopefully final, trip, Jacob noticed that the bear was gone. A mixture of pink snow, sticks, leaves, and dirt had been scraped up to cover what was left of the bear's meal, and the remains of the other hogs had not been touched.

Jacob gathered the remaining meat and staggered on aching legs back down the slope. He had decided to try to smoke the meat and had formulated an idea on how to carry out the task, but first, he needed a soak.

The hot water quickly eased the throbbing in his joints, and with the quiet time came another flood of thoughts regarding his predicament. He'd found shelter and food, a water source that not only provided comfort but a treasure of gold, not to mention the archaeological wealth surrounding him. Would he live the rest of his life here in this maze of caverns, slowly going mad, or would he fall ill or have an accident and die? He was coming to hate the quiet time that allowed these thoughts to haunt him; better to work at something, anything, until exhaustion forced sleep to come quickly.

His gaze rose to look through the dim light up at the Grandfather's Table, as he had decided to call the flat altar-like stone that held the artifacts. Thousands of years ago this place was thriving with life, families living and dying. His mind could almost hear the sounds of human voices echoing throughout the vicinity; children laughing and shouting, the murmurs of a society long forgotten. Then the ice came and closed off the cave forever, but now fate had brought him here. Why?

The hot water succeeded in permeating his body until all the aches subsided, the warm sandy bottom of the shallow pool molded to him with such comfort that he was soon asleep. He did not hear the padding of huge feet approaching. The bear stopped within only a few yards and stared at the pale figure in the water; after a moment, it raised its huge head, turned, and slowly walked back into the darkness.

****

Two days later Jacob stood under another cold gray sky, looking down at the crushed remains of the plane. It seemed ages had passed since he awoke in the darkness of what now had become a morgue. Only yesterday he was convinced the full brunt of northern winter had arrived, but this morning it was as if the hand of God had hit the pause button. The reason for the trek was that he had to retrieve something from the plane.

A million thoughts ran through his mind every night it seemed, and over the past few days, he had been plagued with concern for his journal. Already, he could see as he looked down on the wreck that he may have been correct. The site was almost covered completely in snow and ice. The heavy snows that were sure to come would cover it completely, and after a while, all could become entombed forever in the ice.

He had things to add to the journal now, for when it had been placed in the plane, he felt he had little hope of surviving more than a few days, and even now, things may have only changed a little. Still, while he was able, he would gain comfort from writing his story, though it seemed destined to become only another artifact buried deep in the mountain.

There was an eerie silence as he approached the wreck this time; his boots crunched noisily on the icy snow, and, for the first time, he felt as if he were performing a sacrilege of robbing a grave. The metal protested loudly as he pried it open and crawled inside. A light frost covered everything inside, and the dim light made for a ghostly image. However, the journal was where he had left it. A thin sheen of sweat covered his face, in spite of the cold, as he exited the tomb. Folding back the aluminum flap as quickly as possible, he turned and didn't look back.

Jacob stopped at his old camp on the way down the mountain. He walked around the broken, snow-covered remains for a few minutes, kicking at lumps to see if there was anything he'd missed worth taking. The collapsed tarp sagged to the ground between the huge boulders, covered in snow. He would have never been able to survive here; if not for finding the cavern, he would without doubt be dead by now.

A blustery breeze blew down from the mountain, carrying with it small pieces of ice crystals, the loose snow swirling around his feet. The creepy feeling from the wreck had subsided, but dampness from the sweat caused him to shiver nonstop. Fearing hypothermia and still a distance from the cavern, he felt the need to get out of the wind and build a small fire, but all the dried and broken trees around the old camp had been picked clean, so he continued down the faint trail. A little ways beyond the old moose kill stood a copse of small pine trees hiding a split in the rocks. He knew of this because he'd spent hours here several times, hiding in the deep notch and hoping to ambush an animal heading to the lick.

Shivering uncontrollably now, he crawled into the split and kicked away the thin covering of snow. Pine needles covered the ground, but they were too damp to burn, and no dry wood lay nearby. Desperate, he reached under the rocks and pulled out anything dry enough to burn. Soon a small fire caught in the handful of small dry sticks and pine needles he'd found.

A few of the small pine trees had been broken by heavy snows in the past, but in their tenacity for life, the hardy little trees had survived, growing stunted and crooked. Jacob managed to break a few of the knotted smaller ones in hopes the resinous wood may readily burn. To his surprise, it not only caught, but burned enthusiastically. Soon the shivering subsided as the nearby rock absorbed and radiated the heat.

Until now, Jacob had never tried burning any wood from the small little pines, but as he sat over the fire, he stuck a small sliver into the flame and noticed it ignited eagerly. Holding the stick aloft, he watched as it continued to burn, even when moved around, giving off a bright, if somewhat smoky, flame. It reminded him a lot of the boxes of 'fatwood' fire starters he'd bought in the past. Just a few pieces were sufficient to get the oak firewood blazing in the big fireplace back home. This wood looked and smelled the same; at least it proved to burn with fervor.

He remembered then the small grove of this very same type of trees near the entrance to the cave. Over half of them had slipped down the bank toward the stream when a section of the steep hillside had given way sometime in the past. Most had died, covered now with only a sparse spattering of dried brown needles, another gift almost gone unnoticed!

The following day's activity consisted mostly of cutting and dragging the small pines to the cavern entrance. Once there, he removed the small branches and stacked them, along with the larger limbs and trunks, neatly inside the opening. That evening, with the northern lights dancing across the clear, cold sky, and as Jacob dragged the last pine of the day toward the opening, he heard a faint noise behind him and turned to see the bear not ten feet away. Always startled by these unexpected appearances, both froze and stared at each other, until Jacob spoke, trying to sound braver than he felt.

"Why are you always sneaking up on me like that!" he yelled.

At the sound of his voice, the bear sat on his haunches and cocked his huge head to the side; neither moved until the bear stood and, with a *huff*, turned and walked back along his path. Jacob watched the retreat for a moment, then, as he too turned away, he felt a drop of sweat trickle down his spine.

The next morning, when Jacob stepped outside, he sensed a profound change. The world seemed to have donned an ominous cloak of quietness so intense it could be felt; it was not unlike the day a few weeks back, only this time even more prominent. The sky wore a dark purple-gray color, with not a cloud or blemish to be seen, as if to announce the time had come. Jacob's logic told him that the past inconsistent weather patterns had finally coalesced into the time of serious winter.

The soft snow patches he waded through easily yesterday had frozen overnight into solid lumps that made walking difficult, and when he topped the low rise leading to the little grove of pines, there stood the bear. A great blast of steam left his mouth with the huff at seeing the man.

For an instant Jacob started to turn back, but instead, he decided to gather a few more of the small trees he had already cut.

"And where did you spend the night?" he asked loudly toward the bear. "What did you have for breakfast?" he added, before the thought hit him that just maybe that was why the bear was here.

Trying to remain wary, but still focused on the task, he gathered a bundle and looked up again to notice the bear had again vanished. The situation with this big animal would be a problem to deal with, and again, he thought of killing it. Wasn't it supposed to be hibernating by now? He just assumed all bears went into hibernation when winter came. He had to kill it. What if it became hungry, knowing a warm meal was in easy reach trapped in the cavern? He decided then he would kill the bear the next time the opportunity presented itself.

The next few days, Jacob busied himself with fashioning bundles of the fatwood for use as torches. They proved to burn slowly and give off an acceptable amount of light, in spite of the small amount of dark smoke that soon wafted away in the constant air movement.

Early one morning, as Jacob began his daily ritual of lighting the morning fire, he detected something amiss in the cavern. The normal sounds that he'd gotten used to seemed different somehow. Usually, there was the muted gurgle of water running nearby; that sound was still there, but he also became aware of an additional rush of water, not loud and disturbing, just different. Snatching up a flashlight, he walked the short distance from his sleeping nook toward the ice wall at the exposed glacier and saw that the normal trickle there had increased dramatically and now rushed in a small torrent. Looking down the tunnel in the direction of the exit, he was shocked to see that the normally shallow stream had risen by at least a couple of feet, even covering the path in places.

Chapter 31

Otis had loaded an even dozen of the locust posts into the back of the pickup the evening before, and then decided to go ahead and pull the remaining old posts, along with the jagged stumps of the few broken off at ground level on his way back to the ranch. He stopped at Wetzel's enclosure for a few moments as the sun settled behind the western bluffs, casting a striking orange glow across the cold blue sky.

"Red sky at night, sailor's delight!" he sang out as he approached the gate. "You get a good night's sleep now, big fellow, cause early in the morning, we're gonna get these posts replaced. I plan to take Jude over to Deadwood for dinner tomorrow evenin', then walk around watchin' them fools feed their paychecks into them one-armed bandits."

Sometimes it appeared the big bull understood every word he said, especially the way he gently nodded his great head every time Otis spoke.

"I might even sleep in late Saturday, so don't go a

worryin' 'bout me if I don't show up here early. I'll be here at the same time in the morning, though."

The next morning, after an early breakfast, as Otis started for the door, the phone rang. Jimmy Dent, the caller, an old friend and neighbor who lived on a small spread about twenty miles away near the Piute Creek cutoff, wanted to come over to cut firewood in the river bottom. Jimmy's grandson had a long weekend off and was coming over from Rapid City to help his grandpa prepare for the winter.

An abundance of huge, dead cottonwoods littered the river bottom for miles, as many of the water-loving trees had died over the years as the river changed its course, withdrawing its life-sustaining moisture. The dry, fallen giants provided a great quantity of firewood in an area sparse for trees. Otis readily shared the wood and was usually rewarded to find a large stack cut and left for him as a token of thanks.

Otis assured Jimmy that he was always welcome to come and get the wood and appreciated the courtesy of his calling first. "Jimmy, I might not be around to visit with you, though, 'cause I'm about to go out and replace some posts along the back section; then, when I get done, me and Jude is headin' for Deadwood."

"Tell you what, Otis," replied Jimmy, "if you will just lay out them posts where you want them, me and Joey will stick them in the ground for ya."

"No, no, you guys don't have to do that!" protested Otis. "Besides, a few of the busted butts of the old posts are still in the ground, and these posts I'm usin' is harder than Japanese 'rithmatic; you can hardly drive a new staple in 'em."

"Don't matter none," countered Jimmy. "I want Joey to see that big critter you done turned into a lapdog anyway. It'll give him something to tell the boys over at the cement plant, and besides, he come over to help out with the ranch work, and helpin' out neighbors is ranch work. We'll make out just fine, and if I need anything I'll just get it outta the shop. "

Arguing with Jimmy a little longer didn't change anything, so it was decided that Otis would drop off the posts along the fence line, and then he and Jude could leave early for a rare, relaxing day together. Hanging up the phone, he relayed the good news to Jude, promising to be back within a couple hours, and even agreeing to wear the new cowboy boots she had bought him for his birthday.

He buttoned up his work coat as he got into the pickup, remembering how he never told her how much he hated those new cowboy boots. Heck, they were almost baby blue in color, although she had insisted they were a dove gray. He'd just wear the longest jeans he had and try to cover them up the best he could and hope no one he knew would notice his neon blue cowboy boots.

Wetzel noticed the pickup bouncing slowly down the rough road, kicking up a slight plume of dust, which blew away quickly to the south in the constant breeze. The big beast bumped open the gate with his nose and stood, anxiously waiting for the truck to stop. After a brisk head rub and a short chat, Otis continued a short way through the open gate into what he referred to as the east pasture.

The east and west pasture consisted of an entire flat section of fenced land divided by a cross fence. The separation made for two enclosures of three hundred twenty acres each, these being the only parcels on the entire ranch irrigated to grow hay for the winters when heavy snows covered the other short grass.

During an average year, this part of the country required thirty-two acres to support a cow-calf unit, which made it difficult for even the very largest ranches to carry enough cows to turn much of a profit. It was often joked that a man with a million dollars' worth of land had a hard time making a living, but Otis loved ranching and wouldn't have it any other way.

Pulling along the fence at the first broken post, Otis carefully pointed the pickup at just the right angle, then reached for the dusty, faded bandanna on the dashboard. This he tied in a long loop to the steering wheel at one of the spokes, placed the gearshift in bulldog low, and exited the truck, looping the other end of the bandanna to the side mirror. The old truck started away on its own at a slow crawl, with Otis walking behind, throwing off a post at the required locations. This worked exceedingly well for the first couple hundred feet, but as usual, the truck slowly pulled away from the fence to the right and would require a little steering adjustment, which was still a lot easier than having to constantly get in and out of the truck.

Otis had just grabbed for a post before making the first steering correction when the post caught on an old rusty coil of barbed wire, requiring a tug that caught him off balance. Stumbling backward when the heavy post broke loose, he staggered, trying to steady himself. His left foot dropped into the open posthole, and as he fell to the side, he heard a loud snap, followed by an intense stabbing pain in his lower left leg.

Nauseated with shock and pain, he knew what had happened but couldn't force himself to look down for fear of fainting. Cautiously, he felt his lower leg and audibly winced as he touched the jagged sharpness protruding through the jeans. Quickly, he pulled his hand away and saw his fingers were wet with blood. Afraid to look, he could imagine the stark, jagged bone protruding from his leg Dizzily, he looked up to notice the pickup chugging slowly away, taking the rest of the posts with it.

Otis sat helplessly staring as the truck bounced unhurriedly out into the pasture, knowing for sure he was going to die stuck in a posthole. The loose barbwire behind him provided no support to assist in standing, and he couldn't walk even if he could stand. The ranch house was over two miles away. There was no way he could crawl that far, even in good health. He would die here for sure, and the coyotes would eat him before morning.

He forced himself to take deep breaths, trying to calm his racing heart. Each beat brought intensified pain, and he knew that with every beat, blood was pumping into the hole. Back to his right, a hundred yards or so away, Wetzel stood calmly pulling at the dry weeds by the gate. Otis tried to whistle but only blew air and spittle on his beard. He never had trouble whistling before. Was he dying already? He mustered up enough strength to yell for Wetzel.

"Wetzel, Wetzel, Wetzel!" he yelled at the top of his lungs, almost hyperventilating. "Come here, boy. HURRY!"

Wetzel raised his big head and slowly started toward Otis. Every so often, he stopped to pull at a dry weed; by the time he arrived, Otis was mumbling incoherently. As the huge animal leaned his head down for a rub, the big man grabbed on to one of the big horns in a death grip.

"Easy now, buddy. Just raise up slowly, that's it, easy now!" Otis pleaded as Wetzel lifted his head, pulling Otis upright.

As the pressure increased on the stuck leg, Otis thought for sure it had been pulled loose from his body. His foot came out of the boot, and he nearly passed out from the pain, but something allowed him to hold on.

Standing on his good leg, mostly supported by Wetzel, though still unable to look at the damaged one, he winced and noticed through squinted eyes that the pickup seemed to be returning. The slight turning to the right had allowed for a large circle of travel, and if the vehicle didn't stall for some reason, it should pass within twenty yards of where he now stood. His only hope was to make for it before it passed him by.

Urging Wetzel to turn, he coaxed the animal forward while tightening his grip, each breath causing excruciating pain to shoot up his damaged leg. The animal was moving too slowly. He was going to miss the truck; so, at the last minute, he flung himself forward and hopped on his good leg. Each jolt of his three hundred forty pounds caused the jagged sharpness to tear at his flesh, but he kept going.

The effort proved successful, for with a final lunge, he managed to grasp the side mirror with his right hand. Although being dragged along for a while, he was able to get the door open and crawl inside far enough to turn off the key. The truck ground to a halt. Lying across the seat, on the verge of tears, he panted for breath, but gathering the last of his strength, he was able to get behind the wheel, and with only the use of his right leg, he drove toward the ranch house.

The two-mile drive seemed to last forever; every bump in the road resulted in white-hot stabs of pain. The last thing he remembered before passing out was stopping at the house and falling against the horn, the sound of which faded away as he lost consciousness.

Otis awakened to someone shaking his shoulder. Through blurry eyes, Jude's face wavered, backlit by the sun shining through a window. He was confused and not sure where he was but knew he was lying on his back, maybe in the hospital in Rapid City. After a moment his vision cleared somewhat, and he managed to mumble out a few fear-laced words.

"Jude, were they able to save my leg? Where am I? I know it was bad, but please tell me they didn't have to cut it off!" Tears filled his clearing vision, and her image blurred again.

"What in the world are you talking about, Otis? You're lying on our couch. You didn't hit your head on anything, did you?" she asked as she felt through his head for a knot.

"Don't fun with me now, Jude. They must have me really doped up, cause my leg don't hurt near as bad as it did."

"And it wouldn't have hurt nearly so bad if you had just pulled the splinter out before you drove to the house!" she exclaimed.

"Splinter! I wasn't worried about any splinters with my leg bone stickin' through my pants like it was!"

"Otis, your leg bone is fine! You had a big splinter about six inches long sticking out of your leg. Looked like part of an old fence post. Why didn't you just pull it out? Every time you moved, it just dug around—must have hurt like heck! I cleaned it out best I could, but get back in the pickup, and let's get to the clinic. You may need a stitch or two, and you definitely need a tetanus shot!" She said *tetanus shot* with emphasis, followed by a grin when her back was turned, knowing Otis feared needles worse than a pack of wolves.

Chapter 32

Jacob made his way slowly toward the cavern opening. In some places the water covered parts of the path, forcing him to hug close to the wall. The water still flowed but much more sluggishly, indicating an obstruction. When he had made his way to within a hundred feet of the opening, he heard a distant crash, as if a large china cabinet had fallen over.

Immediately, the water started to flow faster, and by the time he approached the opening, the rush had returned to a nearly normal flow. The reason for the blockage appeared obvious, as huge stalactites of ice hung down from the opening, combined with thick coverings of smooth ice on the walls and ceilings. The warmer water had broken through, and the resulting winter breath of steam froze and fell back to the ground in crystals not long after coming in contact with the frigid air.

Jacob ducked around the hanging ice and could feel his nostrils frosting up with the first breath of the freezing air. He had experienced cold before, but no cold day in his life could compare to the cold he felt now. He'd had no idea there was cold like this! The bare skin of his face burnt with the cold, and within a few steps, the down jacket provided no protection at all. Stumbling, he hurried back inside, reeling from the incident.

A short way inside seemed like stepping into a warm room compared to the outside environment. Immediately, he realized more than ever the fortune of finding this cave system, for there would be no way possible to survive outside in the open. Remembering the day when heavy snow collapsed the tarp at the old camp, he acknowledged that what had seemed like an inconvenience had been a blessing in disguise, for it had forced him to look for better protection from the elements. He had known it was sure to get colder, but he never sensed it would be like this. In his mind, he could envision his frozen-solid body lying gray in a tent.

All things considered, the entire situation could be much worse, and for what he had at the moment, he was thankful. Long-term, though, he wasn't sure; it seemed very doubtful he would ever be able to return home, so keeping himself busy and his mind occupied for the short term would hopefully stave off the insanity that was sure to come.

Blessed as he was at stumbling upon the cave, which, without a doubt, had saved his life, the great fortune in gold that lay around him, as well as the prehistoric artifacts, provided the fodder to keep him active. Never mind the fact that he would never realize one cent from the fortune in gold, but would also never be able to share the thrill of finding the artifacts with his dad. He could only imagine seeing how the old fellow would react to holding and caressing those objects from the past.

Jacob kindled a small fire in the fire pit, added a pinch of fresh coffee into the little pot containing already twice-used grounds. He felt confident the amount of food he had stored would sustain him through the long winter, if he rationed it conservatively.

Coffee was another matter altogether. Having a tasty cup every morning and then suddenly being completely without would be another small disaster, as far as he was concerned. The plan was to reuse the grounds, making his supply last longer, as well as slowly diminishing the flavor; this way, after a while, it would taste so bad that he wouldn't miss it as much when it was completely gone.

After the little meal, which consisted of a few pieces of dried meat and a handful of dried blueberries, heated together in water with a pinch of salt, Jacob sat back with a cup of weak coffee as the fire died down to a bed of coals. Sitting as he was, the dim blue wall of ice glowed eerily, allowing enough light to filter through to make out his immediate surroundings with need of a torch.

Again thankful that at least he could distinguish day from night while entombed beneath the mountain, he found himself hopeful that enough brightness would still filter through in the long months of winter that lay ahead. He'd always heard that the far north experienced six months of light and six months of darkness, but with a bit of luck, the darkness would not be absolute.

Staring at the smooth ice wall, he again could only imagine the view across the valley if that wall was gone. The outside opening to the hot springs should be less than a hundred feet or so to the left if the ice was gone. It was then he decided to forgo his gold mining undertaking for a while and explore every inch of the cavern he could access.

By the dim light, he carefully began a sketched map of the cavern, starting at the entrance at Warm Creek. As he did so, a thought occurred to him of a long-forgotten computer game he had enjoyed playing years ago. The interactive text game was set in a fictional place referred to as The Great Underground Empire. Feeling the connection, he decided to draw his map reminiscent of the diagrams he'd used to navigate through Infocom's Zork games of the early eighties.

A wavy line represented Warm Creek, intersected by another wavy line indicating the entrance branch into the main cavern room. He drew the main room as a crude circle, with indications in perspective as to the locations of the ice wall and the dry and wet channels. Lines from this main circle pointed in different directions; one to the hot spring, another from there to the 'altar stone,' while still another to the room containing the huge pile of dry sticks and twigs. Four other passages that he could walk, or at least squeeze through, led off into other directions from the main cavern.

He would have to be very careful not to get lost, trapped, or injured while exploring, and almost decided not to proceed, but then made up his mind that doing so would at least contribute to mind activity, which he needed as much as air, water, and food.

Digging through his stash of gear produced the fishing reel filled with the thick spool of line, the end of which he tied off at camp. Paying out the line behind him, he entered the first passage carrying a lit bundle of a fatwood torch, seeing himself somewhat as a pitiful version of the Indiana Jones character.

He had shined his flashlight into this low passage several times before, and it appeared to end at a smooth wall about twenty feet in. He had noted the smooth, dry floor and walls and considered using it for storage at some time, but as he approached what gave the impression of being a dead end, the corridor turned sharply more than ninety degrees to the right and continued.

The floor angled upward slightly in a winding path, and soon he was able to stand fully erect. Stopping momentarily to straighten his back, cramped from stooping, he was grateful for the relief. Moving the torch around, its flickering flame dancing on the smooth, layered walls, Jacob surmised the channel had been sculpted by the flowing water over the ages, which still influenced the shaping of the cavern to this day. The oily smoke from the burning torch moved gently away from him, and the lightly moving air could barely be felt on the back of his neck. Somewhere ahead, a crack or fissure must lead to the outside, but this seemed strange, for when standing in the main cavern, the air moved toward the opening above the hot springs.

Carefully continuing, once having to turn sideways to squeeze through a narrow space, he reached a spot where the ceiling sloped down to about three feet from the floor. Stooping to extend the nearly burned-out torch, to which he had already added the last piece of fatwood, he found the dim light it provided was of no more use, so he abandoned it and turned on the flashlight. He could now see that the low ceiling tunnel almost immediately began to rise again as the passageway curved to the right. Crawling through on his hands and knees, within a dozen feet, he was able to stand and walk forward, though he had to stoop his head. The twisting channel soon opened into a small domed-top room about twelve feet wide and just as high; almost a perfect circle, the path continued in the far wall, disappearing into the darkness.

The room appeared to be naturally shaped, except for one area that had the indication of having been crudely tooled to round out the shape, but it was the domed ceiling that gave him a start, for it was covered completely, from eye level upward, with shallow carvings. Figures of men and beasts, mountains, trees, fish, as well as other symbols not recognized, littered the area. Time had not diminished the distinctive nature of the carvings, as each gave the impression of being carved only yesterday.

Jacob stood in awe as he highlighted the figures with the beam of the flashlight. As he turned in a slow circle, trying to take in the splendor of something created untold ages ago, he became aware that he was tangled in the fishing line. Carefully unwinding himself, he set the reel aside and lay on his back to better visualize the carvings.

A grouping of beasts, some with large, curved tusks,

caught his attention, a representation of a herd of wooly mammoth, no doubt. Slightly above them were several stick figures of people depicted in a rough-shaped oval, and to the right of that, another smaller, more flattened oval was drawn, with several wavy, snake-like lines above it. Near the mammoth, smaller animals, deer or elk, with large branching antlers, were carved facing in different directions, as if grazing contently. A long, wavy line bisected the group. Circling around the dome nearer the top, above the other carvings, it ran a zigzag line like a crown. On one side, a half-round circle with lines radiating from it had been carved above the zigzags, and directly across, on the other side of the dome above them, were what looked to be at least a hundred pockmarks or dots.

As he lay there, wondering what ancient hand had created this awe-inspiring display, he noticed the dark soot-like stains covering the area of the pockmarks, evidently from the torches needed by the artist to illuminate his canvas. The floor seemed to have been swept clean, for even now there was minimal dust and grit on the smooth floor.

Then it hit him. He understood why the soot was left in only one area! A night sky — the dots were stars! Across the dome, a sun peeked over the mountains. This wasn't just a random collection of carvings. It represented an actual scene; a panorama of the valley now under the ice! The ancient river ran through the valley where animals grazed! The people were standing in the mouth of a cave, his cave! The snake-like lines above the other flattened circle were the heat waves radiating from the hot springs at another smaller cave opening!

Wishing his father could be here with him to share in this amazing discovery, he just stared in wonder a few minutes longer before deciding to move on. Although he had a spare set of batteries in his fanny pack, as well as a small pen light, it would be better to play it safe and not get stranded in the dark. Later, after mapping the cave system, he would stash small bundles of the fatwood throughout, to be there for emergencies.

There had been no branching channels in this tunnel so far, but he still liked the assurance that the fishing line led back to the entrance; the soft clicking sound of the reel as the line played out echoed tunefully as he walked forward. Counting his steps since leaving the domed room, they numbered three hundred thirty-three when he stopped.

The tunnel had maintained its dimensions, for the most part. The ceiling was a foot or two above his head, and the width was wide enough to walk through without turning sideways. The way still twisted like a snake, and the floor rose and fell, but the ceiling did as well. More and more, he noticed veins of quartz sometimes curving along the smooth walls, only to spiral upward across the narrow ceiling and down the opposite wall, to run along the floor then disappear completely.

He decided to continue on until the count reached five hundred, then go back, returning again later with several torches and some water. He hadn't even brought any with him, and he scolded himself for forgetting.

The count had reached four hundred twelve when he suddenly stepped out into a large, open room. He stopped to listen and could hear water gurgling gently in the distance. From where he was standing at the tunnel exit, he noticed the floor angled upward, as if he were standing in a dry channel long ago carved by moving water. The rest of the floor that he could see was interlaced with dry channels where the water had once flowed.

Moving slowly toward the sound of water, he had not gone far before something unseen touched his ankle enough for him to stumble and fall forward, dropping the flashlight as he broke the fall with his hands. Retrieving the light, he turned to see what had caused the trip and noticed the fishing line wrapped around his ankle. He was wondering how he had managed to get caught up in a loop of the line playing out behind him.

Confused for a moment, it hit him out of the blue as he followed the line into another tunnel opening. He was back where he started! He had stepped out of the second tunnel, only to trip over the line going into the first!

He returned to camp for a rest and a small meal, after which he added the new information to the map, but still feeling restless, he gathered a few bundles of the fatwood, deciding to explore the third tunnel. He had not gone forty feet into this passageway when it abruptly ended. The wide opening angled upward steeply after about thirty feet, then unexpectedly tapered to a smooth walled end. Disappointed, he returned to the main room and headed to the last opening, planning to investigate only a short distance before calling it a day.

The entrance to this channel was situated near the opening to the room containing the pile of dry sticks and more resembled a large crack than the rounded accesses of the other tunnels. Easily missed in the dark confines of the cavern, the tall, jagged notch narrowed to a point about nine feet above the floor and was only a little over three feet wide at its base. Also unlike the others, this one had a damp wall, in some places wet enough to allow water to slowly trickle down, only to disappear into another narrow crack along the wall next to the floor. The other wall, while not wet, still looked damp but felt dry to the touch.

While the entire cavern maintained a constant underground temperature, it felt much colder here, near the mouth of this foreboding crack. The floor slanted a little to the left toward the narrow crack at the base of the wall for the first twenty feet or so before angling upward at a steep incline, requiring Jacob to pull himself upward by searching out handholds along the wall. The one-handed climb proved more awkward while holding the burning torch, but soon became easier when the floor leveled out somewhat.

The soft *click-click* of the reel, along with his labored

breathing, sounded louder in this tunnel than the others, possibly due to the density of the rock and shape of the passageway; at least, that was what he was thinking as he came to a fork in the path. Both ways revealed nothing but an inky blackness beyond the light of the smoky torch.

Choosing the left fork, he proceeded carefully until, a short distance later, the walls narrowed to a point, closing off his progress. An inch-wide crack ran from floor to ceiling, where very cold air could be felt, and the flames of the torch flickered in its rush. The flashlight exposed the crack to be deep, its beam lost in the darkness.

Jacob backtracked to the fork and took the other path, which curved upward through the mountain for a few hundred feet, before leveling out a short distance, subsequently making a dip before continuing upward again. A layer of dark, dried mud covered the path in the low area, revealing animal tracks going in both directions, large animal tracks, bear tracks to be specific. If one were to deduce these to be the tracks of the white-eared bear entering and leaving the cavern, there should be an exit to the outside somewhere ahead.

A few more twists and turns and a hundred feet farther along, Jacob detected a faint light in the distance. The tunnel soon exited onto a ledge through a wide, low opening, requiring him to crawl out on hands and knees. The outside air felt bitter cold, with frozen snow and ice blocking the outside trail along the mountainside. A wide overhang of rock protected the entrance somewhat, but even that was covered in a thin layer of ice. A heavy snow would succeed in blocking it completely.

The dark gray sky, covered in dirty, low-hanging clouds, blocked any view into the distance; no reference points could be seen, and Jacob couldn't tell if it was dusk, dawn, or mid-day. He had no trouble at all knowing that it was cold, though, really cold. He shivered as he approached the edge. Looking down, he could see only jumbles of angular rocks and huge boulders covered in snow and ice; the gaze upward divulged only the steep rock face, disappearing into the haze.

An instant of vertigo and he was falling. Fear seized him as he fought for balance on the icy rock. Twisting violently, he struggled to throw his body away from the edge; it would be certain death to fall onto the rocks far below. Even if he survived the fall, his damaged body would be unable to make the climb back up. He hit the ledge hard, pain lancing through his lower back and down his legs, fingers digging into the ice and rock, trying to find purchase.

All was still except for the wind noise and the sound of his labored breathing. Both his feet and legs, to just above his knees, dangled over the cliff edge, his fingers cold and cramping from trying to dig into the rock and ice. It had happened so fast. He had experienced it many times before when standing upright too fast, becoming lightheaded almost to the point of passing out. He had leaned down to look over the edge and then straightened to look up the rock face, then the dizziness hit. He shivered a moment more before dragging himself forward and into the mountain.

Slowly and painfully, he stood. The pulled muscle in his back made retrieving the flashlight from his fanny pack agonizingly difficult, but after several forced deep breaths, he started back down the tunnel. He didn't even know what happened to the torch. He remembered having it when he crawled onto the ledge and seeing the flames almost fanned out in the wind.

He had just come very close to dying today, over something he didn't even need to be doing; there had been no need to explore the tunnels. That activity wasn't required for survival, but falling over the cliff and being crushed on the rocks would have solved all of his survival issues, for sure. He was glad the instinct for self-preservation had kicked in automatically, and so quickly. Where there was life there was hope, as they say, but all he wanted to do at this moment was to lie near a fire and get warm.

Three hours later the fire had died down to a layer of hot coals. Jacob lay asleep with his open Bible across his chest, dreaming of home. Not far away, in a den above the pile of sticks, another was sleeping the deep sleep of hibernation, wide, wet nostrils involuntary snorting occasionally at the familiar smell of smoke and man.

Chapter 33

Otis eased the pickup down the rough road he'd traveled a million times, but this particular morning, he eased the truck slowly over the ruts, as every jounce brought pain to the new stitches in his calf. The three little stitches pulled at his skin, but it was the remembrance of seeing the needle for the tetanus shot that brought the cold sweat.

Not only that, but he'd had to suffer through a numbing injection at the wound site, and he would have almost sworn the clinic doctor had used a wire brush and gasoline to clean the wound, although he couldn't be sure because his eyes had remained tightly shut for the entire ordeal, after he'd caught a quick look at the nurse filling a syringe.

Surviving the jolt across the cattle guard, he sensed something amiss as he approached Wetzel's paddock, for usually the big beast would be at the enclosure corner nearest the dirt road as soon as he heard the sound of the old pickup. Otis would always call out to the big fellow as he slowly drove the length of the fence, with Wetzel following along on the other side until they met at the gate.

Today, there was no sign of Wetzel. The eight inches of fresh snow that had fallen overnight lay undisturbed as far as one could see into the corral from the road. He had almost reached the gate when he caught sight of the big animal in the far corner of the enclosure, with his enormous head over the top rail, standing nose to nose with a much smaller four-legged critter.

Jennifer and Wetzel appeared to be in deep conversation, which was common every time the little donkey visited, but she was never out of sight of Old Bob, and Otis didn't see him around anywhere. Stopping the pickup, he walked over to the pair and asked, "Where's your partner, old girl?" as if he expected an answer. Looking about as he spoke, he saw only donkey tracks, and they were mostly filled with snow. She had been here for a while.

Otis walked along her back trail, ignoring the sharp pain from his wounded leg until he topped the rise, thinking maybe the old fellow had fallen, but all he saw in the distance was Jennifer's faint tracks. Immediately, he became concerned and headed back to the pickup. Slamming the idling truck into gear and throwing mud and snow, he accelerated across the prairie.

The old man's small dugout shack was situated less than a mile away in a secluded draw, and couldn't be seen until you were close enough to practically jump down on it. In this cold weather, though, the smoke from his ancient stove should be seen at a distance, only Otis couldn't see any smoke!

Racing across the ground a great deal faster than usual and unable to steer clear of the ruts due to the snow, Otis lost count of how many times his head hit the roof, or what tools and equipment bounced out of the pickup bed; ignoring the pain in his leg, he focused solely on getting to Old Bob and making sure the old fellow was safe and well.

A feeling of dread gripped his chest as he skidded the

pickup to a halt and made his way down the slippery path leading to the shack. Falling on his backside when his smooth-soled boots lost traction, he slid the last few feet down the path, until it leveled out near the door. Gathering himself, he shouldered his way through the low wooden doorway into the cold interior.

In the dim light, Otis could see Old Bob lying motionless on his old cot, not even reacting to the commotion caused when Otis burst in. Sensing the worst, Otis placed his hand on the skinny, cold neck of his old friend. Feeling a faint pulse through his callused hand, he hurried out of his big warm coat and tucked it tightly around the frail little man on the cot. This brought a slight flicker of eyelid movement and a feeble groan from the gray, bearded face.

Otis then turned to the old potbellied stove. Opening the door, he found the ashes only slightly warm to the touch. Quickly, he got a fire going, and as the room started to warm, he covered Old Bob with every blanket he could find, then pulled an old, rickety straight-backed chair over near the cot. He had just placed a big, warm hand on the old fellow's forehead when, through the grizzled beard, he heard the old man mumble weakly, "Took . . . you long enough . . . to get here. I thought I was gonna freeze to death."

"I'm here now, Bob!" Otis said, surprised the little man was alive, let alone able to speak. "I'll get you to the hospital real quick, so don't you worry!"

"No. No . . . ain't no need fur that. I . . . just need ya to set still for a few minutes."

The old man took several deep, raspy breaths, then focused on Otis with sad, rheumy eyes before continuing. "This has been a comin' on for a while now." He paused to catch his breath again. "I just been hangin' on till you got here, 'cause I need for you to listen. I tried yesterday to write ya a note in the front cover of that old Bible over on the table, but I doubt if ya can read it, 'cause my hand don't work too good, and now I can't even feel it."

Otis could tell the old man was slurring his words, and the side of his face looked drawn and droopy.

Bob took several more wheezy breaths, then said haltingly, "Otis, listen, I've been feelin' puny for quite some time. I know there is something a-growin' in my head cause my eyes have been getting blurry, and for the past few weeks, it looks like I'm a lookin' through pink glasses. Yesterday, as I went to feed Jennifer, it felt like something broke and spilled hot water inside my head and down my neck." He stopped again to breathe deeply. "But that ain't important. You just got to listen and promise me you'll do what I ask."

"I'll do anything you want, Bob, just let me get you to a doctor!"

"NO! NO! Boy, just listen. I know I ain't gonna live to see tomorrow. I'd already be gone, but I had to wait on ya," insisted Bob with more force than Otis thought possible given his condition.

This outburst left him gasping, so Otis said, "Okay, Bob, I'm sorry. Just go ahead and tell me what you want me to do."

"Otis, ya can't let me get buried in the ground! Get me a little drink of water over there."

Otis gently tried to lift Bob's head to allow him to take a sip, but much of the liquid dribbled into his long white beard. Bob didn't seem to notice.

"When I was a youngin', 'bout eleven years old, me and my ma lived alone in a shack in Lousanna. My pap had died right after I was born, and I don't even know what happened to him. Ma never talked 'bout him much, but she had a picture of him, and I saw her a holdin' it close to her heart a lot when no one was lookin'. We lived okay, mostly off stuff we found in the woods and creeks. Grandma and my uncle and his wife, my ma's sister, lived close by, so we got along okay."

Otis didn't know why Bob was telling him this, and he could see it was a struggle for the little fellow, but he listened carefully, trying to understand every slurred word of the evidently important story.

"One day, Ma was checkin' our crawdad trap when I heard her let out a yell. I hurried down to the bank just in time to see a six-foot cottonmouth slither through the weeds growin' next to the bank. Ma had been bit on the arm as she reached for the trap. Her arm swolt up, and before mornin' she was gone. I had runned to get Grandma, but by the time we got back, it was too late. Ma only lasted another few hours. Before she died, she was sweatin' and moanin' something fierce." Bob paused for a moment, as if reliving it all again as he stared at the ceiling and drew a few more ragged breaths. "Otis, they buried her that same evening. Someone built her a wooden coffin out of old barn boards, and a few of the neighbor men dug her grave. It was rainin' when they put her in the ground. Water was seepin' into that hole as fast as they could get it out. I remember some man puttin' some big rocks on the coffin to keep it down. I kept thinking about my mama drownin' in that muddy hole." He turned to Otis then, and through watery eyes, he said, "That's why you cain't let them put me in the ground. Promise me that, Otis."

"I promise, Bob, but you ain't gonna die yet, just let me get you to a doctor—"

"Hell! I cudda already been dead and my story told, iffin you had got here a little sooner!"

Otis was grateful at once again hearing a little of the feistiness Bob was famous for, but the outburst left the old fellow coughing and gasping. Otis tried to get a little more water down him, but he turned his head away when the glass was brought near his lips.

"Otis," he finally said, "you know that little high point in your north pasture, up near that dog town I've been workin' this year? There's a flat rock on the very top, where the eagles sit."

"Yes, Bob, I know it. The highest point on the ranch."

"Well, there's a jar under that rock with about enough money in it to have me cremated without it costing anybody anything. I want you to have me done that way, and then just pour out my ashes on that flat rock and let the wind blow me away. Will you promise me that?"

Otis was silent for a moment, then, with a strained voice, he quietly said, "I promise, Bob. I promise."

Bob lay there for a moment, then said, "I left that place that very night. I was supposed to stay with my grandma, but she was not in the best of health and spent most of her time with her girl and her girl's lazy husband. My uncle liked to drink, and Ma said he was no good to work, and I shore wasn't gonna stay there and do his work for him. I just started walkin' away from that wet, bug-infested land. I hated it there. Took me . . . surrvvell . . ." He slurred, coughed again, and continued, "Took me several years to git up here, where it's dry most of the time.

"Soon as I stepped out of those Black Hills and saw all this dry land, I knowed I'd walked far enough. Ya know, I stopped for a couple days at a feller's camp over in those hills south of Deadwood, near where they carved those presedents' faces. That feller over there actually pointed to a big rock mountain and said he was gonna carve a Indian ridin' a horse outta that mountain. Said it was gonna be a lot bigger than those faces was. I knowed right then that man was crazy, so I left the next morning afore he woke up. I heard tell later that he almost did it."

Otis noticed Old Bob squint up his eyes and groan for a moment, then he opened his eyes and said, "That hot stuff is runnin' in my head again, Otis. Hurts powerful bad, and I gotta get up in a few hours and get another load of sticks. Is Jennifer okay? Did she go down to visit with that big ugly critter of yourn? You take care of her, Otis. My head's hurtin' real bad now, all the way down my neck and across my chest, and I gotta get up and fix you some grub. You must be hungry. I'll bake up a pan of biskets here in a minute; just let me take a little nap first."

The little old guy closed his eyes, and within a few moments, the ragged breathing stopped. Otis knew he was gone. He just sat there for a while and listened to the crackle of the fire in the ancient cast-iron stove, occasionally wiping away a tear before it ran into his red beard. He reached over to pick up the old worn Bible off the table and turned back the front cover. He found the short, stubby pencil and could see where some scribbles had been made recently, but no words could be distinguished. Bob had just thought he was writing Otis a note. Flipping through the pages, he saw where many notes had been written over the years, and many passages underlined, but in the tenth chapter of the book of Romans, he found an old, faded picture of a young woman. The ninth verse had been underlined, and in the margin were these words: 'I believe in my heart, Mama, and I'll see you again when I get there.'

Chapter 34

Several weeks had passed from the time when Jacob had started mapping the cavern. Exactly how many weeks he wasn't sure, for he had given up trying to count the days. He had also given up trying to count the hours since the watch he usually wore had stopped; the small lithium battery had finally given out. Every day, he had worn the Seiko Chronograph Anna had given him for his birthday a couple years ago.

After the fall on the ledge, he had taken to sleeping whenever he needed to, whether it was a few hours or only a few minutes. The dim light that filtered through the ice only indicated a short period of daylight; sometimes when he woke to it, he didn't know if it was early morning or late afternoon. Often, he went to sleep in the dark and woke in the dark.

The morning after the fall on the ledge, he had awakened practically unable to move because the pulled muscles had stiffened up. At first he feared maybe he had broken a leg or his back, but then he remembered he had managed to walk back through the passage to camp, which probably would have been impossible with a broken back or leg. Later in the day, after he was able to stand, he hobbled to the hot spring and spent a long time soaking.

Sleeping and soaking had been his activities for the following few days. It was during that time of inactivity that he became concerned that he may actually lose his mind. He had heard of people going crazy from being cooped up in a cabin over a long winter, maybe an extreme case of 'cabin fever,' but at least they were able to determine day from night. He remembered being more scared of going mad those days than he had ever been about being eaten by a bear, so from then on, as long as he was able, he'd decided to follow the forced routine he had tried to establish earlier, getting back to the job of being a miner and updating his journal with conversation to Anna and the girls. He was careful not to mention where he thought he was or anything about the gold he'd found.

Also, he planned to make no less than one trip a week to the outside, via one of the two entrances, no matter how cold; a few steps at least would affirm that he was not trapped underground, not a prisoner. He needed to feel he was at least somewhat in control of the situation. At night, before turning in, he would take time to read out loud, maybe a chapter, or at least a few verses, from his Bible.

He paused now from his task, determined to deepen the hole from bank to bank within the dry streambed. The digging had been fairly easy, and the smooth bedrock was less than four feet down. So far, all of the excavated dirt and gravel from the bottom area was piled on the bank to be panned, as this material looked exactly like the material from the last hole he had dug, and all of it had contained gold. Even in the dim light of his torches, he could now envision the pattern and was sure he would find the same all across this section of the wide cavern.

There appeared to be an unusual fold in the rock, running the width of this section of the cavern; any ancient streams would have flowed over this fold in the form of small waterfalls, the exact location of the stream and falls changing over the years, possibly due to the amount of water and where it entered the mountains, to eventually flowing over the fold. In addition to natural percolation, the scouring effect of the glacier advancing and receding also allowed water to penetrate at different rates and in different areas, all the while carrying the gold with it, leaving the heavy precious metal concentrated along a wide area; not counting the striations of gold running through the numerous quartz veins.

While the water feeding the hot spring no doubt came from deep within the earth, leaving the pool to form in its own watercourse, the cold water feeding the other stream entered from the opposite side of the cavern, nearer to the glacier, and it appeared, based on the old dry beds, that the two had flowed together at times; even now, they intermingled in the passage in the flowing warm creek. Jacob was convinced that at one time or the other, water had flowed over every part of the cavern floor.

By the time he felt his shift for the day to be over, he had indeed excavated the full width of the streambed, and the next several days would be spent panning the pay dirt. A few days digging and a few days panning; this was the cycle he had found to be most productive.

Up until this unforeseen 'adventure,' he had only ever attempted panning for gold one other time, several years ago, while on a fishing vacation. That short activity had produced no gold, and he had nearly frozen his hands off in that icy stream somewhere along Skalkaho Creek between Anaconda and Hamilton, Montana.

He really wasn't sure if he was doing it correctly, but his sloshing around had left small pieces of gold in nearly every pan. He had been saving what he found in a large coffee can, and it was now completely full with just the smaller stuff, the larger nuggets, most of which resembled dried raisins, but several as big as prunes, lay in a pile on a flat rock near the can and his gold pan. No doubt, he had stumbled upon one of the richest strikes ever, and all for naught, for no one would ever know.

Jacob stood just beyond the cavern entrance; he could feel the breath frost becoming ice in his beard. This was his fourteenth trip outside, roughly fourteen weeks since he had fallen on the ledge. On his last visit to that exit, he had been unable to go out due to ice and snow blocking his way, and that had occurred five trips ago.

Looking back, the cave entrance gave the impression of gazing into the gaping mouth of some giant beast, thick icicles hanging down as huge, sharp teeth. Warm Creek disappeared into a wide hole beneath the snow; no sign of it in the distance, except for a few vents where the escaping heat frosted in the air like an opaque white smoke.

Today the frigid air was still, and he breathed it deeply into his lungs; the effect caused him to shiver inside the thick down parka. The sky was a dull gray, and he was unsure if it was dusk or dawn, but even this seemed bright compared to darkness of the cavern. The gray remains of the old, dead tree poked up above the drifted snow in sharp contrast to the surrounding whiteness. This sentinel represented his rescuer, for if it hadn't beckoned to him and shared its warmth, his body or scattered bones would be lying under several feet of snow.

A couple hours later, after Jacob had finished a small meal and updated his journal with the most recent account of the outside visit, he became unusually melancholy. Thoughts of his family flooded his mind to the point of becoming physically ill, hot tears rolled down his cheeks, and he wanted to curl up and go to sleep, never to awaken.

The only thing left to do in completing his strict daily directive was to read aloud from his Bible. At first, he chose to forgo this and just surrender to his misery, but on second thought, decided to keep the commitment he made to himself and picked up the worn book indifferently, opening it to read the first verse he saw.

"Trust in the Lord with all your heart and lean not into your own understanding; but in all ways submit to Him, and He will direct your paths." Proverbs 3:5, 6.

He repeated this aloud several times, drawing comfort from the words, but having trouble understanding how they could be applied to his situation. Could it be that the path for him led only to this place, where he would eventually die? As he lay waiting for sleep to come, his gaze focused on the soft light of his small fire flickering reflectively on the growing pile of gold nuggets a few yards away.

Jacob diligently kept to his routine, his hair and beard grew longer, and his body grew leaner. He rationed his food, wrote in his journal, read aloud from his Bible, and rested when he was tired, but mostly, he dug for the yellow stone.

The old bear hide remained across the way, but had not been visited by the white-eared bear for many weeks now. He hadn't even heard the scurry of a mouse. On one occasion, during a trip outside, he had heard the far-off howl of wolves, and another day, he came upon old wolf tracks in the snow near the cavern entrance, but he never once saw an animal of any kind.

Inside his world was mostly quiet and dark, except for the constant soft gurgle of running water and dim glow of his fire. He had become somewhat accustomed to living within the limited light cast by the flickering torches and to the sounds of the glacier movement; the grating groans made it seem alive, but an occasional loud rumble still startled him. Through it all, he dug for the yellow stone.

Stumbling upon a foot-wide vein of quartz laced with gold one day, he followed it until it disappeared deep into the rock under the mountain. A few of the small chunks of the quartz had been uncovered quite by accident, as he was climbing out of a shallow dig site. The edge had given way, exposing a small pocket of the silicate mineral, giving the impression that the area had been 'mined' sometime in the distant past, only to be covered again with the passing of time.

Several chips and larger pieces of quartz lay together, along with crudely made stone tools of a hard, flint-like material he hadn't seen anywhere else while digging; the tool material most likely carried in by the earlier miner. Clearing away the dirt and loose rocks clearly revealed the marks left by the use of the rudimentary tools. The material for the exquisitely knapped artifacts on the stone altar must surely have come from this vein.

Jacob paused in his work to reflect on a time in the far distant past, when another pair of human hands worked at this same spot. Again, he pictured the view of the river valley not blocked by the glacier. Most likely the ancient miner's family was close by, maybe a young son helping him search out the smoothest, unblemished chunks of quartz, only to toss aside the material contaminated by the yellow metal.

Eons later, he now dug at the same spot, tossing aside most of the quartz to keep the yellow metal, which was to some a curse and to others a liberator, but which to him? He looked across the way to where his pile of gold sparkled in the flickering light; a fortune, no doubt, but it couldn't even buy him a piece of bread, and bread he needed, for his food was in short supply by now. He had made it through the coldest part of the long winter, and while spring would soon be approaching, he was anxious to begin hunting again.

The thought of food made him suddenly hungry. He had not eaten today. Climbing out of the dig, he dusted himself off and gathered wood to build up the cook fire. Soon the few small chunks of dried meat boiled in the little pot over the fire, and Jacob added the very last of the freeze-dried vegetables he'd been hoarding away. There were four multi-vitamins left in the plastic bottle, and he took one of those now.

Waiting for his stew to cool, he glanced down from where he sat to see a raisin-sized nugget by his foot. He picked it up, but instead of throwing it back to the pile on the smooth, flat rock, he tossed it toward one of the five galvanized steel drums, where he stored the dried meat. Four of the fifty-five-gallon drums were empty, and the fifth was less than half full. His aim for the empty container missed its mark, and the nugget tinked off the lip and bounced into the shadows.

After the meal, he rinsed out his pot and moved one of the empty barrels over next to his pile of gold. Using the small cooking pot, he began scooping the gold into the barrel. He had also kept seven chunks of quartz laced heavily with gold, the smallest the size of a baseball and the largest a little bigger than a football; these he also placed into the barrel. The flat lid was fastened to the barrel with a curved band fitted with a tightening lever. The chunks of quartz had to be rearranged before the lid would fit. He took a piece of charcoal and wrote on the barrel top: *This gold belongs to Jacob Arrowood, but I will trade it for one ticket to West Virginia.* He tried to move the barrel over next to the others, but, of course, it was too heavy, so he just sat on the ground, facing the dying fire with his back leaning against a fortune he would gladly trade for a way home.

He was thinking of all the good he could do with this treasure when the sound of a deep, low growl snapped him out of his daydreaming. Turning his head, expecting to see the bear, he was stunned to see the visage of a huge wolf standing less than ten feet away. The animal looked as if patches of hair were missing in places, and blood dripped from a torn ear. Willing himself not to make any sudden movements and not taking his eyes from the beast, he slowly reached for the handle of the .44 magnum revolver always at his side. As his hand closed around the grip, he saw the muscles bunch in the creature's shoulders as if getting ready to pounce.

In one smooth motion that would have even impressed John Wayne, Jacob swung the gun around and fired. The heavy slug hit the wolf square in the chest, dropping it in its tracks. Not ten seconds had passed from the sound of the growl to the sound of the gun. Jacob was up before the echo died away, expecting further attack, but no other wolves appeared. Only the soft gurgle of the stream could be heard along with the rapid thump of Jacob's heart and the ringing in his ears.

Chapter 35

Jacob glanced down at the animal only a short moment before easing carefully down the tunnel. The wolf's wet paw prints could be seen on the dry, rocky path, intermingled occasionally with a drop of bright red blood.

The barricade at the cavern entrance should have kept access to the tunnel restricted to much smaller animals, but somehow the wolf had managed to find a way in, and upon arriving, Jacob could see why. The heavy, melting ice had pulled the crude barrier away so much that even he was able to exit with plenty of room. Only one set of tracks could be observed leading up to the opening. He could see where the animal had walked along the creek bank through the melting snow, where it paused intermittently, possibly sniffing the air and then hesitating a short distance in front of the entrance. There, spotting the snow, were several small drops of blood and several more nervous, pacing paw prints.

It seemed fair to assume there was no immediate danger

of being attacked by a vicious pack of marauding wolves as he followed the tracks a short distance along the edge of the creek, then climbed a low bank, slipping slightly on the muddy ground wet with snowmelt. The air on his face was much warmer today, and as he slowly scanned the area within vision, he had to squint his eyes at the brightness.

Walking over to a dead tree, he reached up and broke off a low branch to use as a walking stick. The branch broke evenly with the trunk, leaving a small opening in the hollow tree. As Jacob stood breaking twigs from the branch to better fashion the stick, he noticed slight movement at the hole into the trunk; an amber sap slowly started oozing down the smooth, gray bark. A quick taste confirmed his instant thought: honey! He'd walked past this tree a hundred times and never saw evidence of it being a bee tree! The hive opening must be much higher up the trunk, which meant he stood little chance of having to fight for the sweet prize. A flat piece of stiff bark served as a spoon for a few mouthfuls of the sweet nectar, and a whittled stick provided a plug for the hole.

It didn't seem like that many days had passed since he had stood in this exact spot seeing only dark, cold skies hugging the ground. The deep breaths that filled his lungs felt cleaner and more refreshing, and he soon felt lightheaded from too many attempts to fill them. The sweet honey satisfied a hunger that couldn't be expressed.

Back inside, he skinned the old wolf and tossed most of the lean meat into a pot of water. He knew the animal would be tough and stringy, so a stew would probably be the best way to prepare it. Though he'd never eaten wolf before, the thought didn't bother him in the least. In his mind, meat was meat, and it had been a long time since he had eaten fresh meat. The long, thin backstraps he would try to roast over the coals, for he seemed to suddenly crave a rare bacon-wrapped filet.

As he finished with the old wolf, the evidence revealed that it had been in a fight with a tough opponent, maybe a younger and stronger rival. The overall size of the critter revealed that, in its prime, it would have been a strong pack leader, but all leaders soon must fall and be replaced. He pondered this as he moved the pot to the side of the fire, where it would cook slowly, and then gathered the remains of the wolf carcass to dispose of outside. While there, he hoped to gather a few handfuls of tender pine needles for tea and a cup or so of honey to sweeten it.

Later, after a meal that proved to be every bit as satisfying as he had hoped, he sat back with a sweet cup of pine-needle tea and stared into the dying coals of his fire. This change in the weather meant for a big change in his thinking. He had known it was coming, and had, up until recently, forced the thoughts from his head, but now it was time, time to make a decision.

Against all odds, he had survived most of the winter with his health and mind—as far as he could tell—mostly intact, but now what? Keep digging, hunting, and just surviving? How long until some misfortune rendered it impossible to fend for himself? Then did he resolve to just lie down and die? One thing that had allowed him to get through the winter was to not dwell on these things, but to keep busy and take it one day at a time, but the thoughts were not secreted away very deep into his mind. He merely forced them to hide away long enough to contemplate something else.

He paused in his thoughts for a moment and concentrated on a tiny flame as it tried to remain strong around a small coal that had rolled out of the fire. It danced, hugged, flickered, and died away as the small coal cooled, not strong enough to sustain itself alone. The other coals continued to slowly burn brightly as they shared their warmth and remained strong together. He was like that lone coal, as were most other people. Alone, we would soon give up our life and flicker out. Some people would deny it, but people needed people.

Today had been a good day, and he would force these thoughts away again and settle to be satisfied with a full stomach and a warm fire. His decision had been made for him. He could not plan his way out of this situation. He had to maintain the attitude that had gotten him through and keep vigilant every moment. One day at a time, not seeking an opportunity, but not letting one pass by when it presented itself. He had planned a good soak in the hot spring tonight, which always worked to soothe aching muscles and relax his body for sleep, but the blessing of unexpected fresh meat and the honey had already done the job. He would just sit here a few more minutes and wait for his tea to cool a little, then he would turn in. Tomorrow would be spent on the hunt.

****

Jacob followed the wolf tracks up over the ridge, onto the spine of the mountains. The old wolf kept ahead of him, but would also stop whenever Jacob needed to rest. Always a couple hundred feet ahead, it seemed to know when Jacob needed a breather and would stop the instant Jacob stopped, patiently turning to wait until he was ready to move forward again. Every eight or ten feet along, the wolf tracks in the snow would show a small spot of blood, and whenever Jacob reached the location where the old wolf had stopped to wait, there would be several.

The sky was a cold steel gray, and it was hard to tell if it was very early dawn or late in the evening; no sun, moon, or stars were visible to give an indication. Jacob didn't remember when he started following the wolf or where it was leading him, he just felt compelled to follow. Why had he decided to walk up the narrow cavern path to the ledge in the first place? He had been so warm and content beside the fire, and this was the ledge where he had almost fallen to his death. Then he had seen the wolf and it beckoned him, so he followed.

The snowy path became narrow, only a foot or so wide along the backbone of the mountain, then falling steeply down on both sides so far that he couldn't see the valley bottoms that were hidden in the gloom. Far ahead, he could see the wolf as it continued along the winding course. The animal again stopped when he did, and Jacob blew out a gust of frosty breath, filling his lungs the best he could with the cold, thin air. As he took a step forward, so did the wolf. It soon topped a small rise on the trail and disappeared over the other side.

When Jacob finally staggered to the top of the rise where he had last seen the wolf, the sky had grown much darker, and a stiff wind whipped the fine snow into a dense blanket, obscuring the view downslope to only a few yards. Standing on the point, eyes downcast to protect them from the blowing snow, he could plainly identify where the wolf had stood, even seeing several small drops of blood. A few moments later, as the wind dissipated, he could see no sign of the wolf, except for a line of tracks leading downward toward a yellow light glowing faintly in the distance.

Carefully watching where he placed his feet on the steep descent, he didn't look up until he was almost halfway to the light. By then the wind had died down completely and all was eerie quiet. His breath caught in his throat when he finally saw what the dim light revealed. He stood shock-still as his eyes gazed upon the crashed plane. The tail section was sticking up at an odd angle, and the jagged opening he had chopped in the side with the flap of metal was pushed closed over the opening. Ice and snow covered most of the wreck, so where was the ghostly yellow light coming from?

Mesmerized, he stared as the uneven metal flap started to move little by little, revealing a hand and then an arm. Slowly, a terribly crushed body appeared and, with apparent difficulty, crawled through the opening to stand on the ground. With both hands, it grabbed the edge of the flap and opened it wide. More mangled bodies come into view, all twisting and turning to exit the plane. Soon six were moving about on the ground, tearing and ripping at the ice holding the plane to the ground. Broken bones protruded from gashes in the legs and arms, torn, ragged, blood-stained clothing moved as they worked to free the plane held captive in the ice.

Sections of bone were missing from the crushed skulls, and chunks of blood-matted hair hung by strips of flesh, swinging as they moved. Suddenly, all six of the beings stopped their work and turned in unison to stare at Jacob out of deep black holes where eyes had once been. An instant later they were all moving quickly toward him through the knee-deep snow.

Jacob stood frozen, unable to move as the horrible things dropped to all fours, scrambling up the slope, getting closer, but as they moved forward they changed, becoming snarling wolves, emaciated creatures dripping blood from rips and gashes as they ran.

Turning in panic, Jacob tried desperately to ascend the slope, but every step failed to gain traction, and he only slipped farther down the hill with each movement, until they were upon him. He sensed no pain as the first set of slavering jaws tore into his leg, but felt the hot blood flow down the outside of his thigh.

Chapter 36

Otis sat on the edge of the flat rock where the eagles perched, looking down at the fine coating of dust on his new hiking boots. It was dry and cold this early spring morning, and as he lifted his gaze, he could see far to the south the long, narrow strip of cottonwood trees indicating the meandering flow of the river. Leftover patches of snow dotted the land in the low dips and valleys shadowed from the sun, which felt warm on the side of his face as it rose in the east. One fluffy white cloud floated alone in the vast, deep blue sky, and a quarter mile to the west a small band of antelope fed leisurely in the early morning sun.

Otis rarely came to this particular spot on the ranch. He saw it in the distance every day, but couldn't remember the last time he was actually here, for he never had a reason. Today, however, he did have a reason. He was saying goodbye to a friend. He'd been sitting here for the better part of an hour, occasionally looking down at the little pile of gray ash growing smaller as the gentle breezes carried the fine material out over the landscape.

This was exactly what Old Bob had asked of him, and he vowed to stay here until there wasn't a speck left. Behind him a dog town sprouted a hundred sticks, remnants of the old fellow's handiwork. The way Otis had it figured, Old Bob's ashes would scatter and enrich the soil, which would help the grass grow. New green grass would feed the prairie dogs, and the sticks in the dog town would allow the hawks and eagles a place to rest so they could feed on the varmints. To Old Bob's way of thinking, he was put here to help keep this circle of life in balance. Otis would miss him, and he felt blessed to have known the old codger.

Otis looked down at his new hiking boots again. He had never owned a pair and didn't even want to try them on when Jude had brought them home. It was Friday morning, and this past week had started off bad and kept going downhill. It never seemed to make sense how the littlest of things could cause the most aggravation.

Take Tuesday morning, for example. All he wanted for breakfast was a bowl of Cheerios, a simple bowl of his favorite cereal with honey, and a cup of black coffee. He had awakened earlier than usual and had decided to let Jude sleep in a little. He got his favorite cereal bowl and filled it with Cheerios, then put the plastic salad dressing bottle of honey in the microwave for the required fifteen seconds. Keeping the honey in an empty salad dressing bottle, the kind where you just flipped the lid to reveal a small hole, made for the very best kind of honey dispenser. Funny how he never liked honey until Jude took him off refined sugar now he couldn't get enough of it. In fifteen seconds it had warmed and made his mouth water as it poured over the Cheerios, until he went to the refrigerator and found out there was no milk. There was always milk in the refrigerator. He shut the door and opened it again as if a gallon would magically appear. No milk! He sat down with his coffee and tried to eat his Cheerios and honey without milk. It didn't work, and his grumbling must have woke Jude up, as she came into the kitchen wanting to know what was wrong. When he told her, she reminded him that he had asked her to make him a mug of hot cocoa the night before and she had used the last of the milk. It was his own fault, but he didn't want her to say it, so he just took his coffee to his chair and pulled on his work boots.

When he was halfway across the back porch, the heel on his left boot came off, and one of the tacks jabbed him in the heel of his foot when he stepped down again. He hopped back into the house to change into his dress cowboy boots and informed Jude that he'd planned on going into town that evening to pick up a repaired hydraulic hose for the tractor but needed to go in this morning to get his boots resoled.

"You've already had those old boots resoled twice. They are just worn-out! It's time to buy yourself a new pair," she had said, and followed it up with, "and bring home a gallon of milk."

He didn't want a new pair of boots. The old ones were broke in the way he liked them.

Otis had mostly calmed down by the time he'd reached town and the little boot repair shop he used was closed. A sign in the window said *Gone to Livingston. Be back Friday.* The owner, a semi-retired boot maker, Bob Hein, had a daughter in Livingston, Montana. Across the street was the town's only ranch wear store, so he decided it wouldn't hurt to check out some new boots after all.

Walking in through a door with a dinging bell, Otis nodded to the clerk, who was in the process of telling a little old bent cowboy of a man how fancy he was going to look in the new shiny red-stitched boots he was buying. As he passed by, Jacob could hear the old fellow tell the clerk that his wife just insisted he buy a new pair of boots for church.

Otis walked back to the boot section and was immediately drawn to a stack of boxes that depicted a glossy photo of a Caterpillar Track Hoe on the front of each one. On display was one of the thick black leather 'Cat' work boots trimmed along the sole and heel in bright Caterpillar Yellow trim. A real he-man's work boot. These were lace-up boots and he preferred a Wellington style, but they did have speed laces and were way beyond cool.

Looking through the stack, he found one box labeled twelve and a half, wide, just his size, and he almost upset the stack working the box out. He sat down on the bench and pulled out the left boot and slipped it on. A perfect fit. He laced it up and stood; it felt really good, not too tight and plenty of room, even with the steel toe. If the left one fit he was sure the right would too, so he sat back down and grabbed the right one. As he was ready to slip in his foot, he noticed the tag on the inside: *Full leather uppers, man-made sole, MADE in CHINA*

It was like a punch in the gut. 'Caterpillar,' an American icon! Why would they allow their name to be used on a product made in China? He placed both of the boots back in the box and left the store. He was glad the clerk was busy with another customer so she hadn't seen him leave.

Back in his truck, he had driven to pick up the hydraulic hose needed for the tractor. The high-pressure hose had sprung a leak on the bucket attachment arm at just the moment he had it raised to dump a load of manure into the old dump truck. The hot hydraulic fluid had squirted all over his new Carhartt coat. If the hose had broken with the bucket at any other angle it would have missed him.

This had happened Monday morning, just as he was starting his day. He had driven to the little shop to have the hose repaired, a simple job for Billy, who ran the shop, because the hose ends were good, and all he would have to do would be to have Billy crimp in a new section of hose. As luck would have it, Billy was out on a run, so Otis left the hose ends and a note telling how long a section of hose he needed.

After the disappointment with the boots, he was anxious to pick up the hose and get back to work. Otis paid for the repair, and Billy handed him an oily used plastic bag, saying: "Sorry I missed ya Monday, Otis. I put yer receipt and yer note in the bag with the hose."

Otis thanked him and left. On the way out of town, he stopped at the little hardware store to pick up a new shovel, then drove back to the ranch and straight out to the tractor. He had fastened one end of the hose, and then the other end wouldn't reach; it was about six inches too short! "How in the HELL could that have happened!" he yelled. He checked the note and saw that he had written thirty-seven inches, just as he thought he had. Checking the length the new hose measured came in at thirty-one inches. How could Billy have possibly gotten it wrong, when the length was plainly written down?

Back at the ranch he stormed into the kitchen with the short hose and the note. "Where's the milk?" asked Jude. He had forgotten the milk.

He had tried to explain and handed her the note. She looked at it and asked, "What's the problem? The note says thirty-one inches."

He had looked at her like she had two heads. "Jude, the note plainly says thirty-*seven* inches!"

"Otis, you may have meant to write thirty-seven, but you always make your sevens look like a one. Everybody thinks they're a one, even you sometimes; that's why your checkbook is always messed up. Give me the hose. I'm going to run into town anyway to get some things, like a gallon of milk. I'll have Billy fix it while I'm there."

Jude returned a few hours later with the hose, milk, and another package. Otis grabbed the hose, as it was already late in the day, and by the time the sun was near setting he had the tractor repaired. He dumped the one load of manure into the truck and started to back the tractor into the shed when he heard a cracking sound. He knew instantly what had happened. He had run over his new shovel. He'd used it to prop open the shed door, and as he backed in, the rear tire of the tractor had crushed it. Otis calmly shut off the engine and walked to the house. He didn't even look at the shovel. When he walked in, he looked at Jude and said, "I don't want any supper. I'm goin' to bed."

Before daylight the next morning Otis was in his small shop; he'd pulled the leather heel cup away from the inner sole of his old boot. He had found a half-used tube of construction adhesive hanging on the wall above the workbench. Still in the caulk gun, the dispensing spout was plugged with hardened adhesive. Thinking there may be enough usable material for the task at hand still in the tube, he cut into it with a knife. Sure enough, a pocket of the creamy substance remained serviceable, so he scooped it out with an old putty knife and applied it to the outside heel area of his boot. Five drywall screws later the boot was as good as new, and he proudly wore them back into the kitchen, beaming at Jude as she fixed breakfast.

"What are you grinning about?" she asked. "What have you done now?"

He answered by doing a little two-step, while pointing down to his newly fixed boot.

Jude just shook her head as she placed his eggs and corned beef hash on the table. "Your toast will be up in a minute, so dance over to the refrigerator and get the butter."

After breakfast she removed his plate from the little breakfast table and replaced it with the package she had bought the day before. "What's this?" he asked. "It ain't my birthday or nothing."

"Just open it and don't argue. I'm not going to take them back, and you are going to start walking more."

"What do you mean by walkin' more?" he asked as he removed a new pair of Merrell ankle-height hiking boots from the box, examining them as if they were strange objects the likes of which he'd never seen. "Just what do you expect me to do with these? You know I've never had a pair of lace-up shoes, and I don't want a pair now."

"Otis, you're getting older, and you never walk anywhere. You never get any real cardio exercise. We've talked about this before," she said, as she looked him in the eyes with her hands on her hips.

"I walk all the time and get enough exercise workin' around this danged ranch. I ain't got time to wear fancy boots and go walkin' across the prairie," he shot back.

"Otis, listen a minute," she said, holding her hands out, palms up, to stop him. "I know you work hard around here, sometimes too hard, but the only walking you do is out to the shop or out to the truck. You always ride something, whether it's the tractor, pickup, or four-wheeler if you are aiming to go farther than a couple hundred feet, and don't try to deny it. All I'm asking is for you to walk some each day, to keep your heart strong. Please just try it for a while."

Otis had never refused a request from Jude and couldn't this time, either, especially when she was so concerned about him. So he kicked off his old work boots and laced up the new hiking boots, gave her a peck on the cheek, and walked awkwardly out to the tractor to finish the manure hauling.

By the end of the day, he had to admit the boots were more comfortable than he'd expected, and the aggressive sole lugs gave him more confidence on uneven ground than the smooth-soled work boots he was used to. After supper that evening, he told Jude he thought he might take Old Bob for a long walk to the eagle perch the next morning.

He looked down again at where the little pile of ash had been. Old Bob was gone. Not a speck remained, for now he was scattered across the land he'd walked, the land he'd loved. He wondered for a moment about his other friend, Jacob, and where he might lay scattered.

A few weeks had passed since they had spoken to Anna. He had just said hello, but she and Jude had talked for a while, and after the call, Jude had told him that Anna hadn't given up hope and still hung on to the belief that Jacob was still alive somewhere and would be found. He worried that her resolve might cause her to go mad and she may begin talking to herself. He knew holding so tightly to something and not letting go could play tricks on the mind. He sure hoped not, and he knew she was an extremely strong woman with exceptionally strong faith.

Otis grabbed the broken shovel handle he was using for a walking stick and stood upright, hearing his knees creak. He stretched until his back popped and looked far to the west, where the red roof of the ranch house could be seen through the trees along the river. He looked down the steep trail he'd taken to get here and decided to make his way back to the ranch house by a different route. He just may get into this walking, for it gave him time to see places on the ranch up close that he'd only observed from a distance for many years. He didn't think he had ever actually touched the rock he'd been sitting on, but he had seen it probably thousands of times while driving on the dirt road in the wide valley below.

Behind him to the east the hill sloped gently a short distance to level out atop the high bluff still several hundred feet above the wide valley below. Numerous cattle trails led up and down, so he could take his time until he chose one. Along the way, he passed a few of the steep, jagged draws that ran from the bluff; a few of these had long ago been fenced off, keeping wayward livestock from falling among the tangles of juniper and sage.

Thick, rusty, heavy-gauge barbed wire hung loosely on old bone-gray posts. Walking alongside one particularly steep gully that was deep and wide and almost completely choked with a thick growth of old tangled juniper, Otis noticed the top of an old rusty bucket among the low-growing cactus beside an age-hardened fence post. The ranch had been in his family for several generations, so any one of his ancestors could have left it there. The bucket was half-filled with the sandy soil, and a small cactus had made a home inside. When he picked it up, the bottom and contents remained on the ground, while he was left holding an old, rusty, bottomless bucket.

"So much for rescuing an antique bucket," he said under his breath as he hurled the piece of junk into the deep rift.

As soon as the bucket clanged against the rocks, a huge form burst out of the ravine and over the fence not forty feet away, nearly stopping his heart. The huge mule deer buck cleared the fence with room to spare, stotting away over the uneven ground in typical mule deer fashion.

Otis noticed immediately the coke-can size of the early antler growth, pedicles nearly touching at the base. Of the hundreds of mule deer he had seen in his lifetime, this guy ranked as a giant. He had only seen one other deer near this one's stature, and that was a few days before Jacob was to leave on his bear hunt. Just as the sun was peeking above the horizon and Otis was passing one of the hay yards, he'd caught sight of several deer leaping the fence.

The eight-hundred-pound round hay bales were stacked in two separate yards on the ranch, and a four-strand barbed wire fence surrounded each yard. The fence kept the cattle out, but the deer were always sneaking in for an easy meal. This particular morning, all of the deer jumped out of the yard in the same area, except one that ran the length of the yard and leaped out the far end.

Otis would have completely missed seeing the big deer, except he had just happened to be even with the end of the fence when the big fellow jumped and got the truck stopped in time to get a good look as the deer bounded away. The thing that caught his eye was the heavy rack of dark-colored antlers with long drop points hanging down on each side. They always look bigger running away, but the antlers had to be pushing forty inches in width.

Otis remembered that day as if it was only yesterday, for it was the last time he had spoken with Jacob. He had hardly been able to wait until evening to make the call to tease him about the big muley.

"You really should cancel that bear hunt and come out

here and try for this monster," he had told him. "Not everyone gets the chance to take two Booners off the same ranch. I know he'd make the book and look mighty good on the wall beside that mangy goat."

Jacob had sounded really excited about the big buck and told Otis he'd have Anna send out his two game cams for him to try to get some good photos of the animal. "Try to pattern him!" Jacob had said. "Find out where he's beddin' down during the day."

"Doubt if he'll make it past huntin' season," Otis teased. "Best come out here and get him while you got the chance."

Otis knew this bear hunting trip was Jacob's dream hunt, but how he wished he'd never gone. The cameras arrived the same day they'd received the call Jacob and his party had gone missing. He was just reading the note from Jacob on how to set up the cameras when Jude took the call.

Could this possibly be the same deer? Otis wondered as he walked over to where the animal had emerged from the gully. A steep, well-worn trail led down into the tangle of Junipers. He never would have tried to follow this path wearing his old slick-soled work boots, but he raised his left foot and looked at the rough tread on his new hiking boots.

"I got me some four-wheel drive feet now," he said aloud, as he stepped over the old rusty fence.

Over the years, the infrequent rains had still managed to cut a deep ditch into the gully. Even with his new hiking boots, Otis needed to steady himself by grabbing on to every stick and limb that would hold him. The ditch remained muddy for most of its length, and it was much cooler under the cover of the junipers, with small patches of snow still lying about.

Nearing the bottom, his feet rolled on loose rocks, the thin branch he was holding onto broke with a snap, and he landed on his butt in the muddy ditch, sliding the few remaining feet to the bottom. The curse stopped as it was forming on his lips; being closer to the ground, he was able to see under the lower limbs of the thick growth, and not five feet away lay a shed antler. If he had not fallen, he would surely have missed it. Crawling on hands and knees, he stared at the huge shed a moment before he touched it.

Without a doubt, this was from the buck he had seen at the hay yard; the big fellow had indeed made it through the winter. He picked up the bony mass and carefully examined the long, thick drop tine. His hand barely fit around the gnarly base, even the G1 point or brow tine, usually very small or non-existent on a mule deer, measured at least five inches.

Otis studied the antler, seeming indifferent to kneeling in the cold mud, quickly estimating the total measurements, and raised his head before exclaiming aloud, "This one antler is over a hundred inches or I'm a buck-toothed jackrabbit!"

From his low vantage point, he could see old healed rubs on some of the tree trunks and a few recent antler rubs on others; the lighter, exposed inner bark edged with healing sap. Off to the left a ways lay the rusty bucket he'd thrown into the gully, and what he saw a few feet beyond it brought his breath up short and a big grin to his face: the other shed!

Otis moved the stacked boxes from the top of the old deep freezer; the unit had quit working a few years earlier but still served for storage. Dry and varmint proof, it was one of three in the old bunkhouse. This particular one mostly held Jacob's gear he kept at the ranch: a pair of old steel-toed work boots, a pair of well-used hunting boots, a heavy jacket, orange vest, a few pair of faded jeans, and the two game cameras.

He had made up his mind while walking back to the ranch. He was going to tell no one but Jude about the big mule deer; they really had no close neighbors, and none of them had ever mentioned seeing the brute. He would also set up Jacob's two cameras, one at the head of the draw, and the other just inside the lower entrance.

Jacob had always made a big deal of the advantages of using a game camera to pattern the whitetail deer in the dense woodlands of West Virginia, but had admitted the real reason he was so fond of the cameras was the anticipation of finding out what had been captured, everything from skunks to bears. Otis looked forward to getting some good pictures of the deer's antlers as they continued to grow over the summer. He just wished that Jacob would be able to see them.

He'd filled a plastic five-gallon bucket with a grain mix of oats, barley, and sweetened molasses, knowing Wetzel would enjoy the treat. Parking the pickup a good distance from the draw, he took his time setting the cameras and testing them, planning on returning in a few weeks to switch out the memory card and replace the batteries.

He couldn't get thoughts of Jacob out of his mind. After visiting with Wetzel for a while, he would give Anna a call. It had been too long since he had spoken to her. She and Jude talked often, but he just couldn't seem to find the right things to say. But tonight, he'd call.

Chapter 37

Jacob sat on a high ridge, leaning against a large, moss-covered rock, which shielded him from all but the strongest gusts of cold wind that had blown throughout the morning. No rain had fallen, although the low-hanging steel-gray clouds had looked threatening for the last couple hours.

He had spent much of the last few weeks outside as much as possible. The nightmare had unnerved him immensely, almost to the point of being afraid to go to sleep. Despite the fact that he had awakened violently to the attack, when the hot blood hit him — which in reality had been only hot pine-needle tea spilled down his thigh — the episode had seemed all too real.

Unable to rest for hours after the horrific experience, he had finally fallen into a fitful sleep, only to awaken to find the return of the white-eared bear. The animal had come back sometime during the night and had returned to the old tattered hide. As he had kindled up the dying fire, he noticed the reflection in the bear's eyes as it stared back at him from across the way.

Even now, that same creature stood a mere fifty feet away, pawing at the decaying base of a long-dead spruce that had fallen and rested at an angle against its neighbor; the chestnut-colored hair along its broad back buffeted with gentle gusts of wind, causing the silver tips to dance in waves. He had seen the bear every day since its return. Although it never ventured closer than it was now, it was often in sight.

Jacob turned his gaze far below and to the east, where the mouth of the glacier fell away to the sea. The fjord leading into the bay was crowded with huge chunks of floating ice, its steep sides shadowed in darkness with vast areas still covered in snow.

Just this morning, a large berg of blue-tinted ice had calved, sending a tsunami-like wave coursing through the dark water of the fjord, where it emptied into the wide bay before giving way to the open ocean. Even now, over an hour later, the floating chunks still undulated slightly from the wake.

However, the object that drew Jacob's attention this morning was not the icebergs or the bear, but a large expanse of ice that had at first seemed to be part of the land. The expanse had the rough shape of what he would describe as a bent hourglass. From his vantage point, the hourglass was bent slightly to the left, however, the narrow middle was twice too wide to be a good hourglass shape, and while the bottom part nearest the shore was relatively flat, the upper part looked to be rough, with a tall, prominent peak near its center.

Two days earlier, he had killed a young mountain sheep on this very ridge, and while taking a short break from the butchering, he had rested against this very rock where he now sat and, gazing out over the vast ocean, noticed several black objects moving in the water.

Retrieving his binoculars, he had located the things again,

to identify them as a pod of orcas. He'd watched as they dived and resurfaced, feeding closer into the bay. As they swam alongside the stretch of ice nearing the beach, a few of them dived, and then some suddenly appeared on the other side of the hourglass. At first he'd thought they were part of another small pod, but when he had counted them and watched longer to make sure, there was no doubt they were swimming under the ice. That had to mean the ice was not completely over land, at least not where the orcas were swimming. But maybe the sea ice just connected the beach proper to a sand bar just off shore. He thought this over as he completed the butchering and carted the meat down to the drying rack, leaving the boned carcass for the bear.

That evening he roasted a slab of tenderloin slowly over an open fire outside the cavern, all the while thinking he may have witnessed something important. After the meal, and while the rest of the meat smoked, he knew for certain he would need to spend some more time on the ridge.

Now here he sat again, studying the ice, trying to find and understand the subtle differences between sea ice and icebergs. He assumed all froze together somewhat over the winter, especially if they were bunched together, but how did they thaw and separate? He also knew icebergs were composed of fresh water, and sea ice could be somewhat salty. He believed this particular object of his interest to be a small iceberg surrounded by sea ice, and since only about ten percent of an iceberg was above the surface, the water near shore had to be deep.

He'd also been following the trail of three icebergs as they slowly moved across the water, floating out of the narrow fjord into the bay. The wide bay was covered in small white caps, while beyond the breakwater, the open ocean rolled and tossed violently. The great chunks of ice seemed unaffected by the ferociously pitching sea as they tracked one after the other in an easterly direction.

Where would the currents carry them? How long would

they remain in the open ocean? Would they only float in a large circle, returning near where they started? Would they eventually drift southward and melt away? These thoughts and many others danced around in his mind, along with one in particular that kept pushing its way to the front: would they possibly float within sight of the North American coast? He heard many stories of debris from Japan washing up on the beaches of California and Alaska, but how long did it take, weeks, months, or years?

He was suddenly terrified as to where this line of thinking was leading him. Could he possibly think, even for a minute, that using a chunk of ice as a raft was a rational idea? Would it be suicidal to attempt such a deed? He found himself sweating despite the cool temperatures, and his breath was now coming in short gasps, much as a poor soul with nothing to live for probably felt when looking from a bridge rail into dark water just before the leap. The difference being that he did have something to live for, and this may well be his only chance.

Jacob's somber contemplation was interrupted when a surprised growl sounded, and he looked up in time to witness the leap of a small Siberian squirrel as it landed between the bear's ears and bounded across its back, then up the dead tree and into the safety of another. The squirrel's long, hairy ears stood high as it scolded the intruder, now from a safe distance, for digging into its home. Jacob had to laugh out loud at the comical expression on the bear when it looked at him, as if to say, "He scared the livin' CRAP out of me!"

****

Jacob spent the next few days replenishing his food store. He managed to take four nice trout out of a small mountain pond only half-covered in ice. The pond was situated almost within sight of a trail he frequently used, but he'd never noticed it before the morning he had shot a deer near the edge of a little stream. He'd walked to the stream edge to wash his hands after field dressing the deer, and to his surprise, he saw the pond just beyond a thick stand of spruce.

Through all of this, his mind kept returning to the idea of floating home on a ship of ice. There were two things that caused him reservation. First, he'd never learned to swim; plus, he would get seasick from just *looking* at a boat. But the overwhelming desire to return home convinced him to at least have a closer look at the prospect.

Early the next day Jacob set off. The long hike down to the beach proved uneventful; most of the trek consisted of following narrow game trails along the spines of ridges. One trail led to another, sometimes crossing shallow valleys until the descent led to the steppes adjacent to the shore.

Within a quarter mile after reaching the beach, Jacob stood looking out over the hourglass-shaped accumulation of ice. The waters were extremely calm this day, almost like glass, with gentle wave action that hardly broke at the shore. With a sky devoid of clouds, no perceivable wind moved the tall salt grasses; a gathering of gulls fretted and cawed while sampling the smorgasbord of delicacies washed up on the beach.

To his right, the shoreline curved with the bay, and to his left it led into the narrow fjord. The air was colder here, with the heavy frigid air from the glacier filling the narrow gorge almost like standing in front of an open freezer. The ice pack was nearly the size of a football field, and where it anchored heavily up on the beach, the fjord side ice was nearly five foot above his head, but he could easily step up on the mass on the side near the bay. Here, facing the sun and eroded by the surf, natural steps of sorts led up on the ice. Through the clear water, the ice thickness disappeared into the depths, but about a hundred feet from shore, at the middle of the hourglass, an opening likened to the bottom of a stone arch bridge could be seen allowing the orcas to swim from one side to the other.

With a small camp axe, Jacob chipped a small chunk of ice and brought it to his tongue. It tasted of salt, which meant it was sea ice. Several more samples at various locations revealed the same. Walking past the narrow middle of the floe, he approached the high mound of ice near the center of the outer and largest part of the hourglass. The ice samples here tasted of salt too, until he chipped a small chunk from the mound itself. This tasted fresh, with no hint of salt! He concluded what he had initially surmised: the floe consisted of a small iceberg trapped in sea ice.

The irregular shape of the berg, while over thirty feet high from where he stood, some twenty feet above the water, narrowed at the top to a rounded tip. It was roughly a hundred feet in diameter and allowed for fairly easy climbing. About halfway up, on a wide, flat ledge with an undercut bank, he discovered a foot-deep depression nearly filled with clear melt water. Scooping a handful to his mouth, he found it cold and fresh. With the water problem solved, he sat on his backpack and surveyed the area carefully, trying to find other holes in his plan beyond the obvious ones, like being unable to swim and the unavoidable motion sickness.

A circus of puffins swam not far off shore, diving for the numerous small fish; Jacob could occasionally see one actually flying under the clear water and surfacing with a catch. He was sure he too could catch fish if adrift too long and his food ran out, although he'd probably be too sick to eat most of the time. He also knew he couldn't steer an iceberg, even if he could manage to be on one when it broke free of land, and that too was a real problem, because this one was firmly attached and could well stay anchored here throughout the short summer.

He shut his eyes, leaned back against the cold ice, and immediately felt an almost imperceptible sensation of motion, a placid up and down movement in concert with the sea. He wondered about this for a moment before climbing down to check something out.

Walking slowly back toward the shore, he stopped often, sometimes kneeling to shut his eyes, to better sense the slight movement more clearly. The ever so slight roll continued until he crossed over the underwater arch; on the shore side, the almost undetectable motion couldn't be felt at all. Even when he lay on his back, the ice was stock-still. He guessed that if the slab was ever to break apart it would be at this point, the thinnest and weakest area, but when? The ice at this juncture was still several feet thick, and the seas had been fairly rough only a few days ago, but the bridge had still held. Maybe with the slight movement on the sea side there could develop a hairline crack or something, but did the ice bend and not crack? How could he help to hasten the separation?

Was he convincing himself to actually try to escape this land on a chunk of ice? What options did he really have? He knew he was facing a life-or-death decision and could live with only one, but could die with either. He vowed to make the choice before morning.

As he neared the beach, the sounds of the small colony of seagulls suddenly changed from normal feeding noise to raucous squawking and scolding. Glancing in the direction of the ruckus, he saw a large, dark shape moving through the group at the water's edge, seemingly oblivious to the chaos. The white-eared bear continued walking toward him, only to stop at the edge of the ice and look up. Their eyes met for a moment before the bear turned and started walking toward the mountains.

"Okay, okay," Jacob said aloud. "I know it's getting late. Let's go home."

Home. He'd said it before he thought. Right then, his decision was made.

Chapter 38

Jacob soaked in the hot springs longer than usual this evening. His fingers and toes had wrinkled to look like prunes some time ago. The hike to the beach and back took its toll on his knees, more so than usual. It had been the longest one-day travel he'd made since last fall; about two hours down and a little over three hours back to the cavern.

When he'd at last stumbled to his fire pit and kindled a flame, the flickering light revealed that the bear had already retired to his corner on what was left of the old hide. He had made a small pot of stew by boiling dried meat in a little water; not much of a meal, but he'd been tired and hungry.

The steaming mineral water soothed his aching muscles to the point where he almost felt too relaxed to walk back to his sleeping nook. Through the dim light, he stared across at the ancient altar and thought again of the early people who once lived here. The cavern had provided sanctuary for them, and had allowed him to survive through the harsh winter.

Although he would guess he'd lost at least forty pounds, he still felt good and, by the grace of God, had not sustained any severe injuries.

He was, however, about to put himself in grave danger, for he was now determined to try to escape this otherwise beautiful land on a raft of ice; fully aware that this risk of certain death was worth the threat if he had only one chance in a thousand to return home to his loved ones. It may be that he could survive here a few more years, but still, the yearning to go home was worth the attempt.

Reluctantly, he crawled from the hot spring and made his way back to camp. He was dead to the world in seconds and awoke in the same position as he had fallen to sleep. He lay there in the sleeping bag and planned on the items he needed to gather together; this endeavor must be carefully considered. He would have to carry all the items decided upon to the beach, and needed to make as few trips as possible.

Many of the things Jacob recovered from the plane had not been touched since he'd brought them to the cavern. Clothes, rifles, ammo, tents, and backpacks lay neatly arranged and stored on a natural stone shelf not far from the much-depleted pile of sticks and twigs.

Some of the items still carried tags with prices, like the high-end aluminum framed backpack he now held. One of the zippered sections revealed a watertight compartment in which he could store his precious journal and his small Bible. Once all his chosen items had been carried back to the fire pit, he re-kindled the fire and prepared a meager breakfast, noticing the old hide across the way lay vacant. The bear was gone and might be away for several days. If so, it would return to an empty cavern. By early tomorrow morning, Jacob too would be gone.

An hour after his meal the backpack was stuffed, as well as a large duffle. Over one hundred pounds of the items he wanted to have if he were to spend several days or weeks floating on the open ocean, and even that would only be possible if the ice chunk broke free of land. What if it didn't break free and only melted into the sea? He would have camped on a chunk of ice for nothing.

All these things and others bounced around in his mind as he readied for departure. When the two packs were hauled to the entrance, he walked back and looked around his camp. He had one more chore to do before he left. The gold he had worked the winter to accumulate completely filled the barrel when including several large chunks of gold-laced quartz. He wondered what riches lay within these caverns. He knew he had only scratched the surface of what may be the largest concentration discovered in modern times.

A fortune he could not take with him. Its real value had already been realized, as it had kept him focused throughout his self-imposed confinement. Still, he felt the need to secure it in a safe place rather than leave it exposed in the middle of his 'living room.'

Three hours later Jacob sat on the smooth floor, leaning against the relocated barrel of gold, staring at the ancient carvings for the last time. The dim light from his trusty crank lantern revealed them in all their stark glory. This place he'd chosen seemed appropriate, for it now contained the efforts of men separated by thousands of years. He'd taken another empty metal barrel from the food stores and proceeded to make several trips transferring the treasure, before he was able to fasten the compression ring lid.

He'd torn one of the few blank pages left in his journal and wrote in bold strokes: 'THE GOLD IN THIS BARREL BELONGS TO JACOB ARROWOOD' and placed the declaration on top of the contents before clamping the lid.

He rose now as the light dimmed and cranked the lantern's handle until the room brightened again. With a last look, he walked out through the tunnel.

The next morning, as Jacob stopped at the top of the steep trail to catch his breath, he looked back into the little valley for what he figured would be his last time. Even from this short distance, there was no visible indication of the cavern entrance. He could see the meandering flow of Warm Creek and what was left of the old dead spruce next to the opening, but that was all. It was indeed a miracle that had led him there.

He removed the wide strap from atop his shoulders to check the pack bindings on the travois. The thought of making more than one trip to the beach resulted in his cutting the two long, thin poles. From this point on, the trail would be mostly downhill, allowing the narrow travois to carry the load with very little effort. The poles hung from the wide strap across his shoulders just at his elbows, and extended about two feet in front, providing a good rest for his arms, and served also to keep his rifle within easy reach.

It was nearing noon when he finally reached the steppe above the beach. The waist-high grass hardly moved at all in the still air; hence allowing any large animal walking through to be detected in time to react appropriately. Hopefully the ice would break free in a few days because he really didn't want to be exposed out in the open for long.

His plan was simple: He would set up camp on the ice out at the foot of the freshwater berg and wait. The sea ice would either break free and float him out to sea, or melt around him and force him back to the cavern.

"It will be one of the two, for sure," he said aloud. "Or I could slide into the ocean and drown, or be eaten by a bear in my sleep."

As soon as he heard his own words spoken, he wished he'd never said them. He'd never be able to sleep as long as the ice was connected to land. The most terrifying incident in his life had happened just a short way up the beach, and as soon as he heard his own words, a cold sweat formed on his back, and he gripped the rifle a little tighter.

The aluminum frame on the professional-grade backpack had two bracketed arms at the bottom that, when turned out and locked into place, formed a really handy pack frame that served to haul quite a load of firewood. He had accumulated a sufficient amount from the driftwood heaps along the beach to last through the night, and would haul as much as he could before the ice broke away, if it ever did.

By early evening of his first day on the ice, Jacob had his camp set and a fire burning at the narrow part of the sea ice. The heat from the fire had very little impact on the densely frozen ice; only a little melt water from it trickled away to drip over into the sea. He had also cut and hauled several large bundles of the dry grass to form a thick mat, on which he pitched his tent. He had brought two of the small dome-shaped tents with him. The larger one he'd set up first and was a dark forest green in color with a wide rainfly. He set the small one inside the first and packed his supplies in between. He'd also gathered all the metal tent pegs he could find, along with all the rope and heavy twine he could muster.

The small tent came equipped with a blaze orange rainfly, and he planned to stake it out on top of the iceberg once at sea. Hopefully, during the day, it may draw the attention of any nearby plane, and during the night, he would keep a signal fire burning. Even if a Russian plane spotted him adrift, he could maybe convince them he was a hapless lost fisherman.

He kept a few things within arm's reach or on his person at all times: a firearm and the backpack. He either had the large revolver holstered around his waist, or the rifle nearby, and in the backpack was a small amount of dried food, a compact first aid kit with fire starter, the fishing reel with heavy line, and stored away in the waterproof compartment, his Bible and journal. In his left back pocket, he still carried his wallet, mostly out of years of habit, only now it was carefully contained in a Ziploc bag. His driver's license, credit cards, and a little cash seemed like silly items to carry in his current situation, but he did so only in case a bleached skeleton needed to be identified.

That first night seemed to drag on forever; he dozed a

little, but kept the fire burning bright. By morning he was stiff, tired, and cold despite the all-night fire, which continued to burn, even though an inch of water surrounded the charred wood at the bottom of his fire pit. The heat had melted a shallow bowl in the ice, leaving only the top of the coals glowing red. Since the campsite sat on a slightly higher plane, chipping a shallow trench with his belt hatchet let the water drain. He would need to fill the depression with beach sand, but the melting around the fire pit also gave him an idea.

By mid-day he had accomplished a great deal. The fire pit was now full of sand, and a dry heap of driftwood was stacked nearby. After nearly falling with an armload of wood on the slick ice, he had also decided to scatter sand along the route across the ice and around his camp. Most of the space between the inner and outer tent he'd stuffed with the dry salt grass. It would serve as added insulation and for fire tinder when it rained, which could be any day now. The weather had remained calm and the seas still for the past couple days since he'd arrived, but in the north, dark clouds had started to form.

Every time Jacob crossed the narrow section of the ice pack, he stopped for a moment to study the feasibility of hastening the ice break from the beach. Would he be wasting his time if he hauled grass and driftwood enough to build a large, wide fire, and would it make any difference? The narrow section spanned less than eighty feet, and appeared slightly tilted toward the bay. Maybe if he built a huge bonfire on the high fjord side, the warming melt water would run across the ice toward the bay and weaken the connection. But also, the water could seep into any of the minute cracks and re-freeze and act as glue. The nights were still well below freezing, and this morning, he had to break a thin glaze of ice from his catch basin of fresh water on the iceberg. In the end, he decided to build the fire anyway; the chore would keep him busy, and if the results didn't help, at least they wouldn't hurt.

He had to walk farther along the beach to find dry wood,

as the outermost parts of the driftwood masses were too water-soaked to burn. He was forced to gather from the more protected areas above the tide line. Every time he crawled into the tangle, he couldn't help think of the day he'd done the same to escape the huge bear, only, on that day, he'd crawled a little faster. On his way to this very pile, he'd seen fresh bear sign, and he was less than a quarter mile from his ice camp.

He had just finished securing the latest load of wood to the pack frame when he heard the deep *huff* behind him. Turning quickly with the .44 mag in hand and heart racing, he startled the white-eared bear as much as the bear had startled him. "Don't sneak up on me like that!" he yelled. "I almost shot you!" They stared at each other for a moment, and then the bear gave another, softer huff, turned, and walked away.

For the remainder of that day and all of the next, Jacob carried grass and wood; the dark clouds to the north had dissipated, and on the morning of his fourth day on the ice, the weather remained calm but colder. He had managed to lay a thick bed of dry grass across the narrow section of ice, and on this, he'd stacked the wood. He planned to set fire to the mass right after a meager breakfast, but he had tripped this morning over one of the tent pegs, and it had torn loose. He'd had a difficult time pounding them in the ice anyway, and none of them were fastened tight.

He pondered a solution, then came up with the idea of inserting the tips of a few of the metal pegs into the hot coals of his fire. When the ends were a nice cherry red, he carefully placed the tip of one onto the ice, and it sizzled as he pushed about two-thirds of its length in with a piece of drift wood. As it cooled, the ice refroze and couldn't be kicked loose. An hour later the tent was double staked, and several more of the pegs were frozen into the iceberg, making it easier to climb to the ledge.

Returning to the small fire, he added a few pieces of wood, and as he leaned back, a snowflake landed on his hand. Glancing toward the northwest, he saw a fresh dusting of snow on the high, dark foothills, and the mountains beyond were already obscured by thick snow clouds. The front had moved in quickly, for the sky had been clear when he put the tent pegs in the fire. The snow might stay in the higher elevations, but not wanting to take the chance of getting all his wood and grass wet, he retrieved a blazing brand from the fire. Moving across to light the heap, a sudden loud splash in the water nearby startled him and drew his attention into the bay, where a pod of orcas swam slowly along the beach. As he watched, a huge black tail slapped the water, probably in an effort to scare a meal out of the shallows.

It was already mid-afternoon, and when another snowflake settled on his nose, drawing him back to his task, he knelt at the end of the stack toward the bay and touched the firebrand to the dry grass. Slowly, the fire took, but the smoke drifted gently back on him and out over the bay. He needed to be on the other side and the other end to get the blaze going properly. The colder air off the fjord could barely be felt, but it would move the flame in the right direction.

Wedging a handful of grass into the split end of a dry branch, he made a torch and crossed over to the far side and was leaning in to blow gently on the flame when the deep *huff* sounded behind him. Startled again and nearly setting his beard on fire, he turned to yell at the white-eared bear, but the yell caught in his throat. He dropped the torch, and his breathing and heart stopped. Completely paralyzed, he could only stare at the nightmare standing directly in front of him.

Chapter 39

Not twenty feet away stood a monster on all fours, head down and ears laid back, patches of hair missing from an emaciated body. The cold blood in Jacob's body froze solid when the beast raised its head and stared at him through red, rheumy eyes; for between those eyes, in the middle of a snout swollen and festering, dripping with pus, protruded a sharp, shiny piece of stainless steel!

Bile rose in Jacob's throat as the creature lunged at him, covering the first fifteen feet in an instant. Unable to move or think, Jacob watched in horror as death approached, the hot, fetid breath reaching him before the beast did. At the last instant, bracing for impact, Jacob managed to shut his eyes and brought up his arms to cover his face. A loud roar filled his ears as he was slammed back into the pile of driftwood; he braced for it and prayed death would come quickly, but he felt no pain despite the fact that the roaring continued. He managed to open his eyes to see that another had entered the fray. This one was a bit smaller, but the white ears were unmistakable!

The smaller bear rammed into the monster and knocked the beast off balance, but recovering quickly, the huge bear lashed out with a massive paw, and the five-inch claws caught the younger bear on the side of the throat. Bright red blood spurted from the wound and rapidly covered the ice, some of the hot droplets splashing onto Jacob's cheek.

Gravely wounded, the smaller bear still attacked again, causing the larger creature to slip on the bloody ice. Momentum carried the huge beast to the edge of the ice, and its back legs slid into the water. The smaller bear collapsed and fell against Jacob's outstretched leg and lay still as blood ran over the edge and into the sea.

The big bear clawed at the ice to pull its huge body out of the water. It attained purchase and lifted one dripping hind leg up on the ice, while the other leg kicked in the water, trying to get a grip. Suddenly, out of the sea, a huge set of jaws opened and closed tightly around the flailing leg. The monster bear was pulled off the ice in an instant, thrashing in the water as another giant set of jaws opened and closed over the beast's grotesque head. With a shake, the head was separated from the body just as another of the great orcas clamped down over the shoulders, pulling the carcass under the water; then there was nothing but the sound of the pink water gently lapping against the ice.

Jacob sat in stunned silence for a moment, consciously aware of the moment he started breathing again. It had all happened so quickly. He sat on the cold ice as the last few moments were played back again in his mind. He knew he was in shock, and wasn't sure he could even stand up, but he did notice that his left hand was caressing the soft fur that lay against his leg. He knew the white-eared bear was dead. The blood had stopped pulsing from the gaping wound, which meant the heart had stopped.

He had a jumble of mixed feelings racing through his

mind right now. He realized how close he had come to dying, and he was relieved, but a part of him was overcome with sadness, and he felt like he wanted to cry. He could feel his body vibrating on the inside like a tuning fork, and he wasn't sure his legs would support him if he tried to stand, so he just sat there stroking the fur, his butt growing cold and wet against the ice. This is what eventually made him move. He knew he had work to do, and the gently falling snowflakes were getting more numerous now.

He cleared a way through the long stack of driftwood and, with great effort, managed to drag the dead bear the few feet across to the camp side, a feat that would have been impossible, if not for the smooth ice and a rope attached to the frozen tent pegs.

His fire had failed to catch, which happened to be a good thing, considering the turn of events; so he built up the campfire first, and then lit the dry grass on the fjord side of the heap. Flames caught quickly and spread through the grass bedding, setting the driftwood ablaze.

With his back to the fire, he worked to warm himself and calm his nerves. He shook, and his teeth rattled as he stared down at the still form of the bear. He watched as the first snowflakes landed and melted on the still-warm body; the ones that followed soon gathered as the body cooled.

He didn't know what to do with the bear. He couldn't bury it, he surely wasn't going to eat any of the meat, and he wouldn't feel right just pushing it into the ocean. He thought for a moment and settled on the only practical thing he could be comfortable with. In the light of the fire and with the snow gently falling, he carefully skinned the bear.

He'd originally set out on this adventure to hunt bear, so this would be the bear he claimed as his own. He knew the chances of ever leaving the ice were slim, but he worked the hide from the body with all the skill he knew. In the past, he had helped his friend Jim prepare animals for mounting and had learned a lot in the process, so he tried to remember how to make every cut properly. He couldn't help but feel an unusual kind of sadness as he worked; never before had he felt such a connection to an animal as he experienced now. He'd always been a little sad at ending an animal's life, but he understood hunting and always made use of the meat. This was profoundly different.

It was full dark by the time the hide was removed, and he still had to scrape any remaining fat and tissue from the skin side, and would have a lot of work to do later, like turning the paws, lips, and ears. His back ached from stooping so long, so he carefully placed the fresh hide against the side of the iceberg. Tying it to the tent pegs he'd placed there earlier would allow him to work standing up. He knew he wouldn't be able to sleep, even though he was dead tired, so for a time, he paced alongside the burning line of driftwood, watching as the gentle breezes lifted bright orange sparks skyward. Occasionally, one would be carried much higher over the water, before it, too, burnt out. He stopped at the edge of the ice to stare out over the dark sea, wondering what tomorrow would bring.

Before retiring for the night, in the flickering glow of his campfire, he made the final entry in his precious journal. He wrote of the encounter with the bear of his nightmares and the results that followed. As the tent flapped behind him in the breeze, he filled the last couple of blank pages and completed his thoughts in the margins of others; ending with the statement that this would be his last entry.

He once again sealed away the journal in the waterproof compartment of the backpack. He had removed its aluminum frame after hauling the last bit of driftwood but wore the cloth pack every waking moment. It contained very few items other than the journal, his small bundle with the carefully wrapped artifact, several pieces of dried meat, and the spool of braided fishing line, a pair of gloves, and his Bible.

The snow had stopped completely by the time he crawled into his sleeping bag, but with the snowfall ending, the air became eerily still, so still that he could clearly hear the occasional snapping of the wood in the dying fire and the gentle slap of the water alongside the ice. Lying there, his body began to relax and warm within the thick bag; the soft lapping of the water soon lulled him into a restful sleep.

He slept completely through the night, something he had only been able to do a few times since first exiting the plane after the crash. This night, there hadn't been any dreams, only deep, restful sleep. He seemed to be in the same position as when he had shut his eyes, and now, as they adjusted to the dim light, he noticed how the tent sagged closer to his face. Grabbing the backpack as he exited his tent, he faced several inches of newly fallen snow, which lay heavy under a dark gray sky.

Before attempting to rekindle the campfire, he knocked the loose snow from the fresh hide. He wanted to finish dressing it as soon as possible and thought immediately how foolish it was to be in a hurry to do so. It wasn't like he had a pressing appointment to catch a plane or attend an urgent meeting.

He looked the short distance beyond his tent at the snow-covered body of the bear. Before doing anything else, he needed to attend to it one way or another. He didn't want to simply push it into the ocean. Feeding it to the fishes or seeing it washed up on the beach to be picked at by the birds seemed inappropriate, so in the end, he decided to pack some of the abundant snow over the body.

The coals from the long line of burning driftwood had left a black line across the ice; warm embers still glowed in a few places, while snow covered it in a few others. The motionless air was cold, and he felt the dampness clear to his bones, so he gathered enough embers together and built a small fire near where he worked.

After an exhausting morning, he had the naked carcass encased within two feet of packed snow. As long as daytime temperatures continued to linger in the low forties, any melt would refreeze at night, but he knew his efforts to be only a short-term fix. He would deal with matters as needed, and right now he needed to attend to the bearskin.

By mid-afternoon the hide was scraped clean of all flesh and fat; the paws were turned and free as well. The task had been much harder on the cold, stiff skin. He had saved the work on the head for last, as the snout, lips, eyes, and ears required much care and concentration. The hide now hung head down in a manner that allowed Jacob to rest it on his lap as he worked. He sat on the nylon bag containing the small tent rainfly and its shock-corded fiberglass stretchers; not comfortable, but it kept his butt from freezing on the ice.

Just as he made the first cut to start cartilage removal on an ear, he felt the ice beneath him move ever so gently, followed by an even gentler bump. He more than likely would never had noticed it if he hadn't been sitting. For some reason, he turned to look out to sea when he became aware of the strange color in the sky on the far horizon. Above him, the sky still carried the dark gray color of snow, but far out at sea the color changed to a paler shade of yellow-orange. At least somewhere, far to the south, the sun was shining brightly, and then he felt a soft kiss of warmer air in his face, almost at the same time he detected the rise and bump again.

Some three hundred miles to the south, under a bright blue sky packed with billowing white clouds, the ageless dance of warm air meeting cold commenced. Strong, invisible coils whipped the water into tempestuous waves as it waltzed across the surface, slowly sending rank after rank of deep, powerful currents marching northward. Within another hour the blue sky turned a sinister purple, while the clouds churned together, changing from white to gray to almost black.

Nearer to Jacob another natural event was taking place. At the head of the fjord the seabirds were taking flight, moved by a forewarning honed on instinct. Almost imperceptible, a massive wedge of ice, the size of a twelve-story building, calved from the mouth of the glacier. Falling as if in slow motion, it hit the water with an enormous display just at the last gull took wing. The ensuing displacement of water surged like a tsunami down the fjord toward the open sea, washing the banks free of debris and crashing violently against the exposed cliffs.

Jacob heard what he thought was a far-off clap of thunder. He had just climbed up to the catch basin for a drink of fresh water and to fill his canteen when the little pool of water moved enough to tip a small amount out over the side. Then, suddenly, it felt as if the entire iceberg lifted a few feet out of the water. Jacob instantly grabbed for one of the tent pegs he had driven into the ice, the only thing that kept him from losing his balance and falling from his perch.

The berg dropped as quickly as it had risen, followed by a deep cracking sound, and then the berg slowly spun as it moved away from shore. Jacob managed to regain his balance as he saw the iceberg separate from the sea ice directly along the black burn line. His breath quickened as he realized there was no turning back. He was now at the mercy of the sea.

The huge berg and what remained of the attached sea ice slowly made three complete revolutions before it met with the bay. The water here was somewhat rougher than the water of the fjord, and small whitecaps became more common as he drifted farther away from land. Already, he could feel the discomfort in his stomach as the first indication of nausea hit him. He had suffered from motion sickness since childhood; riding in the backseat of the family car nearly always resulted in his dad having to stop and let him puke. He never liked amusement parks for the same reason.

As the berg moved across the bay to the open ocean, he continued to get worse, and within a few hours he was fully in misery. He tried staring at the horizon, which helped a little but not much. One moment he was looking at the far-off mountains and the next at a huge roll of water. He needed to look up at the sky and focus on a fixed spot in the clouds, but he couldn't just lie on the ice. First he grabbed his canteen and took a deep drink of cold water, then attempted to crawl into his tent. He knew for certain he would throw up if he went inside the confined space, so he just reached in and grabbed the edge of his sleeping bag. Luckily, he managed to pull the whole unit outside, which included the dry, insulated ground cloth the bag lay on.

The effort caused him to throw up, which made him feel a little better. He unzipped the bag and lay back, pulling the loose sides around him, and stared up at the sky. He picked one particular curl of cloud and focused intently there as he took deep breaths. In a while he was feeling better and managed to doze off for a short time.

It was early evening when Jacob awakened. He still felt really sick, but not so much as earlier. Still, the thought of eating made him want to throw up again, so he only took a few sips of water. He knew also that he would not be able to enter the tent and decided to spend the night out by his fire. He had built it on the sea ice right between his tent and where the sea ice met the iceberg. The past fires had melted a hollow in the berg, which now served to keep the fire out of most of the wind. Here, he built up the fire on the old coals and dragged his sleeping pallet near.

He had been out of sight of land for some time now, and he had no sense of direction. No signs of whitecaps could be seen in the diminishing light, but he could feel with more intensity the swells and troughs as the seas rolled.

By mid-morning the next day, after a miserable, cold night, Jacob was again lying back staring at the sky, but this time the clouds appeared to be moving as much as the sea. He knew for sure the sea had become more violent; at times the waves would hit and send a spray up on the ice, and some of the fine, cold mist could even be felt on his face. He was cold and sick, really sick. He had thrown up nearly every hour and couldn't keep a swallow of water down. He even longed to be back in his cave, where he could at least be warm and still.

He wondered how long it would take motion sickness to kill him. Although he had never heard of anyone dying from it, he felt sure he may be the first. It could be that one of the big waves would wash him into the water, where he would drown. He would almost welcome it. Either way, he doubted he would make it through the day feeling this bad.

While Jacob lay in despair, the edge of the storm moved ever closer, wind-driven rain falling in torrents. As the first raindrops reached him, he wondered how things could get worse now that he would be drenched with rain. He fought the urge to puke again and slowly got up to retrieve his parka. As he stood, he heard a loud, dull cracking sound and felt the ice suddenly move violently. A space of open water appeared before him as another crack opened up between his feet! Great panic replaced the sickness as his mind tried to process what was happening. Instinct took over as he saw the loose end of a rope dangle over the edge of the crack before him. Without another thought, he jumped for the rope.

Chapter 40

Jacob leaped the space as the sea ice behind him broke up into several pieces. He caught the rope as he landed hard on the edge of the berg, knocking the wind from his lungs. Frantically clawing at the ice, he slipped over the edge. The rope was connected to the bear hide. He had untied it from the peg as he was working on the paws. He managed to wrap a loop around his wrist as he slipped over the ice, hoping and praying the rope held and the other pegs didn't give way.

The rope grew taut as both legs hung toward the sea. He managed to turn his head to see the water surge up to within six feet below his boots and then recede down to nearly thirty feet below. A chunk of sea ice holding his tent and other belongings bobbed a short distance away. Other pieces of the sea ice tossed and turned and crashed violently against the berg. Seawater soaked him as he scrambled to pull himself up on the berg, but he didn't have the strength in the one arm holding the rope, and the other hand just slipped on the ice.

He would be crushed or drowned within a short time, he knew, as his arms ached and he grew weaker.

He managed to hold on for another moment with his face against the ice, his shoulder burning with pain, forlornly saying aloud, "I'm sorry! I'm so sorry!" A surge of water lifted him up far enough to grab the tent peg with his loose hand, where the end of the rope had been tied. Adrenaline took over and enabled him to pull himself up on the ice. He quickly wrapped the end of the rope around the peg, securing it and the loose corner of the hide to the berg.

As he looked over the ravaging sea, he saw the ice chunk holding his tent raise up on a swell and completely flip over, ripping it away. Food, clothing, and firewood all claimed by the sea, but not everything. He looked to his left, and there held fast to another frozen tent peg, hung his precious backpack. He had failed to take it with him when he had retired in his misery to stare at the sky. In the end, the sickness had been a blessing, for without it, he would not have forgotten to take the pack. Carefully now, he retrieved the pack and placed his arms through the straps. Next, he took the nylon tent bag and squeezed behind the hanging hide. It was a tight fit, but he managed to sit crossed-legged on the bag, the hair side of the hide against his front, with the bag and pack preventing direct contact with the ice.

His pants were made of wool, and they were thoroughly soaked, as well as the lower part of his thick parka. Although his wool sweater and shirt felt dry, he shivered fiercely as he sat there while the storm raged on. The wind-driven rain peppered the other side of the hide, but very little reached him. He was cold, wet, hungry, and more than a little scared, but the thing he noticed most was that the motion sickness was gone, at least for now. He wondered if most of his shivering was from shock. He could feel the rapid beat of his heart and seemed to hear it above the rage of the sea.

With his chin against his chest and the hide against his forehead, he willed himself to take deep, calm breaths. After a while he felt calmer and shook a little less as the storm raged on.

He must have passed out or dozed off because the next time he opened his eyes it was much darker, and the waves looked black as he peered past the hide. He felt as though he may be dreaming, but he reached around and found his canteen wedged under his leg. He drank the last of the water as the cobwebs in his head grew thicker. The next time he opened his eyes it was still dark and the rain had stopped, but he felt colder. He pulled the hood of his thick parka closed more and scrunched his legs closer as the cloud in his mind grew dark once again.

****

Jacob's legs would not move. In his dream they were crossed and bent at the knees, and his feet were numb. But it wasn't a dream. Something was holding him down! He became more aware as his mind awakened from sluggish listlessness. Fearing he was suffering from severe hypothermia, he tried to move them again with more force, and they gave a little. His wool pants were frozen to the ice! As he became fully awake, the false warm feeling faded away as cold returned.

He flexed the muscles of his legs and squeezed his toes, then relaxed and repeated the movement over and over, until his toes burned as feeling returned. He worked himself free of the thin film of ice and managed to crawl unsteadily to his feet. He wasn't sure if he'd been out of it one day or two, but at least he was alive and the sea, while still rolling powerfully, showed no whitecaps, the sky still a dull gray.

Moving carefully, he took in his present situation; most everything he'd needed in order to survive was gone. No way to build a fire and nothing to burn even if he could. His clothes were damp, especially his pants, but the wool held its insulation value when wet, even though they were heavy and uncomfortable. He had access to plenty of water on the wide ledge above and several pieces of smoked fish and jerky in his pack.

In his weakened state, he managed, after a while, to haul the bear skin along with the rest of his meager belongings up on the ledge. In a little niche, he placed the bearskin flesh side toward the ice in a way where he could sit cross-legged and pull the skin around him. Mostly protected from the wind, he sat and stared out over the sea, counting seabirds and other icebergs and trying not to think of anything else.

Chapter 41

Jacob didn't know for sure how long he had been on the ice, but it had been at least twenty days. He knew this by the pieces of jerky he had just counted. The day he climbed to the ledge, he had twenty-seven pieces, and there were seven left. One piece a day, three bites a day. His breakfast, lunch, and dinner. He would take a bite and hold it in his mouth without chewing until it all but melted away. He only did this after he had scrunched his toes, and tightened and relaxed the muscles of his arms and legs for ten sets of ten repetitions.

It hadn't rained at all for the past week; two days ago, the sky had actually been mostly free of clouds, allowing him to see his shadow on the ice a few times. Today, though, gray clouds hung like a dense fog low over the water, casting a depression over him once again.

A thousand thoughts ran through his mind, over and over. He knew the iceberg that had become his home would eventually melt into the sea, but surely he would starve to death before then. His hopes of seeing a plane or boat diminished daily. He'd seen nothing but other floating chunks of ice, not counting the seabirds and whales. The day before, one particular giant had circled the berg several times before blowing right in front of him, spraying a rainbow on that rare sunlit day, only to turn and dive deep, waving with a massive fluke.

He was still cold, his cheeks and any exposed skin red and sore from windburn, and it looked as if the longest dry spell yet was over. His only good fortune was that the niche afforded a little protection from the wind and rain. Today, though, with the low cloud cover, most all the wind had stopped, except for an occasional gust that seemed to originate from nowhere. His ice vessel being mostly wedge shaped, the narrow, pointed end almost always faced into the wind, but it also meant it limited his view of the ocean. The only way to command a three-hundred-sixty-degree view would be if the berg rotated completely, or if he climbed to the narrow, rounded top.

Sitting back against the bearskin, he held the thin orange rainfly, with the intent of waving it frantically in case a boat or plane was spotted, when suddenly, a small gust of wind surged over the top of the berg, nearly pulling the rainfly from his hand. With panic, he increased his grip on the cloth, and in that instant, had an idea. Inspecting it closer, he noted the sewn-in tubes and end pockets intended to hold the thin shock-corded poles. He was sure it would work! And if he ripped the long, narrow bag holding the poles down both sides, it would serve as a respectable kite tail!

Sometime later he beheld a suitable blaze-orange kite, complete with tail and a couple hundred yards of braided fishing line for kite string. The construction of the kite had taken longer than he'd imagined, and this distressed him; he was weaker and less coordinated than he had thought. He fumbled, and his vision blurred at the effort. He worried that just standing to relieve himself may result in becoming faint and possibly even falling into the cold sea. In the end, he tied a section of rope around his waist and to one of the tent pegs.

Huddling in the protection of the bear hide, he folded the shock-corded poles on his kite, lest a gust of wind pull it from his weak grip before he was ready. Trying with all the concentration he could muster, he kept watch on the ocean and in the sky. Soon every bird became a plane and everything floating became a boat. He noticed it was becoming harder to stay awake. During one moment of lucidness, he spotted what he at first thought was a ship in the distance; sitting up straighter, he rubbed his eyes and refocused. It *was* a ship! Excited beyond belief, he willed the vessel closer so he could wave the kite.

His breath coming in excited gasps, he re-snapped the shock cords, prepared the kite, and was in the process of standing, not taking his eyes off the ship, when a puffin landed on it. Gatherings of the pigeon-sized seabirds were observed almost daily and barely noticed, but one had landed on his rescue ship hardly two hundred feet from the iceberg. The ship he was about to hail was only a piece of driftwood floating close by.

The thin, gray clouds immediately gave the impression of descending closer, consuming him in despair. He withdrew as far as he could into the hide, resolving to accept the inevitable. Remorse overwhelmed his spirit more so than the hunger that gnawed at his stomach. He bit off another portion from the piece of jerky he held, breakfast and lunch in two bites. In disgust, he put the rest of it in his mouth, thinking that he may just as well have another piece in a while. While contemplating upon this, the clouds parted a little to allow a weak ray of sunlight to shine down on him.

He looked up, and far off in the distant sky, he spotted another seabird gliding slowly from his right, angling toward his left across the gap in the clouds. Only this was not a seabird! It was a plane, he was sure of it, for he could faintly hear the hum of the engines!

Frantically, his weak hands fumbled to reconnect the shock-cord poles stretching out the kite, while attempting to stand on cramped legs. The plane had cleared half the distance diagonally across the open expanse before Jacob was able to stand on unsteady legs. The constant breeze blew over his right shoulder as he faced the direction the plane flew. Holding the kite high in his left hand, while trying to manage the spool of braided line, he dropped both. The kite started sliding down the ice to his left, while the spool of line bounced and skidded down toward the water on his right.

Panicked by his clumsiness, he froze for a second as his mind fought over which to rescue. He felt a tug at his right heel and looked down to see that the line ran between his legs on the ice; he managed to grab the line and pull hard as the spool bounced one last hop and into the water. The effort allowed the line to tighten on the kite, and it made a sudden leap into the sky, even as the long tail skimmed the waves.

The kite danced unsteadily as he fought for control; diving left and right, it looked for certain to crash into the water, until a saving gust caught and lifted it skyward. The line sung through his damp leather gloves as he applied pressure, until little rivulets of smoke rose from the heat.

By the time the kite reached the low clouds the plane had crossed out of sight. Jacob continued to work the line as the kite soared into the gray mists, and for another fifteen seconds, he held tension, letting it climb, until the line suddenly jerked and went slack. His breathing stopped and his heart beat wildly in his chest as he stared out across the water. Abruptly, he caught sight of a crumpled orange object as it fell from the low clouds three hundred yards out and crashed into the waves like a wounded goose.

Jacob got underway pulling in the line, hoping the kite remained attached. In his weakened state, what should have been a simple task became a chore, and by the time he'd retrieved the remains, he held only a broken shock-corded pole and the kite tail. Adding insult to injury, a fine, misty rain started falling. Sensing the end to his adventure quickly approaching, he once again retreated into the confines of the cold, damp bearskin.

Shivering once again as the adrenaline rush subsided, he took another piece of jerky from his quickly dwindling supply. Adjusting the backpack to afford the best protection from contact with the ice, he held the bite in his mouth, letting it soften, savoring the taste.

With the hair side of the hide next to him, he wrapped himself tightly again, letting the skinned head hang over like the bill of a cap. With his gaze straight ahead, he looked through the two nostril holes as the misting rain turning to sleet.

As time passed, he felt himself growing more sleepy. The shivering had mostly stopped, although he knew it was getting colder because several short icicles now hung from the nose of the bear hide. However, with the temperature falling, he strangely didn't feel as cold as before. Then, somewhere in the back of his fuzzy mind, he remembered that when a body began to freeze to death, the person didn't feel the cold; in fact, they more often felt warm and sleepy, just as he was feeling now. He thought it was a shame to waste the last few bits of jerky and decided he would eat another piece after a short nap.

In the dream came a loud thumping noise and a strong rush of wind! A far-off voice! Unable to move or awaken from the nightmare, he fought his way through the tunnel to find the exit blocked by thick, hanging icicles. Something huge and yellow was coming closer, trying to get at him, but then moving away as if not sure, only to regain courage and then come closer still, until it crashed through the ice barrier, sending a lightning bolt of pain through his head and down his body. Then all was black.

Chapter 42

Commander Mike Arden took control of the HC-144 Ocean Sentry. He wanted to feel for himself the condition of the starboard GE CT7 turboprop. Lieutenant Kenneth 'Ken Dog' Kinder reported the engine had recently developed a high-pitched whine, and he could feel slight intermittent power loss. Commander Arden couldn't hear the whine that Lieutenant Kinder detected due to his much older ears, but he could surely feel if anything was amiss.

Twenty-three years he'd served as a U.S. Coast Guard pilot, most all of it here in Alaska's 17th district, and when flying, he became one with the aircraft. As soon as he touched the controls he confirmed that Lieutenant Kinder's assessment had been correct. There was indeed a slight stutter in the starboard engine. Nothing serious, but it would need to be thoroughly checked out on return to base.

The Ocean Sentry was returning from a routine ice patrol, where the ocean below had been mostly obscured by a low-hanging cloud layer, rendering the patrol mostly a waste of time. Through a rare break in the clouds, Lieutenant Kinder observed several flats of broken sea ice and a few house-sized icebergs. Far in the distance, one in particular held his gaze, for the wedge-shaped chunk of ice contained what looked to be a dark spot not normally seen on most icebergs. He let it go as just a dark shadow, or possibly a rock lump or mass of driftwood beginning to show after being trapped for thousands of years.

Only a moment before the aircraft was to pass again over the clouds, a last glance at the wedge-shaped iceberg gave the impression that the dark spot was moving, as well as color shifting from dark brown to orange. Quickly attributing the sight to sunlight reflecting off the water, he refocused his attention to the instruments showing status of the starboard engine. Satisfied with the readings and with the knowledge that the aircraft was under the control of the very best of pilots, he took the moment to lean his head back into the restraints and close his eyes.

Moments later he was startled to full attention at Commander Arden's raised voice. "What the heck is THAT! Ken, ten o'clock!"

Lieutenant Kinder quickly looked in the direction indicated, to see that a bright orange object had shot up through the cloud cover below! As they both watched, it stopped, hovered for an instant, then collapsed upon itself before slowly falling back into the clouds. They gave each other blank looks before Lieutenant Kinder said, "Was that a kite? In the middle of the ocean!" Then he remembered the iceberg from a few minutes before.

"We can't circle back for a better look because those clouds are laying right on the water. Radio for a Jayhawk and give them the coordinates," said Commander Arden, then added, "Maybe by the time they get here some of the soup down below will have blown away."

The MH-60T Jayhawk arrived on location to find the wind

had picked up sufficiently to thin the clouds and heavy fog enough to make the numerous floating chunks of ice visible through the mist. It took a few passes over the area to locate the wedge-shaped iceberg with the dark shape as reported. Hovering over the target resulted in no indication of life, and the shape didn't resemble a human form. Captain Troy Strambaugh ordered rescue diver AST E-6 Timothy Midkiff be lowered to investigate and confirm. In short order, the diver reported a human form either unconscious or deceased wrapped in what appeared to be an animal skin.

Hauled up and returning in a rescue basket, AST Midkiff directed the unit to the narrow ledge, and while doing so, the unsteady maneuver resulted in the basket colliding into the top part of the still form, causing a loud groan to escape from within. Unable to free the victim from the stiffly frozen hide, AST Midkiff managed, after cutting ropes holding the bundle to the ice, to roll it into the basket. Not completely sure what he was attempting to bring aboard, he gave the haul up signal.

****

Jacob found himself soaking once more in the hot spring, watching the steam slowly rise, only to escape through the opening above the ice wall. He noticed the smoothness of the ice where it had begun to melt and polish from the heat of the steam, forming a yawning concave shape in the wall as it made its phlegmatic slide to the sea. Looking down, he was surprised to notice he was soaking while fully clothed, the loops of his tied boot strings floating lazily above his ankles. For a second he was sure he heard the indistinct sound of a voice coming from across the way, high up near the stone altar.

He was too warm and relaxed to really pay it any mind; he only wanted to sleep. Then came a rush of cold air through the opening above, so powerful as to break off chunks of ice and hurl them down into the water! He was up in an instant, running through the cavern, his wet clothes slowing him down, his wet boots feeling like lead. Looking back, he saw a rushing wall of water pushed by the wind, the water sparkling with thousands of gold nuggets. In slow motion, he ran past his sleeping nook and leaped across the disturbed area of his digging. The wall of water was gaining as he slowly moved forward. Down through the tunnel, it was like running in glue, while far up ahead, he could see the exit was blocked by a wall of icicles, some as thick as his waist. He reached the opening just as the water caught up with him and mashed him up against the ice. The water didn't splash around him, but only held him there as if it was contained within a thick plastic bag. Looking through a space between the icicles, his breath caught as a great yellow bear over twenty feet tall with a festering wound on its snout crashed into the icicle barrier and exploded him backward.

He now lay in the tunnel on his back, looking upward through a hole in the ceiling. He hadn't noticed this hole before, but there was a pinhole of light far above, like looking up from the bottom of a well. If he could stand, he could climb up through it because he could see peg-like protrusions all the way up the rough stone walls, evenly spaced along both sides.

He lay there for a moment staring up through the tunnel, marveling at how far away the light seemed to be, just a speck in the distance like a star in the night sky. He was getting sleepy again. He closed his eyes and heard again the far-off, barely distinguishable sound of voices. He couldn't make out what they were saying, but the sound brought him awake. He looked up again, and the light at the tunnel end seemed to be a little larger, closer.

He attempted to stand, which caused the tunnel to spin around, making him dizzy. He fought off the nausea and, on unsteady feet, stood to find the upper part of his body in the tunnel. In slow motion, he grabbed one of the protrusions and pulled himself up enough to place a heavy wet boot on another, then grabbed another and slowly made his way up through the tunnel. The higher he climbed, the more lightheaded he felt; then something unexpected happened! The pegs bent under his weight like they were made of rubber! He felt himself falling in slow motion back down the tunnel, until he heard the voices again, this time more distinct and calling his name.

The pegs once again became solid, and he stopped his plummet. He held on for a moment, catching his breath, and began the ascent once again. With new determination, he forced himself upward. Several times, he felt himself falter, but somehow, he kept his grip and the pegs held, and although they appeared to be getting farther apart, he persevered. Gradually, almost imperceptibly, he reached the light.

Jacob lay there unable to move. He was on his back, and he could hear, but he could not see. He knew he was alive, for he could feel his heart beating, and he could feel the pain in his head pulse with the rhythm. But it was the voices he lived for. He could hear the voice of his beloved Anna, and it was filled with sadness, as sad as the day long ago when she had to have her little dog put to sleep. She had cried as she handed her sick little pet over to the vet. He was old, and the vet had said the act would be the last gift she could give him, so through the tears, she kissed his little head and handed him over.

Jacob remembered that day clearly, but why was she sad now? Then he heard another voice. He recognized it immediately and smiled, although the smile didn't reach his lips. He heard Otis say, "You heard what the doctor said. He could be in this coma for a week or a year, even though his vitals are good. Go call the girls and get yerself somethin' to eat. You ain't had a bite since yesterday morning."

"Oh, Otis, stay with him. I'll only be gone for a minute, I promise."

"Don't worry, I ain't gonna go nowhere. I got decent cell service down yonder at the end of the hall by the window this morning."

Jacob's thoughts started to link together, and he remembered watching the kite fall into the sea. He remembered struggling to pull the broken thing through the surf, only to recover broken pieces. He remembered the despair he felt and the cold of the ice. He remembered the rushing wind and the sudden pain he'd felt. And now these voices he thought he would never hear again. He willed his body to respond. He prayed and felt the nerves reconnecting throughout his body, slowly, ever so slowly, until he was able to move his left hand.

The weak movement did not go undetected by Otis. The big man practically leaped out of the chair to stand by the bed. Jacob could feel the needle in the top of his right hand. He gradually moved both feet, then opened his eyes to see a big, red-bearded face looking back at him, tears moistening its eyes.

Jacob smiled, and with a weak voice said, "I know I must be alive 'cause heaven wouldn't have an angel that ugly."

The big face grinned and replied, "From a guy who lived through the winter like a penguin on an ice cube, then almost be kilt by folks tryin' to rescue him."

Jacob turned his head to see Anna enter the room. "Now, there's an angel!"

Epilogue

Jacob sat in his old comfortable recliner, staring across the room at the bearskin on the floor by the fireplace. It had arrived two months to the day after he had returned home. He had given up ever seeing it again, yet here it was, beautifully done, despite what it had been through. The guys from Coast Guard Sea Rescue, at the suggestion of AST Midkiff, had gotten together with a local taxidermist to have the skin made into a rug. They had all signed the underside, and added a personal note apologizing that they had almost killed him.

The crew had visited him during his recovery in the hospital and were relieved to find him in such good humor. The young guys took an immediate liking to Otis, who proceeded to invite them all down to his ranch in Wyoming. The crew's gift was a very special surprise, and he was glad the taxidermist had chosen to do a closed-mouth mount. Most all he'd seen had a gaping open mouth, showing huge fangs, but this one gave the impression of a bear in repose. He remembered looking across his camp back in the cave at those white ears and those eyes staring at him as they were now. He found it hard to accept the fact that this bear *and* his mother had both saved his life, on separate occasions — what a story!

He glanced over at Anna, who was nodding off with his journal in her lap. He knew she had read through it at least a hundred times. It had been almost a year since his rescue, and he was still amazed by the fact his backpack had been returned with all his possessions intact. They had found his wallet with his ID and had contacted Anna before the news of his rescue had been made public.

At first, the media circus had been intense. The story of the lost hunters had been played out on nearly every news station and in newspapers across North America when they had first gone missing, and had been rekindled with ferocity after the rescue.

Jacob had been very careful to maintain his story. Keeping vague his recollection, as he had been in the back of the plane during the ill-fated flight and had no knowledge of its true destination. He was forthright with the fact that the plane had crash-landed and been crushed and buried under ice and snow. He related the fact that he was able to chop a hole in the mostly spared tail section, and how he had wandered in the wilderness until stumbling upon a cave, where he spent the winter, surviving on what he could hunt, catch, or trap. In view of the numerous television reality shows regarding Alaska wilderness living, his story soon lost interest.

Life was almost back to normal. He had been offered his old job back, mostly because he had become somewhat of a local celebrity. He took the job, for money had been really tight during his absence, and Anna had struggled to make ends meet. He still hated the job.

He glanced at her dozing and smiled. He was proud of her strength and the fact that she had held things together like a trooper. It had been a good thing when she became acquainted with Hannah Dooley, for they had been able to share their grief and comfort one another as best they could.

Hannah had visited a few months after his return. She had desperately wanted to hear the story from the last person to see Charlie alive. It brought closure to her heartache, and Jacob was careful to tell her the things she wanted to hear. He was surprised to find out that his and Charlie's birthdays were only one day apart. He was even more surprised a few weeks after her visit by the delivery of a completely restored 1951 Ford pickup. Hannah had insisted that she wanted only him to have it. Although he really felt guilty and tried to refuse, she stood firm and said it would make her feel as if it was in some way connected to Charlie.

Last week he had been really excited to watch his dad unwrap the present for his eightieth birthday. The gold-laced quartz point had by some means managed to survive the ordeal unbroken within the secret hideaway. The stiff bottom of the backpack had protected it, as he'd hoped.

His dad was speechless as he carefully turned the object in his work-scarred hands. They had been alone after the birthday dinner, and he felt certain no one else would ever see the object, as long as it was in his father's possession, for he truly treasured the little personal gifts he received. No matter what the monetary value of any gift, they became priceless to his dad, who always marked the gift with the initial of the giver and the date given, then stored it away in a secret place. Jacob planned to show his dad the photos saved on the memory card sometime soon, and he wished then that he could tell his dad what he was planning, but for now, he could tell no one.

It had started several months ago, during Hannah's short visit. After dinner one evening, he had gone to the den to give Hannah and Anna some time for girl talk. He noticed his journal on Anna's chair and picked it up before sitting down. He had not looked inside since he'd made his last entry, and knew it was only filled with the things he had been afraid he'd miss telling his family. Heartfelt writings, nothing about his sadness or depression, nothing about his location or anything about the gold. Writing in an upbeat manner had helped keep his spirits up, like he was really talking to his family. His intent was that if any of his family were ever able to read his words, they would not reflect the rantings of a starving, miserable, nearly mad person.

As he casually flipped through the pages, he noted some numbers crudely written along the inner margins of a page. At first they meant nothing, then suddenly, he remembered the day right after the crash. The day the sun set behind him as he looked out over the ocean! Just before the GPS died, he had written down the coordinates! He could find that place again.

Phone calls, e-mails, cards, and letters had poured in ever since his return. Anna had filtered through all the correspondence, sometimes sharing bits with him, especially if the contact was someone from years back, reconnecting. That particular day, she handed him note where she had written a name and phone number. Casually glancing at the name brought an immediate grin to his face and a flood of memories. He knew he would be returning this call, for the long-lost friend had disappeared over twenty years ago, but that was how it had always been with Tim.

He had met Tim 'Crowbar' Chapman the same year he and Anna were married. Tim worked in a small auto parts store near their small rented house. Jacob needed a carburetor rebuild kit and had taken the old unit wrapped in an oily rag to show the old gray-haired fellow who usually worked the counter. When Jacob entered the old dimly lit building, the older feller wasn't behind the counter. In his place stood a tall, thin young fellow with long, dark hair down to his shoulders.

"Whatcha need?" the young fellow asked as Jacob set the rag-covered carburetor on the counter.

Jacob started to reply, "I need — "

But before he could finish, the young fellow interrupted him. "You need a Rochester Quadrajet rebuild kit for a LS5 big block Chevy."

Surprised, Jacob said, "Yeah, how did you know?"

"You drove by yesterday, and I could hear how it was runnin'. You might want to tweak the jets a little too. It'd help with the new cam and stuff—nice Chevelle, by the way. Can have the kit before noon tomorrow, or if you need to get it on the road sooner, I can fix you up in"—he paused, looking up at the yellowed, cracked face of a Champion Spark Plug advertisement clock on the wall—"about forty-seven minutes."

"Need it to get to work in the morning, but how can you do it in forty-seven minutes?" questioned Jacob.

"Goin' home for lunch in about fourteen. Just live up on the hill and got one just like it in the garage already re-built and re-jetted. Only take me a few minutes to eat a couple baloney sandwiches, get it and get back. Forgot my lunch this morning."

"I can't take your carburetor, buddy," replied Jacob.

"Nah, don't worry about it. The motor's still on the stand. I'll rebuild this one tomorrow, and we can swap back sometime. By the way, name's Tim, but everybody calls me Crowbar," he said as he stuck out his hand for a shake.

And that's how he met Tim. The young fellow not only stopped by exactly forty-seven minutes later, but insisted on installing and connecting the carburetor, still managing to be back at work before his lunch hour was over.

Long, lanky, and strong as a crowbar, he could be bent under a hood, drop a wrench on the ground while working on an engine, and somehow reach down by the motor and pick the tool up off the ground. Always the good sport at six foot three and weighing a hundred twenty pounds soaking wet, he could fix anything. While working on a friend's truck on a hot summer day, he had removed his shirt, exposing a lily-white back. With several of the guys standing around, one said, "Tim, you better not get a bad sunburn. As skinny as you are, you'd look like a thermometer!"

Everyone had a good laugh, including Tim. Jacob remembered that day as if it were yesterday. He had always avoided referring to Tim as 'Crowbar' and thought back to that time when, a few days later, he'd stopped by the parts store, and Tim had told him he would be leaving in a few days for Kansas. His favorite uncle owned a farm a little northwest of Moscow.

"How long you gonna be gone?" Jacob had asked.

"Don't know, but probably not long. My uncle farms a little, but mostly he does some crop dustin' around the area. I don't like dust or farms, so I don't figure I'll stay very long. I just want to get close to that old biplane my uncle has. I'll send you a picture," Tim said with a grin.

True to his word, less than a month later, Jacob received a letter. Inside was a photo of an old biplane, a little bigger than he imagined was necessary for a crop duster, and a tall, thin young fellow with a huge grin on his face was standing by the plane. Tim had written a short note on the back of the photo that read: 'Me beside Uncle Bark's Antonov An-2. A Russian built plane in Moscow Kansas. Ain't that a HOOT!'

That letter had been the last he'd heard from Tim. None of the other guys had heard from him, either, for he would ask every time he had the chance. As the years went by, the memory of Tim faded, as did the old photo of a young kid beside an old plane. He was sure that photo was stashed away in the garage in the old fireproof file cabinet, along with hundreds of others.

Looking down at the note again, checking Tim's phone number, he thought aloud, "Wait . . . 907? 9-0-7—that area code is . . . Alaska!"

He dialed the number, and it went straight to voicemail, "Hey, you've reached Tim. Can't get to the phone now. Leave your name and number, and I'll get back to you as soon as possible, but if you're a bill collector, you've got the wrong number."

Before he could leave a message, his phone beeped with

an incoming call. He answered and it was Tim. "Hey, buddy! Recognized the West Virginia area code and figured it was you! How the heck you been? Well, not counting being lost and all."

The sound of Tim's voice spanned the ages. It was like they had just spoken days ago, instead of twenty years. The conversation was short, due to the fact Tim was in an airport heading to Kansas and his flight was boarding. Uncle Bark had passed a few years earlier, and his Aunt Lucy had sold the farm soon afterward, but chose to keep an acre around the old homeplace, which she had just sold. With no children, she reached out to Tim to help her with the estate sale and then drive her back East to live with her younger sister, who lived just outside of Christiansburg, Virginia. Tim would be flying back to Alaska out of Charlotte, but promised he would call Jacob and they could figure out a way to connect and catch up.

****

Eight days later, true to his word, Tim called on a Thursday evening, saying he would be flying back to Alaska on Sunday afternoon. Jacob offered to come to Christiansburg on Saturday and drive Tim to Charlotte on Sunday morning.

The old friends recognized each other right away. They met for dinner at the Christiansburg Cracker Barrel, and Jacob would be staying at the nearby Quality Inn. Over a meal of broiled trout, wild rice, green beans, and cornbread, they caught up on the past twenty years.

Tim had learned to fly the Antonov An-2 the first year he was with his Uncle Bark. He took to it with such enthusiasm that his uncle sent him to the AG flight school in Bainbridge, Georgia, where he became a legal pilot. He worked for his uncle on the farm and helped grow the small crop dusting business. When farming and flying became too much, his aging uncle decided to lease out the farm and sell the crop dusting business to a competitor. Tim was overjoyed when his uncle announced that he would be giving the Antonov An-2 to Tim. The plane was really too big for crop dusting, and the competitor didn't really want it, as most aerial application planes were of the smaller single wing variety, but Tim loved the old slow-flying beast.

Tim kept the plane in excellent flying condition and made the modifications necessary for it to fly on kerosene. He had always had a longing to see Alaska, and on his first trip, he knew he would be staying. Soon after arriving he was visiting a small airport, checking out the local bush planes, when he noticed a fellow doing a tie-down on a DHC3 Otter. Tim was freezing in his light down jacket, but this guy was walking around the plane in a sleeveless shirt. Tim approached the friendly looking fellow and introduced himself. The man said his name was Dave Smallwood, but he went by the handle 'Highgear' from his days as a truck driver. He proceeded to invite Tim inside the little airport, where the local pilots hung out, for a cup of coffee. "Looks like you're about to freeze," Dave said as he handed Tim a steaming cup of coffee.

"How do you stand it out there without a jacket?" Tim asked as he took the coffee.

"I was born not too far from here," replied Dave. "Not too cold yet, but might be a little nippy about January."

As they continued with small talk, Tim learned that Dave had, until recently, been making long drives to Prudhoe Bay and other places, hauling everything from toilet paper to heavy equipment. He hated spiders and was tired of sliding into ditches. Since he had learned to fly as a young man, he decided he could still haul stuff to the far-off outposts while making a little more money by flying, so he sold his trucking business and had bought the plane outside. He just hadn't counted on being so busy.

Over the next few cups of coffee, the foundation for C&H Delivery had been arranged. 'Crowbar' and 'Highgear' would soon be equal partners in a lucrative air delivery service.

Jacob enjoyed his visit with Tim and asked him if he had ever panned for gold or knew any prospectors. "Too much cold work digging and wadin' in that ice water for me," said Tim. "I've known a few folks who prospect as a hobby and actually find a few nuggets, but only a fool would run into town and scream they've struck it rich like you see on TV."

"What would you do if you happened on a mother lode of gold?" asked Jacob.

"Heck Fire! I'd keep it quiet and sell a little bit at a time. I love my country, but sometimes Ole Uncle Sam takes more than he should, just to waste it on useless crap, and givin' away our money to countries that hate us. The workin' man gets to keep little enough of what he makes the way it is!"

Jacob could see that he'd hit a nerve with Tim, and although he mostly felt the same way, some folks were more vocal about it, so he changed the subject a little. "Tim, neither one of us is getting any younger. Are you planning on staying many more years in Alaska? Do you winter somewhere warm?"

"Naw," replied Tim, "Most of our heavy flying is in the winter. Me and Dave take turns on the worst flights. I'd love to move back down here somewhere and be able to live on a lake, where I could sit on a porch, fish a little, and fly the old plane off the lake. I've managed to save a little, but I'll have to work a lot longer to be able to do that."

They finished their dinner over hot coffee and hot apple pie with ice cream, then made arrangements for Jacob to pick Tim up at seven the next morning for the nearly three-hour drive to Charlotte.

Jacob went to bed that night with a load on his mind. He hated his job, they were living mostly paycheck to paycheck, and his parents were getting by on a small savings and social security. He spoke with Otis about every week and could tell his old buddy was working more hours for less. Tomorrow, he and Tim were going to have a serious discussion.

When Jacob dropped Tim off at his gate in Charlotte, they

were both excited. The more they had talked the past couple hours, the more they looked forward to the adventure. They had discussed the risks and the rewards. They each understood the necessity of the careful planning required, and were both willing to accept the hazards involved. They decided it would be better to have another strong back along, as it would be better to plan for one trip in and then to get out. If all went especially encouragingly and the plan went without a hitch, then they may even plan to do more mining down the road.

As Tim got out of the truck, he leaned in to shake Jacob's hand, agreeing on when to plan further. As he was leaving, he turned back and asked, "When you was lost in Alaska, why didn't you just call me? I would have come and picked you up." With that, he just turned to walk into the airport, leaving Jacob to ponder how he could have answered that question. Just like the old Tim.

Upon returning home, he made a call to Otis, and after a few minutes of chit-chat, asked him if he would be interested in a secret adventure. Otis said he was always ready for an adventure and wanted to know what Jacob had in mind.

"I'll be out soon to explain it all, but right now, I can only promise you a 'barrel' of fun!"

THE END
May 31, 2016

Made in the USA
Monee, IL
16 January 2020